The Witch's Daughter

Also by Paula Brackston

NOVELS

Lamp Black, Wolf Grey

Nutters (writing as P. J. Davy)

NONFICTION

The Dragon's Trail: Wales on Horseback

The
WITCH'S
DAUGHTER

Paula Brackston

THOMAS DUNNE BOOKS
ST. MARTIN'S PRESS
NEW YORK

THOMAS DUNNE BOOKS.
An imprint of St. Martin's Press.

THE WITCH'S DAUGHTER. Copyright © 2010 by Paula Brackston. All rights reserved. Printed in the United States of America. For information, address St. Martin's Press, 175 Fifth Avenue, New York, N.Y. 10010.

Incantation from *The Craft: A Witch's Book of Shadows* by Dorothy Morrison © 2001 Llewellyn Worldwide Ltd. All rights reserved.

www.thomasdunnebooks.com
www.minotaurbooks.com

Library of Congress Cataloging-in-Publication Data

Brackston, Paula.
    The witch's daughter / Paula Brackston.—1st U.S. ed.
        p. cm.
    ISBN 978-0-312-62168-1
    1. Witches—Fiction.   2. Warlocks—Fiction.   3. Immortality—Fiction.   4. England—Fiction.   I. Title.
    PR6102.R325W58 2011
    823'.92—dc22

                                                    2010037441

First published in England by Snowbooks as *The Book of Shadows*

First U.S. Edition: January 2011

10   9   8   7   6   5   4   3   2   1

For Simon, who knows what it took

Acknowledgments

My thanks go to Elizabeth, Anne, Peter, and everyone at Thomas Dunne Books for their enthusiasm, attention to detail, and very welcome efforts in making *The Witch's Daughter* the very best it could be. Thanks, also, to all at Snowbooks. Heartfelt gratitude to Becky Tope for her invaluable input and expert advice. *The Witch's Daughter* would never have been completed without the unflagging support and forbearance of my family and friends, and I'd like to thank them all for their patience with me, and their understanding and encouragement during the long birth of this book.

The Witch's Daughter

Batchcombe, Wessex, 1628

Bess ran. The clear night sky and fat moon gave ample illumination for her flight. She feared the dawn, for with it would come the discovery of her absence, and then the hunt would begin. The fetters still fastened around her legs rattled against her anklebones with every stride, a single broken link on each all that remained of her chains. Metal rubbed through young skin until a thin slick of blood trailed in her wake. Her bare feet slapped through the shallow mud, retracing a route that was so familiar as to be imprinted on her mind, clearly mapped, allowing no false turns as she fled beyond the village boundary and ran toward the woodland. Still the short journey felt longer than it ever had, the trees seeming to recede before her, recoiling from her boiling panic, never coming nearer however hard she ran.

An illusion. Merely a trick of the moon shadows. I must not falter.

Her breath sounded loud in her ears, loud enough to wake a light sleeper in an outlying cottage, her heartbeat surely too thunderous to go unheard. She pressed on, at last reaching the cover of the first slender trees. The darkness in the copse was of a different nature. The early spring foliage admitted only fractured moonbeams, and roots and brambles clutched at her from both sides of the path. On she ran. She gasped as stones scraped her soles. She splashed through a brook, the chill water momentarily numbing her wounds before gritty earth from the forest floor forced its way deeper into the lacerations with every footfall. An owl screeched his disapproval of her presence. A badger drew his snout back into his sett, waiting for the disturbance to pass.

The freshness of the night air stung Bess's throat. Even as it made her cough and fight for breath, she did not slow her pace; nor did she think to care, after so many hours in the stifling confines of her prison cell. Here at least was air to breathe. She crested a small hill and paused, steadying herself against the trunk of a great ash. She could taste the woodland on her tongue: the moss, the silver lichen, the rising sap of the trees. Beyond that, two more things clearly described themselves: her own fear and the sea. Both saltinesses spoke of terror and of freedom. She peered forward along the path and into the heart of the forest. That way lay escape from her captors. That way he would be waiting for her, horses ready, provisions, a plan, a destination to ride for. She pushed herself from the tree, summoning what strength she had left, but something held her back. Something inside her made her wait. *Consider,* it said, *consider the cost of that freedom.*

A distant noise caused her to start. Hounds. They would be upon her in moments; she could not hesitate. Yet still that voice would not be silenced. *Consider,* it warned.

Mother? What should I do?

By way of an answer the night breeze carried the scent of the sea to her nostrils. From the village the baying of the dogs grew louder and was now accompanied by shouts. A movement in the darkness ahead caught her eye. She was sure now she could make out the silhouette of rider and horses. Those who hunted her would take her life, that she knew. But what price would she pay Gideon for her freedom?

No. I shall not go to him. I will not.

She turned and sped down the eastward path, away from the trees, away from the hungry hounds, and away from him. In moments she had broken free of the woods and was racing across springy turf, out in the open, heading toward the one choice left to her: the sea. She felt rather than heard him come after her. She dared not look back now. As she reached the cliff path, a watery sun raised itself above the horizon, bleeding bitter red into the sea. A flat, shadowless daylight replaced the night, leaving Bess exposed. At the cliff's edge, she stopped. Looking toward the village, she could see torches spluttering in the grayness and make out featureless shapes moving rapidly nearer. Even above the hypnotic rasping of the waves on the rocks below, she could feel hoofbeats shuddering through the earth. Though he did not call out, she could hear his voice inside her head, *Bess! Bess! Bess!*

Bess would not turn. To meet his gaze would be to lose her own will. Below her the high tide allowed no glimpse of sand, only deep water and bone-shattering limestone and flint. The sun climbed higher, so that when she lifted her eyes heavenward, it was to see an apocalyptic sky before she stepped forward into nothing.

My name is Elizabeth Anne Hawksmith, and my age is three hundred and eighty-four years. Each new settlement asks for a new journal, and so this Book of Shadows *begins.*

IMBOLG

Awoke at dawn on my first morning at Willow Cottage to a heavy fall of snow. The landscape lay coyly clothed in ermine, waiting to reveal itself to me upon better acquaintance. The sky blushed briefly, lending a fleeting warmth. My bedroom window affords, as I had anticipated, an excellent view of the village of Matravers. Set on a small tump at the far end of the green, my little house is pleasingly separate from the cluster of thatched cottages and the short brick terrace that make up the center of the village. Also situated around the green, which boasts a chalk stream and duck pond, are a post office and small shop, a genteel coaching inn, and a bus stop from which children are taken to school and pensioners go to the weekly market in Pasbury. The church is at the other end of the green, set back and mostly obscured by impressive yews. The lane beyond the church gives access to the canal that runs west toward Pasbury. From the front of my house I have clear sight of anyone approaching, while the modest copse behind gives me seclusion. I can choose when to see and when to be seen.

I do my best to remain as invisible as my admittedly unusual appearance will allow. A woman on her own will always attract attention, particularly if she is in any way different. With this in mind, I keep my long hair tied back loosely and often wear a hat. My father used to say I had autumn hair and that this must have come about because of my September birth date. It is true, the color is a perfect match for that season—a blend of the burnished gleam of ripe chestnuts and highlights of oak leaves turned copper by the falling of the year. In itself such color, even coupled with my hair's exceptional length, would not provoke curiosity. It is the way such deep tones contrast with the broad white streak that runs from the right side of my brow that causes people to look again. This is not some silvery mark of maturity but a snow-pure swathe, an icy sweep, as though the Goddess of Winter has touched me and left her mark. Indeed, I wish that the origin of the feature were so harmless. The truth is so much darker.

I am also tall and, despite my great age, remain vigorous and strong, my outward appearance suggesting I might perhaps be fifty, no more. I dress for comfort, practicality, and so as not to draw attention to myself. These days fashion can be adapted to suit the caprice of any woman, it seems, so that my long skirts, my liking for rich colors and fabrics, and my favorite garments collected over many years of roaming this earth can all be worn without appearing anything more than a little eccentric.

The cottage will, I am confident, serve my needs well, after small alterations. I plan to create a path from the back door directly to the stream, which runs through the willows that give the place its name. The holly hedge on the front boundary needs additional planting, and I must find space for elder, birch, and rowan when the time is right. The garden must be completely dug over, and something will have to be done about the lack of shade to the west of the house. It is perfect for an herbary, but it is a large space and anything else placed there will surely scorch. The house must stay as it is for now unless intemperate weather prevents me from working outside. If there is a clear sky for the moon tonight, I will pace out my kitchen garden and mark it with hazel sticks. I might even venture for a night walk, though I doubt I shall go as far as the edge of the great woods that lie on the horizon behind the house. They beckon, but I am not ready to go there yet. They are of another time.

It is easy on a shining day such as this, when all is newness and future, to forget for whole moments the past. As if it cannot cast its shadow on the taintless snow. Imbolg is my favorite time of year to find a new home, signifying as it does looking forward to rebirth and renewal. But I cannot afford to become complacent. I must not allow myself to drop my guard. These picturesque surroundings are certainly benign, as I predict most of my new neighbors will prove to be. The danger, as always, will come from afar. It does not lie in wait but follows me. I can never let myself be made vulnerable by the illusion of safety.

FEBRUARY 6, 2007—MOON IN THIRD QUARTER

Snow still cloaks the valley, though it has been corrupted now. A trail left by the belly of a badger shows my back garden to be part of a run. I will have to talk him out of digging up my young plants come Ostara. The lane beyond my front gate is black once more, and the village itself is a mess of brown gardens and gray, lumpen effigies the children have abandoned. Cautious pedestrians have worn the pavements to slithers of icy water and dense patches of shrunken snow. All are temporarily afflicted by a curious gait. Each stride falls short of their expectations as it crumps into a shriveled drift or stretches muscles uncomfortably as feet slide through the slush. They have all been much too busy with the weather to bother me.

I have begun work in the garden, but the ground is horribly affected by the receding snow. Aside from planning and some preparatory clearing, there is little I can usefully do. This has forced me to turn my attentions to the house itself. The rooms are curiously small and boxy, two at the front and two at the back, downstairs and up, giving the appearance from the front of a dolls' house, with windows squarely positioned on either side of the door. I dislike the way the entrance opens onto the bottom of the stairs, but there is little I can do about it. The structural alterations required to change it would mean employing builders, and having strangers in the house for many weeks would be too great a price to pay.

The room at the front will be perfectly adequate for my sitting room, though I will rarely use it. The dining room I can utilize for drying plants and storing herb oils and pillows. It is in the kitchen that my most serious work will take place. I spent time there today, considering the best places to store my potions and unctions. The room boasts an excellent solid fuel stove, a quarry tiled floor, and west-facing French windows giving on to the garden. I lit the stove, taking a moment to burn a sage bundle and bless the space with its pungent smoke. As I stood, eyes closed, enjoying the stillness and promise of my new home, I became aware of a light scratching noise. The hairs at the nape of my neck began to rise, and I had the sensation of a caterpillar wriggling its way down my spine. I opened my eyes and looked in the direction of the noise. I need not have been alarmed. At the window a yellow-necked wood mouse was nibbling at the frame. I undid the latch.

'Good morning to you,' I said. 'Won't you step inside?'

He regarded me with dew bright eyes for a second or two before scurrying through the open window. I felt the icy chill of his naked ears as he brushed by. He completed a circuit of the room before settling to wash his paws by the stove. I fetched him a morsel of bread. 'I will strike a deal with you,' I told him. 'Tell your family to let my stores alone, and in return I will set out a daily meal for you on the windowsill. Do you agree?'

He paused in his ablutions. No sound came from the tiny creature; rather, I felt his acknowledgment of our bargain. It will be worth a few crumbs to have my supplies free from the attentions of mice.

I have already positioned my oak table, dresser, and merchant's chest, which fits snugly next to the Belfast sink, and put up shelves on the far wall for my many storage jars. The space succeeds in being both warm and light and will be a good place in which to work. Last night the moon's beams fell through the curtainless glass and washed the room in their pearly light.

Later, I went out into the copse and lit a candle, calling on the spirits and fairies of the woodland. I invited them to show themselves and assured them that they were welcome to stay and that I would not take their rightful home from them. I am a guest in their woodland, and during my stay here I will use it with care and respect.

FEBRUARY 10, 2007—FOURTH QUARTER

The snow has gone and been replaced by an iron frost, which means my gardening continues to be frustrated. Nevertheless, I managed to give the holly hedge some much-needed attention and clear spaces ready for the new plants. I am lucky to have such a protective boundary to my property. Parts of it must have been put in when the house was built, which I understand to be well over a hundred years ago. How long that sounds, and how much the world has spun and shuddered in that century. And yet, for me, it is but a chapter in my life. In truth, I have more in common with the ancient oak on the village green, though I doubt it has seen as many summers as myself.

While I was working on the holly, a squirrel came to see what I was about. He was a fine specimen, with long tail and dense silver fur. I bid him come closer, and he was happy to climb onto my arm and sit on my shoulder. There is comfort to be had in the company of wild things and delight to be found in their trust. I became aware I was being watched. I am, of course, always alert to the sensation of being observed, but on this occasion I was not alarmed. I sensed a peaceful presence, albeit one possessed of great energy. I paused and made as if to stretch my aching back, the squirrel jumping down and hurrying away as I did so. I caught sight of a slender girl standing in the lane. She was dressed inadequately against the cold and fidgeted in her fashionable boots. She looked at me with an open face, curiosity written on her pleasant features.

'Good morning,' I said and waited.

'Hi.' Her voice was soft. 'What are you doing?'

'As you see'—I pointed with my trowel—'repairing the hedge.'

'Bit cold for gardening, if you ask me.' She rubbed her hands together and then began to blow on them.

I wondered how old she was. She was shorter than me, but many women are. Fifteen maybe? Sixteen? The cusp of adulthood shifts from one decade to the next, backward and forward, so that I am unable to guess accurately anymore. Her tight-fitting clothes and obvious desire not to hide her body spoke of a young woman, while her hesitant voice and lack of eloquence suggested an awkward child. Seventeen, I decided. Little more than the age I was when my world collapsed. When I was thrown into an interminable future of hiding and solitude.

'I like this cottage,' said the girl. 'I like the way it sits up here watching the village. Its windows are like smiley eyes, aren't they?'

'You could say that.'

'Saw the smoke coming out the chimney,' she said. 'This place was empty when we moved here. You new too, then?'

'New to Matravers, yes.'

'We've been here a month. Feels like a bloody lifetime.' She began to flap her arms, as much in agitation as to keep warm.

'You don't like the village?'

'The place is okay, fields and stuff, but I mean, there's not much to do here, is there?'

'Not what you're used to?'

'Nah, we come from Basingstoke. Dulwich before that. God knows where we'll end up next. Mum gets an idea in her head and that's it, we're packing. She thinks the countryside will be better for me. Less chance I'll get into trouble. Less chance I'll have a life, more like.'

I looked at her more closely. There was something about this young creature, something appealing, something honest and trusting that is rarely found in a stranger. I caught myself considering offering her a mug of hot chocolate to warm those frost-nipped fingers. But no. It would be so easy to encourage a harmless neighborly acquaintance, but I must not. I returned to my task, turning my back on the girl.

'You should wear a warm coat on a day like this,' I told her.

I felt her watching me for a moment longer, then heard her leave. I confess a coldness gripped me that would not be got rid of by any amount of manual labor. Soon I went inside and busied myself in the kitchen, not wanting to dwell on the hard truth that had made me send the girl away. The heavens know I am accustomed to keeping my own company; it cannot be said to be an unfamiliar state for me. Nonetheless, there is but a spasm between solitude and loneliness. And I live in the knowledge that my friendless state is not a choice but a necessity, for my own safety and for that of anyone who would be close to me.

I put myself to the task of unpacking the last of the boxes. There is something comforting in the sight of well-stocked shelves, so that by the time I had positioned the last of the storage jars of pickled beetroot I had shaken off my earlier melancholy. The gleaming rows of glass and provisions suggested order and security. This evening I lit only candles in the kitchen and sat by the stove with the fire door open, watching a log of apple wood burn. The sight of it warmed me as much as any heat it might have given out. I was dressed, as is my habit through the winter months, in layers of comfortable clothing—a fine silk vest, soft woolen tights, cotton shirt, a heavy cord skirt that skims the floor, and two light sweaters. My sealskin boots were given me by an Inuit fisherman during my time spent in the great ice plains of the north. I peeled off a wool-mix knit. The yarn crackled as I tugged the garment over my head. Small sparks fizzed between the fibers and my hair, visible in the semi-darkness to a keen eye. I turned to the table and set some oil to warm in the burner. Rosemary. Soon the room was filled with the uplifting fumes. As it always did, the scent made me think of my mother. Her eyes were blue as the flowers of the plant, and her presence as powerful and restorative as the essence of the herb. Even now I can see her patiently showing me how to bind bundles of the twiggy stems together and hang them up to dry. I could have been no more than six years old. She would stand behind me and wrap her arms around mine, leaning forward to help my fumbling fingers. I was enfolded in her limitless motherly love, and I would breathe in her own sweet smell. She had such patience. Such tenderness. Such determination to teach me all that she knew, to share with me all her wonderful knowledge. It is the cruelest of the torments of my great age that grief does not abate, not beyond a certain level. It merely continues, my only companion across oceans of time.

FEBRUARY 13, 2007—MOON ENTERS CAPRICORN

Still cold, but the frost is weakening. I ventured into the village today. I was aware I had been putting it off. Whilst I do not wish to encourage more than the most basic of acquaintance with my neighbors, I know it to be a mistake to remain completely distant. To be a recluse is to be mysterious beyond the endurance of villagers of this modern age. Better to allow a polite exchange of nods and hellos and discourse about the weather. I strive to be dull in my conversation, even to the point of rudeness if it is unavoidable. I will impart only sufficient information for those with an interest to construct a dry history for me. That way I may be left in relative peace. However, I had not reckoned upon finding the teenage girl in the village shop when I went there to buy some simple groceries. Clearly not put off by my curtness during our previous meeting, she seemed pleased to see me.

'How's the hedge?' she asked.

'Taking shape slowly, thank you.'

'Are you going to paint the outside of the house?' she asked. 'I saw one like that once done in light blue with white windows and a navy door. Like a fairy-tale house. That'd be fab.' She faced me, eyes bright with her idea.

I wondered at her interest in the place. She was on her own as before. Had she no friends in the village? In my experience, teenage girls rarely did anything alone. I reminded myself she too was a newcomer and might not yet have had time to make friends.

'I hadn't thought,' I told her. 'The color of the walls is not hugely important to me.' I went about my shopping, hoping that would be the end of it, but she trailed after me up and down the aisles like an over-eager flower girl.

'Have you got a dog? Great garden for a dog, with those woods at the back. Mum won't let me have one. Says the hairs would clog up the vacuum.'

'No. No dog.' I took a bag of brown sugar from the shelf.

'Oh, I like brown. Especially the crunchy stuff. On cereal. Do you like cereal? It's over here, look. Honey Crunch or Cocosnaps? No, someone skinny like you'd be more into muesli, I reckon. Do you like muesli?' She held up a packet, beaming now.

I looked at her levelly.

'You ask too many questions,' I said, moving toward the counter, keen to be gone.

'That's what Mum says. But then, how can I learn anything if I don't ask questions?'

'That's another one.'

'Yeah, I suppose I just can't help myself.' She giggled, a joyful sound, like spring rain falling into a dew pond.

A tightness gripped my chest as I realized it was not my younger self the girl reminded me of, aside from her age. It was Margaret, my dear sweet baby sister. Margaret of the light step and easy laughter. Margaret who adored me as much as I did her. Yes, there was something about the openness and innocence of this girl that had also been at the heart of Margaret's character. I nodded hello and thank you to the shopkeeper and handed over my money. As I turned to go, the girl stood looking at me, blocking my path to the door, as if waiting for something.

'Shouldn't you be at school?' I asked.

'Teacher training. We get the day off to study at home.'

'Then shouldn't you be at home, studying?'

The girl had the good grace to blush. 'I came in to get a Valentine's card,' she said, 'only I can't choose. Look.' She pointed to the display near the counter. 'Funny, sexy, or romantic—what d'you reckon?'

'That rather depends on whom it's for.'

She blushed deeper and studied her feet.

'Michael Forrester.'

'Well, what is Michael Forrester like?'

'He's wicked. Everybody likes him. Especially the girls. And he's brilliant at sports. Athletics, rugby, swimming. Wins everything. He's so cool.'

'His ego must be sufficiently inflated already, by the sound of it. I should save your money.'

'Oh no, he's really nice. He held the door open for me once. And he said hello.'

'And how long have you been carrying a torch for this paragon?'

'What? Oh, dunno. Only met him last month, didn't I?'

Her voice had dropped to a whisper, and her whole demeanor told of the torture of unrequited love. She was pretty enough but clearly lacked confidence. And something else. There was an absence of worldliness about her, despite her sham bravado, which, while strangely appealing to an adult, must have been a handicap for her among her peers. I saw now how solitary the girl must be. She did not fit in. She was an outsider. At that moment, with her guard down, loneliness emanated from her in painful ripples. The sound of the shop doorbell saved me from having to advise her further.

'Morning, Mrs Price. Tegan, how are you, my dear? How is your mother? Ah, our newest new neighbor, forgive me for not having called in to welcome you to Matravers before now.'

I looked round to see a stout, bearded man offering me his hand. His eyes shone with the love of life, and his smile was broad and sincere, but the very sight of him made my temples pound. It was not his fault. How could he know how the presence of a priest would affect me? How could he ever imagine the fury that his Church ignited within me? The same Church that had condemned my mother and taken her from me. I took a breath to steady myself, but the smell of communion wine lingered on his vestments. Still his hand remained extended toward me. He waited. The girl waited. Mrs Price behind the counter waited. Such a small moment, and yet it would define my position in the village for as long as I live here. I straightened my shoulders and mustered a smile, clutching my purchases to me.

'Sorry,' I said, indicating my packages.

'Oh, not to worry.' He smiled on and dropped his hand, 'I'm Donald Williamson. You'll find me at the vicarage most evenings. Feel free to drop in; Mary would love to meet you.'

'Thank you. I'm busy unpacking at the moment, but I'll keep it in mind.' I began to edge past him, struggling with the revulsion such proximity to one of his kind inspired in me.

'Any time,' he called after me as I reached the door, 'and hope to see you on Sunday. Ten o'clock. All are welcome.'

I shut the door on his further entreaties and strode for home. Even after all this time I found it near impossible to conceal my feelings for an official of the Church. I had good reason to feel the way I did, but even so

I was angry with myself. It was foolish not to be more in control and ridiculous to experience such fierce emotions toward every harmless reverend who crossed my path. Before I had reached the other side of the village green, I was assailed by a strong sense of foreboding. Unsettled as I was by the meeting with the priest, I recognized this to be a separate threat. I stopped. I lifted my chin and slowly looked about me. There was nothing to be seen. Not a movement. Not a shadowy figure. Nothing out of the ordinary. Silent thatched cottages. A quiet terrace. An empty bus stop. Ducks quacking with reassuring vulgarity on the pond. Nothing to be frightened of. Nevertheless, it was with no small amount of relief that I reached the sanctuary of Willow Cottage and closed the door swiftly behind me.

FEBRUARY 17, 2007—NEW MOON

Clear skies for my first day of trading at Pasbury market. I was up before dawn to load the car with my produce. The vehicle is, by any standard one cares to judge, a mixed blessing. It is an elderly Morris Traveller—small and cheap to run but with a roomy boot and helpful rear doors to allow me to transport my herb teas, oils, lotions, soaps, preserves, and wine hither and thither. It necessitates, however, the most tiresome paperwork. It is impossible to own a car and guard one's identity at the same time. Every few dozen years I am compelled to reinvent myself, largely to be able to comply with the requirements of traffic laws. Nevertheless, I admit to a certain fondness for the vehicle itself. I rarely travel far, but without the car my market trading would be difficult, and the stall is an essential way of generating income. And of allowing those who need me to find me, of course. Even in this supposedly enlightened Age of Aquarius, I am unable to put a sign on the door saying WITCH—SPELLS AND POTIONS FOR EVERY OCCASION. No. I must adjust and adapt and present myself with a more . . . acceptable face to the outside world. The car was reluctant to start but responded to a spell. I left the engine running while I finished loading and secured the doors with string. I was locking up the house when I heard the motor stall. Without thinking, I focused, made myself still, and repeated my spell. There was a moment's hesitation, and then the engine sprang into life once more and chugged on happily. It was only when I returned to the vehicle that I noticed Tegan standing at my gate, her expression all too clearly revealing that she had witnessed my remote motor mechanics. She grinned, her eyes bright. I pushed past her and secured the gate.

'If you'll excuse me, I'm in rather a hurry,' I told her.

'Where are you going?'

'Pasbury, and if I dally, I shall be late setting up my stall.'

'In the market? Cool. Can I come?'

'What?'

'To Pasbury. With you. I could help.'

'I manage perfectly well on my own, thank you.'

'Go on. You don't have to pay me. Just give me a lift and I'll help you unload this lot.' She nodded at the boot of the car before stooping to peer through the rear window. 'What's in there, anyway?'

I looked at the girl. As always, she was wearing too few clothes for the chill weather and had about her a lostness that I could not ignore.

'What are you doing up at this hour?' I asked.

She shrugged, 'Mum woke me up coming in off her night shift. Couldn't get back to sleep. Mum was out like a light.' She kicked at a small stone. 'I didn't feel like staying cooped up in there with no one to talk to.'

'Won't your mother wonder where you are?'

'No.'

I sighed. I would really rather not have had the company of a garrulous adolescent, but she was hard to refuse. 'Get in. And don't fiddle with anything, especially the door handle. It keeps coming . . . there! What did I say?'

'Sorry.'

'And put your seat belt on. The last thing I need is the attention of some nosey policeman.'

The town of Pasbury is unremarkable but adequately supplied with shops and services. The market itself is, in truth, a lackluster affair. A mixture of worthy food, antiques of dubious provenance, pet supplies, heavily glazed china, and clothes that have had their labels excised. I had secured for myself a modest pitch, but in a good position at the bottom of the high street, where most shoppers would pass on their way to and from the car park and bus stop. Tegan put herself to good use helping me set up, apparently in no hurry to leave me. She showed an interest in my stock. So much so that I was quickly weary from explaining things to her. I gave her a handful of coins.

'Go and buy us hot drinks,' I told her. No sooner had she gone than a young woman parked her stroller at the stall and leaned over to scowl at the oils. There emanated from her such agitation, such anger, that I took a step backward. I noticed purple discoloration where her cheekbone met her hairline. She saw the direction of my gaze and turned to let her hair swing forward, but she knew that I had seen the bruise. Her babe was red-eyed but slept on in his stroller.

'What's that for, then?' the girl demanded, prodding at bags of rosemary leaf.

'It is helpful for rheumatism. And to ease period pains. The leaves make a tea.'

'Tea? It smells disgusting. How do you use this?'

'That is an aloe vera unction. A balm for burns, stings, that sort of thing.'

She dropped the pot back on the table. I pitied the poor creature, so young yet clearly so unhappy. I pointed to a bottle of bergamot oil.

'This is very good for lifting the spirits.'

'Huh! Give me a rum and Coke any day.'

'And this gets rid of negative energy.'

'Have you got one for getting rid of cheating bastard husbands?'

Now I understood. I fetched a small blue glass bottle from the box I kept on my side of the table. The label bore only the picture of a half moon.

'You might like to try a few drops of this.' I handed it to her, and she peered at it suspiciously. 'It makes a person more . . . *considerate*,' I explained.

She laughed, then caught my eye.

'How much?'

'See if it works first. You can pay for the next one if you're happy with the results.'

My first day of trading in Pasbury went slowly, but I detected a certain interest. I have found it often takes time for people new to my wares to pluck up the courage to buy them. No matter. Time is something I have in abundance. Tegan stayed with me the whole morning, only reluctantly agreeing to catch the bus home after I insisted she do so. I do not want to attract her mother's disapproval, and I was aware the girl had not asked permission to leave the village. I paid for a pie for her lunch and gave her the busfare back to Matravers. She claims to be keen to accompany me every Saturday. We shall see.

FEBRUARY 24, 2007—FIRST QUARTER

The holly saplings I ordered were delivered this morning, and the ground is at last soft enough to work on. I spent a productive hour planting in the gaps I had cleared and am pleased with the results. I have long reconciled myself to being able only to garden in the short and mid term, as I know I will not be able to stay anywhere long enough for more than this. Still, slow growing as they are, the feisty holly bushes will knit well with the rest of the hedge in a few months. And I have the satisfaction of knowing they will survive long after I have moved on. Holly is one of the most protective plants to set about a garden, and I would not be without it. Whilst not sufficient on its own to guarantee safety, it forms a powerful part of my Wicca arsenal. Later, I unpacked my supply of herbal sachets and hung sweet herbs inside the doors and windows of the cottage.

FEBRUARY 26, 2007—FIRST QUARTER

The weather has turned unseasonably mild, sending bulbs into frantic activity, which they may regret when the frost returns. I have seized the moment and dug over the kitchen garden. The steady toil required to turn such a large area of patchy lawn into beds lifted my spirits. Impossibly ancient I may be, yet I am sufficiently blessed to retain youthful health and vigor. After a morning's effort, I had stripped to my shirtsleeves, and my skirt was hemmed with mud. The soil here is good—loamy and free draining but not so much so as to have difficulty retaining water. I must resist the temptation to plant too early. This is but a false spring. It is curious how my long march through the years on this planet has done nothing to teach me patience. My mother used to chide me for my lack of it, and I still fret and fidget when compelled to wait longer than seems reasonable.

It was while I was leaning on my fork that Tegan arrived at my side. I was startled by her sudden appearance but far more disconcerted that I had not heard her approach. I saw she had abandoned her silly boots and was wearing trainers instead.

She noticed me jump.

'Sorry. I rang the doorbell; then I heard you digging. Wow, have you done all this yourself? You must be exhausted.'

Despite myself, she made me smile.

'I enjoy a little hard work now and again,' I said. 'Do you like gardening?'

She shrugged, 'Never done any, really. Unless you count growing cress on the kitchen windowsill.'

'It's a start, I suppose.'

Again, the girl seemed to be waiting for something. She certainly must be a friendless soul to come looking for the company of a stranger on a mild afternoon, when other teenagers would no doubt be in a gaggle somewhere. I held out my fork.

'Here, you try.'

She grinned, then took it from me. She stabbed ineffectually at the earth, her face registering surprise at how little impact she made. She tried again.

'Lean your weight onto the fork. Look, like this,' I leaned over and re-positioned her hands, showing her how to use her body to drive the tines into the ground. She giggled, that indomitably cheerful sound again, and did as I instructed. It was clear she was a quick learner, and soon she had picked up a rhythm and was making slow but steady progress through the sward.

'Keep it up,' I told her and went into the house. From the window I watched her work. She tired quickly but did not give up. I filled two glasses with hot fruit tea and then went to stand at the door.

'Would you like to come in for a warm drink?'

She did not need to be asked a second time. She followed me back into the kitchen and took the tea from me, sniffing the steam warily.

'What is it?'

'Fruit tea. Rosehip and orange. Drink it while it's hot.'

She sipped, then smiled, then sipped some more.

'Hey, this is great. I'll tell Mum to get some.'

'I'll show you how to make it one day,' I said, surprising myself at the rashness of such a promise.

'You made it? Wow, cool.'

The girl began roving the room, studying my store of bottles and jars. 'This is the stuff you were selling on your stall. I never thought you actually made everything. Did you do all this?'

And so we fell to discussing the oils and incense and herb pillows and sachets that I produce. I explained how I sell them at markets or sometimes to shops. She appeared fascinated, running her fingers along a row of blue glass phials, pausing to sniff a basket of drying lavender.

'These are cool,' she said. 'Is that what you're going to grow out there?'

'Some herbs, yes, and flowers for the oils, and vegetables, of course.'

A thought occurred to her.

'I don't know what to call you. You still haven't told me your name.'

'Elizabeth. You can call me Elizabeth.' I took a sip of my own tea, then asked, 'Tegan is unusual—is it Cornish, perhaps?'

'Welsh. My mum used to go there for holidays as a child, that's all. Another of her whims. To be honest, I think it's the only thing she really likes about me.'

She held my gaze, and the small silence was full of longing and hurt, so much so that I wanted to take her in my arms as my mother would have done me. Instead, I turned to rinse my glass at the sink.

Tegan noticed my journal on the kitchen table.

'Oh, is this for your . . . recipes, and stuff?' She moved to pick it up.

'Put that down,' I said, more sharply than I had intended. The wounded look on her face troubled me, so that I found myself suddenly wishing her gone. I was unused to having anyone inside my home. 'If you've finished your tea, you should run along home. Just because you have no demands on your time, do not assume that is the case for everyone,' I told her, turning to stoke the stove to avoid her crestfallen expression. After she had left, I felt an irritating regret. Even now, I am not sure whether it was because I let her into the house or because I sent her away.

This evening I spent some hours preparing a new batch of oils. I made a dozen or so bottles of lavender and the same of peppermint. It is light and pleasant work and ordinarily holds my attention, preventing my mind from dwelling on things about which I can do nothing. On this occasion, however, I found my thoughts wandering. I was thinking of Tegan. And of Margaret. I cannot think of one without bringing the other to mind. And try as I might to linger only on happy images of my dear sister,

I cannot keep the deathly pallor from her skin when I picture her with my mind's eye.

FEBRUARY 28, 2007—SECOND QUARTER

The mild spell continues, shedding light rain but nothing else. Tegan has proved herself more resilient than I had bargained for and reappeared the next day as if I had never uttered harsh words. Indeed, she has become a frequent visitor. I cannot pretend I have tried to discourage her. I admit I find her freshness and enthusiasm endearing. She soaks up knowledge like bread dipped in broth. She is possessed of such a keenness to learn and has assisted me in clearing the mess of brambles in the far corner of the garden. I have given her an old pair of boots and equipped her with heavy gloves. The poor child had nothing suitable of her own. I asked her why she did not spend time with her new school friends, and she explained none of them lived in the village and that the bus service is irregular and expensive. I ventured to ask if her mother might object to her being out of the house so much—surely there was homework to be done? It seems her mother is a care worker at a home in Pasbury. She works long hours and varied shifts. She is happy that the girl is occupied. There is no mention of a father or of any siblings.

I confess I am allowing myself to feel at ease here at Willow Cottage. Since that sense of threat the day I encountered Reverend Williamson, I have not had any negative sensations or moments of alarm. Could it be that I have at last found a safe haven? Can I have finally stepped beyond the reach of those ever-outstretched claws? The notion is seductive, and I am loath to taint it with caution and care. When we had finished our work, I had Tegan join me in placing a candle and a small circle of pebbles in the newly cleared area. I explained to her that I believe it will make an excellent sacred space. The heavens alone know what the child made of such a statement, but she happily went along with positioning the stones and helping me choose a candle. I will burn sage oil come the full moon and ask for continued protection.

MARCH 2, 2007—MOON ENTERS VIRGO

Heavy rain carried on an icy wind has rendered outdoor tasks unpleasant. Still, I am able to continue with the aid of an old sou'wester and rubber boots. Tegan came straight from the school bus stop to my house this afternoon. One glance told me her face was not reddened merely by the weather. Her eyes brimmed as she stood beside me by the hissing remains of my bonfire. She stared disconsolately into the smoke but did not say what had reduced her to such a state.

'Have you had a difficult day?' I asked, not wanting to pry but happy to offer the opportunity to talk of what was troubling her.

She merely shrugged.

'A nasty chill in the air today,' I said. 'You should have a hat on. Keep those restless brains of yours warm.'

Two tears slid down her cheeks and dripped from her chin. She did nothing to stop them. She looked suddenly so childlike, not a young woman at all, just a sad little girl with a pain she did not know how to share.

'Wait here,' I told her. I slipped into the house and went to my store cupboard. I selected a small blue bottle of oil of bergamot and returned to the now-extinguished bonfire. Tegan barely seemed to have registered my absence. 'Here, take this. Put a few drops on your pillow and one on your heart before school tomorrow.'

She took the proffered phial, staring at it for a moment, frowning, before looking up at me. At last she grinned.

'Thanks. Thank you,' she said. 'Is it . . . ?'

I did not let her finish.

'Off with you,' I said. 'It's too bleak to stand here idle. I've things to do.'

MARCH 4, 2007—THIRD QUARTER

I have no one to blame but myself, which only serves to make my temper worse. How could I have been so foolish? What was I thinking? I hear myself trying to justify my actions, a simple response to the suffering of another by one who could help, but it makes the results no better. Tegan fair flung herself into my garden this afternoon, eyes bright, the light of joy and amazement shining out of her. She jumped about in front of me, waving the blue bottle under my nose with so much vigor I had to tell her to stop.

'But it worked!' she cried. 'It actually worked. You're bloody incredible. How did you do it? Tell me what was in it. What else can you do? I knew it, all along, I just knew you were special. There was something . . . Can you do love spells too? Can you make people fall in love, even if they don't want to?'

I hardly heard the rest. She rattled on while I sought to make sense of what I could have done that could have caused such excitement. At last I raised my hands and spoke sharply.

'Enough! Take a breath and tell me, slowly and clearly, what has happened.'

'Well, I did exactly what you told me—put some of this stuff on my pillow and a few dabs on my heart. Well, quite a lot actually. Yesterday and today. I thought maybe it was a love potion, you know, something to make Michael fancy me.'

'What?!'

'Obviously it wasn't. I see that now. It was something so much better! How did you know? About Sarah-I'm-So-Perfect-Howard? I didn't tell you she'd been bullying me. I never mentioned what she did to my coat, or what she wrote on my locker, or the gross dead frog in my bag, did I? Suppose I might have said something about her teasing me about Michael. Not that she's the only one who does it, but she's the worst. Cow. The others copy her. But not anymore!' She started waving the bottle about again.

I shook my head, 'I'm sorry, Tegan, I don't understand a word of what you're saying. I gave you bergamot oil. It helps build confidence and strengthen resolve. That is all.'

She ignored me.

'Glandular fever! Genius or what?' She all but jumped up and down. 'She'll be off school for weeks, months even. Maybe the rest of this term and half the summer. You have no idea how much I've prayed for something like this to happen. But I never really thought . . . and then you came along. The answer to my prayers.' She gazed at me, the most admiring and adoring expression I have had aimed in my direction for decades. My mouth felt curiously dry as I forced myself to speak. This was going to take some undoing.

'Tegan, what do you think it was that I gave you?'

'Dunno exactly, just something to get rid of Sarah Howard.' She shrugged.
'A magic potion?'

'Well, yes.'

'And why do you think I would have something like that?' I watched her search for the answer somewhere around her feet. 'Tegan?' I persisted.

'Sounds sort of silly now, saying it out loud, but, well, because you're a witch, aren't you?'

She could not have imagined the impact her words had on me. I was relieved she was momentarily unable to meet my eye, for she would have found fear there. How could she have seen so much when I saw so little? I had dangerously underestimated the girl. The rain had become heavy again now, and the two of us stood, a few feet and several hundred years apart, the sound of the raindrops loud in the charged silence. Slowly Tegan looked up and I saw wonderment on her face. It was of the variety only ever found in those young enough to yet have minds as open as the oceans and hearts longing to have proof of magic. If only she knew what proof stood before her.

'Come inside,' I said, and together we went into the kitchen. I bade her sit at the table while I fetched parsnip soup from the stove. I handed her a mugful, and she cupped it in her hands, never taking her eyes off me.

'Watch out for the leg of toad,' I warned.

Her eyes widened for an instant, then she laughed and the tension in the room evaporated with the steam of the broth.

'What do you know of witches?' I asked.

'Oh, usual stuff. They make potions out of herbs. Cast spooky spells. That sort of thing. I know there are lots out there nowadays, well, lots who call themselves witches. It's all the New Age rage, isn't it? But I bet there aren't many like you. Not many that can actually do stuff.'

She blew into her mug.

I opened the fire door of the stove and pushed in another log. The soft wood cuttings from our work of the previous week were sappy and unseasoned and spat crossly but gave out a reasonable heat. I pulled my chair closer and gestured to Tegan to do the same as I rearranged the cushions behind me for more comfort.

'What time is your mother expecting you?'

'She's not. I mean, she's on nights. She won't be home till morning.'

Not for the first time I was struck by the solitary nature of the young girl's life. It seemed cruel. Not deliberately neglectful but cruel nonetheless. I closed my eyes for a moment and did my utmost to still my whirling mind. There existed only two options. Denial, ridicule, making light of events, accepting no argument, and thereafter firmly distancing myself from Tegan. This was surely the more sensible course, but it saddened me, built as it would have to be upon lies and half truths. The other path, however, was one not to be taken without care. It was a journey once started that would require thought and time and consideration, for there would be no turning back. Somewhere deep in my being, I felt a spark of excitement, a scintilla of hope. Could it be, after all this long, long time, that I was going to share my secret with someone? That I would no longer be forced to hide the truth from everyone? This innocent girl had seen through my defenses in a way that no other had, so that now I felt an overwhelming desire to have her know me, to have her understand. And to visit again the events that have brought me here. I opened my eyes.

'If you will listen,' I said, 'I will tell you a tale of witches. A tale of magic and love and loss. A story of how simple ignorance breeds fear, and how deadly that fear can be. Will you listen?'

'Yeah, cool! Bloody right I will.' Tegan nodded energetically.

I held up a hand, 'Really? Are you truly able to be still and quiet and listen?'

She nodded once more, slowly and deliberately this time. I sighed, a long exhalation, a letting go.

'Very well,' I said, 'let me tell you what it means to be a witch.'

Batchcombe, Wessex, 1627

I

That year the harvest was good. Rain early in the season had given way to a dry summer under a fruitful sun, and the last cut of hay from the top meadow was the finest Bess had seen. She pushed up her shirtsleeves, dark wisps of hair from beneath her cap coiling into the curve of her warm neck as she stooped. Her brown skirts skimmed the mowed grass, snatching up stray stems as she gathered armfuls of hay. Ahead of her, her father, John, worked in swift, practiced movements with his fork, digging deep before flicking the hay high onto the rick, apparently without effort. Atop the stack stood Thomas, at sixteen a whole year older than Bess and a head taller, deftly working the hay into the shape required to repel the weather and hold firm through autumn winds. He shared his sister's coloring and angular body, both inherited from their mother, Anne, as was the seriousness that he wore like a cloak about his shoulders, but his practical way of being in the world, his measured habit of facing life, those were qualities handed down to him from his father.

Bess paused, rubbing the small of her back, straightening to stretch tired muscles. She enjoyed haymaking: enjoyed the sense of completion of another cycle of planting and growing, of a successful crop gathered in, of the security of fodder for the beasts and therefore food for the family for the coming winter months. Her enjoyment did not stop her body complaining about the hard work, however. The heat was fatiguing. Her sweat-wet skin was gritty with dust and itched from a thousand grass seeds. Her nose and throat were uncomfortably dry. She shielded her eyes with her hand, squinting toward the leeward hedge. Two figures approached. One tall and lean like herself, striding with purpose and containment; the other a small bundle of energy, dark, nimble, skipping over the ground as if it were too hot for her dainty feet. Bess smiled. It was a smile only her little sister could induce. The child was a constant source of joy for the whole family. This was due in part to her happy disposition, her prettiness, and her sweet laughter that no one could resist. But it had also to do with the painful years that had preceded her birth. Bess and Thomas had been born quickly and without difficulty, but later siblings had not been so fortunate. Twice Anne had miscarried a baby, and two who had survived to birth had dwindled in her arms. Another, a rosy-cheeked boy, Bess remembered, had lived to the age of two before succumbing to the measles. By the time Margaret arrived, the rest of the family were steeled for further loss and grief but soon saw that here was a child who would grasp life with both of her tiny hands and live every day of it, however many or few there might be.

'They're come,' Bess told the men.

They dropped their forks without a second bidding, more than ready for their food after a long morning's toil.

Margaret squealed and ran to greet her sister, leaping into her arms. Bess spun her round and round until they both collapsed dizzy and giggling onto the hay-strewn ground.

'Bess!' Her mother's voice pretended to be stern. 'Have a care.'

'Aye.' Her father dusted down his shirt front with roughened hands. 'The mare won't eat her feed if it's had the flavor pressed out of it.' His attempt at rancor was even less successful.

Together, the family made their way over to the nearby oak and settled themselves in its friendly shade. Anne placed her basket on the ground and began to lift out the meal she had brought for the workers.

'We made oatcakes, Bess, look.' Margaret thrust a cloth bundle beneath her sister's nose, tugging at the corners to reveal the treats.

Bess breathed in deeply, savoring the aroma of the warm cakes. 'Mmmm! Margaret, these smell good.'

'Good?' John laughed as Anne passed him the stoneware jar of cider. 'Why, Bess, doesn't thou know the finest oatcakes in all of Batchcombe when they be under thy nose?'

Margaret jumped with delight, performing clumsy cartwheels of celebration. Bess watched the whirl of skirts and petticoats tumbling across the biscuit-dry ground. The oatcakes tasted of the day itself, of sunshine, and plenty, and loving hands. She wished that it could always be just this time of year, the lazy height of summer, the strong sun, the long bright days, the ease of warm weather and abundant food.

'Why can it not always be summer?' she asked of no one in particular.

'That makes no sense.' Thomas spoke through a mouthful of cheese. 'If it were always summer, there would be no rain, no time to plant, no fallow seasons, no rest for the land, no gathering in. Farmers would be all in a caddle.'

'Oh, Thomas'—Bess lay flat, her hands behind her head, eyes closed, watching the sun's brilliance dance on the back of her eyelids—'do you always have to show such good sense?'

'No person ever died of a surfeit of it,' he pointed out.

Bess laughed. 'Nor did they ever truly live on such a diet.'

'I think you wish to spend all your life as a child, Bess,' Thomas said, more as a plain fact than a criticism.

Bess opened her eyes and watched Margaret dancing across the stubble. 'Surely it is the summer of our lives. Why would I want to leave it? Such freedom. Life is all possibility. And then we grow up and find our choices to be so very few. Everything is set down for us. Who we must be. Where we must bide. How we must live our lives.'

Anne shook her head.

'Most would be thankful to have a place, a home, a position. To be sure of who they are.'

'Not our Bess.' John paused to take a slow swig of cider and then continued, 'Our Bess would sooner go where the wind has a mind to take her.' He laughed. 'Adventure lies o'er yonder hill or else across the ocean, not in Batchcombe. B'aint that so, Bess?'

'Is it so wrong to want to do something different?' Her eyes glowed with the idea of it. 'To change something? To go beyond what is set down?'

'Have a care, Bess,' said her mother. 'There are those would call such notions vanity. They would say 'tis ungodly to wish to be other than He has chosen for thee.'

Bess sighed, wishing that just for once her mother would allow her to voice her dream without trampling it into the hard earth of reality.

'Look!' Margaret had stopped dancing and was pointing excitedly at the far side of the pasture. 'William! 'Tis Bess's William!'

Color flooded Bess's cheeks. 'He most certainly is not "Bess's William",' she said, standing up to hide her discomfort.

'Oh, but he is,' Margaret insisted. 'You know he be in love with you. Everyone knows it.' She laughed with delight.

Bess tried hard to remain stern, but a smile tugged at the corners of her mouth.

'They know no such thing, Margaret.' Bess stole a glance in the direction indicated by her sister's still pointing finger. Two riders were following the narrow path between the grassland and the woods. William, as befitted a young man of his wealth and family, was mounted on a fine animal the color of autumn bracken. The second man rode a simple nag, sturdy and plain. Although they were some distance away, Bess could clearly make out William's youthful but earnest face. The son of Sir James Gould, local squire and owner of Batchcombe Woods, William could often be found about his father's business, helping him manage the estate and lands that went with Batchcombe Hall, which had been in his family for more generations than anyone remembered. He was listening attentively to his companion now, nodding from time to time, his expression serious as ever. Bess's gaze slid to the older man. She knew who he was; his dark clothes and inappropriately proud bearing were easily recognizable. He was nearer her father's age than her brother's yet did not have a similarly worn and rugged appearance, which was strange for someone who lived such a rural and basic life. Gideon Masters. Everyone knew who Gideon was, but Bess doubted that anyone actually knew the man himself. He rarely came into the village, did not attend church or go to the inn for ale, and when he was in company was not given to easy conversation. His life as a charcoal maker meant he would naturally spend most of his time in his cottage in the woods, and yet Bess believed he embraced his reclusive existence, more than likely having chosen his trade because of rather than in spite of it. After all, he had not seen the need for wife or family. He spoke without looking at his landlord, gesturing all the while at this piece of woodland and that. Then, abruptly, he turned and smiled at William. Even from her distant viewpoint, Bess could see the power in that smile, the way it transformed his stern features. As always, Bess found the man oddly fascinating. Watching him reminded her of how when they were small, she and Thomas would lie on their bellies in the grass, hands beneath their chins, bewitched by the sight of a cat chewing on a live mouse. Bess had wanted to look away but could not, finding herself horribly compelled to stare at the sharp teeth of the cat as they sank into the twitching rodent. So it was with Gideon. She would prefer not to see him in the same picture as gentle William, and yet of the two riders it was the man that drew her gaze, not the boy. At that moment, Gideon, as if sensing he was being observed, looked directly at Bess. Even with a broad stretch of pasture between them, Bess was certain he was staring straight into her eyes. She turned away quickly, helping herself to bread. She became aware of another pair of eyes upon her. Her mother was watching her closely.

'There is a man best left to himself.' Anne made the statement for all to hear, but she never once took her gaze off Bess.

'He is a solitary fellow,' John agreed.

'Mibben he is lonely.' As soon as Bess had spoken the words, she wished them unsaid. She could not think what had made her voice such an idea.

'He chooses to bide alone,' said her mother. 'That is not the same thing.'

The afternoon's work went well, the whole family concentrating their efforts on finishing the task. Even so, the sun was disappearing behind the trees as they gathered their implements and turned for home. Long shadows followed them across the enclosure, the last of the day's heat dwindling into evening. As Bess walked she let her ears travel beyond the chattering finches and wheeling rooks so that she could discern the distant sighing of the sea. On a breezy day she could smell it from the open door of the cottage, but in such stillness and heat all that reached her was the exhalation of the harmless summer waves. She loved the fact that their home was so close to the shore. They could not see it from the smallholding, but it was only a short walk to the cliff top. Bess decided she would take Margaret down to the beach to look for cockles and whelks early the next morning.

By the time they reached the cottage, Margaret was dragging on Bess's hand and yawning loudly. The house sat in a small indent in the landscape, its whitewashed stone pink in the afterglow of the sun, its straw thatch a snugly fitting hat pulled low over its windows. From behind the wooden barn came the sonorous lowing of the cows, impatient to be milked. Thomas and John fetched pails while the women went indoors.

The small house was a single storey with a main room, the hall, a parlor, which served as bedchamber for the family, and the dairy. Here the temperature was kept cool by the addition of heavy stone slabs on which the butter lay wrapped in muslin. A wooden rack of shelves held the maturing cheeses. By the window was the butter churn at which Bess had stood for so many hours, helping her mother produce gleaming blocks to sell at Batchcombe market on Fridays, along with the Blue Vinny cheese that was so popular. In these respects the dairy was the same as any other for twenty miles around. Only the far wall and its sturdy shelves were a departure from the commonplace. Here were bundles of herbs tied tight, hanging from the ceiling. Beneath them were baskets of pungent cloth parcels. And on the shelves, regimental rows of small clay pots and stoneware jars stood to attention. Inside each was a concoction of Anne's invention, the recipes known only to her, and some latterly to Bess. There was lavender oil for treating scars and burns; rosemary and mint to fight coughs and fevers; comfrey to knit broken bones; fruit leaf teas to ease the pains of childbirth; garlic powder to purify the blood; and rose oil to restore the mind. Pots of honey from John's bees sat fatly, waiting to treat wounds that were slow to heal or save the lives of infants following sickness. In this dark, quiet corner of this unremarkable room dwelled the secrets of healing and treatments for disease handed down from mother to daughter for generations.

'Leave the door open, Bess,' said her mother. 'Let us have the sun's company while we may. Your father will not begrudge us candles later.'

Bess and Margaret set to laying the table while their mother lit a fire beneath the pottage. They were fortunate in living so close to the woods and having their modest acreage bordered by sizable trees. This meant that with care they need not be short of fuel and could use the manure from the livestock for fertilizing the pasture, rather than having to gather it and dry it to burn in the winter months. Margaret fetched the pewter bowls while Bess took the pitcher to the dairy. She paused a moment to allow her eyes to adjust to the gloom. How she loved this room. She stepped over to the wheels of cheese, sniffing their nutty fragrance, her mouth running at the memory of the creamy sourness of a piece of Blue Vinny eaten with warm bread. She wandered over to the corner of the room and ran a finger along the jars, repeating aloud the names of the contents, memorizing the order in which they were stored.

'Rosemary, thyme, garlic. Feverfew, no . . . comfrey, more comfrey, raspberry leaf tea . . .' Putting down the jug, she prized the stopper from a bottle and breathed in its fumes. 'Ah, sweet dog rose.'

Her mother's gift as a healer was a perpetual source of fascination for Bess. She had seen her prepare infusions and tinctures and unctions hundreds of times, and yet it never failed to enthrall her. Her mother's wisdom had been passed down to her by her mother, and her mother before that had gathered herbs and plants to concoct remedies and tonics. Bess lacked her mother's patience and wished she had more of her levelheadedness so that she might one day take up her work. She knew she had much to learn and at times heard exasperation in her mother's voice when she forgot which tea softened the pains of childbirth or what oil should be given for ringworm.

'Bess?' Her mother called from the fireside. 'Be quick with that cider.' Bess hastily resealed the oil and did as she was told.

They ate their supper in familiar silence except for Margaret's occasional commentary and the spitting of the fire. Light summer evenings were a blessing, but they brought long hours of work in the fields, and none of the family was inclined to energetic talk. With the table cleared, John sat by the last of the burning logs with his pipe. Thomas went outside to tend to the stock before night. Anne lit two candles and sat in her beloved rocking chair by the girls, who had already fetched their lacework and bobbins from the linen chest. Bess disliked the fiddly task and was never wholly satisfied with the results of her labors. Margaret, on the other hand, had a natural talent for the work, her nimble fingers speeding the bobbins this way and that with never a loose stitch or lazy finish. She put Bess in mind of a tiny garden spider spinning its web to catch the morning dew. Her sister became aware she was being watched and grinned at Bess. There passed between the two a silent communication, a tiny nod, a stifled laugh.

'Go on, Bess,' Margaret whispered, *'please!'*

Bess smiled but shook her head, using her eyes to remind her sibling of how close by their mother sat. She tried to focus on the lace. The low candlelight forced her to squint at the fine thread, and the effort was starting to make her brow ache. Irritation began to mount within her. Why should they have to ruin their eyesight and test their nerves with such bothersome work? Where was it written that she, Bess, must spend so many hours engaged in such vexing labor, just to put a few coins in the family purse? The thought of some well-to-do Lady, who no doubt spent her time on far more interesting pursuits, adorning herself with the results of Margaret's handiwork brought a further knot of anger into Bess's head. For a second she failed to keep a tight rein on her temper, and in that second it escaped, an invisible ball of pure energy. At once the candles on the table began to spit. Then, feeding on this rich new fuel, the flames grew, up and up, brighter and brighter. Anne gasped and jumped to her feet. Margaret squealed with delight.

'Yes, Bess!' she cried, clapping her hands. 'Oh, yes!'

The room was filled with light, as if a hundred candles had been lit. The flames towered above the table, threatening to reach the ceiling. John sprang to his feet and was on the point of dousing them with his cider when, abruptly, the candles went out. In the darkness Bess could not see her mother's face, but she was certain she had heard the snapping of her fingers just a second before the flames had been extinguished. The air was heavy with the fatty smell of smoldering wicks. John took a spill from the fire and relit the candles. Anne's expression was stern.

'Press on with your work, girls,' she said.

An urgent knock at the door startled Bess so much she dropped the lace she had been clutching.

John let in a red-faced boy of about twelve. He all but fell into the room, panting heavily.

'Why, 'tis Bill Prosser's nipper,' John said. 'Sit thee down, lad. What devil chases thee?'

'Our Sarah,' he blurted out, 'the baby . . .' He turned tear-filled eyes to Anne, 'Will you come, Missus? Will you come?'

'Is not Old Mary attending your sister?'

'Was Old Mary sent me to find you, Missus. She told me to tell thee she must have your help.'

Bess stood up. She saw her parents exchange worried glances. Although Anne had assisted at many births and was well known for her care and skill, Old Mary had taught her most of what she knew. She was undoubtedly the best midwife Batchcombe could offer. If she needed help, things must be bad indeed.

Anne stepped quickly into the dairy and came back with her bag. She picked up her woolen shawl and handed another to Bess.

'Come with me,' she said, before all but shoving the boy back out the door and bundling him down the path. 'Hurry, Bess!' she called back.

Bess shook herself from her state of shock and ran after them.

The Prossers' home was a fine timber-framed house at the end of the high street. Bill Prosser was a merchant and, unlike John, owned his home. It was neither grand nor ostentatious but rather had about it an understated expense and quality that spoke of a man of money. Indeed, Batchcombe had recently come to boast several such men—merchants who had seen opportunity for wealth and betterment in changing times. So successful had many of them become, Prosser included, that they had acquired not only money but reputation. In the new order, they were not merely mercantile men, little better than market traders simply hawking their wares on a broader pitch; now they were seen as men of commerce and intelligence, men who would be important players in the modern world that was emerging from the dark ages. Mistress Prosser held herself entirely responsible for her own good fortune, having chosen her husband for his fine qualities and coolheadedness, she had been a good wife to him, borne him three sons and three daughters (miraculously all still living) and had been rewarded with financial security and social standing higher than she could have imagined. She had prided herself on furnishing her new home with all the very best and most fashionable items, whilst still, naturally, observing a godly modesty. It was a hard act to carry out successfully, particularly when her husband's merchandise arrived from distant shores—the most exquisite embroideries, the finest linen, the most beautiful glassware from Venice and silverware from Spain. The results were striking, though a little at the expense of modesty. Bill Prosser was proud of what he had achieved and happy for his wife to dress the house with pointers to his success. He was happier still to see his daughters well married. Both he and Mistress Prosser knew very well that their new sons-in-law would have been beyond the reach of their girls only a few years earlier. But society can have its memory shortened by wealth. Nevertheless, disease and misfortune knew no social bounds. Nor did the immensely dangerous business of childbirth.

The scene that greeted Bess in young Sarah's bedchamber was one of panic and pain. The young girl had not yet been a year married and she had returned to her father's house for her confinement. The men sat with stern, pale faces in the kitchen, while the women attended the terrified girl. Her mother, her older sister, and at least two aunts crowded round the bed. Sarah looked no more than a child herself at that moment, her hair damp and tangled on the pillow, her skin flushed and shiny, her body dwarfed by her swollen stomach. The room was lit only by a small lamp and a candle, and in the summer heat the air was fetid and hot. Bess put her hand to her mouth as the door was closed behind her. Anne moved quickly to the window and threw it open.

'Oh!' cried Sarah's mother. 'My daughter will take a chill from the night air in her weakened state.'

'Your daughter will faint away, robbed of breath, if she is to share the rank air in this room with so many people.'

The older woman thought to protest further, but Anne silenced her.

'I am here to help, Mistress Prosser. Allow me to do so.'

Despite the best efforts of Old Mary, the labor had consisted thus far of hours of pain and effort and blood and yet produced no baby. Sarah lay wide-eyed, clutching at her mother's hand, her sweaty face showing a mix of exhaustion and fear. Sarah's sister dabbed at her ineffectually with a damp cloth.

Mary drew Anne to a corner and spoke to her with a muted voice, which she was forced to raise on occasion because of the girl's pitiful cries.

'Bless thee for coming with such speed, Anne. This does not go well. The poor child is all but spent and still no sign of the infant coming forth.'

Anne nodded, listening closely to what the old woman had to say. Bess thought Mary herself looked near collapse. What did she think her mother could do for this wretched girl that she could not? Bess watched the two consulting for a moment longer before Anne stepped over to the bed and laid her hands on Sarah's belly.

'Hush, child, do not fear.'

'Oh, Missus Hawksmith!' Sarah grabbed at her with a clammy hand. 'The babe will surely die, and me besides!'

'No, no. It is just as Mary says. Your infant is lying awkward, 'tis all. We must bid him turn so that he can find his way out.'

She had barely finished her sentence when a powerful spasm gripped Sarah's body. The girl let out a shout that grew into a shriek until it trailed off to a heartbreaking whimper. Anne placed her hands on Sarah's belly once more, gently but firmly working to manipulate the baby, to change its position. For a moment it seemed she might succeed, but then, just when the child seemed ready to engage with the process of being born, it would spin upward and sideways again. Anne persisted. Three times she almost won, but on each occasion the infant swiveled at the last minute. Anne straightened up as Sarah endured another agonizing convulsion. Bess marveled at how her whole body was taken up as if by some unseen force. A force that should be aiding the unborn child's delivery but instead seemed only to be hastening its death.

Anne spoke softly to Mary.

'Have you tried turning it from inside the girl?'

'I have'—Mary nodded—'but she is a lissome lass. There is no room for my crooked hands.'

The two women looked at her bent, arthritic fingers, and then at Anne's own straight but broad palms. Anne turned to Bess.

'Show me your hands.'

'What?'

'Quickly, Bess, show me.'

Bess did as her mother bade her. Anne and Mary examined her hands closely. They looked at each other and then back at Bess. Anne lifted her daughter's hands up and squeezed them as she spoke.

'Bess, you must attend to my words. Do precisely what I tell you, no more nor less. Move with care but firmly.'

'You mean . . . but, I can't, Mother. I cannot!'

'You must! Only you can do it. If you do not, both mother and babe will die this night. Do you hear me?'

Bess opened her mouth to protest further but could not find the words. She had delivered calves for her father, who had also seen the value of her small hands. She had assisted at lambing time. She had even been present in the room when Margaret was born, though she remembered little past her mother's determined face. She saw that same fixed expression now and knew it was not in her power to change it. Before she could think further, her mother called for a bowl of hot water and had Bess wash her hands. Anne dried them on clean linen, then rubbed them with lavender oil. All the while Mistress Prosser and the attendant women looked on with disdain at such unfamiliar practices. Anne led Bess to the bed before positioning herself at Sarah's side, placing her hands on her belly once more. She nodded at Bess.

Bess looked at the young girl who was lying before her. Her chest heaved with the effort of labor and of pain. Her cheeks had taken on an alarming pallor. She looked up at Bess, her eyes pleading. Bess leaned forward and slowly eased the fingers of her right hand into the girl.

'What do you feel, Bess?' Anne asked.

'I cannot be certain . . . not the head, nor any limbs.' She looked at her mother, brows creased, trying to picture in her mind how the baby could be arranged in its mother's womb. 'I think . . . yes, I feel the child's back, and here, its shoulder.'

Old Mary cursed quietly, ''Tis as I feared—the babe lies crossways.'

Mistress Prosser began to weep.

Anne held Bess in her gaze. 'Feel for the top of the shoulder. Work your fingers over the bone. I will aid you from outside, but you must turn that baby so that his head is drawn downward.'

'There is no room. I cannot take a hold . . .'

'You must!'

Bess searched with her fingertips, finding her way to the nape of the unborn child's neck and then over its tiny shoulder. She pulled, gently at first, then with more force. 'It will not move.'

Old Mary stepped forward to whisper in Anne's ear, but her words were audible to all.

'Anne, I have the hooks . . .'

'No!' Anne was adamant. 'Not while the infant still lives.' She turned to Bess again. 'Keep trying,' she said.

Bess did as she was told but feared her efforts would prove fruitless. The slippery baby seemed stuck fast in its impossible position. A terrifying image came into Bess's mind. She recalled with frightening clarity the time her father had failed to deliver a particularly large calf. After battling for hours, he had thrown up his hands and sent Bess to the dairy to fetch the cheese wire. He had used it, with slow and deliberate movements, to slice the calf into pieces so that they might take it out and save the cow. No one could be certain the creature had been dead before he started dissecting it. Bess could see now the pathetic limbs and hooves lying in a gory mess beside its mother. The cow herself had died the following day. Bess blinked the picture from her mind. She must stay calm. She must be steadfast. If she was not, Sarah would pay the price with her life. Bess redoubled her efforts, shutting from her thoughts the notion that she might harm the child—it had to come out. At last she began to detect some shifting in its position. Anne noticed it too.

'Do not let it slip back,' she said.

Bess prized the shoulder to one side and felt the head moving downward toward the birth canal. At that moment, a powerful contraction swept through Sarah's body. The girl was now too weak to scream and instead emitted an eerie wail.

Old Mary stepped forward.

'Bear down, child! Do not falter now. Push!'

Now she screamed. With one last, gargantuan effort, with strength summoned from an unknowable place that exists hidden within every mother, Sarah screamed and pushed.

Bess gasped as her hand and the baby were driven out. Everything happened with such speed she barely had time to grab the infant as it slithered onto the blood-soaked linen.

'Look!' Bess cried. 'He's out! A boy!'

Anne examined the child who protested loudly, much to the relief of everyone in the room.

'The Lord be praised!' whispered Mistress Prosser, raising her daughter's hand to her lips.

Old Mary smiled a toothless grin, 'The Lord and young Bess here,' she said. 'She surely be her mother's daughter.'

Bess watched the baby wrapped in warm swaddling and handed to his mother. Sarah kissed the top of her newborn's head, her face transformed, the cloud of death removed and replaced by the warm joy of life. She looked up at Bess.

'Thank you, Bess,' she said.

'I need no thanks beyond seeing you and the babe safe and well, Sarah.'

'I will never forget what you have done for us,' Sarah said, before closing her eyes.

Bess felt her mother's hand on her arm.

'Come, Bess. Let us leave her to rest.'

'I feared I might fail,' she confessed.

Her mother smiled. It was a smile that from anyone else might have been said to betray pride. She shook her head. 'You did well, child,' she told her daughter. 'You did well.'

2

A week later, at the start of the day, with dawn barely progressed sufficiently to light her way, Bess took a basket and headed into the woods to gather moss and lichen for her mother's pharmacopoeia. The early daylight cast not a shadow and gave soft edges to tree and stone so that the world appeared somehow gentler and more yielding. As Bess reached the limit of the pasture, she hesitated. She loved the woodland and yet had always the sense that in stepping into its leafy embrace she was entering another realm. Here things were hidden and secret. All manner of possibilities dwelled in the tangled roots and verdant undergrowth. The trees provided a place unknowable and mysterious for shy and mythical creatures to abide in. It was a place of fairies and sprites and wood nymphs. A place of magic.

Bess found herself treading thoughtfully as she threaded her way deeper and deeper into the forest. She was not afraid, nor even nervous; rather she felt she should show a certain respect, a reverence even, to those woodland deities whose stores she now plundered. She stooped to peel moss as thick as wolf fur from a shady rock. She laid it carefully in the bottom of her basket and continued. On a blackthorn she found an abundance of silvery lichen. She plucked the brittle antlers from the lower boughs until she had sufficient. A narrow brook provided perfect conditions for more moisture-loving mosses, all good for speeding the mending of open wounds. She was picking her way over stepping-stones when she heard, or rather sensed, a disturbance. It was not as if a sound had reached her ears, more that she noticed a change in the air about her. A subtle shift in the energy. She cocked her head and listened, then pushed slowly into the woods in the direction of whatever it was that she detected. A few paces farther and she could indeed discern sounds. There were grunts and groans, animalistic and gruff. Now she could plainly hear gasps and moans. A movement up ahead made her stop. She brushed aside a curtain of ivy that was obscuring her view. What she saw made her start. Two figures, one darkly dressed, tall, and powerful, the other a woman—no, a girl—all but naked save a few dove-white strips of her torn slip. They were standing, the girl pressed up against an ash tree, the man with his back to Bess. She dared not move, afraid they would discover they were being watched, but at the same time she realized they were far too involved in their energetic lovemaking to be so easily distracted. She was about to turn and slip silently back into the trees when something caught her attention. A frayed piece of rope. The girl was bound to the tree. Now she looked again, Bess could see that the girl's moans and wails were not of ecstasy but of anguish. She was not enjoying the attentions of an ardent lover but was being raped. Bess opened her mouth to shout out but checked herself. She must do something to rescue the poor young woman, but a man capable of such a thing would not give up his prize easily. She had no weapon with which to protect herself or to threaten him. She cast around for a strong stick or heavy stone. At that moment she heard shouts coming from a way off to the west, deeper into the forest. The man heard them too and turned to look over his shoulder. Turned so that Bess could clearly see his face, and there was no mistaking the stern features of Gideon Masters. Features distorted by a bestial lust and eyes inhumanly red with anger. The girl heard the voices of her would-be rescuers and called out to them. Gideon stepped back. He placed a finger under the girl's chin and raised her face. He stared into her eyes, his lips moving quickly as if uttering some prayer or incantation. The girl's lids grew heavy and she slumped forward, her weight taken by the rope that tied her. Gideon took a pace onto the eastward path but then hesitated. Swinging round, he narrowed his eyes in Bess's direction, scanning the undergrowth. But Bess had already dropped to the cover of the forest floor. She heard him turn again and make off through the forest. She stayed where she was but peered through the foliage in time to see the searchers find the girl. She recognized them as the family of gypsies who had passed through the village some days before. The mother flung herself at her daughter and clung to her, weeping loudly. The father stormed about, cursing in a tongue unknown to Bess and shaking his fist at the sky, before untying his daughter and carrying her away in his arms. Bess abandoned her basket and slunk back the way she had come, not daring to stand and run until she was sure she was out of sight, clear of the terrible scene, one which would stay imprinted on her mind forever. She was in reach of the sunshine at the edge of the woodland when Gideon sprang out in front of her, blocking her escape. Instinctively she recoiled from him, but then anger gave her courage. She would not let him see her fear.

'Why, it is young Bess Hawksmith. I was certain it was you I saw.'

'Let me pass.'

'How long had you been hiding, I wonder? How long were you watching, hmmm?'

'I was out gathering moss and lichen.'

'Really? I do not see any.'

Bess cursed herself for abandoning her basket like a frightened child. Gideon stepped closer. The warmth of his body was clearly discernible and gave off an earthy odor. Bess turned her head away from him. When he spoke again, she could feel his breath against her ear.

'The girl was not so unwilling as you think,' he said.

Bess swung back to face him.

'She did not bind herself to that tree, I think.'

'Mibben she asked me to do it.'

'Mibben you forced her.'

'What manner of force would that be? Did you see a single mark on her ripe young body? A single bruise or sign of brutal treatment?'

'I know what I saw. I know what you did.'

Gideon smiled.

'Have a care, Bess. That tongue of yours will talk you into trouble one day. Do you plan to run home and speak of what you have seen? Do you think you will be believed?'

'I will speak for the gypsy lass if she asks me.'

'Ah, then the matter is closed. For she will remember nothing of her . . . experience. I have seen to that.'

He placed his finger beneath Bess's chin just as he had done to the girl. Bess wanted to look away but found her gaze locked to his. She set her jaw, resisting the curious swirling that had begun to stir her thoughts. Gideon's voice reached her as if through a November fog.

'Most yield without a struggle. Some minds are easily influenced, easily bent to a stronger will. Others, like your own, not so.' He dropped his hand.

Bess pushed past him, head down.

'Oh, Bess,' he called after her softly, 'do not leave without what is yours.'

Despite herself, she turned, then started. Gideon held out her basket, filled to overflowing with the greenest of mosses and the most delicate of lichens.

'My basket! But how . . . ?' She could not bring herself to form the question, for she knew that there was no sensible answer. Instead, she snatched the wicker handle and strode for home, fleeing Gideon's gentle singing of "Greensleeves," the melody too lovely to bear from such a dark and disturbing soul.

The village of Batchcombe was, in truth, sufficiently large to be called a town, but the memories of the families who inhabited the place were long and slow to change, and so it was still referred to as the village. As such, it was well supplied with stores and facilities. There were more than enough ale houses to slake even a harvest thirst. There were two butchers, a well-patronized baker, a blacksmith's forge, and a tailor's shop. These emporia were arranged along both sides of the broad main street, which itself hosted the weekly market, where all and sundry came to sell their produce. In the center of the street stood the courthouse, an imposing stone building. The ground floor served as magistrates' court and council meeting place, the top provided rooms for local records and government matters, and beneath the whole was a subterranean jail. The growth of Batchcombe had allowed for the inclusion of fads and fashions where buildings were concerned, so that a lack of continuity or conformity of style existed, giving a wide-ranging variety to the façades that lined the streets. There were stone cottages, some whitened, some bare brown sandstone. There were houses of warm brick, and others of timber with wattle and daub. Next to these stood a terrace constructed painfully out of flint. Thatch of straw or reeds covered some, while others sheltered from the wet winters beneath tiles of stone. Every taste had been accommodated, every innovation tried. Yet the overall impression was one of slight decay and disintegration. It was as if each building was a separate dwelling placed close to another merely by chance, rather than a matter of cohesion and community.

It was fair to say that Batchcombe stood as a portrait of the preceding century of flux. The winds of political change had buffeted it this way and that, and throughout it all, the village and its people had seen survival in acceptance and flexibility. And the monument to their malleable nature was the raw ruin of the monastery to the west of the village boundary. It was as though the centuries of existing side by side for the Church and the godly people of the area had never happened. As if they had never worked in the monastery gardens, or gained employment assisting the monks with the harvest, or apprenticed a clutch of boys every year as stone masons to work on the glorious home of God's servants, or held out their hands for alms in times of poverty and disaster. When Henry VIII had broken from Rome, and the monasteries were sacked, Batchcombe turned its face away, and not a pitchfork was raised in protest. The monks' place of worship and home for centuries was raped, plundered, and defiled, left a craggy heap of stone.

By contrast, the modest church at the southern end of the high street had flourished. It was simply built of stone, with most of its windows plain. Only one had the indulgence of stained glass, depicting Christ's raising of Lazarus from his tomb. The church had become the focal point for most social gatherings and, of course, worship in the area. A succession of canny church wardens had spirited away any signs of popery or undisguised wealth, leaving a spare, understated interior, in keeping with the wishes of first one monarch, then the next, and portentously interpreting the spartan tastes of the years that were to come. The parishioners had slipped quietly into the cushionless pews and counted themselves lucky not to have been delivered into the dubious care of one of the more radical itinerant preachers who roamed Wessex in search of receptive ears for their puritanical beliefs. The parson, who had by this time established himself firmly at the heart of matters both religious and secular in Batchcombe, was the Reverend Edmund Burdock, a thin strip of a man whose flimsy frame and soft voice belied a steely will.

Bess enjoyed attending the Sunday service at the church. After tending the livestock and finishing their household chores, the Hawksmith women, in keeping with all other women in the area, put on their least-worn gown if they had one, or fresh collars, cuffs, and apron if they did not, fastened their bonnets, and set out for the church. If the weather was kind, they would walk; otherwise, John would persuade the mare between the shafts of the wagon and they would ride to the village.

On this occasion, the sun was arcing upward into a cloudless sky and the happy group trod the dry path to Batchcombe, enjoying the prospect of a little socializing. For Bess, this was the one opportunity the week afforded to watch the people of the village and to listen to their gossip. Her mother had spoken to her about the perils of eavesdropping, but there was something irresistible in those snatches of conversation, those glimpses into lives other than her own. Lives that seemed to offer so much more variety and excitement. Even loving her family as she did, Bess harbored a secret yearning for something more. Quite what that might be, she had no idea, but she was certain it was out there, if only she knew how to set about finding it. In the meantime she made do with learning what she could of her mother's skills and nourished her desire for adventure with tidbits of other people's lives. The act of worship itself did not interest her. She had a distant memory of a time when musicians had accompanied the hymns and dazzling hangings and tapestries had glowed from the walls of the church. Now, however, the whole event was a somber affair. The interior was unadorned, except for the color added by the congregation—though even the dresses of the women had subtly altered to keep in step with the trend for modesty and simplicity. Disappointingly so, to Bess's mind. From the pulpit, the parson, the very embodiment of restraint and humility, called on his flock to live godly lives in an ungodly world. Bess was willing to accept God's presence in her life and did her best to behave in a way she had been taught to understand would please Him. She envied those with a true faith. She saw their radiant faces when they prayed or sang in the pews. She watched them nod and smile as the preacher reminded them of God's benevolence and His love. Although she would not dare voice such thoughts to a living soul, Bess herself could not see evidence of all this love. Where was it to be found? Not in the poverty and hunger that afflicted everyone if the crops failed and the harvest was bad. Not in the cruel stamp of disease as it strode through families, crushing the weak and the old beneath its feet. Not in the agonies suffered in childbirth nor the grief of losing children.

As she joined in with the closing hymn, Bess felt Margaret nudge her. She looked down to see her sister grinning and inclining her head toward the end of the pew opposite. Glancing up, Bess's eyes met the pale gray gaze of William Gould. She saw him blush almost as deeply as she herself did in that moment. She cast her eyes down, then slowly looked up again. He was smiling at her now, all pretense at singing abandoned. Bess pointedly put her nose in the air and sang with much more conviction than she felt. She was aware that he continued to watch her, which was no less than she expected.

With the service over, the godly began to file out slowly. Margaret could not contain herself.

'Mam, did you see? William is here. He must have come just to see our Bess.'

'Hush, Margaret!' Her mother took her hand.

'Surely he has,' the child persisted. 'Why else would he choose our plain little church over his own pretty chapel?'

Bess caught her mother's stern glance, but they both knew there was truth in what Margaret said. The Goulds had worshipped at the chapel at Batchcombe Hall for as long as the great house had stood.

Anne sought another explanation.

'The Reverend Burdock is known for his fine sermons,' she said. 'It may be, as a young man of learning, he has an interest in what the reverend might say.' She began to pull Margaret toward the door.

Behind her, John offered Bess his arm and smiled. 'Mibben he does,' he said with a mischievous lifting of his eyebrows, 'or mibben Margaret speaks the truth of it. I'll wager there be nothing so pretty to look at in that chapel of his than what he could gaze upon from the pew 'cross the aisle from where our Bess stood.'

Bess feigned indifference, but she enjoyed the idea of William's affection for her. What young girl would not? True, he was quiet and did not have an exciting manner or clever way about him, but he was kind and gentle. And she was not immune to the fact that he was wealthy and highborn. Too high for the likes of Bess, her mother would frequently tell her. A statement that only served to make the boy more interesting than he otherwise might have been.

Once outside, Margaret skittered about, finding other children to play with while her parents were engaged in conversation with the Prossers. Thomas was quickly bored by the business of other people and took himself off to lean against a shady yew. Bess noticed Sarah showing off her new baby, now nearly one month old, and felt a wave of pride. She still marveled at what she had managed to do that night. It was good to see mother and child happy and well and know that she had played a part in their well-being. Bess wandered about the churchyard, ears pricked. The tail end of summer still held some heat and cheerful light, so that the scene was one of brightness and color, a pleasant contrast to the interior of the poor church. At the western boundary, a late-flowering honeysuckle trailed over the wall of the churchyard, its buttery blooms resting against the glossy leaves of the ivy beneath it. Out here, even the restrained fabrics of the women's dresses were charming and colorful. A little girl hurried by in periwinkle blue, chased by a boy in doublet the color of crushed cherries. Bess passed Widow Digby and Widow Smith, both reliable mouthpieces for village gossip.

'By all accounts, they found him running down the high street wearing nought but his hat and his silver-buckled shoes!' declared Widow Smith in a stage whisper.

'For shame! His poor wife, that she should endure such behavior. And him a vicar's son.'

''Tis no more than is to be expected. There have been complaints aplenty to the magistrate over the strength of the ale at the Fiddler's Rest, but nothing is done, Sister, nothing is done. Oh, good morning, Bess.' Whatever Widow Smith had been about to say further on the matter, Bess would not now hear. She silently berated herself for stepping too close before learning the identity of the poor man with the silver-buckled shoes.

'Good morning, Widow Smith, Widow Digby. What a pretty day it is, do you not agree?'

Widow Smith puffed herself up, inflating her already considerable bulk to menacing proportions.

'Pretty? 'Tis the Sabbath, child. Have a care.'

'Would the Lord take offense?' Bess asked.

'He may,' Widow Digby warned, 'if He believed that fair head of yours was full of nothing but frivolous thoughts.'

'Instead of thoughts of Him, which is what thou shouldst be concerned with on this day,' agreed Widow Smith.

'Upon my oath, Ladies, I have only to look at such a blue as that sky be to think of our Lord,' said Bess with a disarming smile, before turning on her heel and stepping quickly away. She walked quietly around the edge of the churchyard until she neared the lychgate. There stood the Reverend Burdock and the church warden, Amos Watts. Bess had thought to walk straight past them but paused when she discerned the subject of their conversation.

'I will have to make a note,' the church warden was saying. 'I cannot refrain from doing so any longer.'

Reverend Burdock nodded sagely, 'Of course, you must. It is incumbent upon us to be vigilant. I had hoped that after my brief conversation with him at last Tuesday's market . . . but no, it seems Gideon Masters wishes to remain firmly outside of our flock. It saddens me. To see a man, a man of quiet intelligence I believe, to see him turn away from God.'

'Gideon has always been a man apart. I've never known him attend a service in all the years I've lived in Batchcombe, which is a fair few, Reverend, as you know. Time was, a man's conscience was his own concern.'

'And God's, of course.'

'Well, now 'tis the business of government, and government says all those failing to attend church on the Sabbath must have their names noted in the church records. They will be dealt with at the quarter sessions, like it or no.'

'You must do your work, and no person here will think badly of you for it. Be that as it may, I might yet attempt a second meeting with the reluctant Mister Masters . . .'

'Bess?' William's voice made Bess start. She had not noticed him come to stand next to her. She frowned, annoyed that she would not now be able to follow the reverend's conversation further.

'Ah, William. Good morning,' she said, not bothering to disguise her irritation.

William smiled warmly. 'I had hoped to see you here,' he said.

'A safe hope, after all, my coming here every Sabbath.'

'Yes. I suppose so.' William fidgeted, tugging at his short cape, which had become tight around his neck instead of sitting neatly on his shoulders. He continued to smile at her. 'Might we walk awhile?' he asked.

'There are many people here doing just that.' Bess began to stride on. 'It is not for me to say that they might or might not.'

William scurried along beside her, apparently immune to her sharpness. Bess was on the point of saying something else withering when she caught sight of her parents watching her. She slowed her pace immediately so that William was in step with her and treated him to a bright smile.

'So, William, tell me. All are well at Batchcombe Hall?'

'Very well, thank you.'

'And your father?' Bess disliked the man, but William no longer had a mother living for her to inquire after.

'Quite, yes. Taken away often with matters of government, of course.'

Bess nodded, 'Leaving you to run the estate?'

'Well, there is my brother Hamilton. He being the eldest . . .'

They drew level with the Widows Digby and Smith. Bess enjoyed the scandalized expressions they wore. She couldn't decide whom they despised more: Bess herself for having ideas above her station or William for having notions beneath his. The world they had known had been turned on its head in recent years, and nothing could be relied upon to stay as it was. It was a situation not helped by people choosing to step away from the position on this earth the good Lord had seen fit to give them. Bess inclined her head toward the ladies with an innocent smile. Widow Smith pursed her lips so hard they lost what little color they had. Bess waited until they were out of earshot before continuing her conversation with William.

'But it was you I saw about your father's business the other day,' she said, 'on the edge of Batchcombe Woods?'

'Oh, quite possibly. You saw me? What could have so occupied my thoughts that I was unaware of your presence?' William looked genuinely appalled at the idea.

'You were conversing with Gideon Masters.' Bess did her utmost to keep her voice level but saying the evil man's name out loud disturbed her.

'Oh, yes. We were discussing over which trees his rights extended. It seems the demand for charcoal is ever increasing. I believe the man would have the entire woodland stumps if he could.'

Bess looked at William. It was the first time she had ever heard him speak so plainly of anyone.

'You do not like Gideon Masters?'

'I did not say so.'

'You don't disagree, though?'

'What would you have me do, argue with you or . . . ?'

'Or have the courage to speak the truth?' Bess finished his sentence for him and waited.

William stopped walking and stood squarely facing her. His face was altered by his determined expression. So much so that he looked considerably older, the man replacing the boy.

'If you will press me, no, I do not find anything to like in Gideon Masters. He has a way about him, a manner, a . . . disposition that leaves me unsettled.'

'Upon my word, his manner.'

'Mock me if you must, Bess. You asked for the truth. There is something bad in that man. Something I would rather not be in the company of, and I advise you to stay away from him.'

Bess felt her temper getting the better of her. She was in fact pleased to hear that William was wary of Gideon, that she was not alone in knowing him to be dangerous. Even so, she could not help herself bridling at the young man's presumption that she should do as he said.

'Why, thank you kindly for you advice, but I am afraid of no man.'

'I did not think for one moment that you were,' said William.

Later that same afternoon, Bess took Margaret down to the shore to collect shellfish. They descended the twisting path from the cliff top and stepped onto the beach. The tide had turned an hour before so that the rocks were pooled with water and bristling with all manner of crustaceans. Bess and Margaret unbuttoned their boots and left them on a dry rock. Margaret's feet slapped onto the wet sand as she ran ahead, a soft breeze tugging at her braided hair. Bess followed her sister, basket in hand, stooping to fish cockles and whelks from the pools. Above them, gulls swooped low, raucous and bold. One or two alighted on the beach and hopped after the girls to see what might be had.

'Look! Bess, a crab. A great big one!' Margaret stood knee-deep in a pool, snatching at the sandy water she had stirred up in her excitement.

'Be still, Margaret, he will hide from you in all that caddle.'

Bess quieted the girl and they peered into the settling water.

'I see him!' Margaret was irrepressible. She began to laugh and soon had Bess giggling loudly too. Both girls squealed as they splashed their hands into the pool after the crab. Margaret squealed even louder when she caught it. Bess plucked it from her and dropped it into her basket.

'I'm going to find another!' sang Margaret as she danced on to the next pool, her waterlogged shift and skirt clinging to her skinny little legs.

Bess straightened and watched her go, enjoying the leisure and simple happiness of the moment. The beach was long and wide, a tawny crescent stretching as far as Batchcombe Point. On the other side of the promontory, the beach changed. A strange combination of tides and currents and layers of rock decreed that beyond Batchcombe the beaches in the area were not of sand but of smooth pebbles, large ones at the near end, each bigger than a goose egg, dwindling to sandy-colored damsons a mile farther on. Bess let the hissing of the lapping waves lull her into a gentle daydream. She noticed something now, at the far end of the beach, just at the water's edge. It was a dark shape, too distant to be clear. As she watched, she could see that the shape was moving slowly toward her. She half closed her eyes, shading them with a hand, straining to focus. Now she could see it was a figure. A man, dressed in dark clothes with a wide-brimmed hat. He walked with purpose but seemed barely to advance across the wet sands. Bess heard Margaret chattering behind her about tiny fish, but she felt compelled to watch as the man drew slowly, slowly closer. She could not be certain, but she believed she knew who it was. The somber clothes, the tall stature, the methodical, assured movements. It was Gideon Masters. What could he be doing here on the beach? He had no basket or fishing rod. Bess could not imagine him a man to wander idly by the sea. He continued his approach, so that she began to make out his stern features and realized he was looking straight at her. She was transfixed. She licked her dry, salty lips and noticed that her breath had shortened. She remembered what William had said. Something bad in that man. Was that why she felt like this?

'Bess, come here, help me catch these little fish. Daddy will be so pleased! Bess, come now!'

Bess tore herself from the object of her fascination, turning to answer her sister.

'A moment, Margaret, don't frighten them away before I get there.'

She peered back down the beach, part of her hardly daring to look, expecting to see Gideon only paces away. But he had gone. The beach stretched out empty before her. Empty and undisturbed. She ran forward, searching the sand for footprints, but there were none. She could hear Margaret calling after her, but she searched on, splashing through the shallow foam, scanning the beach and the rocks that led up to the cliff. Nothing. She tried to convince herself he must have been walking in the wet sand. His footprints would have filled in quickly, all trace of his walking instantly erased. That seemed logical. Still it did not explain how he had crossed the expanse of dry sand between the water's edge and the path to the cliff top. Nor how he had covered the space with such speed that she did not see him go. That she could not see him now toiling up the winding track.

'Bess?' Margaret was becoming anxious.

With a furiously beating heart, Bess hurried back to her sister.

3

The year turned the corner away from summer and began the fertile rot of autumn, and the family put their efforts to the apple harvest. The trees were not young but were reliable and healthy and had produced another fine yield. The ground was beginning to soften with the increasing rain, but the branches still held their leaves, though they were more copper than green now. Bess and the others worked carefully through the orchard. John had parked the wagon in the gateway, and each basket of apples was tipped gently on to it, ready to be transported to the barn. From there, Anne and Bess would spend many days putting the apples through the press to produce strong, sweet cider that would slake thirsts and lift spirits throughout the following twelve months. Thomas and John climbed wooden ladders with round rungs to reach the higher parts of the fruit trees. Bess and Anne took the apples from them as they were passed down, while Margaret was given the task of collecting windfalls. The harvest would be painstakingly picked over and spread out in a dry, airy part of the barn. It was slow work, but the time invested would pay dividends.

'Have you fallen asleep up there, Thomas?' Bess was becoming impatient standing at the foot of the ladder, apron stretched out, waiting for the fruit.

From the next tree her father laughed, his head deep among the foliage. 'Ah Bess, mibben Tom be struggling to choose. This is important work we are about. I favor my zider free from maggots.'

Bess began to tap her toe in exasperation. 'Mibben he's waiting for them to move on,' she muttered.

The branches above her head parted. Thomas frowned down.

'Cease chiding, Bess. I be going fast as I'm able.'

Bess sighed. 'Better let me up there if the task be too vexing for thee.'

Anne walked past with another laden basket. 'Bess, leave him be. He shan't work faster for you nagging him.'

Bess opened her mouth to protest at what she was being asked to put up with, when without warning Thomas came hurtling past her. He crashed wordlessly to the ground. For a second Bess was too stunned to move, then the sound of Margaret's screams brought her to her senses.

'Thomas?' Bess stooped over her brother. She repeated his name, but he lay motionless. Anne pushed her way to him.

'Thomas! Here, let me to him. Margaret, step out of the way, child. Thomas?' She knelt beside him. At last, the boy groaned and opened his eyes. The family let out a collective breath of relief.

'How do I come to be down here?' he asked, attempting to get to his feet.

'Hush! Lie still,' Anne told him, stroking his forehead. She flinched, drawing her hand away as if his skin had burned her. She looked up at John. 'He has a fever.'

'That caused him to fall?'

Anne nodded. 'Help me get him to the house and put him to bed.'

They raised him gently to his feet, an arm around the shoulders of each parent, and half carried him to the cottage. Bess made to follow, but Anne called back, 'Help Margaret with the windfalls. Come in when you're finished.'

Bess bridled at being so excluded. She wanted to help tend to Thomas, not to be left out in the orchard. But she knew work had to go on. And, more important, Margaret must not be alarmed. She would do as she was told and take a turn in nursing her brother later.

A low cot was made up for Thomas in the main room so that he might benefit from the fire. When dusk fell and Bess at last took Margaret in, she was concerned at the sight of her brother. In a few hours he appeared to have gone from a pale but strong young man to a clammy, fever-ridden boy with ragged breath and dull eyes. Bess took her turn in gently sponging his face. Anne had added a few drops of rose oil to the water, but they could not mask the increasing odor of poor Thomas's overheating body. Despite the fire that seemed to be raging within him, he shivered, moaning at the pains in his limbs and joints, complaining that he was colder than a cow's tail in winter. When Margaret was asleep in the other room, Anne had John and Bess help her strip Thomas. They bathed his whole body and put him in a soft nightshirt of his father's.

'What is it, Mother?' Bess asked.

'A fever.'

'Born of what ailment?' Bess pressed her for a more detailed answer.

'Too soon to say. We must bide with him. Time will reveal to us what it is that makes him suffer so.' Anne would not meet her daughter's questioning gaze. 'Go to the dairy. Fetch me the tea in the tall jar on the top shelf.'

'The nettle tea?'

Now Anne looked at her. 'Yes. You remember how to prepare it?'

Bess nodded.

'Quickly, then.'

Bess left her brother's side with reluctance but with purpose, pleased her mother considered her able to make the infusion for him. As she reached the door to the dairy, she glanced back. The three of them made a poignant tableau—mother kneeling at her stricken son's side, father standing beside her. As Bess watched, John, without taking his eyes off Thomas for an instant, reached down and stroked Anne's cheek. Anne placed her own hand over his and gripped it tightly against her face. Bess knew, in that tiny moment, in that one small but telling gesture, she knew that her brother was in mortal danger.

By the next morning Thomas seemed neither better nor worse but had lost the ability to sleep. Instead, he fidgeted on his bed, shifting his weight this way and that in a vain effort to find a less painful position. Margaret was out collecting the eggs. John had gone to Batchcombe market to sell the cheeses. Anne and Bess worked at their lace so as to be close to Thomas. All at once he swung his legs to the floor and struggled to his feet. Both women rushed to him.

'Thomas'—his mother put her hands on his shoulders—'you must rest. Do not try to raise yourself.'

'No!' Anger tinged his curiously slurred words. 'I must be about my work, Mother. I cannot leave all to father.'

'You are not well,' Bess told him. 'Father will manage until you are recovered.'

He would not be quieted but fought against them with some new-found strength.

'Leave me be! I will go out,' he said, staggering past them to the door, oblivious to his state of undress. His gait was shambolic and precarious, so that he clutched at furniture and walls as he went.

'Thomas!' Anne called after him. She and Bess tried again to persuade him back to his bed but without success. He was ranting now, a stream of incoherent words, as if talking to some unseen person in the room. At last he took hold of the latch and wrenched the door open. Bess feared what might happen to him if he started to fall about outside, but he was prevented from leaving the house. John stepped over the threshold, guiding his son back inside. He turned him, firmly but gently, not back to his bed but through the door into the bedchamber.

'Come, Thomas,' he spoke softly, 'thou'st been working hard. Rest yourself now.'

Bess and Anne followed and helped get him into his own bed. Thomas seemed exhausted from his exertions and fell into a fitful sleep at once.

John took Anne's hands in his. 'I have been to the village,' he said.

Anne's face asked the question, though she could not bring herself to say the words.

'Others are ill,' he confirmed. 'Some already dead.'

'How many?' Anne whispered.

'Eleven so far.'

'O dear Lord.' The color drained from her face.

Bess could stay silent no longer. 'Mother? What is it? What is happening?'

Anne could only shake her head, for a moment robbed of speech. Then she took a shuddering breath and faced Bess.

'Gather the bedding.' She gestured at the room. 'Take everything from here that does not belong to Thomas. Your father will move the beds. Then fetch me candles, no, tallow and a pail, and I shall have need of water. And sage to burn . . . Quickly now, Bess, there is no time to stand gawping.'

'But, I don't understand.'

'Listen to what I tell you, Bess. Once I have my things about me here, you are not to come into this room again. Do you hear me? Nor let your sister so much as set one foot through that door. You must look after her yourself and keep her from this room and from me. Promise me!'

'I promise,' said Bess, her tears blurring the sight of her wheezing brother as he shivered on his bed. She understood now, though no one could tell her plainly what she wanted to hear. In her heart she already knew the truth of the news her father had brought from the village. She knew the truth of it, and she felt more afraid than she had ever been in her life before. People in the village were dying. Her brother was dying. Many others would endure the same slow, painful fate. Plague had come to Batchcombe.

The next few hours passed in a whirl of activity. Bess did as her mother had instructed and then, keeping Margaret close by, set about Thomas's chores with the animals. There were cows to be milked, swine to be fed and watered, wood to be gathered in. Bess made herself concentrate on her tasks and deflected Margaret's ceaseless questions with vague assurances. She could not let herself think that while she fetched kindling, her brother's life was ebbing away. Such thoughts would either paralyze her or send her into madness. As she returned the cows to the byre she saw her father lighting a bonfire. Onto it he was piling Thomas's bedding from the previous night, as well as all his clothes. The sight moved Bess near to tears. She stood and watched her father, her heart breaking at the sight of his slumped shoulders and bowed head.

That night she lay on her makeshift bed in the hall and listened to Thomas's pitiful moaning from the next room. She had seen her mother only briefly, when she had emerged to go outside for a moment's air and stillness.

Bess had watched her go outside. The door to the bedchamber was ajar, and the need she felt to see her brother was stronger than she could bear. She pushed the door and stole into the room. She stood beside Thomas's bed and peered down at him. The room was gloomy, and he lay with his face turned to the wall.

'Thomas?' she whispered, then 'Thomas?' a little louder.

At the sound of her voice, he rolled over. Her first sight of him forced Bess to stifle a cry. One side of his face was blue-black and swollen, the other pale and somehow shriveled. One eye was bloodshot, the other a crimson mess. The stench of his wheezing breath made bile rise in Bess's throat. It took all her self-control not to run screaming from the room.

'Bess? Is that you?' He lifted a hand, searching for her.

Bess steadied herself and took his hand in hers. His grasp was not that of a strong youth but of an old man.

'I am here, Tom. Be still.'

'It is good to see you again. I feared . . .' He was unable to finish the thought. Hot tears brimmed up in his wretchedly grotesque eyes. 'Forgive me, Bess,' he sobbed.

'Forgive you? For what?'

'For not being braver. I know I should be, for Mother, for all of you. It's only that . . . I be so afraid.'

Bess knelt beside him and clasped his hand to her breast. 'Oh, Thomas, there is no courage in being fearless. Do you not know that? A person who knows fear and yet can still think of others, well, he be a brave man.'

Thomas looked up at her, a crooked smile distorting his face further.

'Do you truly believe that, Bess?'

'I do.' She nodded, her own tears falling to join his on the damp coverlet.

'Bess! What are you doing?' Her mother's shout from the door forced Bess back on her feet.

'I just wanted to see him, Mother, just for a moment.'

Anne grabbed her arm and hauled her to the door, pushing her roughly through it.

'You promised me, Bess!'

'I'm sorry, I only wanted . . .'

'What you wanted is of no importance, girl. Do you know what you could have done? Do you?' Anne slammed the door shut.

Bess shuddered at the memory of her mother's fury and of the suffering of her poor brother. She gave up chasing sleep and pulled Margaret closer to her. Somewhere before dawn, Thomas began to wail, a nerve-jangling noise that Bess knew would haunt her the rest of her days. As a feeble dawn broke through the unshuttered window, the wailing stopped and with it Thomas's heart.

Groggy from lack of sleep, Bess pushed off the covers and stirred herself. She shook Margaret gently, but the child did not wake. Looking down in the scant light, Bess saw now that her sister's face was the color of unripe cheese. She heard a shrill scream, and it was some moments before she realized the noise came from herself.

O dear Lord, what have I done? What have I done?

Life disintegrated into a mess of fever and panic. Bess found it hard to believe what was happening could be real. Surely it was some hideous nightmare from which she must soon awake, gasping and afraid, only to be quickly calmed and restored by the ordinariness of everyday life once more. Only it was not a dream. Margaret lay muttering and sweating in her bed in the hall, Bess at her side, whilst Anne prepared poor Thomas for his grave. Into this madness came the sound of a wagon outside and a brutal hammering on the door.

'Open up! Mr. Hawksmith? Come to your door!' a gruff voice demanded.

Anne appeared from the bedchamber. She looked at John.

'The searchers!' she said.

'Mother, what do they want?' asked Bess.

'Thomas' came the reply. 'They would take our boy away.' Anne looked fit to faint.

'Not while I live,' said John, his voice drawn up from a deep place of suffering and loss. He marched to the door and shouted through it. 'There be nothing to concern thee here! We will see to our own.'

'You have the plague in your house, Mr. Hawksmith. We must see for ourselves and take any bodies to the pit.'

'No!' Bess shouted. 'Father, you must not let them.'

John grabbed the end of the kitchen table. 'Help me, Bess.'

Together, they dragged the heavy piece of furniture so that it braced the door. John leaned against it.

'Open up, Hawksmith. We will only come back with an order from the governor and more men, you know that.'

'Come back with the whole of Batchcombe, for all the good it will do thee!' John roared, 'No child of mine will be laid to rest in a plague pit, d'you hear me?'

There came a muttering from outside and then silence.

'Have they gone?' Anne asked.

'They have,' said John. He went to the window and watched for a while, then spoke firmly to Anne. 'We must bury the boy tonight. It cannot be left any longer.'

Anne took a turn in nursing Margaret while Bess tended the beasts. The cows had not been milked properly for days and were surly. Bess wept tears of grief and frustration and fear as the oldest kicked the pail of milk from her hands for the second time. She thought she had never shed so many tears and feared she would never stop. Thomas was dead and Margaret was dreadfully ill. Had that been her doing? Had she taken the illness from Thomas to Margaret herself? The thought of it made her heart constrict. She hurried out to check that there was still sufficient water in the meadow for the cows. Walking back to the cottage, she saw her father digging Thomas's grave. She stopped and watched him, unable to drag herself away from the sight of her beloved parent doggedly turning shovelfuls of wet soil, digging ever deeper, preparing the place for his firstborn to spend eternity. As she watched, he finished the grave, a dark, muddy wound in the grassy orchard. He straightened up and she saw him wipe a tear from his eye with the back of a grimy hand. For a moment she thought he might be praying, he was standing so still. Then, without a sound, his legs folded beneath him and he fell forward into the grave.

'Mother!' Bess yelled as she flung down the milk bucket and ran toward her father. 'Mother, come quick!' She reached the grave and stared down into it. 'Father!' He lay moaning on the floor of the gritty space. Bess climbed down and tried to raise him to his feet. He drifted in and out of consciousness, muttering sounds that were not clear enough to be words. His hands were clammy and his face flushed and hot. Anne peered down from the top of the grave.

'O Lord save us!'

'He fell in. He is ailing, Mother. Father is unwell! He is too heavy for me to lift.'

Anne slithered down next to Bess, and together they hauled him to his feet.

'Push, Bess. Come on, we must get him out.'

It took the better part of an hour for the two women to heave and drag John out of the slippery tomb. By the time they had him back in the house, all three wore coats of mud. Bess barely had the strength to fetch water, but she knew they must wash her father and themselves. Margaret wriggled restlessly on her cot, calling out for her mother and for something to make the pain stop. Anne and Bess put John to bed. Anne lit sage to burn in the hearth, and they rubbed both John and Margaret with lavender oil. As Bess sat next to Margaret, stroking the girl's tiny arms gently with the fragrant oil, she wondered again about God's love and decided there was none of it in the Hawksmith house that night. She was so tired she all but fell asleep on the floor where she sat. Her mother roused her with a gentle shake.

'Bess, we must bury Thomas. The bearers will be back soon enough if we don't. I won't have them take him,' she said.

A numbness fell upon Bess as she fetched the barrow. Anne had wrapped Thomas tightly in his winding sheet; there was no time for coffins now. The women shifted his body onto a board, which they shuffled onto the barrow, and took him outside. It had started to rain, and since it was October, the water did not content itself with falling downward but descended at such an angle as to creep under every coat or collar. Bess and Anne did their best to move Thomas gently, but such was their fatigue and so hampered were they by the now sludgy graveside that they were reduced to simply tipping him into the watery hole. Wordlessly, they shoveled and scraped at the earth until the grave was filled. They stood silently contemplating the mound of soil in front of them. The rain ran unchecked down their faces. It coursed down their backs and dripped from their every hem. Bess waited for her mother to say something, some words of comfort or farewell or some attempt at commending his soul to God. But nothing came. Bess had not the heart to try. Where was the use in talking to God now? She reached out to touch Anne, but her mother swung about and strode for the house.

'The living need us' was all she said.

As Bess reached the cottage, she noticed for the first time the mark the searchers had left on the door. It proclaimed to the world that this was a plague house. Not a farm, not a home, not a cottage where people lived and were loved. Just a building harboring disease, a place to be despised and spurned. As Bess went inside, she wondered how many more graves she and her mother would have to dig. And who would be left to dig their own.

That night Bess and her mother sat by the fire, too exhausted to work at their lace. Too low in spirit to bother to heat some pottage. They had finished a dry wedge of cheese and drained the final flagon of last year's cider some hours before. Bess felt her stomach threaten to reject even that. She looked at her mother. The uneven light of the fire illuminated one side of her once-handsome face, casting deathly shadows beneath her eyes. A vision of how Thomas had looked the last time she saw him came into Bess's mind. She shut her eyes against it, but still it persisted, worse in the darkness behind her closed lids. Instead, she looked toward Margaret. She was sleeping peacefully now, while John in the next bed moaned and turned over fitfully.

'She does not seem to suffer so much now,' Bess said to her mother.

Her mother continued to stare into the flames. 'She is sleeping.'

'That is good, surely? With rest can come healing.'

'It can.' Her mother's voice carried no conviction.

Bess could stand her evasion no longer. 'Will she live, Mama? Tell me she will.'

Now Anne changed the direction of her gaze. She looked first at where Margaret lay, then turned to face Bess. Even such small movements seemed to involve enormous effort.

'She has the plague, Bess.'

'But some survive it, do they not? Some live on.'

'Some do. The strong and the grown. Those most likely to succumb are the weak. The old. And the very young.' She had not the energy for emotion. The fire took her attention once again.

Bess got to her feet. 'I will not let her die. I will not!' she said. She swung the kettle over the heat, then fetched honey from the dairy. She poured hot water into a bowl and stirred in the amber syrup. She took it to Margaret. Propping the child up on bolsters, she spoke to her softly.

'Come now, little Meg, see what I have for thee. Here.' She lifted a spoonful of the warm liquid to her sister's cracked lips. Margaret's eyelids fluttered but did not open. Her neck was disfigured and swollen by the buboes on it. And those hideous lumps in turn bore a mass of red spots. Her skin was beginning to darken with the bleeding beneath the surface that gave the disease its nickname of the Black Death. Bess pushed such thoughts from her mind and gently prized open her sister's lips, tipping a tiny sip of the honey-water into her mouth. It dribbled back out. She tried again. This time Margaret spluttered, but the taste stirred her a little so that she opened her reddened eyes.

'Bess?' Her voice was a dry whisper.

'I am here, little one.'

'Bess . . .' She struggled to focus, a hand reaching out for Bess's face. 'You can make me better . . . I know you can . . . use your magic, Bess. Your *magic*.' The child's eyes met Bess's now, imploring, entreating, begging, filled with fear and yet with hope. With expectation.

Bess fought back tears of grief and frustration. Her tricks were no use to her now. The small conjurings and illusions with which she had secretly so delighted Margaret all her life were powerless against the ferocity of the plague and Bess knew it. She shook her head, not wanting to admit to her beloved sister that the magic was not going to help her.

'Later, dear one. For now you must drink some more. There, that's good.' Bess dipped the spoon into the bowl again. 'Here, now. A little more. It will make you strong again.' She continued to feed her sister, the little girl's gaze all the while upon her until she thought she would not be able to stop herself weeping again. Once the bowl was empty, she laid Margaret down and made her comfortable. She sat on the floor next to the low bed, her arms around the child, willing her to be well. Willing her to live.

The next morning Bess woke where she had fallen beside her sister. The cockerel crowed hoarsely from the roof of the barn. A gray dawn suggested another night had been endured, another day lay ahead. Bess raised herself to her feet stiffly and moved to the fire to stoke the embers.

'Bess.' Her mother stood behind her.

'Morning, Mother. Do not disturb yourself. I will see to the fire and fetch Margaret some more honey-water. She liked it, I think. I know it will help her.'

'Bess.' Anne stepped forward and placed a hand on Bess's arm. 'Your sister is dead.'

All the blood drained from Bess's head so that she felt she might fall into the fire. She opened her mouth to scream but found she could not. She ran to Margaret and flung herself on the child's cold body. Now Bess's voice returned to her.

'No! No, no, no, no! Not Margaret. Not my little Meg.' She grabbed the lifeless girl. 'Sit up, Meg, come on, now. You must wake up. Wake up!' She shook her roughly, beyond knowing what she was doing.

Anne pulled her away. 'Leave her be, Bess.'

'I should have stayed awake! I should have saved her!'

'There was nothing to be done.'

'But I did it! O dear Lord, I killed her. I went in to Thomas when you told me not to, and I brought the plague to poor sweet Margaret and now she is dead! Let me die too! Let me go with them!'

Bess glimpsed her mother's hand only briefly as she raised it and brought it with great force down upon her cheek. The power of the blow knocked Bess to the floor. Shocked, she wiped blood from her mouth with her fingers. She looked up at her mother, stunned by what had happened.

Anne's voice was level as she spoke through closed teeth.

'Listen to me, Bess. Listen well. You no more killed your sister than did I. She fell ill with too much speed for you to have taken the sickness to her from Thomas. Do you understand? Do you?'

Bess nodded.

'You must be strong now. You must reach deep inside your heart and find a strength you never knew dwelled there, Bess. You must show courage. As must I.' She helped her daughter to her feet. She held her arms firmly as she continued to speak. 'Fetch your cloak, child, we have work to do outside.'

'But one of us should stay with Father.' Bess sniffed, still trying to stem the trickle of blood from her lip.

Now she felt Anne's hands tremble, though her grip did not loosen and her eyes did not waver in their steady gaze.

'Your father has no more need of us here,' she said. 'Come, we must make haste before the bearers return.' So saying, she strode across the room, snatching up her shawl. At the door she waited. Silent tears washed the blood from Bess's face now. She went to where her father lay motionless and cold as a slab of butter. His face looked peaceful, despite its livid color. She fancied he still wore a trace of his impish smile. She stroked his cheek with a shaking hand and then followed her mother out of the cottage.

4

It was not until two days after they had buried John and Margaret that the merciless rain stopped. Bess went to the edge of Batchombe Woods and gathered what few wildflowers there were to be had. The air was still heavy with water, but the sun shone boldly down. From the woodland came the scent of damp moss and fungus spores. Bess stared into the gloom between the close trees and found herself thinking of Gideon Masters. Had he escaped the plague? His cottage was well apart from any other, and his solitary habits meant he may well have not come into contact with a person carrying the sickness. It would be terrible, she thought, to be so alone. She imagined falling ill with no one to notice. But then, if Gideon had no one to love, that meant he had no one to lose. Not for him the dull ache that haunted the empty chambers of Bess's heart now or the brutal clutch of pain that assailed her in unguarded moments, such as when she came upon Thomas's walking stick or spied her father's pipe or caught herself muttering Margaret's favorite nursery rhyme. At those times she would be brought to her knees by grief, the breath knocked from her body as if by a physical blow. She saw her mother suffering in the same way, and both of them knew that no remedy existed. Nothing would ever make them whole again. Bess walked back to the cottage and took the flowers to the graves. The mounds of earth were still wet and would not grass over for many months. There was no money for headstones. Instead, Bess and her mother would fashion something from wood on a distant day in the future, when they could risk doing so without fear of collapse. Bess felt Anne's presence beside her.

'Come inside, Bess. It does you no good to stand here so long.'

'Have I stood a while? I didn't know it. Look, I fetched flowers.'

'They are very pretty. Margaret would like them.'

'She should be here to see them.'

'I do believe she is still here, Bess. Do you not?'

'I mean here.' Bess wrapped her arms around herself as if still hugging her little sister. 'Warm and alive and full of joy and sweetness, so that I might hold her . . . not cold and quiet in her muddy grave.'

'We have to keep her alive in our hearts, Bess. That is where she truly dwells now, not in the earth, in our hearts. In us.' Anne's gaze fell upon John's grave. 'They are all safe in our hearts.'

'I thought they were supposed to be with God.' Bess could not keep the bitterness from her voice. 'In his loving arms—isn't that what we are taught to believe? Do you believe it, Mother? Do you?'

'Bess . . .'

'Do you?' Bess began to weep.

'Hush, child. No more tears. No more.' Anne reached out and wiped her daughter's cheek with her finger. Her expression changed to one of alarm. 'Bess . . .'

'You don't believe it any more than I. Where was the Good Shepherd when Thomas's face swelled up like the belly of a dead sheep? Where was our Lord when Father cursed us all from his deathbed?'

'Bess! You are hot.'

'Where was our loving God when Meg clawed the air for breath?'

'Bess!' Anne took hold of Bess by the shoulders and spoke earnestly. 'You are not well—you must come inside.'

'What?' Bess tried to take in her mother's words. 'Not well?'

Time froze in that moment. The two women stood leaning against each other, fear and grief threatening to overwhelm them. Somewhere in the orchard a magpie fought with a crow. A thin wind began to tug at the flowers Bess had laid at the graves.

Anne drew in a deep breath and turned her only living daughter toward the cottage. 'Come,' she said, 'let us go in.'

Fever quickly robbed Bess of all sense of time or knowledge of reality. She was aware of her mother's presence, of being washed with rose water and stroked with fragrant oils. She registered a spoon being held to her lips or a cup tipping liquid into her mouth. Beyond that, the world did not exist for her. All that she knew was pain and delirium. She felt at once such heat that she imagined the thatch of the cottage had caught fire, and yet such cold that she believed she must be already dead. Her body became somehow separate from herself, as if she had neither control over it nor use for it. It was a conduit of agony, nothing more. She heard a ragged rasping sound. Was it wind down the chimney? Or wood being sawn. No, she came to realize it was the sound of her own breathing. The air was dragged in and out of her body as if from a worn set of blacksmith's bellows fanning the flames of her fever. At moments she felt a calmness, an acceptance that she was going to die. It was right that she should. Why should she be the one to live on? Hadn't she hastened poor Margaret's death? She would be with the others soon. Once, in the darkness, she heard her mother's voice. She fancied she spoke of living, not dying, though her words made little sense. Then, strangely, Anne was gone. Bess had no real way of knowing she was not in the house, but she was quite certain she was alone. Not alone for ten minutes while her mother fetched wood or water, but alone for a great, empty, silent stretch of time.

And in that time Bess dreamed. It was a dream as real as any living memory. She found herself back in Thomas's empty grave, rain washing down the steep sides so that a pool of liquid mud rose up to her knees. She clawed at the slippery soil, struggling to pull herself out but never able to gain a sure foothold. She slithered down, falling onto her back in the mire, submerged for an instant. She sat up choking, spitting out mud, rubbing the gritty water from her eyes. When she did so, she saw Thomas, as he had been during the worst ravages of the plague, sitting up opposite her. He stared at her with his grotesquely bulging eyes and blackened face. She screamed and started climbing again, but this time she was knocked down by Margaret's body as it was thrown into the pit. The child turned an angry face to Bess, shouting at her, 'You did this to me, Bess! You killed me!' Bess shook her head, scrambling backward, screaming until she had no voice left. Beaten, she cowered in the corner, her arms over her head, and awaited death.

The first indication Bess had that she was in fact alive was the sound of singing. It was such a curious and unlikely noise that it took some time for her to believe she was awake and listening to a real sound, not a product of her fevered mind. She opened her eyes. It was day. The fire in the hearth burned quietly. Winter sun fell through the unshuttered window. She glimpsed the shadows of movement and found she was able to turn her head a little. She saw then that the song came from her mother. Anne had her back to Bess and wore her shawl up over her head as she stood at the kitchen table. She was entirely focused on a solitary candle burning in front of her. There were unfamiliar objects positioned around the candle. Her arms were raised as if in supplication, and her body rocked slightly from side to side as she continued to sing the low monotonous notes over and over again. Bess could not discern the words. They seemed strange, as if of some foreign tongue. It was certainly not a song she had ever heard her mother sing before. The melody, if such it could be called, was eerie and discordant yet strangely hypnotic. Suddenly, as if sensing she was being observed, her mother dropped her arms to her sides and was silent. She stood still for a moment longer, then blew out the candle and turned around.

Bess gasped as she saw now that her mother's hair had turned completely white. Not a strand of gold remained. The effect was to make Anne appear a decade older than she had only days before. Bess struggled to raise herself onto an elbow, but her mother hurried forward.

'Bess! There, be still, my little one. All is well,' she said, kneeling by the low bed. She touched Bess's cheek and smiled, the first smile Bess had seen on her mother's face since the day of the apple harvest.

'Mother, what has happened to you? Your hair . . .'

'It is of no importance. What matters is that you are well, Bess. You are well.' She squeezed her daughter's hand.

'But how?' Bess sat up, examining her arms and hands, feeling her face for lumps or swellings, for signs of the disfigurement the rest of her family had borne. There were none.

'Be assured,' her mother said, 'you are just as you were. The plague has left no mark upon you.'

'Oh, Mother!' Bess flung herself into Anne's arms and wept tears of relief and of grief. For a short time she had felt close to Margaret and been convinced she would see her again soon. Now the news that she was to live was tainted by the pain of being torn away from her sister anew.

Anne dried her daughter's tears. 'Come now, this is not a moment for weeping. I will make you some pottage. You will be strong once more very soon. You will see.'

As Bess watched her mother moving about the room, preparing the food, she struggled to make sense of what had happened. She had been afflicted by the plague, yet she and she alone had survived. Had her mother effected the cure? What had she tried with Bess that she had not given to the others? What powerful remedy had she concocted, and if it were so efficacious, why had she not used it sooner? She saw now that her mother's hair was not the only thing to have altered so dramatically. She seemed to move differently, to inhabit the room in an entirely new way. A way that was strange and unsettling. Something profound had changed in her mother while Bess had lain on her sickbed. Some transformation had occurred at the root of her being, Bess believed, something had changed forever in her very soul.

That winter was the bleakest Bess had ever endured. The chill of grief in her heart was matched by the icy winds and cruel frosts that assailed the farm. She and her mother battled to tend the land and the livestock, but it was an impossible task. The smallholding had been stocked and planted to require the labors of four adults, not two. It quickly became clear that they could not manage the acreage alone, and as there was no money to hire help, they were forced to part with some of their beasts. And fewer beasts meant less food. Together, they slaughtered the old sow, laying the meat down in salt. The remaining pig wandered the yard morosely for days and threatened to pine away to nothing before their eyes. The youngest cow they sold to a neighbor. The oldest proved to be barren, which meant there was only one left to give milk. Such a low yield meant an end to their cheese-making at least until the following autumn.

Christmas passed unmarked in the Hawksmith household. Neither Bess nor her mother could face the cheery traditions and customs that would mark the day out as special and remind them of their lost loved ones. Had they but had the time or energy to care, they might have realized that many in the village now ceased to celebrate the yuletide festival. The fashion of the land was for quiet observance of God's will, not for showy rituals that gave an excuse for gaiety and often drunken excess in His name. None of this mattered to Bess or Anne. They rarely ventured into the village now, save to sell or buy something. Neither of them had set foot inside the church since the plague. It had crossed Bess's mind that this would not go unnoticed. She remembered Reverend Burdock's words to the church warden. What a long time ago that seemed—back to a sunny, light, hopeful time. All parishioners were required to attend Sunday worship, and their absence would be recorded. For now though the inclement weather and privations inflicted on the village by the plague gave people other things to concern themselves with. For now.

For two whole weeks in the darkest days of the season, snow covered the land almost to the sea itself. Bess had never seen the cliff tops white before. The warmth of the sea had always kept such weather at bay until now. Looking out at the beautiful, frigid land, Bess felt as if the earth itself had gone into mourning. Would spring ever come again? she wondered. It seemed to her things might stay this way forever. Before Christmas, she had helped her mother press the last of the apples and set the juice to ferment. Now the cider was ready, and Anne decided they should sell some of it.

'I want you to take those flagons to the Three Feathers. Ask for James Crabtree. Agnes will want to bargain with you herself.' As she spoke, Anne fastened her own heavy cloak about Bess's shoulders. 'Do not be drawn into dealing with that woman; she will have the lot off you for nothing. Insist on speaking with James, do you hear me?'

Bess nodded. She felt an unfamiliar sensation in the depths of her bowels and eventually recognized it as excitement. She had never been in an alehouse before, and the Feathers had a reputation as the wildest in the village. After being so long cooped up in the farmhouse, she felt a certain thrill to be going out in the world and to be charged with something so adult and important. At once Bess felt sick with guilt, as if it was wrong to feel anything akin to pleasure. Would it always be wrong? she wondered.

The snow had gone, but the ground was frozen to rock and a mean wind stung Bess's face as she stepped outside. She pulled the hood of her cape up over her cap and tied it tightly. She fetched the old mare, who was surly and reluctant to be dragged out of her warm barn. Anne helped her sit the flasks of cider into the panniers on the horse.

'Don't dawdle,' Anne said as she tightened the girth strap and handed Bess the reins of the bridle. 'I know Whisper will go slowly on the outward journey, but you can ride her once you have delivered the cider and she will step quickly enough coming home.'

Bess took the reins. 'Come on, old girl, I'll find you a handful of hay when we return.'

'And do not linger in the alehouse, Bess,' her mother called after her. 'Talk to no one but James Crabtree!'

The Three Feathers was a large building constructed of stout timbers and a scruffy thatch. The upper floor had small windows set into the roof. The rooms here were used for lodging, a place for passing travelers to endure a night of little comfort and much noise. Bess had heard of all manner of uses for these rooms other than sleep. She tied Whisper up to a hitching ring on the front wall of the alehouse and went inside. At once her senses were assailed. The smoke produced by the greenwood on the fire and the numerous clay pipes being puffed and pointed with fervor rendered the air thicker than a sea fog. Bess shut the door behind her, doing her best to ignore the lecherous looks thrown her way. The ground floor of the building consisted of one low-ceilinged room filled with an assortment of worn tables and benches. A large settle beside the fire was regularly occupied by elderly drinkers of indeterminate age and failing mental capacity. The seats by the windows were taken by loud women dressed in bright colors, who entertained glint-eyed men. The raucous laughter of these drunken pairings ceased only when they slipped away to one of the rooms upstairs. At the opposite end of the room from the fire, a bar was constructed roughly of salvaged wood. Barrels stood in the corner. Tankards, jars, and jugs sat waiting on grimy shelves. The barks and roars of the inebriated competed with the shouts for ale or cider directed at the increasingly bad-tempered landlady and the serving wench who spent more time batting away unwanted hands than filling beer mugs.

Bess straightened her shoulders and stepped quickly toward the bar. She blushed as lewd observations regarding her long legs and full lips were lobbed at her as she made her hasty progress through the throng. More than once she felt a hand upon her, but she did not respond. On reaching the bar, she was dismayed to see no sign of the innkeeper, only his disagreeable wife. She felt a crowd of men begin to press in around her.

'I am come to speak with Mr. Crabtree,' she said to the ever-moving figure of Agnes Crabtree.

'Well, now'—the woman spoke without bothering to look at Bess—'Mr. Crabtree be engaged at present, so thee'll 'ave to address thyse'n to me.'

The smell of hot and unclean bodies was beginning to permeate the smoke and reach Bess's nose. She gave no outward sign of the revulsion she felt.

'I would not trouble him more than a moment. I have cider to sell.' She kept her voice level but pleasant.

Now Agnes turned to frown at the provokingly attractive young girl before her.

'Doesn't thee think I know about zider, then?'

There was a murmur of interest from the men standing close. Bess quelled panic as she felt one man stand so near behind her she was aware of his body against hers.

'I see that you are yourself busily occupied, Mrs. Crabtree. I would not wish to bother you. My mother told me . . .'

'Oh! Well, if thy mother told thee!' Agnes cruelly mocked Bess, causing the drinkers to let rip a cacophony of laughter and coughing. Some joined in the taunt. 'Mother told her! So she did, Mother told her!'

The man behind Bess pressed himself shamelessly to her. Bess blushed as she distinctly felt the hard length of him against her buttocks. At once, any fear she had felt was replaced by fury. What right had he to treat her that way? What right had any man? She spun on her heel, startling the man with her swift movement so that he staggered back a little.

'Sir! I did not invite your attentions, and I do not welcome them!'

A chorus of surprise and delight rose from the assembled group.

'Hard luck, Davy!' mocked one, laughing. 'The lass doesn't welcome thy attentions!'

'At least she called thee *sir*!' put in another.

The man himself bridled under the ridicule. He stepped forward, pinning her against the bar.

'Mibben thou favors a more direct approach,' he said.

Bess felt physically sick at further such intimate and aggressive contact.

'Step away from me, sir.' She felt her own fury building and knew she must keep it in check, no matter what the provocation.

'Think thyse'n too good for the likes of me, then? Fancy thyse'n to be mistress up at Batchcombe Hall one day?' As he spoke, fine drops of foul-smelling spittle rained on Bess's face. She resisted the urge to wipe them away.

'I warn you . . .'

'Warn me, girl?' He laughed at her. 'What must I fear? That simple brother of yours going to come for me, is 'e? Or will I be set about by old man Hawksmith himse'n?'

At the mention of her father's name, many standing near fell silent. It was clear some of them knew of her family's fate, even if her tormentor did not. Bess opened her mouth to speak, but such a rage boiled up inside her she could find no words to express it. She had never felt such fury, and now the loathsome man was moving his hand toward her breast. She wanted to unleash her anger, but there was a small part of her that was afraid to do so, unsure of what the consequences might be. Instead, she snatched up a stoneware jug from the bar and swung it through the air. When it connected with Davy's face, there was a fearsome crash as the pottery smashed, quickly followed by a thud as the man toppled sideways to the floor. Shouts and peals of laughter filled the space. Agnes elbowed her way through the crowd.

'Get 'im out of here, somebody, afore there be more trouble, and you'—she scowled at Bess—'if thou has such a desire to see my husband get through that door, and quick about it.' She jerked her head in the direction of the far corner of the room.

Bess did not wait for further bidding but hurried through the door, her heart racing at what she had just done, at the power of her own anger.

On the other side of the door was a narrow passageway. In the gloom Bess could make out steps to the cellar on one side, and another door at the far end. She felt her way along the wall and pushed open the second door. A scene of wild excitement greeted her. The space, which might once have housed beasts or been stabling for horses, had been altered to accommodate a circular pit. Around this arena was assembled an agitated crowd intent on the action within the circle. Bess edged forward through the shouting, gesticulating men so that she could see what it was that whipped them into such a frenzy of yelling and swearing. In the center of the pit, two cocks hurled themselves at each other. Both were bloodied, and both wore viscous false spurs of bone strapped over their own. The birds seemed evenly matched in weight, but one had far more vigor than the other. The stronger cockerel had feathers of copper and purple that stood out in a great ruff about his neck. He leaped into the air and launched himself, talons and spurs foremost, at his weakening opponent. As the failing bird fell beneath the attack, blood poured from a fresh wound in its side, eliciting a cheer from the audience. Bess looked from the hapless creatures to the men around her. She saw money clutched in fists and eyes gleaming. Was it the gambling that excited them so or the sight of blood so cruelly spilled? Her nerves already greatly affected by her experience inside the inn, Bess now found herself near overwhelmed by the lust for violence all around her. Her anger returned. She looked at the glistening faces of the men and the pitiful state of the birds and could stand it no longer. She closed her eyes. Uncertain of what precisely she was trying to do, Bess followed her instincts and summoned her will, her strength, her rage. She gathered it up and then released it, her eyes snapping open as she did so. The doors on either side of the room flew open. A frenzied wind blew through the enclosure, stirring up a storm of dust and straw, blinding the shouting mob, swirling in a vortex of chaotic noise and choking detritus thrown up from the floor. It lasted no more than half a minute and then stopped as suddenly as it had started. Amid much coughing and swearing, the air cleared, revealing the pit to be empty. The birds were gone. After a collective intake of astonished breath, the crowd began hurling abuse and accusations at one another, whilst a fruitless search was mounted for the missing cockerels. Bess stood calmly amid it all, scanning the throng for Mr. Crabtree.

As she let her gaze rove the room, she caught her breath at the sight of a tall figure in a wide-brimmed black felt hat at the back of the room. Gideon Masters. What drew such a solitary man to an event of this nature? He met her eye and a small smile played on his face. Bess looked away again quickly, certain that he and he alone was aware of what she had done. She was jostled by the men as the atmosphere grew more and more violent. Fights broke out, and very soon the scene was that of a riot. Bess spotted James Crabtree standing next to Gideon, shaking his head in disbelief at the madness around him. She took her courage in both hands and made her way to him.

'Mr. Crabtree.' She had trouble making herself heard. 'Mr. Crabtree!'

He looked at her now.

'Lord's truth, what 'ave we here?'

'Bess Hawksmith. I have some cider to sell, if you are interested.'

'Has thee now? And where might that zider be?' He glanced about her as if expecting her to produce it from beneath her cape.

'Why, on our mare, to the front of your . . . inn.'

Crabtree laughed. 'I dare say mibben that be where thou left it, Bess Hawksmith, but I'd wager my night's winnings it be there no more!'

'What?' Bess was appalled. 'What do you say? Surely no one would take it?'

The landlord began to walk away, still laughing to himself. 'Count thyse'n lucky if they left you the nag, lass! 'pon my word!'

Bess stared after him, then at Gideon. She was certain he was enjoying her distress, even though his face remained unmoved. She turned and fled through the back door. Outside, the wind had strengthened. She ran round to the front of the building. Whisper stood asleep, resting a hind leg. The panniers were empty.

'No! Oh no!' At that moment Bess could not decide who she hated most, the thieves who had robbed her or herself for her own stupidity.

She sensed she was not alone and then heard soft humming, a familiar tune sung in a low voice. Even without the words, she knew the song to be "Greensleeves." Her father had often bade her sing it herself. Bess stiffened as Gideon came to stand next to her. He stopped singing and watched her. Bess fought back tears, determined she would not humiliate herself further in front of him.

'It seems there are people hereabouts not to be trusted,' he said, his words softly spoken but in a voice that contained unmistakable strength.

Bess ignored him and untied the horse.

'Such a pity,' he went on, 'that a trusting nature should be so taken advantage of. It is a rare thing to find innocence in these dark times. I do not enjoy seeing it abused.'

Bess looked up at him, unsure whether he was mocking her or showing genuine concern. She could not read his expression. She finished untying the reins and started to turn the horse.

'What will you tell your mother?' Gideon asked, making no attempt to move from her path.

'Why, the truth of course.'

'Will she not berate you for your foolishness?'

'Would you have me lie to save face? What sort of a daughter would I be then?'

'A clever one, maybe?'

'Better foolish and honest than clever and false.'

'Fine sentiments, Bess. I applaud your integrity.'

There was something about the way he spoke her name that Bess found deeply unsettling.

'I have no need of your approval, sir.'

Now he smiled properly, plainly amused by her show of defiance. His angular features and dark eyes were softened and transformed by his wide smile. His eyes crinkled, and it would have been easy to believe in that moment that the man's natural disposition was one of gentleness and merriment. Bess found this new, pleasant, charming version of the man more unsettling than his usual self. She looked at the ground and made as if to push past him. He held up a hand, stopping her silently with the gesture.

'I will buy your cider, Bess,' he told her.

Bess felt renewed anger lending her strength but reminded herself that he had witnessed the results of her rage. The knowledge that he had seen this secret part of her, that she had somehow unwittingly revealed herself before him disturbed her.

'Will you stand aside, or must I drag the mare about for your further amusement?'

'Why so cross? All I did was offer to buy your cider.'

'When you know full well I have none to sell.'

'Really? Are you certain?'

She frowned at him, then turned back to look at the horse. The panniers were full. She grabbed at them, unable to take in what she was seeing. A moment ago they had been empty—she was certain of it. Yet now the flagons were returned to the pack, and each, judging by the weight, was full. She plucked out a stopper and sniffed the contents. There was no mistaking the sweet fruity scent that greeted her. Bess felt the skin over her spine wriggle. She turned slowly back to Gideon, who was casually stroking Whisper's ears.

'What trickery is this?' she asked, her faint words snatched up by the wild wind that pulled at her cape and caused her eyes to water.

Gideon watched her as he spoke. 'Not trickery, Bess. Just simple magic. You do believe in magic, don't you?'

'I believe such talk is blasphemous and people have been hanged for less.'

'That is because you are a God-fearing young woman who has been taught well the ways of the world. Between all those books your mother forced upon you and the dry words of Reverend Burdock, what else are you to think?' He stepped closer to her, his body blocking the wind so that between them was a small pool of stillness amidst the wildness of the fading day. 'But you know, Bess, in your heart, you know the truth. There is magic all around us. In the boiling clouds. In this wicked wind that even now delves beneath your clothes to set its chill fingers on your soft young body. In the cider that goes away and comes back again.' He lifted a hand slowly and lightly touched a lock of hair that had come loose from under Bess's hood. 'And you, Bess, there is magic in you.'

'I do not know what you mean.'

'I think you do. I know what I saw. I know what you did. Do those words sound familiar? They should. You spoke them to me not so very long ago. We are not so different, you and I, Bess. I wish you would see that. Don't pretend to me you haven't wondered why you survived the plague when the others did not. How often do you hear of anyone so ill, so taken by the vile disease, how often do you hear of them returning to good health, hmm? With not a blemish upon their pretty pink skin.'

'I was fortunate.' Bess could hear the tremble in her own voice.

'Fortunate? Do you think God spared you, perhaps? Why would he do that? Are you better than the others, d'you think? Is that it?'

'I know only that my mother nursed me back to health.'

'Indeed she did. Indeed she did.' He nodded, then let his hand drop. 'Surely that must have been strong medicine she found for you. Has she told you how she did it? Have you asked her what herbs she used?' He made the word *herbs* sound ridiculous.

Bess could not make sense of what he was saying. He seemed to be implying that her mother had used magic to save her. But that was nonsense.

Her mother knew no magic. Her mother was no witch. And yet it was as if he knew more than she, as if he had some knowledge of what her mother had done. Of how she had done it.

Gideon reached into his pocket and took out four coins. He pressed them into Bess's hand.

'For the cider,' he told her. 'Hurry home now, the light is dwindling.' So saying, he touched the rim of his hat as he inclined his head toward her and then brushed past her, striding away. Bess looked at the coins. It was a good price.

'But, the cider . . .' she called after him. 'You have not taken the cider.'

He replied without looking back, 'Oh, I think you'll find I have. Good day to you, Bess. Until we meet again.'

Bess whipped around, her mouth gaping as she saw the panniers empty once more, hanging loose and flat against the mare's flanks. She turned back, her mind in chaos, but Gideon had gone.

5

When Bess returned home, she had intended to tell her mother the full tale of what had happened. Why should she not? And yet, when the time came, she found herself reluctant to mention Gideon Masters at all. Her own reticence puzzled her. In the end she simply said she had sold the cider, and her mother, being pleased with the price, had not questioned her further. As the days slipped by, the moment for telling more went with them, so that Bess soon convinced herself there was nothing more to be said. In quiet times, however, when she had occasion to let her mind wander back to that wind-beaten place in front of the inn where she had watched magic performed, Bess knew there were a hundred questions screaming for answers. What powers did Gideon possess that he could do such things? And what did he know of how Bess had been saved from the plague? Bess turned such queries over and over inside her head, yet something prevented her from voicing any of them to her mother. This, she knew, was the most perplexing question of all: Why could she not bring herself to speak to her mother of what Gideon had told her? What was it that she feared to hear?

The long winter plodded on with leaden feet toward an ever-retreating

spring. The barren cow sickened and died. The chickens showed no inclination to resume laying. The solitary pig had quite lost its mind and
added to Bess's heavy workload by regularly escaping the confines of the
yard and having to be retrieved from any number of haunts. It was on just
such an occasion, when Bess was shoving and shooing the wretched animal back along the lane, that a visitor came calling. There was no wind or
rain that day, so that Bess heard the thud of approaching hoofbeats. She
left off cajoling the pig and peered down the twisting path, watching the
gleaming mount cantering closer.

William, she thought. Just that. She had not the energy to form an opinion of his presence after so many months of not seeing him. He brought
his horse to a halt and slipped from the saddle, greeting her with a formal
bow. Bess stood impassive, watching him. As he straightened and came to
look at her properly, she saw in his reaction how much the preceding
months had taken from her. She had known, of course, that she could not
endure all that had happened without some outward sign of her suffering,
but it was hard to see it so clearly declaimed on William's handsome
young face. It was true she bore no marks of the plague itself, but grief
and heartbreak had been compounded by a winter of hardship. She knew
well she was not the same girl William had walked with in the churchyard the autumn before. Her skin had lost its youthful glow, her figure its
early promise of fecundity and pleasure. Indeed, her flesh hung loosely on
her bones, her naturally angular frame now looking poor and frail rather
than lithe and elegant. She put a hand to her hair, knowing it to be sullied
and unkempt. She let her palm fall against her skirts but made no attempt
to brush the dirt from her clothes. She set her jaw. Let him find her as she
was. There was no purpose in pretense.

William stood before her with restless eyes.

'Bess, please accept my condolences. I was truly sorry to hear of your
misfortune. Your father was a good man, and your brother and sister . . .'
He left the words unspoken, his practiced politeness failing to provide
him with the means to properly express his sympathy.

Bess gave a small nod by way of answer. The silence between them
quickly became as solid as a stone wall. She dearly wanted to break it
down, but she felt unable to do so. It was for William to reach out to her.
It could not be the other way around. She waited.

'I would have come sooner, but I am only recently returned. From

France, indeed. My brother and I were sent there on business. For my father.'

'Many who were able fled the plague.'

'Please, do not reproach me, Bess. It was not my choice to leave.'

Bess thought he looked so much younger than she remembered. Still a boy. Whereas she was no longer a girl. Her youth had been buried along with her family. She sighed, knowing that yet another gulf had opened up between her and William. Something more to keep them separate.

'And you?' William tried a smile. 'You are well, Bess? And your mother?'

'As you see.'

'I see you have suffered. I wish to help you, Bess. Sincerely.' He stepped closer. 'I know it must be very difficult for you both, trying to work the farm without . . .'

'We do what we must.'

'But it is surely too much, Bess. You look so very weary.'

'No more nor less than any other person with beasts to tend to and fields to work and not much sustenance to fuel their labors,' said Bess, failing to keep a bitter edge from her voice.

'Won't you let me help you? You know, I think, that I have always had an affection for you, Bess. That I hope you have counted me a friend.'

Bess was astonished. Had he chosen this moment to declare his feelings for her? Here she stood, shabby and wretched, a pauper among peasants whose prettiness had been all but snuffed out—was he now going to speak of love? Of marriage? A marriage that had, even before her beaten state, been a farfetched notion, and one that would have raised objections and questions. Could he truly believe his father would permit him to choose such a woman for his bride? Bess felt a sob catch in her throat. Whether it came from the thought of rescue from the relentless struggle of poverty or the idea of the warmth and comfort of William's affection for her, she could not say. Her legs weakened as if she might crumple onto the ground. Seeing her frailty, William slipped an arm about her shoulders to support her.

'Do not be troubled, Bess. I will not let you suffer so. You will see. I came to tell you that Lily Bredon, who was maidservant to my dear mother for many years, has left our employ. After my mother's death, Lily became housekeeper, but she is no longer young and has gone to live with her sister over in Dorchester. At once I thought of you and your mother. We have need of a housekeeper, and another kitchen maid would be a boon, now that my brother looks set to marry. The quarters are cheerful enough and warm. The work is not over-arduous, I think, and you would not be hungry ever again. Is it not the perfect solution? Say you will speak to your mother about it at once.'

Bess stared up incredulously at him. His eyes shone with the joy of offering such a wonderful opportunity of salvation. She could see only sincerity and kindness in his expression, of that she was certain. It was clear to her that in his innocence he had not the slightest notion of the pain he had just inflicted upon her. Somewhere deep within her a strange sensation stirred, accompanied by a curious gurgling sound Bess did not recognize at first. Only when it grew louder and stronger did she know it to be laughter. Not a gentle chuckle or a nervous giggle but a forceful belly laugh, so raucous and unexpected it caused William to take a step backward. Bess laughed so her body ached and tears fell unchecked from her eyes. William stared at her, clearly concerned he had somehow prompted a madness to overtake her. She waved a hand at him helplessly.

'Forgive me, William,' she said. 'I am no longer able to contain my baser emotions, as you see. And after all, is not a fool supposed to cause mirth?'

'Do you call me fool?'

'No.' She shook her head as she dabbed at her eyes. 'Not you, dear, kind William. It is I who am the simpleton here. I deserve that title. And none other. As half the village did their utmost to inform me, though I would not hear it.'

'I fail to comprehend you, Bess. I had thought to offer you hope, to assist you in your time of need, but you laugh at my suggestion.'

'Your offer is a fair one. It is of sound sense, as I would expect from you. It is that very sense I lack, which sets us apart from each other more than any other thing. You are more worldly wise than I had allowed for, William.' She recovered her composure and began to feel a heavy sadness settle about her. She had not, until this moment, understood the strength of her own affection for William. She had overestimated her worth, failed to heed the words of those who knew better the order of things, and now she had caused her heart to be bruised by her own stupidity. How could she ever truly have believed William Gould of Batchcombe Hall would consider her for his future wife? 'I am sorry, William,' she said at last. 'It is a kind offer, genuinely made, but it is not one I could accept.'

William shuffled his feet, fidgeting before he raised his eyes to hers with a tentative smile. He reached out and took her hand in his. Bess was harshly aware of how calloused and roughened her own fingers were against the smoothness of his own. When he spoke, there was longing in his voice.

'Can you dismiss so quickly the chance to be near me?' he asked gently.

Now she understood. She let out a snort of amazement as she snatched away her hand and shook her head. 'I swear I do not know what more astonishing words will come from your mouth this day! First you bid me enter your house as a servant, though you call me friend. Now I hear your plan was to install me as mistress, to be at hand when whimsy turns you in my direction, ever eager for what crumbs of affection you might choose to give!'

'Bess, I . . .'

'No! I beg you say nothing further. I see I misread your character, William. I had foolishly seen goodness and innocence in those smiling eyes of yours. How mistaken I was.' She spun on her heel, her heavy boots sucking at the sticky mud of the track as she strode toward home.

'Bess, do not turn away from me. Let me be your friend still!' he called after her.

Without pausing or looking back, Bess told him, 'I have no need of a friend who thinks me good enough to share his bed but not his name. Good day to you, William Gould!'

When Bess reached the cottage, she found herself still unable to contain her rage. She slammed into the house. Her mother heard the door rattle in its frame and came through from the dairy.

'Bess? What has happened?'

Bess tore the shawl from her shoulders and hurled it onto the settle.

'I have been taught a lesson about the true nature of men,' she said, pacing the floor.

'Oh. And who was your teacher?'

'None other than William Gould, heir to Batchcombe Hall, soon to be lord of all he surveys. A lord like any other who will take what he wants in his high-bred hand and twist it to his will.'

Anne's expression changed to one of alarm. 'Did he harm you?'

'Oh, quite the contrary, Mother. I should thank him, indeed, for opening my eyes. Let me tell you what caused him to come calling after his long absence. Was it to be in the company of a friend, mibben? Or more, you might be thinking, was it to express the depth of his true feelings for me? No, neither of these. It was to give us a gracious offer of employment. Tell me, Mother, how would that sit with you? Are you ready to be housekeeper at Batchcombe Hall? To serve the Gould family? To one day soon have William as your lord and master?'

Anne surprised Bess with her reaction. She did not at once dismiss such an idea; nor did she take offense. Instead, she sat on the bench and rested her arms on the table. Bess saw that she was taking in this news.

'Mother, am I to believe you would consider such a fate for us?'

'I am not in a position to reject it out of hand, Bess. We are failing to manage the farm. You know this.'

'Is that what you want for us? To be servants?'

'Do you think yourself better than those who do such work? When you wallow in the mire to rouse an ailing hog, or pull the lice from your hair that the infested ewes have shared with you, or fall filthy to your bed in soiled linen, do you see yourself too good to be a housemaid, Bess?'

Bess could not believe what she was hearing.

'That is not all,' she told her mother. 'William had a wider role in mind for me. He saw me as his future mistress, so conveniently placed in the servants' quarters. What do you say to that?'

'I say every woman must choose a master. William is a good man. He would protect you.'

'I swear I am driven quite to madness by the words of others! To hear my own mother counsel me to accept such a fate! Is this the low opinion you have of me?'

'You are my dear-heart. You are my all, Bess. I seek only to see you safe. To see you secure.'

'And you care nothing for my reputation?'

'Reputation is for those who can afford it.'

'And my freedom?'

Anne narrowed her eyes at her daughter.

'Have I instructed you so poorly? Do you not know that no woman is free, Bess? Indeed, the only freedom she possesses lies in her choice of master.'

'Was Father then your master?'

'Certainly he was.'

'No! He treated you as his equal!'

'You are mistaken, Bess. There can be only one ruler in the house.'

'So now that you have freedom thrust upon you by courtesy of death you would give it up and see me debased for a new master?'

'The Goulds are a fine family.'

'I do not think their morals fine.'

Anne leaned heavily on her elbows and spoke with a sigh in her words. 'You are ignorant of the ways of the world, Bess, and that is due to my shortcoming, not yours. I should have better taught you. I should have clearly shown you your place. Instead, I encouraged your strength of character, your spirit, your wits. I see now I have done you a disservice.'

'No, Mother. You have not.' Bess came to sit opposite Anne and took hold of her hands tightly. 'You have raised me to be who I am, and I will not see us both crushed into nothing. I will not see us reduced further. We will find a way to stay here and to work the farm and to rebuild our lives.'

'Bess, your courage cannot be doubted, but it gives false hope to deny our limits.'

'I will show you we have need of no man.'

Anne shook her head. 'Daughter, without a man's help, you would share your sister's grave.'

Bess felt a chill grip her heart. She waited for her mother to explain.

'When you were stricken with the plague, I saw that I was losing you. I tried everything I could to heal you, but to no avail. I came to see that you too would slip from my grasp. As your brother and sister had done. As your father. I could not sit and watch you die, child. I could not. I went to Gideon.'

Bess frowned. 'But why? Why did you think that he, of all people, could help?'

'There are things about Gideon Masters you do not know. Few people are aware of the truth of that man. Indeed, it is not something many would understand. But I knew. I have always known.' She squeezed her daughter's hands but could not meet her gaze, keeping her eyes cast down as she spoke. 'Your grandmother was known for her healing powers, as was her mother and her grandmother before that. The knowledge they had was passed down to me through instruction and practice, as I have sought to pass it on to you. The women in our family have done good work, Bess. They have seen generations of babes safe delivered into this world; they have treated their ailments through cradlehood; they have eased the suffering of all and any who looked for their help. There is nothing ungodly in this. No witchery. No magic. Simple remedies, herb concoctions and tinctures and unctions. That is all. But sometimes, as you saw with your sister, sometimes, Bess, it is not enough. I could not save Thomas. I could not save Margaret. I could not save your poor dear father. I knew I could not save you. Gideon was the only hope left to us. I went to his cottage in the woods and begged him to cure you. I said I would do anything, give him anything, pay any price, if only he would make you well again. I knew he could do such a thing. And he saw that I knew.'

Anne let go of Bess's hands and straightened up as if unable to say what she had to while touching her daughter. Bess wanted to ask a hundred questions but forced herself to be quiet and let her mother tell the tale.

'He took me inside. He warned me there would be no going back from the journey we were about to take. He made me tell him twice more that this was truly what I desired, at any price. Only when he was certain of my resolve did he act.' Anne shook her head and rubbed her eyes. 'Oh, Bess, to see such power in the hands of a single man, it is a thing of wonder and of terror. I stayed there the whole night watching him about his incantations, his chants and prayers, his rituals and strange processes. There were flames of white fire dancing in the room, and sounds . . . unearthly sounds the like of which I have never heard. Nor can I describe them to you now. For the most part I was required to do nothing. Then, toward dawn, Gideon drew me forward to stand in a circle he had marked upon the floor. Within the circle he had drawn a five-pointed star. He made offerings; he spoke in strange tongues. The very air in the place that night tasted of magic, I swear it. All about me swirled shapes and colors and sounds not born of this world.' Anne stood up now, her eyes glowing at the memory, her gaunt faced framed by her chalky hair looking wild and distant. 'I felt it. I felt the power that Gideon summoned. It was a fearsome thing. A thing like no other. A force from without that traveled into my very soul. I tell you I have never been more afraid in my life.' She looked down at Bess, her expression altered to one of ecstasy. 'Never more afraid and never more alive!'

Bess found a small voice. 'You used magic to cure me? Gideon gave you this magic?'

'Yes. And it worked! As soon as I felt it enter me, I knew it had the power to heal you. I knew you were saved. I returned home and did as Gideon instructed. I made offerings. I lit candles. I repeated the strange songs and incantations. And you lived!' She smiled now, her face radiant with the joy of what had happened.

It was some moments before Bess could speak, but speak she must. There was one more question that demanded an answer.

'Mother.' She stood up and chose her words with care. 'Tell me, what price did you pay for this magic?'

Anne looked away, shaking her head.

'What price!' Bess persisted.

'No! Do not ask me that.' Anne raised her voice and held up a hand as if to ward off further interrogation. 'Never ask me that, Bess. Never.'

Bess wanted to press her further but found she could not. The revelations her mother had made were enough for now. Her head was already in turmoil. She needed time to consider what she had been told. Further explanation would have to wait for another day. But that day would come. Bess would have her answer.

The following morning the pair arose before dawn in order to reach Batchcombe in time to set up their stall at the market. They had no cheese to sell, nor butter, nor eggs. They took, instead, a small bundle of lace collars and the solitary pig. The animal seemed to sense the futility of resistance and allowed itself to be herded up a makeshift ramp onto the back of the old cart. Whisper trod the ground with slow and steady hoofbeats so that they arrived at their allotted corner of the high street a little after eight o'clock.

They had not attended such a gathering since autumn of the previous year, and Bess was shocked to see how reduced the event was. Gone was the usual hustle and bustle, the good-natured banter between stallholders, the gossip of the women and the posturing of the men. The brutal winter weather and the merciless progression of plague had rendered Batchcombe a town of shadows and ghosts. Couples were reduced to lone figures. Families had once filled the street, but now grim-faced parents walked with spaces beside them where their children should have been. Many had lost the sole provider, forcing women to sell articles of their own clothing and furniture or to part with precious livestock. The fish stall was empty, there being no men to spare to send out in boats. The door of the baker's was shut and locked. There was, as there had always been, drunkenness, but it was no longer of the ribald and merry variety. Instead, men tipped ale and cider down their throats and sat in gloomy silence, awaiting respite from their own personal torment. Few elderly people had survived, and even fewer babies, giving the scene a curiously unbalanced and unnatural feel. The children who had been spared looked haunted now, bereft of siblings and weary from grief and overwork. It was a look Bess knew she wore herself. Even the weather seemed tired and could not be bothered to blow or bluster as it had done. Everywhere there was a sense of absence and of loss. The sky remained flatly gray. The ground was damp mud and dull stone. The people of Batchcombe themselves had lost their color, with not a crimson coat nor scarlet cape to be seen, so that the market presented a drab and sorry spectacle.

Bess stood beside the hapless sow while her mother did her best to persuade a well-dressed woman to buy some lace. As she watched the procession of sadness drift by, she wondered idly if there would ever be joy in the village again. A couple she recognized paused in their progress up the street. Bess mustered a smile, but the man stared stonily and the red-eyed woman looked fit to dissolve into fresh fits of weeping. Bess frowned at her mother who put a hand on her arm as the couple walked on.

'Goody Wainwright had all her children taken by the plague,' Anne explained.

'I am sorry for their loss, but why do they regard us with such hate in their eyes?'

'It is hard for them to reconcile themselves to their lot. My daughter lives still. Theirs does not. That is all.'

As if to underline the truth of this, Mr. Wainwright slowed his step to hawk heavily and spit in the direction of Anne's feet. Bess wanted to respond, to say something in their defense, but she noted her mother's forbearance and stayed silent. She was so unsettled by what had happened it took her a moment to realize she was being spoken to. She turned to find William standing beside her.

'Good morning to you, Bess. I had hoped to find you here.'

'William, if you have come to press me further . . .' She found herself uncomfortable in his presence.

'No. No, please forgive me for offending you, Bess. I . . . I had not given the matter proper consideration. I see now that I misjudged your feelings for me. I am sorry. I had no wish to cause you distress.'

Bess looked at him. What was the point in trying to make him understand? He and she had grown up separated by a divide that could never be crossed.

'There is nothing more to be said on the matter,' she told him.

Anne moved closer to her daughter. 'Good morning, William,' she said levelly.

He responded with a stiff bow, clearly unsure of how his proposal had been received. His eye lighted on the pig.

'Ah, you are selling her?'

'Why, no,' Bess snapped, 'we fancied the ride to market might improve her temper.'

Anne stepped between William and Bess.

'Yes, William. We are selling the sow.'

'Good, well, we could use another such animal. She looks . . . well enough.'

'She is a little lean,' Anne said, 'but she is young and has produced fine piglets in her time.'

'Excellent. I will take her.'

Bess could not help herself. 'Now you insult us with your charity!'

'Bess!' Anne hissed. 'The young master merely wishes to purchase the pig.'

'The young master has not even asked the price of the pig.'

'I assure you, Bess, I have need of another sow. This is not charity but business.'

Bess opened her mouth to give her thoughts on William's business but was prevented from doing so by a sudden commotion at the bottom of the high street. There was a sound of clattering hooves and barking dogs as a party of riders swooped around the bend and up the hill. Market-goers crowded to look and then quickly flattened themselves into stalls and doorways to avoid being trampled by the fast-moving entourage. There were six men mounted on good horses. All were somberly dressed but in clothes of good quality and with swords at their hip. One rider stood out. His garb was similar to that of the others in most respects, save his noticeably fine boots. His black hat had no feather, and his wide leather belt was fastened by a gleaming silver buckle. His horse was white as a newborn lamb and moved proudly, seeming to float above the cobbles. Bess thought there was an air about this man, something in his bearing, something in the understated elegance of his outfit, or the confident set of his jaw, that put him apart from the others. There was nothing flamboyant about him, nothing that could be criticized in these times where plainness and modesty were virtues, and yet for all his simple cape and unadorned livery, he had an unmistakable presence.

A murmur rippled through the crowd. It started as a hesitant whisper but quickly grew to a chorus, so that when the party swept past Bess, she clearly heard the announcement. The village was now host to Nathaniel Kilpeck, magistrate, coroner, and witchfinder. Bess's mouth dried and she found herself unwilling to meet her mother's eye. Instead, she silently took her hand, and the two women stood wordlessly watching as the group cantered toward the coaching inn at the top of the high street.

6

Two days later, Bess and Anne sat at their kitchen table and ate a meager breakfast of watery pottage in silence. They had not spoken of Nathaniel Kilpeck or of the nature of his purpose in coming to Batchcombe. Bess felt to voice her fears would give them more weight, would somehow bring them into being. And yet not broaching the subject of the witchfinder left her in private torment. She had heard of witch hunts in other parts of the country. Thomas had even entertained his sisters with tales of the witches' spell-casting and evil deeds. And of the eventual hanging of those same women after they were brought to trial and condemned. Bess watched her mother finish her meal. Her once-handsome face now showed the skull beneath the flesh, and the intense blue of her eyes had faded. Even so, there was still a strength about her. A power. As Bess struggled to make sense of all that had happened in a few brutal months, she heard a horse gallop into the yard. She and her mother exchanged anxious glances and hurried outside to find Bill Prosser reining in his brown mare.

'Good morning to you, Widow Hawksmith. Bess.' He nodded hurriedly, clearly not intending to dismount.

'What brings you to our door at such speed, Bill Prosser? Is someone in your household unwell?' Anne asked.

'No, thanks be to God. We were spared. The plague passed through the village, but the good Lord saw fit to protect us. I come to you on another matter, at the urging of my wife and daughter.'

'Another matter?' Anne's voice gave away nothing of her fears.

'You are aware Nathaniel Kilpeck is in the village? He has been sent here on government orders, to seek out witchery and try the accused. Old Mary has been arrested.'

At this news Anne gasped, her hand flying to her mouth.

'No!' Bess stepped forward. 'But on what charge?'

'The charge of witchcraft.'

'Mary is no witch,' said Bess, 'She is a good woman. A godly woman. She has saved lives aplenty in the village. Everyone knows this. Who accuses her?'

'Mistress Wainwright. And Widow Digby.'

'That woman has a serpent's tongue!'

'Bess!' Anne sought to silence her.

Bill had more to tell. 'Mistress Wainwright claims Old Mary put a curse on her children and that because of it they fell quickly to the plague.' He paused awkwardly, then added, 'She names another in her accusations.'

'Who?' Bess demanded.

Anne put a hand on her daughter's arm. 'There is no need to press our good neighbor further, Bess.' She looked up and gave him a nod. 'My thanks to you for coming to give us this news,' she said.

'It is as I told you, my wife and daughter bade me warn you. Good day to you both,' he said, turning his restless horse about and spurring it quickly into a scrambling canter.

Bess clutched at her mother. 'He meant you! You are accused! Mother, we must leave here at once; we cannot stay. It is not safe. We must take what we can and go this very instant.'

'Hush, child,' Anne said, her eyes fixed on the horizon. 'Fleeing will avail us nothing.'

Bess saw a look of calm resignation on her mother's face. She squinted into the distance, following the direction of her mother's gaze. Bill Prosser had disappeared into the woods, but still hoofbeats could be heard. They came, she saw now, from the fast-moving group cresting the hill and thundering down the path toward the cottage. At the head of the party rode Nathaniel Kilpeck.

The meeting that had been called at the courthouse was essentially to determine whether or not the accusations brought against Anne had sufficient credence to warrant trying her. In fact, to Bess's mind, it was a trial in itself. Anne was held by a constable, standing in front of the high bench at the far end of the room. The public gallery was full of murmuring, whispering people from the village. Everything had happened so quickly Bess still could not fully take it all in. Here she sat, in the echoing courtroom, surrounded by familiar faces she no longer recognized. These were neighbors, fellow farmers and stallholders, people she had known all her life, and yet here they were, crowding the wooden benches, straining forward the better to see the supposed witch in their midst. A door opened and a procession of earnest men strode to their places on the magistrate's bench. Bess recognized Nathaniel Kilpeck and two of his own men. With him were also the town councillor, Geoffrey Wilkins, and Reverend Burdock. As soon as they were seated, Councillor Wilkins banged his gavel three times for silence. A hush fell.

'This meeting is called to order,' he declared, 'for the purpose of inspecting the evidence against Anne Hawksmith. Presiding is Magistrate Nathaniel Kilpeck, sent directly on the authority of Parliament in his position as witchfinder.'

Nathaniel Kilpeck waved aside further introductions.

'Thank you, Councillor,' he said in his curiously high, tense voice. He paused, narrowing his eyes to take in first Anne, then the gathering of onlookers. 'Many of you here will have heard my name, and you will have heard of deeds associated with that name. Grave deeds. I make no apology for them. These are dark times. The devil walks the earth, and we are none of us safe from his unholy grasp. It is incumbent on all of us, each and every one, to be vigilant. To be awake to the dangers that lurk within our midst. It is only through such vigilance that we can root out the putrid rot of evil from our society and cleanse our land of Satan's influence. To rid it of creatures as the witch who stands before me, if witch she be, or else no child can be raised in safety and in God's name in this town.'

This drew assenting nods from the reverend and a ripple of ayes from the crowd. Bess's palms were already damp with sweat. She had known her mother to be in great danger, but until that moment she had not realized the enormity of her peril. Here was a man out to show the world that ungodliness would not be tolerated. Here was a man, it seemed to her, who had not come to listen, to hear evidence and testimony, but to condemn whoever was put before him, regardless of their innocence or guilt, merely to further his own cause.

'Rest assured I will be rigorous,' he continued. 'Rigorous in my interrogation of both accused and witness. And rigorous in my application of the law in these matters. I will not bend to mob rule. I will see to it that the evidence is correctly gathered and examined. Then and only then will I commit the accused for trial, and that trial will be conducted with the utmost propriety. However, should I find Satan has indeed corrupted this woman, that he has defiled her, taking her from the handmaid of God she was born to be and turning her into something vile and malevolent, then I will show no mercy. Witchery is against God. It is against the law. I aim to see that it is stamped out so that God-fearing citizens may live in peace and safety once again!'

This time there was a cheer. In just a few moments Kilpeck had won the support of the majority in the room, and already Bess could see the frightening fervor with which hitherto gentle people now shook their fists and banged their canes on the floor to show their agreement. Through it all her mother stood straight and still, her eyes fixed at some distant point, looking at once both vulnerable and strong.

Councillor Wilkins was on his feet.

'Who accuses this woman?' he demanded.

There was a shuffling to one side of the gathered throng. Mistress Wainwright stepped forward.

'I do, sir,' she said.

Nathaniel Kilpeck addressed the woman directly.

'And what do you say she has done?'

'I say that she, along with that beldame Mary, did put a curse upon my four children so that they suffered terribly and died of the plague.' Mistress Wainwright's eyes were reddened and puffy. Her skin was dry and pinched, as if all the juices had been sucked from her body. Bess could feel the woman's rage and pain as she spoke.

Reverend Burdock cleared his throat. 'If I may . . . ?' He received a nod from the magistrate, 'Mistress Wainwright, we are all deeply sorry for your loss. I know how you have suffered. But surely it is the nature of that dreadful disease that little ones are lost. If God saw fit to take your children, why would you think that Old Mary or Anne Hawksmith here had any part in it?'

'Everyone knows the two of them are cunning folk. They use potions, they even sell them. They make no secret of their black arts.'

The reverend risked a smile. 'But for healing, surely. From what I know of these women, they have assisted at a great many births and eased the suffering of numerous members of our parish. What could they have to gain by wishing harm on your children?'

At this, Mistress Wainwright clenched her teeth so that she had to spit out her words between them. 'Anne Hawksmith's daughter did not die.' She pointed a bony finger at the accused, her extended arm shaking as she did so. 'Her child was stricken with the plague but lives still. She should have died, but that woman made a pact with the devil to save her, so she did. She gave him my babes so that hers might live!'

There were gasps of horror from the crowd and curses uttered. Kilpeck raised a hand to silence them once more.

'Is this true, Mistress Hawksmith? Does your daughter live still, even though she had the plague upon her?'

There was a tremor in Anne's voice when she spoke, but she kept her tone level and her eyes fixed forward.

'My eldest daughter, Bess, did indeed fall sick, sir. And yes, we are blessed that she is recovered,' she said.

'Blessed or cursed!' came a shout from the gallery.

'Silence!' demanded Councillor Wilkins.

Anne went on. 'My younger daughter, Margaret, my sweet babe, was not so fortunate. She died. As did my son, Thomas, and my dear husband, John.'

'So, Bess alone was spared?' asked Kilpeck. 'Bess and yourself, of course.'

'It is as I say, sir. Bess fell ill but recovered fully. I myself was not afflicted.'

'That is strange, wouldn't you say? A house so riven with death, and yet you resisted its advance without so much as a fever?'

'It is what happened.'

'Indeed. And where is your daughter now? Is she here?' He scanned the public gallery, 'Bess Hawksmith, show yourself.'

Bess pushed her way through the crowd, finding that people quickly stepped out of her path. She came to stand next to her mother.

Kilpeck and the others on the high bench peered down at her, regarding her closely.

'I see not one sign of your suffering,' Kilpeck told her. 'No pockmarks or scars. Indeed, you appear in remarkable health.'

'I thank God and my mother's tender care, sir. Though I had at one moment wished to join my brother and sister.'

'Did you think you were going to die?'

Bess hesitated, then nodded. 'Yes, sir. I did.'

'I see. So, you were so gravely ill that you considered yourself about to be taken into Our Lord's arms, and yet here you stand. What kept you on this earth, do you think? What medicaments and prayers did your mother offer?'

In the silence of the courtroom all Bess could hear was the beating of her own heart. She thought of how she had woken to find her mother chanting and singing before a candle. She thought of how her mother had spoken of Gideon Masters and the powerful magic he had given her. The magic that had saved her. Was she about to condemn her own mother? Would it be her own words that would place the noose about her neck?

'Come, child,' said Reverend Burdock, 'tell us what you know.'

'I am sorry, Reverend, not to be of any further help in this matter, but I was, as the magistrate has said, gravely ill. I do not remember any treatment nor details of my cure. I know only that I have God's will and my mother's love to thank for my life.'

Kilpeck said nothing for a moment but sat watching Bess closely, as if he knew that the real answers he sought lay with her. At length he whispered to Councillor Wilkins, who stood up and demanded, 'Who else accuses this woman? Step forward.'

Widow Digby, handkerchief in hand, forced her way to the front of the assembled group.

'I do.' She addressed Kilpeck tearfully. 'My name is Honoria Digby, and I was forced to watch helplessly as my dear sister, Eleanor, was taken from this world. In her delirium she clung to my hand, and she spoke of the vision before her poor blinded eyes. "Honoria," she said, "they are coming for me. I see them!" I implored her to tell me who it was that terrified her so and she said, "Old Mary and Anne Hawksmith! Here they come, swooping on their brooms, naked and shameless, suckling their imps at their breasts!"' Widow Digby swooned into the arms of two nearby men and could say no more. A shudder of revulsion worked its way through the crowd. Nathaniel Kilpeck looked at Anne.

'Well, Anne Hawksmith, you have heard testimony against you. What have you to say in your defense?'

'Am I to be condemned by the rantings of a fever-addled old woman and the jealousy of a mother whose mind has been poisoned by grief? Am I to be punished for nursing my own child back to health?'

'It is precisely how you succeeded where so many others would have failed that is of concern here,' Kilpeck told her. 'It will go badly for you if you do not tell us what methods you used to effect her cure.'

Anne paused. She turned to look at Bess and smiled gently at her. She turned back to Kilpeck.

'You have no daughter, have you, sir?'

'I am not the one being investigated here,' he said.

'I know that you have none,' Anne went on, 'for if you had, you would know that you would do anything to save her. There is no power on this earth or any other that you would not use if it would end your child's suffering and bring about her recovery.'

The crowd grew restless.

Reverend Burdock sought to counsel Anne, 'Have a care, Mistress, you do your case no good with such statements.'

'My daughter was close to death,' said Anne. 'I had already watched my first and last-born die. I had buried my own husband. What sort of mother would I be to do nothing if it were within my power to save my last remaining child? Death had her in his clutches, and I pulled her from his grasp, that is all.'

Kilpeck frowned at her. 'Do you say you brought her back from the dead? Had she departed this life when you effected your cure?'

'I know not how deeply into that pit of endless night she had fallen, only that I was able to raise her up again.'

There were further gasps of shock around the room.

Reverend Burdock paled. 'You would have us believe you raised your daughter from the dead? Do you claim to perform miracles now?'

Anne smiled softly, a look of resignation on her face. 'Our Lord's work you call miracles; mine you say is magic.'

'Blasphemy!' cried Widow Digby.

'You go too far, Anne Hawksmith!' The reverend could not conceal his fury. Anne was unmoved by it.

'Why, Reverend Burdock, you have on the window of your church Christ raising Lazarus. Would you have cried "Witchery!" at Our Lord?'

At this, the room collapsed into turmoil. There were shouts and curses from the gallery, which Councillor Wilkins's gavel failed to silence. The reverend was unable to stay still in his seat. Court officials and two constables were forced to restrain the crowd from pushing forward. Bess feared they were to be swept away by the furious mob. She looked at her mother anew. Why had she spoken so boldly? Why had she made no attempt to conceal the facts or at least to make light of them, to throw herself on the mercy of the magistrates? The more Bess stared at her mother, the less she recognized her. She seemed so calm, so resolved, and in no way disturbed or terrified, as Bess was, by the frenzy of the crowd nor the possible consequences of her words.

At last, order was restored. Nathaniel Kilpeck waited for complete quiet before making his pronouncement.

'I am satisfied that there is substance to the accusations of *maleficia*. I therefore decree that Anne Hawksmith's body be searched for known signs that she be a witch and that she be returned to her house and there watched for two days and nights. I will accept further testimonies should they be forthcoming, and a trial will be held in this court five days from now.' He finished speaking and rose quickly from his seat. As Anne was bundled out of the side door down to the cells below, the members of the bench filed out. Bess's heart filled with fear at the sight of her mother being taken from her.

'Mother!' she called out, but the door had slammed shut behind the last constable.

Bess was not to learn until some time later what her mother had endured at the hands of the searchers. Ordinarily such work was undertaken by local midwives, but clearly in this instance someone else had to be found. Isabel Pritchard, a woman of dubious integrity, was brought in from Dorchester to perform the task. Anne was stripped and strapped to a table with leather cinches. Under the scrutiny of Councillor Wilkins and Nathaniel Kilpeck, Mistress Pritchard inspected every inch of Anne's flesh. After some time, she announced the discovery of two dark moles, which she proceeded to prick to see if they would produce blood. They did not. Kilpeck was not satisfied with Pritchard's efforts and undertook to search Anne's body himself. No part, however private or immodest, was left unprobed. At last he found, deep between her legs, what appeared to be a small, flat teat. Kilpeck had the recorder note this down in detail, saying it appeared to him to have been recently suckled.

From there, Anne was taken back to her farm. Bess had been told that the watching would take place in Anne's home, where familiars and imps would be more likely to present themselves. Old Mary, having no real home of her own, was to be watched there also. The furniture was pushed to one side, with Anne and Mary tightly bound to chairs in the center of the room. To the sides were placed other more comfortable seating, upon which sat the official watchers. These were Isabel Pritchard, no doubt happy to accept a fee for further services; Councillor Wilkins; Reverend Burdock; and the witchfinder. A constable was placed at the door. Bess was permitted to stay, but it was made clear any interference on her part would result in her being thrown out.

After much fuss and settling in, the watchers fell silent. Bess found a space in a shadowy corner where she was able to see her mother's face clearly, as the light from the fire and the carefully positioned candles fell upon it. She was at a loss to understand what was expected to happen. Did anyone really believe that curious creatures and small spirits would visit her mother? It was beyond comprehension that someone of sound sense, such as Councillor Wilkins, could truly believe he was about to witness such things. He had known her mother all her life. He had seen her attend church regularly, as had the reverend. And yet now, here they were, sitting in the silent room, waiting for unearthly beings to appear. Old Mary looked close to fainting. Her lips moved ceaselessly, as if she were praying, and her eyes appeared to have lost their focus. Anne, by contrast, sat straight and still, impassive and serene. Bess marveled at her composure and forbearance.

The hours passed, notable only for their emptiness. There was no weather to speak of and no conversation, so that the only sounds to be heard were the gentle hiss and spit of the fire and the occasional screech of an owl behind the house. After two more hours, these sounds were increased by the ragged noise of Councillor Wilkins's snoring. Bess shifted stiffly, knowing herself to be in no danger of falling asleep, even though she was exhausted by the anxiety of the past few days. The candles burned low, suggesting dawn would soon put an end to the ridiculous night. Then, quietly at first but quickly gaining volume, sounds could be heard. Scratching sounds. Kilpeck stiffened in his chair. The reverend frowned and looked about him. The scratching noises continued and seemed to be coming from the door to the dairy. Just as Bess was convincing herself it was nothing more than a hungry mouse, the sounds changed to banging and the door could be seen to rattle in its frame.

'Lord save us!' whispered Mistress Pritchard.

All in the room kept their eyes fixed on the door. Even Councillor Wilkins was shaken from his slumbers by the racket.

Now the banging was accompanied by strange squeals and yelps. Reverend Burdock started to pray. Councillor Wilkins moved to stand up, but Kilpeck put out a hand to stop him.

'Do not move!' he instructed.

The yelps grew louder. They were unlike any sounds Bess had heard in her life before, somewhere between the yapping of puppies and the babbling of babies. Old Mary whimpered and strained against the ropes that bound her to her chair. Her eyes widened as the wooden latch on the dairy door began to lift, seemingly of its own accord. Through it all, Anne did not move.

Bess found herself holding her breath as the door slowly swung open. At first, she could see nothing, then low, undulating shapes slipped out from the darkness of the other room and slithered into the light. Now Bess's breath left her in a gasp of horror. The creatures were clearly not born of any animal on God's earth. There were four in total, all roughly the size of badgers, but their bodies were twisty and sinuous like overlarge weasels. Their coats appeared to consist in part of coarse fur but also of toad-like skin. Their eyes were rheumy and dull, and saliva drooled from their slack, toothless mouths. The aberrations crept forward, their stomachs low to the floor, still making their eerie sounds. Old Mary began to shriek and soon Mistress Pritchard joined in.

Councillor Wilkins would be restrained no longer and leaped from his chair. Reverend Burdock had stopped mid-prayer to stare, appalled, as the creatures circled the room before finding Anne. At the sight of her they began to squeal with glee. They flung themselves onto her lap and about her neck, licking her face and snuffling into her hair. Bess thought she would be sick, but still her mother did not move: nor did she give any outward sign of horror or revulsion. Indeed, it seemed to Bess that she was not at all surprised at what was happening, rather that she had expected it. Could it be that she knew these abominations? That they were indeed her imps? Her familiars? Bess's head reeled as she tried to take in what she was seeing. Old Mary had quite lost her wits and was screaming madly, twisting desperately in her chair to try to get away from the creatures. To get away from Anne.

Kilpeck stood up and drew his sword. His constable was about to leave his post at the door, but the witchfinder signaled for him to stay where he was.

'Hold fast your position!' he cried. 'Let no living thing quit this room.' He raised his sword and brought it slicing down upon one of the animals at Anne's feet, cutting off one of its legs. It squealed horribly, a ghastly sound which did not stop even when a second blow severed its head from its body. Both halves continued to writhe and wriggle. Reverend Burdock vomited copiously. Mistress Pritchard swooned onto the floor. Councillor Wilkins, having no sword, took up a stool and began to beat wildly at the creatures as they darted about the room. Bess put her hands over her ears to shut out the dreadful sounds, unable to take her eyes off her mother. One of the imps sought refuge beneath Anne's skirts.

'See! See how the foul creatures cleave to their mistress! These are the spawn of the devil! This woman is no sister of Eve; she is a vile instrument of Satan!' He raised his sword above his head and Bess saw that he meant to bring it down upon her mother.

'No! No!' she cried, flinging herself forward. She threw her arms around her mother, ignoring the fleeing imps, covering her mother's body with her own. 'No!' she screamed up at Kilpeck, locking eyes with him. For a moment, his sword wavered, suspended, threatening to end the lives of both Anne and Bess with one mighty blow. In that moment, the imps fled. In the blink of an eye, they were gone, and with them the noise and chaos they had caused. Bess held Kilpeck's gaze, challenging him, knowing, as he knew, that he had no right to take her life. Slowly, with great effort, he harmlessly lowered his sword. Isabel Pritchard sat on the floor weeping. Reverend Burdock began to pray once more. As a steaming pool appeared beneath Old Mary's chair, the sour stink of hot urine filled the air.

7

Word quickly spread through the village of the events of that night. By the time Anne and Old Mary were brought from the cells to stand before the magistrates a second time, there was not a space to be found in the courtroom, and the constables had difficulty keeping order. Councillor Wilkins hammered long and loud to obtain silence. Old Mary had recovered her wits sufficiently only to emit a babbling confession. It seemed she had given up all hope of being spared but clung to the hope that her soul might yet be saved. Her testimony on top of that of Goodwife Wainwright and Widow Digby would have been enough to condemn both the accused. After what the watchers had seen, such evidence was hardly necessary.

Bess was dazed from lack of sleep and from fear. Fear that she was losing her mind. Fear that her mother was beyond saving. And fear of what power it was that had sent those creatures to her mother. What did it mean? What had her mother become? Was this the price she would not speak of? The price she must pay for Gideon helping her to save Bess's life?

Nathaniel Kilpeck held up his hand for silence. At last, when all the restless onlookers had been stilled, he began to speak, his reedy voice betraying an otherwise well-concealed excitement.

'We have heard testimonies from the witnesses, both godly women of good standing in this parish. We have listened to the confession of Mary, who stands before us, an admitted witch.'

A hiss of hatred and agitation came from the public gallery.

'Last night, I myself, along with others here present, did witness the unholy spectacle of four loathsome imps coming to suckle at the privy parts of this blatant, dangerous witch before me!' At this, he pointed a trembling hand at Anne. The crowd gasped and stamped and shouted. The witchfinder waited for quiet before continuing. 'Such were the horrors and so strong the evidence that I sent word to the high court and pleaded the case for immediate and swift action. I can tell you now that I have received notification that it will not be necessary to wait for the quarter sessions or to transport these . . . *women* to the court at Dorchester. I have been empowered to pronounce a verdict on the evidence collected and to pass sentence here in this place and on this very day, such is the nature of their crimes.' A cheer went up. Kilpeck forced his voice to be heard above the crowd, not waiting for them to settle this time. 'Mary, midwife of this parish, we have heard your confession and accepted your plea of guilty. May God be merciful upon your soul. Anne Hawksmith, you have heard the charges brought against you. You have been searched and found to bear the marks of the devil and the wherewithal for suckling your familiars. I myself have witnessed Satan visit you in the form of these vile imps. All present there saw them delight in your company. Have you anything to say in your defense?'

At last, silence returned to the courtroom. Every ear strained to hear what Anne would say, every neck craned for a clearer view of the devil's bride who had lived undetected in their midst for so many years. Bess began to tremble. Anne took a moment to gaze about her as if studying the faces of those who had come to witness her condemnation. When her eyes met Bess's she smiled weakly, then turned her attention back to the magistrates.

'There is nothing I can say that will soften hearts of stone,' she said.

'Do you still claim innocence? After all that we have seen?' Kilpeck asked.

'I am innocent of the charges made against me by Widow Digby and Goody Wainwright, yes. I have harmed no one.'

'The charges of *maleficia* are but one aspect of this trial. Witchery itself is a capital crime, this you must know.'

Anne said nothing.

Reverend Burdock leaned forward on the bench, hands clasped.

'For the love of God, woman, and to save your soul from certain damnation, will you not confess and plead for the mercy of this court and of Our Lord?'

Anne looked at him levelly. 'I have nothing more to ask of God,' she said.

The reverend recoiled as if she had struck him, 'How can you have come to this wretched, godless state, woman?'

'Not woman—witch!' came the cry from the room, so that soon a chant had been taken up. 'Witch! Witch! Witch!'

Wilkins banged his gavel in vain. Only Kilpeck getting to his feet finally restored order.

'Midwife Mary, Anne Hawksmith, you have both been found guilty of the charges of *maleficia,* in particular with regard to the Wainwright children and Widow Smith, and in general that you do follow the practice of witchery. It is the sentence of this court that you be taken from this place at sunrise, two days from this date, and that you be hanged until you be dead.'

The court descended into chaos. Bess heard the sound of her own screaming and thought she would lose her mind in that moment. She tried to push forward, to reach her mother, arms outstretched, but it was hopeless. She felt dangerous madness welling up inside her but could not see what to do. Despite the force within her reaching almost unmanageable levels, she could see no way it could be employed to save her mother. The crowd shouted and jeered fit to riot, so that Kilpeck gestured to the constables to remove the convicted women while his men held back the increasingly wild villagers. Bess was jolted and jostled by the mob so that she managed only one last, brief glimpse of her mother as she was led away.

Batchcombe Hall was a fine example of the craftsmanship of its day. Its glowing red bricks and gleaming timbers declared its owner to be a man of substance. The front door itself had much to say—wax-smooth wood told of wealth and strength; intricate iron hinges demanded to be noticed for their beauty rather than function; the muscular lock suggested this was in fact a fortress, as did the seven dozen black studs protruding from the wide wooden boards. It was to this door that Bess came early on the day following her mother's trial. She left Whisper to snatch at the abundant grass beside the drive and took a steadying breath before mounting the steps. She had thought long and hard about seeking William's help. She was far from certain that there was anything he could do, but she had no one else to turn to. She had no choice. Having made up her mind, she had then to decide at which door she would present herself. She was uncomfortable at the thought of arriving at the front of the great house. She had never set foot inside such a place. Would she even be admitted? And yet, she was neither a servant nor a tradesman. Nor did she care for the notion of slipping into William's home unannounced through the back door. There was something furtive about such an action. Her situation was grave, but whatever the court had decided regarding her mother she refused to feel shame. No, she would go to the front door and ask for William. This was no time for delicate manners.

She lifted the heavy iron knocker and banged hard four times. After a worryingly long wait, she heard footsteps and the door was opened. A neat woman with sharp features and tiny hands cocked her head at the sight of the unexpected caller.

'What business have you here?' she asked.

Bess inwardly bridled at the speed with which this woman had summed her up as having no possibility of being a friend of the Goulds.

'I wish to speak to Master William Gould.'

'Master William is engaged at present. On what matter did you wish to speak with him?'

'A matter of a personal nature.'

The woman remained motionless for a moment, as if considering whether or not this was sufficient reason to disturb her master.

Bess went on. 'It is a matter of some urgency,' she added, then, seeing no weakening in the guardian's resolve, 'I would consider it a great kindness if you would inform Master William I am here.'

Without a word the woman disappeared back into the house, shutting the door behind her. Bess stood staring at the impregnable barrier, wondering if she had been dismissed. She waited, a knot tightening somewhere beneath her breastbone. At last the door opened again, and this time William came hurrying forward. He took her hand and led her inside.

'Bess,' he said, 'my poor, poor Bess. I have heard the terrible news, of course.' He spoke as he whisked her through the grand entrance hall, past the polished wooden staircase, and through another door. The comfortable room contained more furniture and wall hangings than Bess had seen in her lifetime. It also contained a fair-skinned young woman seated on a low chair by the fire. Bess stopped, thrown by the sight of this unexpected stranger. William drew her on to a carved oak seat made restful with tapestry bolsters and cushions.

'Bess, you have not yet met Noella Bridgewell.' He turned to the woman. 'Forgive me, my dear, I fear this is not the time for formal introductions. Bess Hawksmith is a neighbor and a good friend.'

Noella gave a short nod by way of greeting.

'I have heard the name, of course,' she said.

Bess took in at a glance the girl's fine clothes, the expensive Spanish lace at her throat, the rich silk of her gown, the pearl-encrusted band in her hair. This was a lady of some standing, considerable wealth, and undeniable beauty. Bess sat down, conscious of her roughened hands and drab clothes.

'I am pleased to make your acquaintance,' she said, unable to concentrate on thinking up social pleasantries to exchange. 'Forgive my bluntness, but I am come on a matter of life and death.'

Noella nodded again, taking out an ivory fan to keep the warmth of the fire from her face. 'I am certain my fiancé will afford you any assistance in his power,' she said.

Fiancé! This woman was to be William's bride? Bess felt her head spin. She wanted to run from the room, but she needed William's help. He was the only hope left to her mother. She drew a deep breath and raised her chin.

'How fares your mother?' William asked.

Bess did not know how to answer. She no longer felt she knew who her mother was or how she might be feeling. She dug her nails into her palms to stop herself giving in to tears.

'I have not been permitted to see her since the trial,' she told him, shaking her head. 'Oh, William. They will hang her tomorrow!'

William still had hold of her hand. He squeezed it, showing no signs of wanting to let go, despite the constant gaze of his fiancée.

'The world no longer lives by any rules I can understand, Bess. Your mother is a good woman, a God-fearing woman of modesty and prayer. A loving mother and wife. She has helped so many people. I am at a loss to explain how such a thing can have come about.'

'Many in Batchcombe have suffered greatly, William. They look for someone to blame. It was my mother who made me see that.' She hesitated, then added, 'People fear what they cannot explain.' She felt her heartbeat quicken and knew that she herself was frightened. Not of the mother who had raised her and loved her and instructed her all her life but of this new power inside that same beloved woman. She looked up at William. 'Will you help us?' she asked.

'But what can I do?'

'Your family is well regarded. Your father has influence. If he were to make a plea for mercy, surely . . .' She stopped at the sight of William's bowed head.

'My father will not intervene.'

'You know this?'

William nodded.

'But you could approach him, ask him yourself, make him see that these are innocent women. The plague took so many; surely enough people have died. What is to be gained by more death?'

Slowly William's grasp on Bess's hand began to loosen until at last he let his own hand fall by his side. He could not look at her. At last it was Noella who spoke. She stood and stepped forward to stand beside her future husband.

'You should know that it was William's father who sent for Nathaniel Kilpeck,' she said, her voice level.

Bess could not believe what she was being told.

'What? Your father sent for the witchfinder? But I do not understand. What possible reason could he have for concerning himself with such matters? Why would he bring such ruthless injustice into our midst?'

Still William could not look at her. He paced as he spoke, his hands raised in despair. 'There are wider issues at stake, Bess,' he said. 'Things you cannot know of. Parliament is a place of unrest and intrigue. Every man has to prove himself, to prove his loyalty. My father treads a perilous path. Should he step too far to one side, he may be called traitor and lose his head. Should he veer to the other, he may find himself on shifting sands a short time from now, and the end result would be the same. In these dangerous times, the winds of change turn from north to south and back again between sunsets. There is pressure on the nobility to maintain firm control over their own regions. People feel this state of flux in the country and they fear it, Bess. They want to see strong government. They want to know they are in the hands of men of action. That they will be protected. If they cannot be saved from plague or starvation, they must at least know they are in God's keeping and the devil is not among them.'

In the silence that sat between them, Bess was reminded of how different her life was from William's. Here was a man whose father would sacrifice anyone to maintain his position. How could she ever have entertained the thought that he would have allowed that position to be weakened by letting his son marry a girl of no wealth or standing? And indeed, William had never harbored such a wish himself. She saw that now. All along he had known where her place was, and it was never going to be at his side. Not publicly at least. Noella was precisely the sort of woman his father would have chosen for him. She would enrich the family's standing and no doubt its fortune. She was important. Bess and her family were expendable. She closed her eyes against the dizzying colors of the fine tapestries around her. She did not belong here. There was nothing William could do to save her mother. There was nothing he would be allowed to do. She stood up, mustering more composure than she felt.

'I see now I was wrong to hope for your assistance for my mother. I am sorry to have brought this to your door, William. Good day to you.' She strode from the room, uncertain how long she could hold back the tears of anguish now pricking her eyes.

'Wait.' William sprang to his feet and hurried after her. 'Please, Bess. There must be something . . .' He barred her way to the door.

'What? Shall I take up your kind offer and install myself as your lover in the servants' quarters, William? Or am I no longer even suitable for that position now that my mother is condemned?' She pushed past him.

'Will you go to your mother now? Let me at least accompany you . . .'

'They will not permit me to see her,' she said without stopping, her hand already reaching for the front door latch.

'Not see her? But surely . . .'

Bess swung round, anger lending her the strength she needed. 'Yes, she will hang in the morning, and they will not admit me so that we might say our good-byes. There is greater cruelty in that one denial than my poor mother ever committed in the whole of her good life.'

'Then there is something I can do. Please, wait here but a moment.'

William sprinted back into the room they had just left. Bess was on the point of leaving when she noticed the maid who had let her in watching. She straightened her shoulders. She would not be made to feel ashamed. Why should she? William scurried back to her.

'Here.' He pressed a leather pouch of money into her hand. 'Take this. It is sufficient to pay whom you must so that you can spend a moment with your mother. It is the very smallest thing for me to do. I pray it brings you both peace of mind.'

Bess closed her fingers around the bag, still struggling to control her overwrought emotions.

'Thank you' was all she managed to say before fleeing the house, knowing as she ran back to Whisper and snatched up the trailing reins that she might never have peace of mind again.

The entrance to the jail beneath the courthouse was down a twisting stone staircase barely the width of two men. Bess followed the jailer down the dimly lit spiral, the light from his smoking lamp falling nowhere useful to her own faltering feet. Here was a man corrupted by the company he had been paid to keep for so many years. Bess detected a darkness emanating from him beyond even the foul stench of the breath that belched out between his blackened teeth.

'Nobody gets to see the prisoners the night before an execution,' he had told her flatly. 'Nobody.'

Any hopes Bess had harbored of appealing to his Christian spirit were quickly dashed.

'I only ask a few brief moments.'

He leaned back against the bolted door and folded his arms. 'I'd lose my job. I'd be out on my ear. And where would you be then, eh? Would you come a-looking for poor old Baggis, jobless and starving, mibben? Eh? I think not.'

'Perhaps, if I could provide you with some . . . insurance. Against such a terrible consequence . . .'

He grinned, taking in her simple clothes and young body with a leisurely stare. Without any sense of hurry, he stepped forward and reached out a grimy hand. 'And what could a maid such as you have that old Baggis might want now, eh? What d'you think?'

Bess took a step back and held up the purse of money.

'Half now,' she said, 'half when we have been permitted time together. An hour.'

He frowned at her and at the bag dangled in front of him. With a shrug and a grunt, he held out his hand. Bess quickly counted half the coins into his filthy palm.

The gloom and airlessness in the cells was not the worst of it. With the accused confined to their prisons day and night for the length of their stay, the air was thick with the stench of piss-soaked straw and loosely emptied bowels. Bess could only begin to imagine how much worse the jail in a town the size of Dorchester must be. These were merely cells for holding those accused of crimes and awaiting the assizes for their trials. An exception had been made for Anne and Mary. At least they had been spared possibly months of incarceration in such a hell-like place. When Bess saw Old Mary, she doubted the ailing woman would have survived more than a few days. She sat in the corner of the cell rocking back and forth, her fetters jingling as she did so, still muttering to herself, having aged a decade in a few days. Anne saw Bess and came quickly to the metal cage door, the shackles around her ankles slowing her progress. The jailer rattled his key in the rusty lock and let Bess in, slamming the door behind her. Bess fell into her mother's arms.

'There, child. Hush now.' Anne stroked her back.

'Oh, Mother, I feared I would not be allowed to come to you again before tomorrow.'

'Indeed I am greatly surprised to see you here. Who was it who gave you permission?'

'It doesn't matter now.' She pulled back to look at her mother. Her hair hung loose about her shoulders, a veil of white. Her face was tight drawn but somehow serene. Not for the first time Bess was struck by her mother's self-possession and apparent lack of fear. The memory of how she had sat unperturbed through all that had happened on the night of the watchers came back to her and spread a chill over her heart. She shook her head slowly.

'There is so much I want to ask you,' she said, 'so much I do not understand.'

'But you will, one day, Bess. One day. Do not judge me too harshly.'

'Never! How could I judge you? You have given everything for my sake, that much I know.'

'I am so sorry, my dearest one, to leave you so alone. Forgive me.'

'There is nothing for me to forgive.'

Anne glanced toward the door to make sure they were not overheard.

'Listen to me, Bess. You must make me a solemn promise.'

'You have only to ask it.'

'After tomorrow . . . no, do not weep . . . after tomorrow you must go to Gideon.'

'What? Mother, no!'

'Yes, you must ask for his help.'

'But have we not suffered enough for his help already? Have you not paid a higher price than any other would?'

'You know so little of the minds of folk, Bess. Do you not see that those who have condemned me must in turn persecute you?'

'Me? But for what?'

'You are the daughter of a proven witch. These are times unlike any we have known. People live in fear, though they do not know of what. For now it is witchery. By disposing of Mary and myself they will feel a little safer. For a short time. But it will not be many days before panic is stirred up anew, and the mob will lust for another killing. Gideon is the only one who can protect you.'

'By what means? Would you have him turn me into . . .'

'. . . a loathsome creature such as your mother has become?'

'No! That is not what . . .' Bess left the words unsaid and gave up trying to control her sobs.

'Bess, heed my words, child. You are all that is left of me. Of all of us. You have your father's good heart, your sister's love of life, your brother's fortitude. Survive, Bess! Live on, so that we all can continue. If you do not, then I die defeated. If you give your word you will do as I bid—then and only then can I go to the gallows content.'

'Oh, Mama.'

'Your word?'

Bess gave the tiniest of nods. 'If you must have it, then yes, I give you my promise. I shall go to Gideon and ask his protection.'

Anne sighed and Bess fancied some of the tension and tautness went from her body. She put a finger beneath Bess's chin and tilted her daughter's face up to her own.

'Let these be the last of your tears,' she said, 'so that you will have none without me there to dry them for you.'

'Oh, Mother, I am so . . . powerless. If only I could tear down this terrible building and bear you away to a place of safety. How can I watch you die?'

'You have more strength than you know, Bess. Do not grieve for me. I go to join our family, and I will take your love with me. I am not afraid.'

Bess stopped crying and touched her mother's cheek. 'I am,' she said.

'I know. But I will always be at your side, Bess. Know that. You are clever. You are resourceful. You are steadfast. There is a world waiting out there for you. I know you will do wonderful things.'

They were interrupted by the wheezing cough of the jailer as he thumped down the passageway toward the cell.

'Right you are,' he barked. 'Time's up.'

'What?' Bess clung to her mother's hand. 'You said an hour!'

'No, lass, t'was you said an hour. I mentioned no such time. Come on, out with you before I lose my job.'

'I won't give you a penny more till we have had the full hour.'

'You will if you don't want to end up locked up in here yourself, you cocky little vixen. Here, give me that.' He stepped forward and grabbed the purse from her belt. 'Now move your pretty young backside up those stairs before I find another use for it.'

Bess turned to her mother, who quickly kissed her hand.

'Go now,' she told her after they had embraced, 'and remember, no more tears.'

From some hidden place within her, Bess found a small, brave smile. Then she turned, fearing her courage might fail her. On leaden legs she forced herself to hurry after the jailer.

8

Being a place of no great significance, Batchcombe did not boast its own gallows, and there had not been time to construct one. There was, however, a stout oak to the west of the village, which had for as long as any could remember been known as the Hanging Tree. In less civilized times, the hapless and the wicked were summarily hoisted from its convenient boughs. There had been no steps to mount and no platform for the priest to say his words of comfort, but the convicted had ended up nonetheless dead at the end of their ropes. It was to this tree that the cart carrying Anne and Old Mary made its tortuous progress. It seemed to Bess the whole of the parish had come to witness what she saw as the murder of these two poor women. Peasant families, merchants, and nobles alike had turned out and jostled for a position with a good view. The cart carrying her mother was pulled by two mules. The women were still shackled at the ankles, with nooses already placed around their necks. They stood leaning against each other to ride the rough track without falling onto the cruel wooden spikes that surrounded them. Every step of the journey was accompanied by the jeers and taunts of the crowd. Bess looked at the wild faces and raised fists and was taken back to the cock pit where last she had seen such frenzied and brutish behavior. She had not slept but had hitched Whisper to the farm wagon and found a place on a small hillock to one side of the hanging tree. From here she could see her mother, and her mother could see her. The two women exchanged looks of longing and sadness, but true to her mother's wishes, Bess did not cry. Indeed, she could not. It was as if over these past dreadful months she had cried the tears of a lifetime, and there were no more left.

The crowd grew noisier and bawdier as the Reverend Burdock intoned his prayers. The cart was positioned beneath the tree, and the trailing ropes of the nooses were quickly looped over the branch above. To the front of the tree sat Nathaniel Kilpeck on his fine white horse. He held up his hand for quiet as the preacher finished commending two more souls to heaven.

'Let it be known,' he said in the thin voice that now inhabited Bess's nightmares, 'that there is no victory here today. The wretched creatures you see before you were corrupted by the devil himself, and they are deserving of our pity.'

There were murmurs of dissent at this. Kilpeck continued: 'Nevertheless, I know that all here will believe me when I say that Batchcombe is now a safer place, a more godly place, a better place, because it is free of witchery.'

This brought a cheer and cries of 'Hang the witches! Let them dance with the devil if they love him so much!'

Kilpeck turned to the women in the cart. 'Have you any words?' he asked.

Mary merely whimpered and shook her head. Anne remained composed and said only, 'I go to my family.'

Kilpeck seemed irritated by her calmness. If he had hoped for desperate pleas for mercy and last-minute confessions, he got none. He raised his hand again, signaling to the constable at the head of the mules. As he brought his hand swiftly down, the man dragged the animals forward. Both women were hauled off the back of the cart by the ropes attached to the tree at one end and their own necks at the other.

Bess felt all the breath leave her body and heard no sound but that of blood rushing in her head. She watched in despair as Old Mary kicked and jerked, her body more animated as it neared death than it had been for many years in life. By contrast, Anne slipped silently from the boards of the moving cart, her face as serene as ever. There was a crack, but she did not so much as twitch once. It was clear to Bess she was dead in less than a heartbeat, even though her beautiful blue eyes remained open, gazing benignly on the mob that screamed for her death.

During the slow journey home with her sad cargo in the wagon, a calmness overtook Bess. It was over, at least for her mother, and all that remained for her to do were practical things. Things within her control. The sun shone down with inappropriate cheerfulness as Whisper came to a halt in the farmyard. Bess went into the house and fetched what she needed—a shroud for her mother and a length of cloth that would serve as a winding-sheet for Old Mary. She had accepted both bodies, not being able to stand the thought of the poor kinless woman being buried outside of the churchyard, alone and unmarked. It took the rest of the day for Bess to gently prepare the two women for interment and to dig their graves. She shut her mind to the cruel memories of how she and her mother had buried first Thomas, then her father, and then little Margaret. She worked for hours, chopping at the dry soil with her spade while birds flitted overhead with twigs in their beaks. Here she was at the start of another spring, when all about her was burgeoning and budding, signifying new life, and yet she was entirely occupied with the matter of death. A soft movement of the air carried the scent of the sea with it. Bess felt a sudden longing to go to the shore and gaze upon the soothing water. She promised herself that when she had finished her grim task she would do just that. She was in no hurry to re-enter the empty house that had once been such a loving home. It took draining effort to drag the bodies from the cart onto the barrow and then lower them as gently as she was able into their earthen tombs. By the time she had replaced the soil, she was trembling with exhaustion. She knelt beside the fresh graves that lay alongside the three earlier ones, not in prayer but in a state of near collapse, her legs unable to support her a moment longer. She felt she must say something meaningful, something to mark the tragic moment. But neither words nor tears came. Instead, into Bess's benumbed mind came the sound of distant voices and the rumbling of cartwheels over hard ground. Squinting into the lowering sun, she could see a small crowd, some on horses but most on foot, and one scruffy wagon. The procession moved without urgency but with determination, and soon arrived at the farmyard.

Bess hauled herself to her feet. She saw Widow Digby sitting on the cart, along with Mistress Wainwright. She recognized a constable among the men and familiar faces from the market. She braced herself for whatever might come next.

A man stepped forward, who she now saw was Mr. Wainwright. He pointed at the dark mounds of earth.

'Be they the graves of the two witches?' he asked.

Bess spoke through gritted teeth. 'They are the resting places of my mother and of Old Mary.'

There was some activity near the wagon. Wainwright signaled to the other men.

'Bring them here!' he called.

The others unlatched the rear of the cart and slid out four broad flagstones, each big enough to require two men to carry it. They approached the graves. Bess was stung into action.

'What are you about? Take those away!'

'Stand aside, Bess,' said Wainwright. 'Let us do what must be done.'

'No!' But even as Bess protested, she was shoved from the path of the men. There were heavy thuds as the stones dropped into place on top of the graves.

'Can't you leave them be?' Bess cried. 'Even now, when they are dead, must you harry them still? Can you not let them rest?'

One of the stone carriers turned to her. 'Aye, we'll let them rest,' he said, 'and we'll see to it that they stay resting an' all.' He paused in his work only to spit noisily. Others followed suit.

'Get away!' Bess screamed, 'Get away! Go from this place, I tell you.' She flung herself on top of her mother's grave, emboldened by fury, 'Are you satisfied now? Can you sleep easier in your beds knowing you have sent my mother to her death and pinned her soul with your wretched stones? My mother who showed you only kindness. My mother who saved your sister's life, Tom Crabtree, and eased your pains in childbirth, Betty Tones, and drew a poison nail from your foot, Mistress Baines.

Have you truly such short memories? My mother was a good woman! My mother was a healer.'

Wainwright stepped forward, close enough for Bess to smell the whiskey on his breath and see the madness in his griefstricken eyes. His voice was a slow growl.

'Your mother was a witch!'

Silently the mob turned their backs on Bess and left her kneeling on the cold slabs they were content would prevent the witches rising from their graves and riding naked on their broomsticks about the village.

Bess watched them go. Only when the last of them had vanished from sight did she stir herself. She could see now that her mother was right. These were people in the grip of a fever every bit as deadly as the plague, and it would not be long before they came looking for Bess herself. She went quickly into the house and fetched a small bundle of possessions. Her hand hovered over treasured items, such as her father's pipe, but she left them. They belonged in the cottage. She took her mother's best shawl and tied it around her shoulders. She paused in the doorway for one last, lingering look at the only home she had ever known, then went out, latching the wooden door behind her. She turned the livestock out into the fields, opening the gates between enclosures. The cow trotted for a few paces, then settled to grazing. Whisper swished midges away with her tail and browsed for tender shoots. There was plenty of grass to be had and access to spring water. The chickens would have to take their chances with the foxes. Bess stood awhile by the graves, still unable to form words, merely letting her heart speak to the departed. As the dusk deepened, she set off with determined steps, not knowing when or if she would ever return. She had a promise to keep.

Bess knew Batchcombe Woods well. She had played in them as a child and scoured them for their treasures as an adult. She had sneaked in to pick wild garlic or collect moss or flowers for her mother's remedies. She and her brother had climbed many of the knuckled oaks and peeled strips of silvery bark from the birch for its fire-lighting properties. She found her way without difficulty, despite the failing light. By the time she came within sight of Gideon's cottage, owls were raising the alarm and hedgehogs had begun to rouse themselves for their nighttime activity. The cottage itself was small, wooden, and unremarkable. Its weathered timbers were a perfect match for the trunks around them and seemed to merge with the woodland, sinking into the scratchy embrace of the trees and undergrowth. To the left of the house, though, was a sight that drew the eye. Now, in the darkness, there appeared to be two slumbering dragons sitting, heads bowed, their smoky exhalations echoing the slow rhythm of their sleeping hearts. On closer inspection, these wonders turned out not to be fantastical creatures but the work of man, for these were Gideon's charcoal clamps. Day and night there would be at least two of them burning, while round about others cooled, their crumbly harvest calming from flaming wood to brittle bits of blackness, waiting to be lifted from their ashy beds. As Bess neared the rumbling pits, she could detect their frightening heat, despite the layer of turf that covered them and kept out the air. It was a wonder to her that the infernos did not escape and devour the cottage and indeed the entire wood. She stepped quickly past these fearsome objects and made her way toward the cottage. Her hand was raised to knock when the door was wrenched open. Gideon must have seen her approaching. The two regarded each other wordlessly, the distant rumble of the burning charcoal the only sound in their heavy silence. At length, Gideon moved aside and gestured for her to enter. Even at that moment Bess found it hard to believe that she was willingly putting herself in the care of a man she knew to be capable of rape and cold-blooded murder. It was a measure of her distress, of her grief, of her unshakable feeling of hopelessness, that she no longer cared what happened to her.

The single room, which constituted the whole accommodation of the house, was dimly lit by two lamps. The only other illumination came from the fire burning in the stone hearth. There were two chairs by the fire, a small table and bench, an assortment of cupboards, and a large feather bed in the far corner of the room. Bess turned to face Gideon. She was about to speak when he said, 'Your mother is dead.'

It was a statement, not a question, and so devoid of sentiment it was impossible for Bess to take either comfort or offense from it. She merely nodded, then said, 'It was my mother who . . . She told me to come to you.'

Gideon moved closer, letting his eyes rove the length of Bess's body, cocking his head a little on one side. Despite her weariness, Bess found she had the energy to feel indignant at his treatment of her. Here she was, recently bereaved, alone in the world, distressed, and exhausted, and he had not a civil word or offer of sympathy. What had made her mother believe he would even wish to help her?

'If I am not welcome here, I will leave, of course,' she said.

Gideon waved away the suggestion.

'Forgive me,' he said, 'I am being a poor host. I am unaccustomed to company. Please, sit.' He indicated a comfortable chair to the left of the fireplace.

Bess slipped the shawl from her shoulders and placed it with her bundle on the floor. The chair was soft with cushions, and the moment she lowered herself into it, tiredness began to swamp her.

'Rest awhile,' said Gideon. 'When did you last eat?'

Bess rubbed her temples. 'I do not recall.'

'I will fetch some food. You will need your strength for what lies ahead.'

Bess closed her eyes, intending only to rest them, but within moments she was asleep. She dreamed of dragons flying above Batchcombe Woods, flames spouting from their fanged mouths as they sent Nathaniel Kilpeck running for his life. The dream altered, and the dragons turned on Bess. She awoke with a start, sitting upright in the chair. The strains of "Greensleeves" seeped through her bleary consciousness. The woolen blanket that Gideon had placed over her slid to the floor. Her eyes regained their focus to find him sitting still as stone in the chair opposite, pipe in hand, humming the melody as he watched. Watched and waited. He gestured with his pipe at the table.

'Go and eat,' he said.

Bess did as she was told. She was surprised to find herself ravenous. There was a tasty stew of rabbit and pungent herbs, with bread to soak up the gravy. She ate greedily, not even caring that she was all the while observed by Gideon. When she had finished, he stood up and began to pace unhurriedly about the room. Bess wondered what would happen next. Here she was with someone who was, in fact, a stranger to her. She had never been alone in a house at night with a man before. There was no one left to protect her. She was at his mercy and had no notion of what to expect from him, aside from knowing him to be capable of taking from her whatever he desired. She straightened her back. She would not let him take from her the small amount of dignity she still retained. He noticed her unease but made no move to put her mind at rest. Instead, he stood, fingering a curious wooden carving. In the gloom Bess could not quite make it out. It appeared to be of some sort of goat. Abruptly he returned it to its place on the shelf.

'Tell me, Bess, how do you think I might protect you, hmm? Do you imagine these flimsy wooden walls will repel your persecutors? Do you think they will listen to me when I tell them to leave you be?'

'I do not know. I had not thought.'

He lunged forward, slamming his palms down on the table directly opposite her. He leaned toward her so that his face was only inches from hers.

'Then you must begin to do so! I have no interest in a frilly-headed maid who has not the wit to help herself. I can assist you only if you show yourself equal to the task.'

'I'm sure I shall do my best, sir.'

'Let us hope your best is good enough, then.' He stood up slowly, never once taking his eyes from her. 'It would be a great pity to have that delicious neck of yours scarred with the burns of a noose. Your mother sent you here because she meant you to learn what she herself learned. And more. She sent you here to be my pupil. The same power that saved you from the plague will save you again, Bess. But there can be no turning back, be sure you understand that. Once you have embarked on this journey, you may not return to the place you previously inhabited on this earth. You will be forever changed.'

Bess felt her mouth dry, but she forced herself to speak. 'And what price must I pay for your help?' she asked.

Gideon shook his head and allowed himself the smallest of smiles. 'We will not talk of that now. Enough for one night. Sleep, and we will begin in earnest in the morning. I must tend my charcoal fires. You may take the bed.' He picked his black hat off its hook on the wall and began to walk toward the door.

Bess was on her feet. 'You would have me strike a bargain blind?'

He paused, his hand on the latch, not turning to look at her as he spoke.

'You are in no position to bargain, girl. You will take what I offer and not argue terms. Because if you do not, you will break your promise to your mother. And because if you do not, you will most certainly twist in the wind beneath the Hanging Tree, just as she did.'

The next two days and nights passed for Bess in a whirl of strange-sounding names and unfamiliar words. Gideon showed her books the like of which she had never encountered before. For the most part, they were not in Latin nor English nor French nor any language she might recognize. He had her repeat curious words over and over until she knew them and her tongue was fat from stumbling over the unknown sounds. He was a hard tutor, not letting her pause for rest or sustenance until he was satisfied she had learned what he wanted her to know. To begin with, Bess failed to see a use for these unintelligible utterances. She did, however, understand how much importance Gideon placed upon them and quickly realized he would explain nothing until he deemed the moment right. Sometimes they worked at the table in the cottage. Other times they marched through the darkest parts of the woods. Occasionally, he had her sit outside and study while he tended his charcoal stacks. Bess found the process fascinating. Gideon sang as he worked, in a low, curiously melodic voice, always the same tune. Always "Greensleeves."

> *Alas my love you do me wrong*
> *To cast me off discourteously;*
> *And I have loved you oh so longer*
> *Delighting in your company.*
> *Greensleeves was my delight,*
> *Greensleeves was my heart of gold,*
> *Greensleeves was my heart of joy,*
> *And who but my Lady Greensleeves.*

Singing the strangely hypnotic love song, he would tend his charcoal pits. He started by clearing a space for the hearth, then hammered in a charcoal burner six feet in height. Around this, he constructed a chimney formed by a triangle of strong sticks. Around this chimney, he laid cords of wood, sometimes oak or sweet chestnut. Other times willow, all coppiced from the forest around them. At length, he would complete a dome-shaped stack, which he then covered with loose earth and turf, damping the hole down. The motty-peg was removed, and into the space he poured burning charcoal to ignite the heap. The chimney was capped off with more wet turf, so that the only escape for the steam and smoke produced was the vent he gouged out in the side of the stack. To Bess's mind, these were nothing more or less than the nostrils of those slumbering dragons. The nights were still fresh, but the days were warmed by a smiling spring sun. The work was hard so that Gideon often stripped off to his breeches, his sinewy torso tensed with the effort of lifting the heavy wood. On the days when he uncovered a finished kiln, the air was full of gritty steam as he poured water on the fresh charcoal. The dust from the powdery black remains of the wood mixed with his own sweat, so that soon he appeared as if he himself had climbed out of the pits. It still disturbed Bess that though he was not a young man, his body was not weathered or weakened from such work. Despite his harsh labors and simple existence, he had the appearance of a member of the gentry, with his fine features and firm, smooth skin. All this time he charged her with committing to memory lilting incantations or bizarrely rhythmic passages from one of his books. On the evening of the third day, he bade her sit at the table and he produced a new volume. This was the most beautiful book Bess had ever laid eyes upon. Its cover was of the softest red leather, tooled with gold, covered in a pattern of stars and a curling, sinuous script. For the first time Gideon sat beside her. She was acutely aware of the pressure of his leg against hers.

'This,' he told her, 'is something wonderful, Bess. Something sacred.'

'It is a Bible?'

'Of sorts, perhaps. But not the kind familiar to you.' He let his fingers glide lightly over the lettering on the cover before gently, with great care, opening the book. 'This is my *Book of Shadows*.'

As he let the first page fall flat under the pulsing light of the candle, Bess could smell sweet incense and feel a warm breeze against her face, even though the windows were tightly shut and the weather outside near to frost. Gideon turned the pages, handling the book with a tenderness Bess had not seen him display before. She peered closer at what was written and found the words were English. As she read them, she let out a small cry.

'Spells! These are all spells!' she said

'Naturally, for that is what a *Book of Shadows* is, Bess, a book of spells. As well as being a journal, and a record of magic used and encountered. In here are words to ease suffering and end pain. There are spells to lend courage to the weak and melt the hardest of hearts.'

Bess read as he spoke.

'And curses,' she said. 'Look, this concerns striking down a neighbor's beasts. And this one, to banish a rival in love.'

'Curses, yes, and hexes too. There is nothing that cannot be addressed by the power of magic, Bess, you of all people must surely know that now.'

'I know my mother would have had nothing to do with wishing ill on anyone. She was hanged for just such a thing, and she was innocent.'

'Bess, Bess, you are the innocent one. She was hanged for being a witch, something I believe she never denied, did she?'

'What?'

'At her trial, did you ever once hear her say she was not a witch?'

'She was not guilty, she said so.'

'Not guilty of cursing those wretched children or hounding the silly widow, of course. Why would she waste her energies in such ways? But being a witch? Come now, this is neither the time nor place to be coy, Bess. Do not deceive yourself further. What do you imagine we have been about these past few days? What power do you believe I have spoken of? What power did your mother use to bring you back from the clutches of Death himself, hmmm? Let us once and for all speak plainly on this matter. Your mother was a witch. I helped her become one. And now you are to take that journey.'

'I will not put curses on people! I will not use evil! My mother was a healer. She was good and kind.'

'Indeed she was. But she was also a mother, recently bereft of most of her offspring. She would not see you die, Bess, even if it meant damning her own soul to save you, she was prepared to do it.'

'How can you stand there and tell me she was damned! I will not hear it!' Bess stood up, scraping the bench on the flagged floor.

'Happily, you may be at ease on that matter. She might indeed have damned herself, but she chose instead to die to save you and so redeemed her soul. I'm sure she is at peace with the rest of your family at this very moment.'

Bess frowned, shaking her head as if the thoughts in it might drive her mad.

'She put herself in your debt to save me,' she said, 'but she did not have to die for my sake.'

'I am sorry to tell you that you are wrong on that point. Your mother had a great gift for the dark arts, Bess. She was a willing and talented pupil and made great progress in the very short time available to us. Had she wanted, she could have escaped her jail, set herself free, and evaded her pursuers with relative ease.'

Bess sat down again heavily.

'But I do not understand. When I saw her the night before she died, I lamented that I could not do those very things for her. That I could not break down the prison walls and take her from that awful place. If she could have done so herself, why would she not?'

'And who do you think the great and the good of Batchcombe would have turned on then? Had she effected such an escape, she could not have taken you with her, Bess. She knew that. She would have left you unprotected. She chose to hang so that you would come here and be given the power to survive. That is what she wanted you to do, is it not? Survive?'

Bess recalled her mother's words to her the last time they had spoken. 'Survive, Bess,' she had said. 'Live on.' How could Gideon know what she had said? Had he somehow been listening to their conversation? Had he been watching them?

Before Bess could respond, Gideon reached out and took her hand in his. At his touch, her body tensed and a curious warmth spread through her, as if her very bones were softening. She was shocked to find the sensation was not unpleasant. She wanted to withdraw her hand but found she could not.

'You must not torture yourself with things about which you can do nothing,' he told her, smiling gently. 'Your mother made her choice, and you freely made your promise to her. Do not be afraid. I will be your guide.' He lifted his other hand and softly stroked her hair. 'I will see no harm befalls you. There is greatness in you, Bess,' he whispered. 'A greatness that until now has lain dormant. Once awakened, you will be magnificent!'

Bess stared at him, reminded again of the way a cat cruelly plays with its prey before feasting on it. How could she trust such a man? What terrible things might he be capable of? As if reading her thoughts, Gideon let go her hand and turned back to the *Book of Shadows*.

'Come,' he said, 'there is much to be done, and we may not have many days left.'

The time that followed was the most wondrous of Bess's life. Had she been able to organize her thoughts, she would have been forced to admit that she was intrigued by what she was being shown. Not only intrigued—but soon enthralled and beguiled. Her initial resistance quickly began to fade in the face of dazzling acts of magic. Gideon showed her how to produce fire where there had been none, using nothing but a spell and the force of his will. He conjured up fantastic creatures. Not the hideous imps that had visited her mother but delicate fairy beings who danced for her around the charcoal pits. He summoned an invisible choir who sang the sweetest music she had ever heard, so sweet it made her weep with joy. He showed her how to heal her own wounds. She had recoiled in shock when he had sliced into her palm with a knife, but her shock had turned to wonder as he made the laceration vanish with a few words and a touch of his own hand. And what a touch. She had felt herself more and more drawn to him. More and more succumbing to his own spell. He fascinated her as he had always done, but slowly the equal measure of revulsion she had felt for him began to dwindle. Soon she found she enjoyed his praise when she executed some task well. She glowed with pleasure when he applauded her attempts at some new trick. And she quickly came to wish for his touch. He never tried to force himself upon her or even to kiss her, and yet she knew herself to have been seduced. She was his for the taking, and he must surely have known it. And yet at night when she fell exhausted into the feather bed, he left her unmolested and went outside to tend the charcoal. On one occasion, she spoke to him as he was about to open the door.

'Wait,' she said. 'Must you go out? Cannot the charcoal do without your attentions a little longer?' She stood in the center of the room, shocked by her own boldness, not knowing what it was she expected of him, only wanting him to stay. Aching for him.

Gideon paused. He smiled at her, a knowing smile. He walked over to where she stood and placed a hand on each of her shoulders, his face only inches from her own. Bess could feel the warmth of his body close to hers. Gideon leaned forward and his lips touched hers. It was the lightest, most restrained of kisses, but it had a power and irresistible sweetness that took Bess's breath away. She wound her arms around his neck. Gideon pulled back gently. He took hold of her hands, disentangling them, and held them to his chest instead.

'Patience, my love,' he said quietly. 'Our moment will come.' He smiled again, then turned and left the room.

Bess remained where she was, her face burning. She felt ashamed, stunned by the power of her own feelings and how willing she had been to throw herself at him. At the same time she was astonished at the strength of the desire he had awakened within her. Desire for a man she knew to be capable of terrible things. She thought of the gypsy girl in the woods all those months ago and she hated herself even more. She hurried to her bed, where she lay restless and confused for many hours before finding sleep.

On another warm night some days later, she again found herself unable to sleep. She turned and fidgeted beneath the heavy covers. Although winter had barely departed and the night was chill, her skin burned. Her body was alight with desire and would not let her rest. At last she got up. She threw her shawl about her shoulders on top of her shift and went barefoot out of the cottage. She had expected to find Gideon stoking the fires or damping down the finished charcoal, but he was not there. She became aware of the sound of distant music drifting faintly through the trees. As she walked on, she recognized the melody of "Greensleeves," but it was played with such roughness, such urgency of rhythm and such chaotic volume it was rendered the sound of madness—insanity made music. The moon was high though not yet full, but there was enough light for her to make her way carefully in the direction of the sounds. After walking for a short time, she caught glimpses of flames between the trunks. There was a fire burning in a clearing up ahead. Cautiously Bess approached, getting as close as she dared, not wanting to be discovered spying. She reached a wide-girthed oak and peered out from behind it. What she saw forced her to press her fist to her mouth to stifle a scream.

There was indeed a fire—a large, angry one that burned with unnatural brightness and ferocity. Around it danced a collection of creatures so gruesome they must surely have stepped straight from the very worst of nightmares. One had the head of a lizard but the body of a sheep. Another slithered snake-like on its belly but was covered in coarse, matted hair. Bats the size of turkeys dropped, swooping, from boughs. Unearthly screeches and shrieks accompanied the music, which in turn came from a pox-ridden, hairless giant. He hammered on an enormous drum, his great arms swinging down with frightening force. Beside him a beautiful boy with the lower body and legs of a goat played a set of pipes. A man old beyond comprehension strummed a harp, his grime-encrusted brows wriggling in concentration. Other creatures whirled past in a blur of madness, dancing and yelping. A litter of imps suckled from a vast pig as she dozed. Two weasel-like creatures fell to fighting with such vigor that one bit entirely through the neck of the other, severing its snarling head. At the far side of the fire, a figure stood, his back to Bess, his arms raised in supplication. He wore a long cape. From him came an incantation Bess recognized from her studies. The voice was also unmistakable. Every nerve in Bess's being screamed for her to run, but she could not pull herself away from watching Gideon. As he finished chanting, he turned so that the light of the flames lit up his face.

At that moment, the flames of the fire doubled in height. They twisted and roared as two shapes writhed within them. The shapes took the solid forms of two naked women as they stepped from the fire. The women draped themselves about Gideon, kissing him and fawning on him, undoing the clasp so that his cape fell at his feet, leaving him as naked as they were. He pushed one of the women to the ground, spinning her round so that he might thrust himself into her from behind. The she-devil let out a dreadful scream of pleasure as he pounded between her buttocks. The second woman fell to her knees and busied herself licking his thighs as he continued to gain pleasure from the squealing creature in front of him. As his own passion mounted, he began to emit a terrifying growl. Then, as Bess watched, his face began to twitch and pulsate as it underwent a terrible transformation.

It was now that Bess was swamped by fear. Gone were Gideon's harsh but noble features. In their place was the face of a beast, a goat-like apparition with scrofulous flesh and protruding fangs. Bess fought for breath, telling herself this could not be the very man whose touch she had craved. But his eyes left her in no doubt. There could be no mistake. This was Gideon, transformed into something unspeakably evil. Or was it? Could it be that this was the truth? That this was Gideon uncovered and revealed to her as he truly was, and that the handsome man she knew was merely a disguise? The thought brought from her an unchecked cry.

Gideon looked up, his hideous visage still contorted with ecstasy, and in that instant he saw her. Bess spun on her bare heel and flung herself, stumbling, through the woods. Even as the brambles whipped at her face, she knew Gideon was coming after her. She heard him bounding through

the undergrowth. As he grabbed hold of her, she screamed uncontrolla-
bly, averting her eyes from his face, terrified of what she would see.

'Bess!' He shook her. 'Bess, look at me.'

She could not.

'No!' she cried, 'Let me be! Let me go from this terrible place!'

He clutched her chin and yanked her round to face him. She could no
longer avoid looking at him and found that he had reverted to his human
self, though there remained a sickening redness to his eyes. He held her
tight against his naked, aroused body.

'This is for you, Bess. This is all for you. I have asked for you to be
blessed by our Lord Satan, and tonight we celebrate his generosity. You
will become as I am. No longer will you fear death or pain. You will be
beyond the reach of those who would take your life. We will leave, move
to another place where we are not known. Together we . . .'

'No! I cannot!'

'You know that we are alike, you and I, we are of a kind.'

'No, that is not true!'

'But it is. Think of it, Bess. Think of your own power. You have the
force of magic within you, we both know it; I have seen you use it. It is
not some flowery trickery, not some remnant of your mother's teachings
as a healer. You know I speak the truth . . .'

'No . . .'

'Yes! You know that force comes from a dark place inside you, for you
can only ever use it when you are angry. That is the truth. It is a black
force and it will be magnified a thousandfold once you take the step, once
you embrace the craft and join me.'

'I would rather die!'

'You are meant to live. To continue, as your mother wanted you to.'

'She would not have delivered me to . . . this!' Bess struggled in his
grasp.

'She knew what price would be asked of you. But do not fear. Our
master rewards his loyal disciples. You see how strong I am; you have
noticed my vigor, you cannot deny it. It is his gift, and he offers you the
same. Life, Bess, not death but eternal, youthful life, my love!'

'Love? What can you know of love? I do not see love here.' She shook a
fist at the abominable company that leaped and danced about them. 'I see

only evil!' She wrenched herself from him and ran back through the woods, slamming the door of the cabin behind her and barring it with the table before flinging herself onto the bed. For an hour or more she sat rigid with terror, waiting and listening. When no sound or movement could be detected, she gave in to weariness and fell into a fitful sleep.

9

By the time she awoke the following morning, the table had been returned to its place in the center of the room and pottage was simmering on the fire. Gideon sat cleaning out his clay pipe as if the events of the night before had never taken place. On seeing her stir, he gestured at the pot.

'Come, take breakfast. We have little time.'

'Time?'

'You must be word perfect before the moon is full. Only then can you intone the ancient verses that will complete your transformation. Only then will you be empowered.'

'I will not say them.' Her voice was little more than a whisper. 'I will not.'

He ignored her words and placed his pipe back on the shelf. It was an unremarkable action but one that almost brought Bess to her knees. How often had she watched her dear father do the exact same thing before he set about his work on the farm or prepared for bed? How could she have traveled such a short distance and yet come so very far from that loving home and simple, good life that was once hers? What had become of her now? Gideon took his hat off the peg. He was about to open the door when horses came thundering into the clearing outside the cottage. Shouts rebounded off the trees.

'Gideon Masters! Come out!'

Bess recognized the voice of the witchfinder at once.

'Come out. We know you have Bess Hawksmith with you. I am required to arrest her and take her now to be tried for witchery. Bring her out.'

Bess scrambled from her bed and grabbed her shawl. She expected Gideon to bolt the door, to do something to protect her, but instead he opened it.

'Be assured, Magistrate,' he called out, 'she is preparing herself. Come now, Bess,' he said to her, holding out a hand.

Unable to make sense of what was happening, Bess put her dress and shawl over her shift and hastily pulled on her boots. She could not stay in this dreadful place with whatever Gideon was, but for him to hand her over to Kilpeck—knowing as he must what fate awaited her—was astonishing. What outcome could he envisage? Trembling and ignoring his hand, she stepped out of the door. Kilpeck sat on his white horse. With him were six of his men and two town constables. Bess struggled to find her voice.

'Who accuses me?' she asked at last.

'Bill Prosser.'

'What? But he knows I saved the life of his grandson and that of his daughter, Sarah.'

Nathaniel Kilpeck took obvious pleasure in being the bringer of devastating news, 'Sarah Prosser fell into a delirium for three days, during which time she was heard to repeat your name over and over. The good Lord in his infinite mercy took her from this life two days ago. Come. You will have the opportunity to face your accusers in court.'

Two of the men had already dismounted and now strode toward Bess, who stood where she was, frozen with fear. She felt Gideon's hand on her arm. He leaned close to her ear, his warm breath on her neck making her shiver.

'The full moon,' he said. 'Be ready. I will be waiting for you.'

She stared at him, her face showing a mixture of horror and defiance, and then she was led away.

Less than an hour later, Bess stood where her mother had stood in Batchcombe Courthouse, a restless crowd eagerly awaiting the start of her trial. The constable called for order, and Councillor Watkins, Reverend Burdock, and Witchfinder Kilpeck entered the room and took their places at the high bench. Bess heard her name read out, along with the charges against her, but it was as though she were removed from what was happening. She felt as if she were once more watching her mother being accused, while at the same time knew herself to be the one they were prosecuting. Even so, she had difficulty focusing on what was being said. Bill Prosser had indeed accused her of putting a vicious curse on his daughter, claiming Bess must have planted the seeds of death in her when she had attended her confinement all those months ago. Bess looked at the familiar face of a man she had known all her life and saw clearly how the dementia of grief had altered him. Next, she heard testimony from Davy Allis, whom she recognized as the lech from the Three Feathers. He claimed she had put the evil eye on him and he had not enjoyed good health since the day she assaulted him at the inn. He had even found witnesses willing to testify to the event. Bess listened to it all with a fatal detachment. There was nothing she could do or say to reason with these people. She had been tried and found guilty before ever she had been dragged into the courtroom. The heavy weight of resignation to her awful fate pressed down upon her shoulders. By the time the magistrates declared their judgment, she was almost relieved for the sham to be over. She heard Wilkins bang his gavel and felt rough hands propelling her toward the door to the jail. She was taken to the same cell where her mother had spent her final days. Although empty, the room stank and the straw was wet and rancid. The single window was too high to allow so much as a glimpse of freedom and admitted very little air through the iron bars. The jailer allowed himself the pleasure of invading her body with his hands as much as was possible as he shackled her feet.

'Old Baggis be pleased to see thee again, witch wench. Do not fret thys'n in these short hours left. I shall see you do not spend them lonely.' He left with a throaty laugh still rattling around the room as the door clanged shut and the key turned in the lock.

It was a relief to be alone, even in such a place. Here at least, for this moment, there was no one to jab an accusing finger in her face or spit at her as she passed by. She sank to her knees on the rancid straw, trying to summon some of the courage and forbearance she had seen her mother show. At least they would all be reunited once more. It would not be long now. The execution had been set for dawn the following day. She had only to endure this night and the ordeal of the gallows, and then she would be at peace with those she loved. She had already made up her mind that this was the only path left to her. She believed Gideon when he said she could have the power to save herself, that it was there for the taking. But she would not. How could she? Could her mother truly have wished her to become such a vile creature as Gideon? She refused to believe it. No, she must have hoped only that he could keep her persecutors at bay long enough for some other salvation to present itself. Had she hoped William would come to Bess's rescue? It was possible, her mother not knowing the full truth of the Gould family's involvement in her own end. Bess's head throbbed with the effort of reasoning the unreasonable. She pulled her shawl over her head and lay down, thankful to find herself quickly drifting into sleep.

It did not seem moments later, although it must have been several hours, when she was woken by the sound of the door being opened. Baggis staggered into the cell. Even in the fetid air Bess could smell the alcohol on his breath as he approached her.

'Well now, here be Baggis, good as 'is word, come to keep thee company.'

Bess scrambled to her feet. 'Leave me be, please.'

'Don't be shy, little lass.' He stepped close to her, reaching a hand toward her breast. Bess batted it away. He laughed. 'You 'ave no business being picky, you mibben better take comfort where 'tis offered. I heard,' he said in a conspiratorial whisper, 'that the witchfinder be so sure thee be a wicked, wicked creature, he be planning a little surprise.' Baggis paused to wipe his dribbling mouth with the back of his hand. 'Seems he favors the Scottish method of ridding the parish of witches. Should draw a crowd bigger than a summer fair. Years since we've 'ad a burning at Batchcombe.' Seeing fear in Bess's eyes, he went on. 'Never mind, witchy, I dare say thee'll make a right pretty candle.'

Bess tried to dodge past him, but he lurched sideways and grabbed her by the hair, falling to the ground with her. 'Now then, you be gentle with old Baggis, witch wench, and 'e'll be gentle with thee.' He pinned her down, leaning his great weight on top of her. Bess struggled wildly, but she was hampered by her shackles and not strong enough to push him off. He lowered his mouth toward hers. 'A little kiss, shall we 'ave, mibben?' he slobbered.

Bess moved her face at the last moment and sank her teeth deep into his bulbous nose. Baggis let out a scream and sat up, blood gushing from the bite. He swore unintelligibly before swinging his right fist down with brutal force into Bess's cheek. She heard her own jaw crack.

'Bite me, would you, you vixen? Lie still or I'll knock every tooth from that pretty mouth!'

Bess was still reeling from the blow but quickly became aware of him fumbling beneath her skirts. Now the fetters were hampering her attacker. Bess squirmed and wriggled, not thinking now, simply reacting. Baggis swore and brought his fist down a second time. Bess screamed as it connected with her cheek in the exact same spot as the first. The pain rendered her immobile until she felt Baggis reach his goal. He let out a series of porcine grunts as he moved to force himself inside her. A different pain, sharper than that which possessed her face, more intense and somehow far more unbearable, stabbed through her body. Bess looked up to see the leering face of her attacker made even uglier by his selfish lust. At that moment the clouds shifted in the night sky, exposing the moon. Its silver beams fell through the high prison window, slipping between the bars and reaching into the darkness. Bess felt the light cover her. The full moon. This was the moment. Now she must decide. Baggis lunged into her, spitting saliva onto her face. Bess thought of Gideon and of what she had witnessed in the woods. Then she recalled how he had spoken of freedom from pain and freedom from death. She thought of her mother's words. *Survive! Live on.* She made her decision. She tried to say the words Gideon had taught her, but her mouth no longer responded as it should. She coughed out blood and tried again. Every word was wrenched painfully from her throat.

'*Fleare dust achmilanee . . . achmilaneema . . . Eniht si eht modgnik.*' She spat out a tooth and continued with a little more strength. '*Eniht si eht modgnik,* my Lord. *Fleare dust achmilanee, dewollah eb yht eman! Fleare dust achmilaneema. . . . Rewop dna eht yrolg! Fleare dust achmilaneema!*'

Her attacker was too absorbed in his own pleasure to pay any heed to the strange sounds Bess now chanted, louder and louder, stronger and stronger. She repeated the verses three times, just as Gideon had instructed, terrified that at any moment the clouds might rob her of the moon's rays. But they did not. She spoke the last syllable of the last utterance and waited. Nothing happened. Nothing to stop the relentless defiling of her body. Nothing to mask the repulsive noises coming from the drunken jailer. Had it all been a fantasy? Had she really to submit to this and then to suffer the torment of being burned alive? Bess closed her eyes and formed one more word. She used all the breath that was in her body to scream it.

'Gideon!'

The room became suddenly preternaturally still. Even Baggis paused.

In the distance, Bess could hear a high whine that grew and gathered force until it became a deafening roar. The soft light of the moon was replaced by a dazzling glare. The jailer looked about him in panic, then back at Bess. He cried out in terror, struggling to get away from her, falling backward in his haste to disentangle himself.

'Witch!' he shouted. 'Witch!'

With the filthy man out of the way, the pulsating light enveloped Bess. The noise was terrifying now, like the battle cry of a thousand regiments or the roar of a hundred fighting dragons. Baggis's mouth stretched open in screams that could not be detected in the cacophony. Bess could feel the power surging through her body. It washed away the pain, stopping the blood and mending her broken bones. She stood up, feeling herself weightless and free as the chains to her fetters snapped. Now she understood. She understood the ecstasy of power. The beauty of it. The glory of it. The sensual joy of it. Her entire being glowed and shone with it. She regarded the cowering man in the corner of the cell. How quickly the tables had been turned. This time it was she who raised her hand. Baggis covered his head with his arms, whimpering. Bess wanted to test her strength, to take her revenge, to feel for the first time in her life what it truly meant to be the one with the power. She knew she could squash him like an ant beneath her foot if she wished. She began to rise up, floating toward the window.

'Mercy!' Baggis screamed.

Bess lowered her hand slowly.

'You will receive precisely the mercy you deserve,' she told him, pointing a finger in the direction of his groin.

As the pathetic man's screams rose to shrieks, Bess turned and pushed her way effortlessly through the bars of the window. Once she was in the street, silence returned. She looked about her, suddenly spent and weak once more. She had not been observed. The village slept on. Clearly only the occupants of the cell had heard anything at all. Keeping to the moon shadows, Bess ran.

Extract from
Batchcombe Court Records,
March 21, 1628

On this day, shortly before dawn, the accused and convicted Witch, one Eliza-beth Anne Hawksmith, did use Witchery to escape her gaol. The same did grievously afflict the gaoler, one Jonothan Baggis, as he attempted to restrain her. He was in fact rendered simple-minded, and his privy member was seen to turn black and wither. The Witch did, according to his testimony, scale the walls of her cell with all the ease of an insect before using the strength of the devil himself to pull the bars from the window. She did then shapeshift, trans-forming her body to that of a lizard so that she might effect her escape via the narrow portal, which is indeed too small to permit a grown woman to pass through it.

Let it be recorded here that the said Witch did then flee the village. Upon the discovery of the distressed gaoler near to sunrise, the alarm was raised and she was pursued to Batchcombe Point, where the party, despite speedy response and valiant efforts, did fail to apprehend her. Those present have borne witness and testified to the fact that the convict did then step from the cliff top, spreading her arms and taking to flight.

BELTANE

It has been several weeks since Tegan sat in my kitchen and listened to the tale of Bess and her family. Ostara came and went on swift westerly winds that have at last begun to chase away the darkness of winter. Since the equinox, the weather has been mild and damp, bringing about a lushness and early spring splendor to rouse us all from our vernal hibernation. I have found myself strangely uplifted by the sharing of my history, as if I have let go some of the pain and loss that I have carried with me all these years. Of course, Tegan is unaware that the story of Bess is in fact the story of my own beginning. Why would she make such a connection? She has assumed that Bess was perhaps a distant relative of mine, and I have been content to let her believe so. The story has, however, ignited a passion in her for all things magical. She quizzed me endlessly on my own knowledge of the arts so that I eventually agreed to instruct her in the ways of the hedge witch. I have searched my heart and can find nothing wrong in doing this, so long as I believe I am truly free of my pursuer. Certainly I have seen no signs that my new settlement is unsafe. My intention is to teach Tegan what it means to work with nature, to heal and protect. The craft of hedge witchery is benign and good, and I believe she will take to it. Indeed, she has already shown herself a willing pupil, spending more and more time with me, listening attentively and carrying out my instructions with care and interest. I confess I am enjoying both her company and her enthusiasm. Of course, it is out of the question that I would allow her to wander into the darker realms of the craft. Such magic has no place in her life. I would not wish upon anyone the price I have paid for the power that I chose to take. And it was a choice, however much I might care to blame circumstance and misfortune. It was my choice. And it was a choice my mother turned away from. The only way I have been able to reconcile myself to my decision all these years is to have continued her work. To heal. To tend. To support the weak. These are the good things a witch can do. A witch must do. These are the skills I will impart to Tegan. We have already started our preparations for celebrating Beltane. How I long for that day to come, when the sun god takes his place as majesty over the year and all is warmth and growth and abundance. I have given Tegan books to read on the subject, all the while reminding her that her schoolwork must not suffer. Her mother, whom I have still yet to meet, might at last become resistant to her spending so much time with me if she were to receive bad reports from school.

APRIL 19 — FIRST QUARTER

The first swallows have arrived, and a pair have returned to an old nest in the eves of my garden shed. The daffodils have ceased their nodding and begun to recede. The dance of spring has been taken up in turn by the blossom, which is particularly good this year. The pussy willows and apple trees in the copse are a delight, and I can easily lose hours wandering among them. But there is work to be done. I continue to take my place at the weekly market at Pasbury. There is another market I could attend, in a town close enough for me to pass signposts to it. A larger, more prosperous town, where no doubt I would find a more abundant supply of customers for my products. But it is not a place I can bring myself to revisit. The memories are too vivid and too painful, even after all these years. I must focus on my stocks. I have plenty of flavored and scented oils but wish to prepare a quantity of lavender bags and bowls of potpourri. And the birch sap wine is ready for labeling. My needs are simple, but my savings have dwindled after the long winter. There is no avoiding the necessity for money. Much as I dislike the activity of selling, I must force myself to peddle my wares. At least it offers the chance to treat those I might otherwise not come into contact with. Tegan is determined to join me as often as I will allow, though I have warned her not to expect too much.

APRIL 23 — SECOND QUARTER

What a success! I had no idea the people hereabouts would have such a desire for my products. It seems word has begun to spread. Tegan hugely enjoyed the day and gained almost as much satisfaction as I did from seeing the last of the basil oil snatched up before three o'clock. We celebrated with an ice cream from the neighboring stall. The day was remarkable for something other than my modest financial gain, however. Just before midday an attractive woman with gentle eyes and pretty hair approached the table. She feigned interest in the bottles of bath oil, but I sensed immediately she had another reason for standing before me. At the same moment I recognized what was familiar about her features. Tegan spoke.

'Mum!' she said, 'What are you doing here?'

'I begged a long lunch break so I could come and see how you were getting on.' She paused and looked at me while continuing to address her daughter. 'Aren't you going to introduce us?'

'Oh, course. Mum, this is Elizabeth. Elizabeth . . . my mum. Helen.'

She held out a hand and I took it. Only now did I notice the uniform beneath her mac.

'I'm pleased to meet you at last,' I said.

'Tegan talks about you nonstop. Elizabeth this, Elizabeth that.' She smiled, but I could not read her true feelings on her face.

'How embarrassing,' I said, then, 'She has been a great help to me today.'

'Yeah, look, Mum, we've sold heaps of stuff. Everyone loves it. You should try some of this.' She picked up a pot of oatmeal body scrub. 'It's lush and only a couple of quid. Go on.'

'Quite the salesman,' Helen said, taking the pot and digging in her purse. She handed Tegan the coins without looking at her purchase. 'Well, I'd better leave you to it then. Keep up the good work. I'm on a double shift, remember. There's cold chicken in the fridge. Don't wait up.'

Her visit seemed to have little effect on Tegan beyond her initial surprise. I think she was pleased her mother had bothered to seek her out and that she had bought something. I am very sure, however, that her purpose in coming to the market was not to please her daughter but to see me. It was, after all, the ideal neutral ground on which to size me up. There was no need for the awkward niceties a visit to my home would have required. Instead, she could satisfy her curiosity with the briefest of meetings. I felt too that she was in some small way staking her claim on Tegan. Or rather, reminding me that she was her mother and that any time she spent with me was on her sufferance. Or was I placing my own needy interpretation on a harmless gesture of friendliness? It is hard for me to tell. I know I have become fond of Tegan. I look forward to her visits and find instructing her a joy. I am all too aware that her mother could put a stop to her seeing me if she wanted. What would she say if she knew her daughter was learning the craft from me? I do not know the woman, and yet I am more than a little certain that she would disapprove. Which means we must keep secrets, Tegan and I. And secrets are dangerous. They start small but grow with every evasive answer or outright lie that protects them. Nevertheless, I confess to finding the closeness such conspiracy breeds irresistibly delicious.

APRIL 25—SECOND QUARTER

Last night, after a long day's toil in the garden, I invited Tegan to join me for the evening in a thanksgiving to the Goddess and the elements. As darkness began to fall, I picked up my staff and we made our way to the clearing in the center of the small copse. I have already used the shallow fire pit several times and have arranged two fallen logs around it for seating. We gathered some kindling and larger fuel and lit the fire. I placed candles on stones in a bigger circle about us. I had Tegan stand beside me as I began the prayer to consecrate the circle.

> *I cast this circle in the names of the Mother of Life and of the Green God, nature's guardian. May it be a meeting place of love and wisdom.*

Carrying my staff, I paced the circle three times deosil, holding in my mind the image of a blue flame burning atop the staff. I then returned to the center of the circle and took Tegan's hand. We raised our arms and eyes heavenward. I intoned:

> *I call upon the elemental spirits of Ether, the wraith of life, to watch over us and assist us with magic. You who are everywhere, in all directions, in Fire and Water and Earth and Air, sustaining, I bid you hail and welcome.*

We sat down and I passed Tegan warm cheese scones and cold ginger beer from our picnic. Her face glowed as much from the uplifting nature of the small ceremony as from the heat and light of the fire.

'That was so cool,' she said, biting into the scone. 'Weird but bloody cool. I really felt something, as if someone was listening. Is that daft?'

'Not at all. It is a sign that you are beginning to let down your guard and be open to the craft. It is no small step to accept that we are not alone on this earth. And that we are not the all-powerful creatures most people believe themselves to be. You are learning to still that frantic mind of yours at last.'

'When can I try a spell? Nothing major, just a little one. Will you let me have a go?'

Her overflowing eagerness made me laugh.

'All in good time, Tegan. You can't rush these things.'

'There must be something you think I wouldn't screw up.' She swigged on her bottle and stared grumpily into the fire. I knew she was a long way from being ready, but it was hard to refuse her.

'After Beltane,' I said. 'If you finish the reading I gave you.'

'I will! I will. Wow, that's gonna be ace. I can't wait. What will it be? Can I choose something?'

'Wait and see, and no, you can't choose. Leave that up to me.'

We ate in silence for a moment, reminding me that she had indeed begun to temper her youthful restlessness and learn to listen and to think. There was something wonderfully companionable about sharing a small moment such as this with someone new, someone open and without cynicism who was willing to learn. I was quite moved by the closeness I feel exists between us. It is such a very long time since I have allowed myself to care about another living soul. I relish the luxury of such a friendship. I treasure it, acutely aware of how precious and rare such a thing is.

Tegan finished her food and lay back on her elbows, prodding the edge of the fire with her foot.

'Tell me again about Beltane,' she said. 'Tell me what we're going to do.'

'Beltane is the festival of the sun and of fire. It heralds the coming of summer and fertility.'

'Do we have to get naked?'

I shot her a look, 'That's up to you,' I said. 'Personally I prefer to keep my clothes on at this time of year. As I was saying, Bel is the god of light and fire. We celebrate the fact that the sun has at last come to free us from the bondage of winter. We will collect the nine sacred woods for our fire and smudge our faces with the ashes. We keep vigil all night. Some believe the dawn dew at Beltane carries blessings of health and happiness. I suppose you could take your clothes off for that bit if you must.'

Tegan laughed. 'All night, wow. Never mind getting naked—think I'll bring a sleeping bag.'

'The fire will keep you warm. And I'll make us some mead; that always keeps out the cold.' I threw another log on the fire. Sparks danced up into the evening sky. A bat swooped daringly close, no doubt attracted by the moths hell-bent on self-destruction in the flames. I watched Tegan's reaction and was pleased to see her simply observe the creature. Only a few weeks before its arrival would have brought shrieks from her and flippant comments about vampires. 'Beltane will be an important night for you, Tegan. It is one of the most magical events on the witch's calendar. At such a time, the veil between the otherworld and our own terrestrial existence is gossamer thin. Spirits of all natures and persuasions may visit. You must be open to what happens, but do not allow yourself to give way to an overexcited imagination.'

'Is it dangerous?' she asked, almost hopefully I thought.

'No. But we must not be complacent. There are dark forces abroad as well as light. We will dress the doors and windows of the cottage with rowan branches, and I will ask for the Goddess's protection.'

APRIL 28—MOON ENTERS LIBRA

Tegan did not come today. I admit I am surprised. She is so keen to be a part of the preparations for Beltane, and today she was to help me decant the mead and then collect wood to stack for the Bel fire. Still, no matter. I am, after all, accustomed to working alone. I am getting to know the little woods well now and am enjoying watching them shake off their winter drabness. The first of the bluebells have nudged above the soil and are already beginning to flower. Was there ever a plant more suited to fairies? I look forward to wandering among them as soon as they are in bloom.

APRIL 29—SECOND QUARTER

Tegan showed up after school today full of apologies. She was unable to stand still for a moment, hopping from one foot to the other, tripping over her words as she babbled on about meeting someone the day before and not noticing the time slip by, and she hoped I didn't mind but she couldn't stay today either. She proudly showed me a mobile phone her new friend had given her. She was evasive about the identity of whomever it is she is rushing off to see, but I suspect a boy. Who else could engender such a feverish state? I suppose it was to be expected, but I confess to being disappointed. If she becomes attached to a boyfriend at this point in her instruction, she will most likely give up her studies. All the knowledge and wonder on this earth cannot compete with the frenzy of young love. We shall have to wait and see what happens. I reminded her that if she misses Beltane, she will regret it later. Perhaps her new friend would be prepared to forego seeing her for just this one evening? She reassured me, but I have my doubts. I shall make provisions for two but expect to be alone.

MAY 1—MOON ENTERS SCORPIO

I write this as the glow of my Bel fire is replaced by a glorious sunrise. The crimson slashes pulsate with healing power. I sit on a mossy log, my bare feet bathed by the dew. This should be a moment of exquisite joy and hope for the future, yet I cannot rid myself of a sadness. As I predicted, Tegan was absent last night. I am sorry for her, sorry that she missed such a magical and moving experience. I am sorry for myself, too. I should never have allowed myself to become so fond of the girl. What am I to her? A passing interest, that is all. A whim. Someone to help build her confidence so that she might engage with the wider world. So that she might build important friendships of her own. It is ridiculous to see myself in competition with some raw youth. I have no romantic interest in

Tegan, after all. It is only right that she pursue the desires and needs of all girls her age. But I wish it could have been a little later. Just a little.

Another successful day at market. I have, it appears, garnered good reports among the shoppers of Pasbury. The number of customers at my stall has grown steadily, and some have become regular faces. The young woman from my first Saturday of trading returned today. Her bruises were gone and her toddler trotted in front of her on reins this time. She fingered objects set out on the stall until there were no other people within earshot.

'It worked,' she said quietly, 'that stuff you gave me. Sorted him out. Hasn't been out since, not without me. Wanted to, he did. Got as far as the front door last Friday night, but he came over all funny. Turned pale as you like and said he felt sick. I sat him down and made him something to eat. He cheered up. Thanked me. Thanked me! No cursing and shouting and getting handy with his fists. Just thanked me. Next day we all went to the beach.'

'I'm glad,' I said.

'So, how much do I owe you?'

'Call it a free sample. And you might like a bottle of my birch sap wine. Five pounds a liter.'

She took the bottle I held out to her. 'Is it . . . ?' She left the question unformed.

'It's quite strong,' I told her, 'but nothing more. Just wine.'

After she had gone, an elderly couple from the retirement flats pitched up for the third week running. I was wrapping a collection of treatments for arthritis, plus a little something of my own devising to aid memory, when I noticed Tegan, hovering by the cake stall opposite.

She approached slowly, her body language eloquently telling of a guilty conscience. I felt my spirits lift at the sight of her but reminded myself to keep a distance between us.

'You're really busy today,' she said.

'I've been running the stall for a few weeks now. Word has got round.'

'People like coming here.'

'My wares do seem popular, yes.'

'It's not your stuff, not really. It's you. It's you they come to see.'

I ceased fidgeting with the lavender bags and looked at Tegan. The gauche girl was fading, and a newly confident woman was taking her place. Only love could lend such instant confidence and bring about such a rapid transformation. I had been right in my assumption. She was lost to me, then. Her study of the craft was surely not far enough advanced to hold her attention when faced with the distraction of youthful lust.

'Thought I might call round tomorrow, if that's okay,' she said.

'Won't you be busy with your new friend?'

Surprise altered her features. 'How did you know?'

'It doesn't take magical powers of divination to see when a person is in love.'

She blushed and grinned.

'He's performing in Batchcombe tomorrow.'

I flinched at the unexpected mention of the town of my origins. Tegan noticed my reaction and I turned away, anxious she should not think the disconcertment written on my face was connected with her romance. There was a pause where she waited for me to respond. Fortunately, two new customers presented themselves, and I gave them my attention. Tegan lingered for a while longer and then slipped away. I felt a painful tugging in my chest. I knew I had snubbed her and she had felt that rejection. What choice did I have? Better that I give up the idea of her as my pupil, of ever sharing with her the beauty and the blessing of my magic. She is just a girl, and I must let her be one.

MAY 6—THIRD QUARTER

I must say I admire Tegan's thick skin. She arrived at my front door a little after twelve this morning.

'I would have come earlier, but, well, me and Ian had a late night. He's gone to Bournemouth now. He's got this cool motorbike. Says he can make shed loads of cash on a Sunday lunchtime this time of year. He plays the guitar brilliantly.' She ventured a coy smile, 'I think he loves me.'

'I'm happy for you.'

'You've gotta meet him. I know you'll love him. He's . . . special.'

'Of course he is.'

She shifted from one foot to the other. A blackbird in the garden behind her began to sing.

'Well, are you going to invite me in or what?'

I stood aside and she brushed past me. In the kitchen, she fell to idle chatter, clearly trying to regain some of the ground she had lost. It is not in my nature to be sullen, but I did my best at least to be uninteresting in the hope that she would get bored and give up. She did not. Eventually she got cross.

'Look, what did I do that's so wrong?'

'Do you need to ask?'

'So I missed some stuff. I'm sorry. I'll do it next time.'

'Stuff!' Now it was my turn to be angry. 'You missed Beltane. You passed up on the opportunity to experience one of the most exciting and spellbinding Sabbats of the wiccan year. One of the most important rights of passage any apprentice witch can take.'

'What did you say?'

'I said Beltane is of huge significance, not to be treated as a casual event . . .'

'No, *witch*. You said *apprentice witch*.'

The air in the pause fizzed.

'I might have.'

'You did! You really mean you are going to show me how, to train me up to be like you. Me! A witch! It's not just a few bits of New Age larking about and some smelly oils, is it? This is so mad.' She sat down heavily in my chair by the unlit stove, not taking her eyes from me for an instant.

'I don't think you even know what the word means,' I said, embarrassed by my own petulance.

'I do. I've been reading the books you gave me.'

'When you thought it was all just, what did you call it, "larking about"—I'm surprised you bothered.'

'I did. I am. Look, never mind what I thought before. It was always cool, I mean, I wanted to learn. And d'you know what? I think that's because I always knew. You tried to pretend. Admit it, you tried to make out it was just, like, a lifestyle choice or something. Hippy values. Natural way of living. Grow your own veg. Make your own herb oils. Culture your own yogurt. I knew that stuff you gave me fixed Sarah Howard. I told you then I'd sussed what you are, but you were having none of it. Told me about your ancestors and all that but wriggled out of it, didn't you? Tried to get me to believe it was all just a bit of fun, just old remedies and fairy tales and superstition.' She narrowed her eyes at me. 'But it's more than that, isn't it? Much more.'

I had been so determined to push her away, but I felt my resolve weakening in the face of such fascination. The ego is a dangerous thing.

'To be brutally truthful with you, Tegan, I no longer believe you have what it takes to be my pupil.'

'Bullshit!'

'Must you use that language?'

'If you didn't think I could hack it, you wouldn't have started showing me stuff in the first place.'

'To learn the ways of the craft demands dedication. Commitment. Sacrifices have to be made.'

'You're saying I can't have a boyfriend?'

'I'm saying you have to prioritize.'

'Choose, you mean?'

'Not necessarily, no.'

'What then?' She sprang up from the chair and strode over to me. To my surprise, she took my hands in hers. 'Tell me what I have to do to prove myself. I want to do it. I want to learn. I want to be like you. What do I have to do?'

I wondered: If I had asked her to give him up, would she have done so? Was she daring me? Challenging me? Or did she know me better? Know me well enough to be certain I would not, could not, ask that of her. How could I? The child had barely known love her whole life, who was I to take it from her now that she had found it?

'You would have to devote far more time to your studies.'

'I will.'

'Serious study, not simply leafing through books and treating the whole matter as a pleasant diversion from your schoolwork.'

'Serious. I can do serious.'

'Why do I doubt it?'

'Test me, go on.' She hurried to the sideboard and fetched my *Grimoire*. 'Ask me something. Anything. I *have* been reading.'

'Your commitment cannot be so easily tested.'

'Let me show you what I know.' She shoved the heavy book into my hands. 'Go on.'

'Very well.' I put the *Grimoire* down on the kitchen table and folded my arms. 'Tell me the difference between a wand and an athame.'

'Easy. A wand is for moving energy and directing it; an athame is for sacred rituals and ceremonies and for banishing negative energy. Ask me another.'

I pursed my lips. 'Which tree is sometimes called the Lady Tree and must never be cut down.'

'The elder! Come on, ask me something harder than that.'

'List the Sabbats in the order they occur in thirteen moons.'

She did so. She also listed the Esbats, the Equinoxes, the festivals of the pagan deities, and wiccan lore. She went on to explain the plants associated with each Sabbat ceremony, as well as the colors and foods that should be used. When she had finished, she sat back down, a triumphant smile on her face.

'Go on, you're impressed, admit it.'

'Learning things by rote is hardly a sophisticated skill.'

Temper flashed in her eyes, but she mastered it well. Taking a breath, she said, 'I am serious, Elizabeth, really.'

I sighed. I so wanted her to be in earnest.

'We shall see,' I said. 'You can start by making me lunch while I consider what is to be done.'

'No problem.' She jumped up again and wrenched open the door of the stove. She peered into its cold interior. 'We'll have to get this thing lit first,' she said.

I focused, then blew gently in the direction of the kindling I had laid earlier.

Tegan leaped backward as the fire burst into life. Despite myself, I was unable to conceal my amusement. Tegan slammed the firedoor shut and turned to frown at me. 'Serious, you said. I'm lucky I've got any eyebrows left.'

Tegan busied herself and cooked a dhal for us. As we ate, she continued to try to impress me with the knowledge she had so far amassed of the ways of a hedge witch. I was pleasantly surprised, both by what she had learned and by the quality of our lunch.

'Your cooking has improved,' I told her, when at last she fell quiet.

'Wow, Elizabeth, don't go wild with the praise, will you!' She wiped her bowl with a piece of bread and pushed back her chair, stretching out her legs. 'I'm stuffed,' she said. I sensed her hesitation before asking me. 'Will you tell me more? About what it's like. Being a witch, I mean. What it's really like.'

'What do you want to know, specifically?'

'You know, do you ever curse people? Put hexes on them? Has anyone ever done it to you? Do you know lots of other witches? I mean, they could be everywhere, couldn't they? All around us and we just don't know it. Do you belong to a coven? That sounds seriously scary. And what about men, can they be witches or are they wizards, or what was that bastard in Bess's story? Warlocks, are they always warlocks? And can you really heal people? I mean, I know you have your potions and oils and you don't have to persuade me they work, but what about bigger stuff? Real illness. Can you mend people? Can you?'

'Healing is the reason for being a witch, Tegan. If you are truly of the craft, of the sisterhood, you cannot *but* heal. Sometimes with more success than others.'

'So, you could cure cancer, that sort of thing? Wow, you could go into a hospice or a hospital and just . . . make people better! Couldn't you? Could you?'

'It's not that simple. There is a great deal you don't yet understand.'

'Tell me.' She leaned forward again, holding my gaze. 'Please, tell me.'

The afternoon had begun to wane and sultry summer clouds darkened the sky. I waved my arm in a slow, expansive movement and the candles placed around the room gained tongues of fire. Tegan gasped but sat still.

'There are witches who use their healing magic to great effect, Tegan. And there are those who would use it in the very opposite way.' I shook my head. 'Such power is terrible. It is against nature. It is a desecration of the craft. It is to be feared.' I let my eyes be taken by the dancing flames of the candles and started to tell my tale.

Fitzrovia, London, 1888

I

The cadaver had already begun to stink. Eliza stepped aside to allow the men to manhandle the corpse off the handcart, through the doorway, and into the coolness of the morgue. The left arm of the deceased brushed against her brown skirt as he was carried by.

'Put him over there, please.' She pointed at a vacant wooden table in the near corner. 'Gently now.'

'Don't you fret yourself, ma'am.' The older of the two men treated her to a toothless grin. 'The odd knock or bump ain't going to bother this fella no more.' He grunted as they swung the body up onto the scrubbed surface.

Eliza peered down at the figure. In the low gaslight, his features were softened, but there was no mistaking the face of someone who had lived a cruel life. All his woes were etched around his eyes and across his forehead, and his own aggression dragged down the corners of his thin mouth. Small flecks of light glinted off the backs of the lice that inhabited his hair. The noose that had dispatched him to another place had burned a vivid line around his neck. His clothes were filthy. Eliza pitied him his lonely end. What had brought him to the gallows she did not know. Whatever his crime, it seemed unreasonably cruel to deny the man a burial. But such was the fate of murderers with no one to claim the body or pay funeral costs. His destiny was to be an instrument of instruction for the medical students of the Fitzroy Hospital, who would pore over him, greedily slicing his organs, delving and probing and dissecting without a care for who he was or where he had come from. Eliza wondered how she herself would look if the story of her own life were so clearly written on her face. She fancied she would be too hideous to contemplate. Instinctively, her hand went to her hair. She let her fingers trace the broad sweep of pearl white that she did her best to conceal, tucked into her neat bun. It was indeed a mark of her history. A legacy of the moment of her transformation all those dark years ago. Aside from this memento, her appearance had changed little. She was no longer a girl but a woman. It seemed her body had continued to grow into maturity, and then the aging process had slowed. The magic that sustained her, which give her the eternal existence Gideon had spoken of, also gave her continued youth and strength. Eliza had observed that she aged outwardly no more than five years or so for every century she lived.

She became aware that the two men were still standing behind her, shuffling their feet.

'Oh, please go up to Mr. Thomas. He will see you get your money.'

'Thank you, ma'am.' They touched their caps and scuttled away.

Eliza checked the watch she wore pinned to her dress. She must not keep Dr. Gimmel waiting. She hurried up the stairs from the basement into the main body of the hospital. The Fitzroy, as it was known locally, had been open as a teaching hospital for only four years, but the building was not new. Funds had dictated that part of a street of townhouses be bought and modified to produce a space that could accommodate both patients and students. Consequently, with its many floors and narrow hallways, the Fitzroy presented unusual challenges when taking patients to and from the operating theater, or to the mortuary. The theater itself had been constructed for the purpose of surgical procedures and was well planned and equipped. By the time Eliza entered by the side door to collect her white apron, the room was already a-buzz with eager pupils. The smell of carbolic mingled with that of sweat and polished wood. A short oak partition screened off the area where the nurses, dressers, and surgeons donned their theater garments. Nameplates above a row of pegs identified the owner of each apron or coat. Once a week, all the blood-stained clothes were taken to be laundered, though some doctors became superstitiously attached to a particular coat and would rather proceed with it in its gory state than give it up. Eliza harbored no such sentimentalities. She had learned a very long time ago, from her mother, that cleanliness was inseparable from healing. It astounded her that the medical profession had only recently woken up to this fact, and some still stubbornly persisted in their own dirt-ridden ways. She wrapped her spotless apron around herself and tied it tightly at the small of her back. Despite being better qualified and more experienced than many of the medical staff working at the hospital, she knew it would be provoking to dress in a surgeon's gown rather than a nurse's uniform. It was hard enough gaining acceptance in such a man's world without drawing avoidable criticism. She covered her hair with a fresh white cap and went through to the theater proper. There was barely a space empty in the rows of tiered stands that formed a semicircle in front of the operating table. Since it had become a legal requirement that a practicing doctor should have a minimum of two years' anatomical instruction, there had been no shortage of students. As was her habit, Eliza briefly searched the muddle of faces, checking for new students, for someone unfamiliar, someone set apart. She had felt safe since coming to the Fitzroy, but the habits of suspicion and wariness were deeply established after all these years. She had never fully shaken off the sense of being pursued. She knew it would be dangerous to do so. She was accustomed to ignoring the ribald remarks thrown in her direction. Aside from an elderly nurse who was now busy pouring sawdust into the blood box beneath the operating table, she was the only woman present. She was aware that some of the young men saw her only as a female, as someone to be seduced or ignored depending on taste. She was also conscious that many resented her presence, and some were fiercely jealous of the regard in which she was held by Dr. Gimmel. It was no secret that he saw her as his protégé and took pride in her skill as his most talented pupil. In truth, Eliza believed he enjoyed scandalizing some of his fellow surgeons. She counted herself fortunate to have such a mentor. So fortunate that she had so far decided against going into practice herself. While women were now permitted to work as doctors, they seldom practiced as surgeons. By staying at the Fitzroy as Dr. Gimmel's assistant she had the opportunity to perform operations she would never have been able to carry out anywhere else.

As Eliza sprayed quantities of carbolic over the table and into the air, she continued to search the faces looking down at her. She noticed two new students sitting together, both possessed of the same abundant red hair, and remembered there were two brothers starting their studies that morning. Then, on the edge of her vision, a lone figure caught her attention. He sat near the back of the amphitheater at a distance from the others. He was tall and wore a dark frock coat with restrained but elegant collar and silver buttons. He carried a black cane on which he now rested both hands in front of him. Even in the clammy confines of the amphitheater, he had chosen to remain in his cape and top hat, the silk of which gleamed under the gaslight. Eliza knew at once that he was watching her. Not in the casual, time-passing way some of the others might but intently. Closely. With acute interest. She tried to shake off the sudden feeling of unease that had settled about her and was relieved to see the door of the theater open. Phileas Gimmel, FRCS, strode into the room followed by an orderly wheeling the hapless patient.

Dr. Gimmel was a man who commanded respect without ever appearing to wish for it. He had about him the air of one who was driven, one with boundless enthusiasm for his profession and a genuine desire to impart his wisdom to others. He had also a roguish gleam in his eye and a ready smile that had quelled the nerves of many a student and patient alike. An awed hush descended as the great man took center front, addressing the students as if they were his audience in a rather different sort of theater.

'Gentlemen! How happy I am to see so many eager and attentive faces. It gladdens my heart to know that such fine young men have the vocation to come here and to learn all that medical science has to offer. One day, some of you will, God willing, be standing on this very spot, poised on the threshold between life and death that all surgeons must tread. It is upon the arrival of that moment that I ask for your most earnest concentration today, gentlemen. For when that moment comes, you will stand here alone. The responsibility for your patient will rest on your shoulders, no matter how ably you are assisted.' He paused to glance at Eliza. 'All that you will be furnished with is the knowledge and experience that you gain in this place of learning. I can teach only those who would learn, gentlemen. To learn, you must be humble. You must be prepared to admit your ignorance. You must allow yourselves to be filled with the vital information presented to you via the skills and dedication of those who have gone before you down the long path to enlightenment.'

He turned and nodded to the nurse. She and the orderly raised the moaning patient out of his chair and onto the table. The man was gray with pain and clutched at his stomach with both hands. Dr. Gimmel continued. 'We have a straightforward case before us this morning, Gentlemen. Our patient, as no doubt even the slowest among you will already have observed, is a young man of lean build, in good health except for the severe abdominal pain that has brought him to us. After a thorough examination, I have concluded that the appendix is inflamed, dangerously so, and to leave it in situ would be to pass a death sentence upon this poor fellow.'

On cue, the patient let out a plaintive cry. Dr. Gimmel nodded.

'It is a misfortune, without a doubt, for any man to find himself with such an ailment. It is, however, this patient's great good fortune to find himself so afflicted within the reach of the ever-outstretched arms of the Fitzroy. Fear not, my good man.' He laid a palm briefly on the patient's brow. 'Your troubles will soon be at an end.'

Eliza stepped forward with a tray bearing a blue glass bottle and a piece of lint. She watched the doctor as he carefully placed the lint over the patient's mouth and nose and applied measured drops of chloroform. An image flashed through her mind of another operation some fifty years or more earlier, before she had come to the Fitzroy. Before surgery had been blessed with effective anaesthesia. She remembered the haste with which the surgeon had been forced to proceed. She remembered the screams rising to shrieks as the bone saw had hacked its way through the patient's thigh. She remembered the terror on the young man's face and the way he strained and struggled against the ties that bound him until pain and exhaustion mercifully caused him to lose consciousness. Those had been dark days for surgical procedures. Eliza had quickly learned, however, that there were ways she could ease such terrible suffering. Mesmerism had been widely practiced for years, and though frowned upon, it was legal. She had been able to present herself as a mesmerist and so use the craft to benumb the patients and render them in all ways senseless. As mesmerism became outlawed, she had been forced to cease the practice for fear the true nature of her skills would be uncovered. It was only the use of first ether and then chloroform that had allowed her to resume her work.

Now she watched as the young man on the operating table slipped peacefully into a deep sleep. It was later his true courage would be tested, during the dangerous days of recovery. If indeed he was to survive the surgery itself.

Dr. Gimmel proceeded confidently, continuing to address his students as he worked. He took a scalpel from the tray and made a deft incision. The nurse leaned forward to clear blood from the wound. Eliza placed a set of retractors in the surgeon's outstretched hand.

'As you can see, gentlemen, however effective the applied anaesthesia, the surgeon still faces the ever-present hazard of blood loss. Indeed, uncontrolled bleeding remains the second most common cause of fatality in the operating theater. No doubt you will have read all this many times in your studies, but there can be no substitute for seeing it for yourselves.'

As he spoke, blood ran in a syrupy stream off the table and onto the doctor's shoes. Without pausing in his work, he used a foot to nudge the sawdust box into position. One of the paler students fainted.

'Happily, the area in which our efforts are focused today does not involve any of the major arteries, and therefore we can continue secure in the knowledge that what we are seeing here, though dramatic, is in fact superficial in terms of blood loss. Ah, there is the offending item.'

Eliza passed him a scalpel and a clamp. He grasped the gut above the swollen appendix and then attempted to make another incision to remove it. To Eliza's horror, she saw him miss his target and nick a piece of healthy intestine. The doctor hesitated, then tried again, frowning, head low, peering into the abdominal cavity. More blood flowed. Seconds passed in unusual silence. A droplet of sweat followed the curve between Dr. Gimmel's eye and nose and stopped, dangling, at the edge of his nostril. At last his scalpel found its mark. Eliza caught the removed body part in a dish while the surgeon stitched the severed gut. He straightened up. 'My assistant will now close the wound for me. Observe and learn, gentlemen. Acknowledge that needlework is no longer the preserve of the female of the species. You yourselves will be required to produce such neat and effective sutures as Eliza is now so ably doing.' He wiped his forehead with the back of his hand, leaving a bloody smear across his brow.

Later, in the doctor's study, Eliza sat at the small desk by the open window and wrote up notes on the morning's work. From the street came the clanging of the omnibus headed for Shoreditch and the rattle of the ever-busy wheels of the hansom carriages behind sleek horses. The weather was warm, and Eliza thought briefly of how pleasant it would be to walk through the leafy coolness of Regent's Park. The rose garden was past its best by this time of year but was still scented and full of cheerful blooms. She promised herself a trip there on her next free day. Behind her, seated at his broad mahogany desk, Dr. Gimmel was atypically subdued. Eliza watched him as he sat, spectacles in hand, rubbing his closed eyes. She knew he was troubled by what had happened during the appendectomy, but it was not for her to broach the subject. Had his mistake been an isolated event, she might not have given it much thought, but this was not the first time she had witnessed him make an error at a sensitive moment in surgery. He was still the brilliant, visionary man who had inspired her nearly five years earlier. He still emitted the same verve and courage that pushed him to pioneer techniques and procedures other surgeons might shy away from. But something had changed. Something in his abilities had altered in recent months, and the results were alarming.

He became aware of her watching him and hastened to recover his more usual humor.

'So, Eliza, my dear, let us see what challenges await us tomorrow.' He picked up the appointments book in front of him, squinting at his secretary's writing. 'A kidney removal in the morning—a private affair, not for our students, alas. And after luncheon, aha, a new patient. And an interesting one. Her own doctor has referred her to me. He writes, "Miss Astredge is a young woman of good family whose life has afforded her thus far every care and privilege, and yet she fails to thrive. Indeed, her general health seems to be failing with alarming rapidity. She does not complain of any pain or even discomfort, but she is clearly suffering, and if matters are not addressed, well, we can assume the outcome will be tragic." He offers no suggestion as to what malady the poor woman suffers from. That we shall have to determine for ourselves.'

'Do you suspect cancer?' Eliza asked, crossing the room to stand before him.

Dr. Gimmel smiled, the sage with his favorite pupil once more.

'And if I do,' he asked, 'where might I look for it in this case?'

'I would suggest the liver.'

'Your hypothesis being?'

'It is well known that cancer of this organ may not present pain until late in the progression of the disease. The symptoms are also concurrent with the failure of the liver, allowing the patient to take no nourishment from food, despite a normal appetite.'

'Excellent, Dr. Hawksmith. I fear you will have my place at this desk before very long if I do not keep my wits about me. You will assist me in my examination of this young woman on the morrow. For today, we have achieved sufficient, I believe. You may take the afternoon off.'

'But your ward rounds . . . and I understood there was a further procedure scheduled for three o'clock.'

Dr. Gimmel waved aside her protestations. 'Nothing that will not wait. I fear I am not at my best today. Fatigued from our busy week, no doubt, nothing more.' He stood up. 'Nevertheless, I will surprise Mrs. Gimmel by arriving home early, and so allow her the pleasure of fussing over me, just this once.'

Eliza picked up her large leather bag, dropping an anatomy book into it before snapping shut the clasp. For a fleeting instant, she considered taking that walk but quickly decided the park would wait. There were more useful ways she could employ this unexpectedly vacant afternoon.

She stepped lightly out of the main door of the hospital and turned left along the noisy street. A bat-eared boy selling newspapers shouted from atop an upturned box. A gypsy woman attempted to press lavender into Eliza's hand. Even in the wide avenues around Fitzroy Square, there was a rush of traffic. Carriages, hansom cabs, omnibuses, and wagons jostled for position, ignoring shouts from pedestrians who struggled to negotiate the mêlée. Eliza walked the two short streets to the Tottenham Court Road, where she caught the eastbound omnibus, paying sixpence for an inside seat. The vehicle clattered over cobbles and past lofty buildings, clearing a path through the constantly moving landscape of figures. It headed up the incline through High Holborn and made its halting progress through the city. Eliza was unaccustomed to traversing London at times other than rush hour and was pleasantly surprised by the relative lack of people. It was not until she alighted on Whitechapel Road that the swirling humanity around her became more familiarly dense and frenetic. Here were narrow alleys and crowded routes, not the broad avenues of Fitzrovia. Gone were the elegant tall houses with their raised ground floors and imposing front doors. Here the dwellings were built with consideration only for quantity and a degree of shelter. Rows of small cottages stood backs to one another as if braced against assault, feet in the street, two small rooms downstairs and two smaller and low-ceilinged up. Aside from these were the dour tenements and the workhouses, the breweries and the warehouses, and the almighty factories, those machines of commerce that drove the engine that carried the wealth from the aching muscles of the poor to the velvet-lined coffers of the rich. Eliza picked her way through the fast-moving current of people. She found a certain security in being among such a mass. Here, women, men, and children alike became part of a huge single body, no longer individuals, rather pieces of a colossus, the living, breathing, breeding giant that was the city's poor. Here, she was hidden. Here, she could remain undetected. Undiscovered. Safe. What hope had any man of seeking out a solitary figure in such chaos? Even one possessed of such powers as Gideon Masters. Here at least, Eliza could let down her guard, if only fractionally.

She weaved through the small market that filled Cuthbert Street on Fridays, pausing to buy an apple from a barrow. As she paid for her purchase, she caught sight of Benjamin David standing in the doorway of his draper's shop, enjoying the warmth of the late August day. The tailor and his wife had been kind to Eliza, making her welcome when she first arrived. She enjoyed the company of the elderly couple and often dined at their home above the shop. The two exchanged waves before Eliza pressed on. The organ grinder on the other side of the street played a waltz to which everyone seemed to move as they did their best to avoid bumping into one another. Minutes later, Eliza arrived at her own front door. Or rather, the front door of the house belonging to Mrs. Garvey, where she had lodged for nearly three years. The house had once been a sweet shop and sported a deep bow window that protruded into the street. The silhouette of Eliza's landlady could be clearly made out behind the lace curtain at the window. It was her favorite place to sit and watch the comings and goings of the neighborhood. Very little of note escaped Mrs. Garvey's avaricious eye.

Eliza's hand was on the door handle when she had the strongest sensation that someone was watching her. She stood frozen for an instant, then whirled round. On the other side of the street she glimpsed a dark figure, or maybe even the shadow of that figure, as he slipped into the narrow alleyway that ran alongside the bakery. The street was a fast-flowing river of people, and yet she was sure she had seen someone who should not be there. A shudder gripped her body. She pushed open the door and went inside, shutting it with a slam. Mrs. Garvey sprang from her room faster than a bolting hare. She was a statuesque woman who enjoyed dressing her figure to accentuate its curves. Even if she had not been wearing a crinoline, her frame would still have filled the slender hallway.

'You are home early, I see. Are you unwell, Dr. Hawksmith?' Her concern was not so much for her lodger's health as for morsels of drama.

'No, not at all. Dr. Gimmel was indisposed. He sent me home.'

'Ah! I always held the good doctor would wear himself to a scrap of meat the way he runs after those patients of his. Such a good man. Please be sure to give him my very best regards for a speedy recovery, won't you?'

'Of course.' Eliza edged past Mrs. Garvey, her senses almost over-whelmed by the smell of violets. Mrs. Garvey made no attempt to step aside. She whipped out her fan and began to work it vigorously beneath her jowls.

'Oh, this heat,' she moaned. 'Is it any wonder people fall ill? There is no air, I tell you. It has all been used up. There will be cholera again, mark my words, Dr. Hawksmith. Mark them. I will be proved right.'

'No doubt, Mrs. Garvey, now if you'll excuse me, I wish to open the clinic.'

'What? Now! In the hours of daylight! No, no, Dr. Hawksmith, I think not. That was not our arrangement. Clinics to be held in the eve-ning, that was agreed. Nothing was said about afternoons.'

'I appreciate it is irregular . . .'

'Most!'

'. . . however, it does seem such a provident opportunity. The clinics have been so busy of late.' She met the older woman's horrified gaze and tried one of her brightest smiles. 'Perhaps just this once, if you wouldn't mind?'

Mrs. Garvey pulled a face, then sighed deeply, the lace at her bosom fluttering beneath the exhaled breath.

'Very well. On this occasion. But this is not to become a habit. I have my reputation to consider. Ask your ladies to be discreet, if you please.'

At the rear of the house, there was a small, square room with a modest window giving onto a cobbled yard. A lobby of sorts connected the room to the outside with a sturdy door. It was through this door that Eliza received her patients. Three evenings a week, from eight o'clock onward, she did her best to see, advise, and treat as many women as came. The women presented a variety of ailments, injuries, and complaints as wide-ranging as they themselves were in age, shape, and size. What they had in common, however, was a profession, for these were all prostitutes. When Eliza had first moved to London many long years before, she had been shocked and saddened by the wretched lives led by these women. They were forced to walk the streets selling their bodies and their dignity, risking their safety and their health, at the mercy of every drunk with a few shillings to spend, reviled, excluded, despised by everyone, cared for by none. The injustice of the censure society inflicted on these women moved Eliza to action. She could not change what people thought of those less fortunate than themselves or alter the way people judged others. She could do nothing to temper the disdain or even violence the men who used these prostitutes inflicted upon them or to redress the balance that allowed the men their pleasure without judgment or criticism. What she could do was help to heal these women. She had persuaded Mrs. Garvey, with much badgering and not a little money, that this was a godly and worthy thing to do, that her standing in the community would not suffer as a consequence of the clinic being held on her property. On the contrary, it would be elevated. The women would only ever use the back door, would never call when Eliza herself was not present, and would not present themselves in an intoxicated state. When word had spread that there was a woman doctor prepared to treat unfortunates for whatever donation they could muster, girls as young as twelve and toothless grandmothers made their way to 62 Hebden Lane. Once there had been trouble when an overeager client had tired of waiting outside the high wall of the yard and had barged his way into the house. The girl he sought was furious and set about him with a table lamp, until the other women present hauled the pair from the building and out of earshot of Mrs. Garvey. Even so, Eliza was warned that a second such occurrence would see the clinic closed. Since then, the ladies of the night had themselves policed the area, never allowing their beaux to venture anywhere near the house or their beloved doctor.

Eliza jammed open the window before propping wide the door and unbolting the little yard gate. She hung upon it a small wooden sign bearing her name, then returned inside. She had, at her own expense, furnished the room with a desk and chair, both of which Mrs. Garvey had insisted on inspecting for fear of worm or rot before letting them cross the threshold. There was also a narrow bed behind a makeshift screen, where she could examine her patients. A stout cupboard with a padlock contained bandages, dressings, and Eliza's own remedies and ointments, as well as such conventional medicines she could afford to buy from the apothecary at the hospital.

Despite the unusual hour, it was not many minutes before a young woman entered the clinic. Eliza recognized her at once and bade her sit down.

'How are you today, Lily?' she asked, taking her hand, both to comfort the girl and to tactfully check her pulse. As Eliza had anticipated, it was racing.

Lily gratefully sat on the hard chair, tugging her shawl about her even though the room was uncomfortably warm.

'I don't know, Doctor, I really don't. One minute I's feeling quite well, chipper even, then the next I'm tireder than a staggering mule. Can't 'ardly put one sorry foot in front of the other.'

'Have you been taking the medication I gave you last time?'

'Course, yeah, look.' She pulled an empty bottle from the drawstring bag at her waist. 'See? Not a drop left. And I've been using that cream an' all. Don't make much difference though.'

Eliza gently turned the girl's head to one side and examined her neck. 'The sores look better.'

'Oh, yeah, they're better. Don't give me no more pep, though, do it? How am I supposed to make a living if I can't 'ardly get off me bed, eh?' The girl ceased talking and let herself slump farther down in the chair.

Eliza took note of how much thinner Lily was than the last time she had seen her. It was true the progression of the sores and the disfiguring corruption of the skin had been checked, but now the girl seemed to have lost all strength. Eliza smiled at her and patted her shoulder.

'Don't worry,' she said, 'I'll give you something.' She went to the cupboard and took a large key from her pocket. She undid the padlock, swung open the door, and stared at the rows of jars in front of her. She knew in truth there was little she could do for Lily. She was all too familiar with the relentless advance of syphilis and painfully aware of how limited her ability to treat it was. All she could do was alleviate the symptoms. It was clear to her that Lily had entered the depressive stage of the disease. The pattern was not rigid, but it rarely varied greatly. It was only because the girl had so far escaped the most obvious ravages that often affected the face that she was able to continue working. Eliza had instructed her about the contagious element of the disease and that she must guard against spreading it among her clients and therefore ultimately her friends too. But she knew the girl had no other way of supporting herself.

The gloomy prospect of delirium, madness, and a painful death lay ahead. When the time came, Eliza would do her best to find the wretched creature a bed in one of the more tolerable sanatoriums. She handed Lily two bottles.

'This is more of what you had before,' she told her, 'and this is a draft to help your strength. Take it with care, Lily. Too much will have the opposite effect.'

'Thanks, Doctor. You're a good soul.'

It was at moments like these, when faced with such pitiful suffering, that Eliza was tempted to use the stronger elements of her craft. She knew it was not beyond her capabilities as a witch to prevent the inexorable march of the disease. She could not completely cure the girl, but she could rid her of the curse of the illness and spare her a miserable and short future. But long ago Eliza had made a promise to herself. A promise that she felt sure was the only thing that kept her beyond Gideon's reach, for to connect with that power would inevitably connect her to him. A promise that meant she could endure the lonely life she had inherited. She would not use the dark arts. Ever. She would use only her own talents as a healer and the skills and remedies her mother had taught her. Nothing more. Not even now. Not even for poor Lily.

Brisk footsteps in the lobby told of the arrival of another patient. A lithe figure, brightly dressed, her hat at a cheeky angle, a smile lighting up her features, strode into the little room.

'I was told there was a doctor here would see me without getting paid. That right, is it?' she asked.

Eliza was about to answer when she was silenced by an overwhelming sense of foreboding. Fear swamped her, so that for a moment she could not speak. There was something about the girl who stood before her, some connection with terrible violence. An image flashed through Eliza's mind of the same girl lying covered in freshly spilled blood, her body grotesquely mutilated. Eviscerated. She closed her eyes and shook the horrific vision away. Collecting herself, she went to her desk for her ledger.

'You were informed correctly,' she said, picking up a pen. 'I will see you just as soon as I have finished with Lily. Will you give me your name?'

'Mary,' the girl replied. 'My name is Mary Jane Kelly.'

2

It was after ten o'clock when Eliza at last reached the peace of her own room above the clinic. She had taken a light supper at her desk and now wished only to fall into bed. She took off her outer garments and sat a moment in her slip and petticoats at the dressing table by the window. She had never learned to feel comfortable in a corset and considered it one of the worst fashions she had had to endure. In the looking glass, her tired reflection gazed back at her. However satisfying she found it to help those who could not otherwise afford medical care, and however much she enjoyed her work at the Fitzroy, by the end of each day she was invariably weary. It was not simply the long hours that wore her down. It was the lack of companionship in her life. She had long since accepted that she could never have children of her own. She was as certain as she could be that her immortality had rendered her infertile. It had taken many years to fully come to terms with this, but she knew it was in fact a blessing. How could she raise children, only to watch them age and die as she continued her endless journey? No, she had come to see she was never meant to be a mother. Besides, she had her patients to nurture and care for. Many of them were indeed like motherless children, alone and unloved in the world. It was within Eliza's gift to help them, and she did so willingly. But it was her own family she missed. Even after so many years, the pain of their deaths and the void they left in her life did not lessen. And as for a man to love, someone to hold her close, to make her feel like a living, feeling woman and not some unnatural creature . . . There had been lovers, of course, but Eliza had quickly learned not to let herself care deeply. How could she ever stay with one man, be his wife, his soulmate? How many years would it be before he realized she could not offer him children and that she was no longer mortal? What then? Would she nurse him through old age and then move on? She had never been faced with such a situation. Gideon had seen to that. Every time Eliza had come close to finding happiness, he had taken it from her. No matter where she went, how many times she changed her appearance and her name, in the end he always found her. It was just a question of time. How could she put someone she loved in the path of such danger, of such evil?

Eliza unpinned her hair and brushed it rhythmically, remembering how she had done the same for Margaret, whose hair shone like a blackbird's wing. She climbed into the high narrow bed, casting off the covers since the night was almost as warm and airless as the day had been. She fell into a restless sleep. A sleep troubled not so much by dreams as by memories. So many memories. So many lives she had led. So many corners she had turned, ever hoping to shake off the one who would claim her. The one who would never let her be free. Into her dreams stepped the phantom-like figure she had seen watching her, reminding her she would always see herself as one man's quarry.

The following day was no fresher than the one before. It was a mercy that no students were present in the operating theater, for the atmosphere was fetid and uncomfortable enough with just the few who stood at the table. A man of good family but poor health lay prone before Dr. Gimmel and Eliza. One of the more experienced students, Roland Pierce, had been selected to attend and stood at the patient's head ready to administer further chloroform should the need arise. Nurse Morrison stood opposite the doctor. Between them, a broad incision had been made in the patient's back to provide access to a kidney harboring a particularly large stone. Eliza watched in wonder as the doctor bent low over the patient to navigate the area below the rib cage, gently finding his way to the vital organ.

'Here we have it,' he said. 'Aha, yes . . . in tolerable condition except for the stone. Scalpel, if you please, Nurse Morrison. Thank you. Now, a small amount of cutting is all that is needed . . . yes . . . and here . . . Damnation!'

Abruptly the doctor stopped cutting. As he straightened up, a fountain of deepest crimson spouted up from the abdominal cavity. In a second, it fanned into a plume, spraying the nurse with glistening arterial blood. Eliza expected the doctor to react, but he stood transfixed. Roland gasped and paled.

'Dr. Gimmel.' Eliza touched his arm. 'The renal artery has been severed.'

'What?' The doctor appeared unable to continue. He dropped his scalpel onto the now slippery floor and clutched at his head, staggering backward.

'My Lord!' Roland roused himself. 'Eliza, the patient will bleed to death.'

Eliza snapped at the nurse. 'Attend to Dr Gimmel. Roland, more chloroform.'

'More? But this man is surely at the limit.'

'Do as I say!' Eliza grabbed a small clamp from the tray of instruments and struggled to locate the source of the gushing blood. 'We must slow his heartbeat, if we can.' She continued to delve in the cavity, but there was so much blood now, it was near impossible to find what she was looking for. At last she gave a cry. 'I have it! There, it is secured. Roland, pass me a needle. I must attempt to suture the artery. It is cut but not detached. If I repair the opening, leaving enough room for sufficient bloodflow . . .'

'Never mind.' Roland did not move. 'It is too late now.'

Eliza looked up, her own face dripping with the patient's blood. Roland had a hand to the man's throat to confirm there was no pulse. He shook his head. Eliza looked down at her hands inside the body of the dead man, hands thick with gore, as if she had been trying to murder rather than save the poor wretch. For a second, she saw again the image of Mary Kelly, the girl from her clinic, equally doused in blood.

'No!' she cried out.

Roland stepped to her side.

'It wasn't your fault,' he told her. 'There really was nothing more you could have done.'

As Eliza shook her head, she noticed the tiers of seats were not completely empty. Sitting in the top row, still as a stone and with an expression as unreadable, was the new student she had noticed the day before. What was he doing sitting in to observe a private operation? Everyone knew the theater was closed to students when fee-paying patients demanded it. Eliza grabbed Roland's arm.

'Who is that?' she whispered.

'What?' Roland was understandably surprised that she should be concerned with a stranger at such a moment.

'Up there, sitting in the top row.'

Roland glanced up just in time to see the man leaving via the rear exit.

'Oh, that fellow. New student, I think. Italian, as I recall. Name of Signor Gresseti.'

An hour later, Eliza sat with Dr. Gimmel in his room. Mr. Thomas had brought them tea, but it was scant comfort. Eliza thought she had never seen the doctor look so old.

'The fact of the matter is, Eliza, my eyes are troubled. And lately I have been experiencing severe headaches. They come on with frightening swiftness, as you saw today. And when they do, my vision is seriously impaired.' He placed his cup on its saucer and sat back in his chair. 'In short, my dear, I am losing my sight. I think I have known it for some time, to be perfectly candid with you. I confess I was afraid to speak the words out loud.'

'I am so very sorry.'

'You are a kind girl, Eliza. And an exceptionally fine doctor. You will make a splendid surgeon when the time comes. But it is I who am truly sorry. My stubbornness in refusing to accept my condition has just cost a man his life. No'—he held up a hand—'don't try to convince me otherwise. We both know the truth of it.'

They sat in silence awhile. It seemed a cruel blow for such a talented man to be robbed of his skills when all his life he had used them to heal others. Now there was no one to heal him.

'What will you do?' Eliza asked.

The doctor shrugged and shook his head. 'I cannot work as a surgeon, that much is certain. I may continue in my capacity as a consultant until such time as that too becomes . . . untenable.'

Eliza opened her mouth to offer some words of comfort, but they were interrupted by Mr. Thomas at the door.

'Excuse me, Dr. Gimmel, but your next appointment . . . ?'

'Yes, yes. Of course. Show them in.' He stood up and cleared his throat, extending a welcoming hand as two figures entered the room.

Thomas presented them. 'Mr. Simon and Miss Abigail Astredge, sir.'

'Thank you, Thomas. Come in, come in. This is my assistant, Dr. Eliza Hawksmith. Please, be seated.'

While pleasantries were being exchanged, Eliza watched the new patient. She was a slender, delicate girl, barely out of her teens, with skin the color of candle wax and hair of autumn gold. Her pallor and two spots of color on her cheekbones suggested she was indeed unwell. Her brother, a broad-shouldered yet angular man with soft green eyes was quietly solicitous, helping his sister to a chair before placing himself to stand behind her. Eliza was touched by this protective behavior, but when she offered him a smile, she gained none in return. Embarrassed, she turned her attention to what Dr. Gimmel was saying.

'Now, my dear Miss Astredge, please be assured, we will do all in our power to cure you. I have had details of your condition from your own doctor and I am happy to welcome you into the care of the Fitzroy.'

'Thank you, Dr. Gimmel, you are most kind. I am sure you are just the man to heal me,' said Abigail in a small voice that lacked conviction.

'My sister has withstood her illness with uncommon courage.' Simon Astredge placed a hand on the girl's shoulder. 'But, well, let us say she has lost confidence in the medical profession's ability to help her.'

'Now, Simon . . .'

'No, no, Miss Astredge, let him say what you yourself must surely wish to tell us. It is absolutely understandable,' said Dr. Gimmel, 'that you should feel this way. There can be nothing more alarming than to find oneself in failing health with no proper diagnosis and therefore no correct treatment. Please, allow me and my staff to restore your belief in what medical science has to offer you.'

'For myself, Doctor'—Abigail smiled, but there was a sadness about her eyes that would not be lifted—'I admit I would happily go to my bed and let the good Lord take me in my sleep. My brother, however'—she glanced up at him and patted his hand—'will not have it. Indeed, he has such determination that I will make a full recovery I feel it my duty as a sister to oblige.'

Now at last, Simon smiled too. Eliza could see that it was his fear for his sister's life that so clouded his face.

Dr. Gimmel was full of optimism.

'Then we must not disappoint, must we? I propose that, after a thorough examination in which, with your permission, I will be assisted by Dr. Hawksmith, we admit you to one of our private rooms so that we may observe your health under a strict diet and regimen of medication for some weeks before deciding on any surgical procedures.'

'Oh'—Abigail looked alarmed—'I do not wish to appear for a moment unhelpful, Doctor, but the idea of staying in a hospital . . .'

'She is set against it, Sir.' Her brother finished her thought.

Eliza sat next to Abigail and did her best to reassure her.

'We have several very pretty rooms, Miss Astredge. All are light and well ventilated, and you would be encouraged to walk in the hospital gardens. It may not be as disagreeable as you have feared.'

Abigail turned to face Eliza.

'Please understand, Dr. Hawksmith, it is not that I doubt the quality of the facilities at the Fitzroy. It is simply that I am happiest at our home overlooking the park. That is where I believe I will heal best, and that is where I wish to be. With my brother. Whatever the future may hold.'

'I should explain,' put in Simon, 'that Abigail and I have no parents living. We are all and everything to each other. I am as keen as she that we not be separated. Our minds are quite made up.'

Dr. Gimmel nodded. 'It may well be that home is more important in this case than the unfamiliar walls of an institution, however well equipped. The fact remains, however, that for treatment to be effective, there must be regular monitoring and observation. Only by such means can we ascertain the nature and progression of the illness and therefore acquire prognosis and prescribe the most efficacious treatment.'

'Could not such observations be made at our house?' asked Abigail.

'By a resident nurse, you mean?' Dr. Gimmel was unconvinced.

Simon shook his head. 'Forgive me, I do not think a nurse sufficient to the task. If a doctor could be found, perhaps?'

'A doctor's time is hard put upon, Mr. Astredge.'

'If I might suggest . . .' Eliza spoke up, 'Regent's Park is very near. I would be more than willing to undertake to visit Miss Astredge on a daily basis and to undertake any examinations or tests that may be necessary.'

Dr. Gimmel considered the idea.

'It would be a solution, that is clear, but, Dr. Hawksmith, your clinic in Whitechapel places many demands upon you, as do your duties here assisting me.'

'My clinic will not go neglected. And I recall, Dr. Gimmel, that you had considered taking a break from surgery for a short time, is that not so?'

Dr. Gimmel struggled to adjust to what Eliza was telling him, then smiled and nodded.

'Quite so, Eliza. You are the voice of cool reason, as always. Well, Miss Astredge, Mr. Astredge, will Dr. Hawksmith do for you?'

Abigail's smile illuminated the room and she squeezed her brother's hand.

'I think she will do very well indeed,' she said.

Simon looked at Eliza directly now, his green eyes holding her own gaze. She felt herself blushing a little and was surprised to find the experience a pleasant one.

'Dr. Hawksmith,' he said slowly, 'we would be delighted to welcome you into our home.'

That night, well after nine o'clock, Eliza finished her clinic feeling even more exhausted than was usual. The hot weather had turned close and thundery, with distant drums sounding out a warning of the approaching storm. She followed out the last of her patients, Lily and her friend Martha, who had come to support her. The women exited the little yard laughing. Though she was seriously unwell, Lily's spirits had been raised by the care Eliza had shown, as well as by the draft she had made her drink. This was not something she might have found in the local apothecary. This was a remedy of Eliza's own concoction and was not for treating the poor girl's disease but for lifting the malaise that came with it. Eliza took the sign from the narrow gate at the back of the yard. As she did so, a noise in the shadows of the alley made her heart race.

'Who's there?' she called out, attempting to sound bold even if she did not feel it. 'Mary Ann? Sally, is that you?'

There was no answer, but Eliza was certain somebody stood concealed in the darkness. She waited, but whoever it was chose not to reveal themselves. Once again, she began to feel cold dread seeping into her body. She wanted to run inside but was too unnerved to turn her back on the unseen figure. All at once, she heard a sharp double snap. The small sound, which might have been a watch being closed or the top of a hollow cane being pushed home, jolted her from her state of immobility. She slammed the gate shut and raced across the yard, not looking back. Once inside, she bolted the door top and bottom and leaned against it, her breath ragged, her mind refusing to form the idea that yet again her place of safety might have been discovered.

3

That night the weather broke into a wild but short-lived storm. Less than an hour of cacophony and lightning gave way to steady rain, which lightened to drizzle and then fog by the time the gray dawn came. The damp coolness was a relief after the sultry days that had preceded it, but the streets were now awash with dust turned to mud by the rain. Gutters over-flowed so that small rivers ran beneath iron-clad hooves and leather-soled boots, bearing all manner of flotsam that clung to ladies' long, broad skirts. Eliza found that even the floor of the omnibus had become a filthy mess of wet straw, mud, and crushed rubbish. The smell in the crowded wagon was enough to turn the strongest of stomachs. She was thankful to reach the tended cleanliness of the Fitzroy. It was her habit in the mornings to go directly to Dr. Gimmel's rooms. She entered without knocking, took off her bonnet, and set about removing her shawl and shaking the water from it. She was on the point of hanging it up when she realized she was not alone in the room.

'Oh!' She took a step backward, her mind momentarily rendered empty of polite words as she recognized the man who stood in front of her. He whipped his top hat from his head and bowed low.

'Forgive me, madam, it was not my intention to startle you.' His accent was full of sharp consonants, dancing vowels, and misplaced stresses, but his English was excellent. 'May I present myself, in the absence of another to provide introductions? My name is Damon Gresseti.' He remained bowed and reached forward to take her gloved hand and plant the driest of kisses on it. Eliza snatched it away far more quickly than manners dictated.

'Who let you in?' she demanded. 'These are Dr. Gimmel's rooms.'

Signor Gresseti straightened up unhurriedly, returning his hat to his head and leaning slightly on his black cane. His silk-lined cape was flicked back over one shoulder, revealing exquisitely tailored clothes. He was tall, and his features were curiously inexpressive. Even now the faint smile he wore did not appear to reach his eyes.

'Mr. Thomas was kind enough to admit me. I am early for my appointment with the eminent doctor. You would surely not wish me to be late and keep him waiting?'

'No. Of course not.' Eliza moved to her desk and placed her bag by the chair. 'Naturally, if you have an appointment, Mr. Thomas would want you to wait in comfort. It is more usual, I must say, for visiting students to remain seated in Mr. Thomas's room.'

'Quite so. Once again, I can only ask your forgiveness—it was my suggestion that I be allowed to enter before Dr. Gimmel's arrival. I would not wish Mr. Thomas to be upbraided for granting me my wish.'

At that moment, the door opened, and Phileas Gimmel fair bounded into the room.

'Ahh! My good friend, you are here already. Must I always be late for every appointment?' He grasped his visitor's hand and pumped it enthusiastically. 'But, no matter, I know you would not have noticed my tardiness whilst in the company of my invaluable assistant, Dr. Eliza Hawksmith. Eliza, allow me to present Signor Gresseti.'

'I would have arrived earlier myself, Doctor, had I been aware a new student was to be joining us for this morning's surgery.'

'Student?' Dr. Gimmel gave a bark of a laugh. 'My dear me, no. This is Damon Gresseti of the Milan Institute of Medical Research, here for an exchange of insight and methodology at the suggestion of the senior surgeon of that great place himself.'

Eliza felt flustered. Not a student but a medical scientist of no small standing, judging by Dr. Gimmel's regard for him. 'The Milan Institute? We are honored.'

'Indeed we are,' said Dr. Gimmel.

'The honor is mine,' Gresseti insisted.

'Please, be seated, let us not stand on ceremony.' Dr. Gimmel ushered Gresseti to a chair. 'We are to be working together for some weeks. There will be no time for formal niceties in the operating theater.'

'But, Doctor'—Eliza remained standing—'I understood you were to take a short break from surgery.'

'Yes, yes, quite so. Dear me, Dr. Hawksmith, I always believed it to be my wife's affair to fuss over me, not that of my colleague.' He shot her a reproachful look. 'I intend to oversee procedures and guide the junior doctors who have proved themselves equal to the task. I count your good self as the first of these, Eliza, naturally.'

'Dr. Hawksmith will make a fine surgeon, I think,' said Gresseti. 'I have already observed her work. Yesterday morning. The removal of the kidney stone . . . ?'

Dr. Gimmel was silenced, his jaw dropping. Eliza was both shocked and angered. How could the man be so unkind as to raise the matter of the procedure that had proved fatal for the patient? What possible reply could Dr. Gimmel be expected to make? It was unforgivable of Gresseti to be so insensitive. Eliza stepped forward, putting herself between Gresseti and her mentor.

'I recall you were present during that particular procedure, Signor Gresseti. Regrettably the outcome was not what any of us would have wished for. However, as a man of medicine, you will appreciate that no surgery is without its risks. The fact remains that under Dr. Gimmel's care many more patients have survived to make full recoveries than might have done so at the hands of a less gifted surgeon.'

'I do not doubt this.' There was that shallow smile once again. 'And I must add that you acquitted yourself admirably, Dr. Hawksmith, in your attempts to correct the . . . *risk* that occurred. Valiant efforts, sadly unsuccessful.'

Dr. Gimmel looked as if he had been struck. He sat down heavily. Eliza felt fury rising. On first seeing Gresseti, she had been unnerved and suspicious, as she always was of a singular stranger. She had believed him alone and unknown, a combination that invariably caused her alarm. Now, however, his credentials had been revealed, so that she no longer feared him. He came recommended by a surgeon Dr. Gimmel had known for many years. His provenance could not be questioned. Fear, then, had been removed and was now replaced by a fierce dislike coupled with anger at his treatment of the doctor. How could either of them be expected to work with such a man?

Dr. Gimmel was struggling to recover himself. 'Well, let us hope you will observe happier conclusions to those procedures we have before us today.' He shuffled through some papers and found his appointments book. 'Ah, yes. I see there is the removal of a malignant tumor from a young woman this morning. At ten o'clock. Dr. Hawksmith and Roland Pierce, one of our finest students, will be assisting. I trust you will find the operation interesting, Signor.'

'I am sure of it, Doctor.' He rose, picking up his cane. 'Until then,' he said, bowing low.

After he had gone, Eliza and the doctor sat in silence for a full minute before Thomas entered with a tray of tea.

'Ah, Thomas.' Dr. Gimmel tried a small laugh. 'You are as always the master of intuition. If ever refreshment were needed . . .'

Eliza poured the tea and handed some to Dr. Gimmel. His hand shook slightly as he took it, causing the cup to rattle in its saucer. He hastily set it down on the desk.

'Dr. Gimmel, you called Signor Gresseti "good friend"—did you meet him on one of your trips to the institute?'

'What? Oh, no. Merely a figure of speech. Professor Salvatores, the senior consulting surgeon at the Institute is, of course, a dear friend of mine. But I had not met Signor Gresseti until this morning. He is not, I will admit, what I had been given to expect by the professor's letter of introduction.'

Eliza saw weariness dull the doctor's features. These were dark times for him. It seemed a harsh twist of fate that had decided this was the time the odious Gresseti should be sent into their midst.

Later that day, to the collective relief of all present, the scheduled surgery went smoothly and was declared a success. Roland proved a diligent student and did well, assisted by Eliza, with Dr. Gimmel directing. The inscrutable Signor Gresseti stood a few paces from the table. Eliza found working under the unsympathetic scrutiny of their visitor deeply unsettling and was glad Roland had not been present for the meeting earlier in the day. As soon as the operation was over, Eliza changed her clothes, made her excuses, and left the hospital. She set off on foot across Fitzroy Square in the direction of Regent's Park. This was to be her first visit to Abigail Astredge, and she found she was looking forward to it. It was certainly a relief to be out of the strained atmosphere of Dr. Gimmel's presence. More than that, she realized with some surprise the thought of seeing Simon Astredge again pleased her. The weather was gray and damp and the streets still wet, but the air was fresh now that the earlier fog had lifted. She turned the corner out of Cleveland Street onto Euston Road. At a stand on the pavement a boy was selling newspapers. Ordinarily she had neither the time nor the money to spare for a paper, but the headline he was calling out made her stop and pull a coin from her purse. She stepped out of the stream of pedestrians to stand against the railings of a garden and study the front page. A lurid banner read: WOMAN BRUTALLY SLAIN IN WHITECHAPEL. She read on. A girl had been attacked and murdered. Her body had been found on the first floor landing of a tenement block in the Whitechapel area. There were nearly forty stab wounds and slashes on the poor girl's body. She had been found drenched in her own blood. Eliza's breath caught in her throat. The girl's name was Martha Tabram. The same Martha who had accompanied Lily on her visit to the clinic the night before. Eliza had seen her only a few hours before her death. She might have been one of the last people to see her alive. She recalled the girl's laughter as she left the clinic. And now she was dead. Cut to ribbons and horribly mutilated. Eliza folded the paper and thrust it into the hands of a passerby.

'Take it,' she said. 'I cannot bear to hold it a moment longer.' So saying, she forced herself to walk on with no small effort. One foot in front of the other, she made herself continue her journey to the edge of the park. She could not shake off the sensation she had experienced the night before that there was someone watching the entrance to her clinic, someone standing in the shadows. Had that person followed Martha? Eliza found herself at the front door of the Astredges' house. She took a moment to compose herself and retrain her thoughts. It was Abigail who mattered at this moment. There was nothing anyone could do for poor Martha now. She must turn her mind to the needs of her new patient.

Number 4 York Terrace was a handsome Georgian house of white stucco with high windows, a portico supported by slender pillars, a raised ground floor, and broad steps leading up to the royal blue front door. Eliza tugged at the bellpull and heard footsteps inside. The door was opened by a smartly turned out butler, whose head was as hairless and shiny as the marble floor of the entrance hall. On seeing her card, he confirmed she was expected and asked her to follow him to the morning room. As they crossed the elegant space, Eliza thought how grand the house was for two people, with its sweeping staircase, central atrium, marble columns, and stately busts peering out from behind gargantuan ferns rooted in huge brass urns. The butler opened a door off the hall and announced her as she stepped past him. Abigail got to her feet at once and came toward Eliza.

'Please.' Eliza held out a hand. 'Do not trouble yourself to rise on my account, Miss Astredge.'

'Now I insist you call me Abigail,' said the young woman, 'and why would I not greet you properly, when it is so good of you to undertake the tedious task of visiting me every day?'

'Firstly,' said Eliza, allowing herself to be led over to the seat at the open window, 'because you are my patient, and as such I am far more concerned with your rest and recovery than with etiquette. Secondly, please do rid yourself of the notion that it is in any way a task for me to come here. I often make house calls for patients from my own clinic, and none offer quite such lovely surroundings.' As she spoke, she looked about the most charming morning room she had ever set foot in. The formality of the entrance hall had given way here to upholstery of fresh stripes against cheerful paisley wallpaper. There was an abundance of greenery; asparagus ferns with feathery fronds brightening every corner, bolder aspidistras on either side of the fireplace. There were two comfortable sofas, an elegant chaise longue, a deep window seat with sumptuous cushions and numerous small tables bearing pretty pieces of china or silver. There was a deftly embroidered firescreen and delicately etched glass shades over the gaslights. In the far corner was an escritoire with crisp notepaper and a silver inkwell, next to which sat a highly decorated paper knife. Every item had been chosen for its prettiness or charm, and the effect was delightful. This was a woman's room. 'What is more,' Eliza went on, 'I welcome the chance to be released from the confines of the Fitzroy for a short time.'

'Oh?' Abigail sat down and patted the cushion beside her, smiling as Eliza sat stiffly next to her. 'Is it not a happy place to work?'

'Ordinarily it is.' Eliza hesitated, untying the ribbon of her bonnet. 'Let us just say Dr. Gimmel is under certain . . . pressures at present that put a strain on him and are matters of concern to us all. Also, we have a visitor to the hospital. An observer.' She stopped, wondering what it was that made her chatter on so to someone she hardly knew and who was a patient to boot.

'And?' Abigail quizzed her. 'Don't stop there, I beg you. I have a nose for a story; my brother says it. I can sniff one out like a bloodhound. There is more to this than you are prepared to tell me on your first visit. No matter, I shall winkle it out of you, Dr. Hawksmith. You will see, I am an incorrigible gossip. Now, shall we have tea?'

Eliza at last began to relax. The news of Martha's death was starting to recede a little in her mind in Abigail's presence. She slipped her shawl from her shoulders and nodded.

'Tea would be very welcome,' she said, 'and, please, call me Eliza.'

'Is that your first instruction for me, Doctor?' Abigail's wan face was warmed by her grin.

'Indeed it is.'

'Then I must obey'—she laughed—'and after tea, you can inflict Dr. Gimmel's horrible medication upon me as much as you please. I aim to be the least troublesome patient you have ever encountered. Though I may feel that a short game of cribbage might help my constitution. Don't you think it might?'

The afternoon passed quickly for Eliza. She was enjoying Abigail's easy company so much it would have been easy to forget the seriousness of the young woman's condition. Eliza examined her thoroughly, made notes regarding her symptoms, and adjusted her diet and medication accordingly. She reflected on the cruel nature of diseases of the liver. The patient gave the outward appearance of frailty and pallor and had little energy but otherwise appeared well. In truth, she was fading away. Dying, in fact. Unless something could be done to arrest the deterioration of her vital organ, she would not live through the summer. Eliza understood Dr. Gimmel's plan to try to treat the condition without risky surgery. To attempt to remove a tumor or indeed part of the liver itself would be highly dangerous, particularly with Abigail so weak. Their best chance of success was to first increase her vigor and health in general and try to arrest the advancement of the disease with medication. Even so, Eliza could not help wondering if Dr. Gimmel's reluctance to operate was in part due to the fact that he would not be able to carry out the surgery himself. Was there anyone else at the Fiztroy sufficiently skilled and experienced to do the procedure? Eliza had never even observed surgery on the liver. The memory of the renal patient dying while her hands were still inside his body haunted her. How would she feel if Abigail were to die because of her inexperience?

As she was readying herself to leave, an eerie noise drifted in through the open window.

'Good heavens,' she said, 'what is that curious sound?'

Abigail smiled. 'I chose this room because it overlooks the park. Beyond those trees are the zoological gardens. What you can hear now is the wolves singing. Isn't it the most wonderful thing you have ever heard? Listen. How mournful and yet how thrilling.'

Eliza stepped closer to the window. The wolves raised their voices in a discordant chorus of howling. The noise seemed to fill the room. It was unsettling to be standing in a town house with every comfort and modern convenience, yet to be bathed in the song of wild and dangerous animals. Eliza shivered. At that moment, the door opened and Simon appeared in the doorway. He smiled on seeing Eliza.

'Ah,' he said, 'our very own Dr. Hawksmith. How do you find your patient today?'

Eliza gathered herself and took his hand. 'I was on the point of leaving,' she told him, releasing his hand and picking up her bag. 'Your sister's condition remains unchanged as yet,' she added, 'though I am pleased to see her in good spirits.'

'I'm sure she will do her best to be a model patient. She greatly appreciates your undertaking her care and agreeing to pay house calls. We are both of us indebted to you.'

Eliza found herself looking at him, holding his searching gaze. His gentle green eyes were still smiling. She became aware of the fact that the wolves had stopped singing, and she felt her unease lift.

'As I have already told Abigail, it is far from a duty for me to come here. Your sister has been a solicitous hostess, despite my best efforts to remind her she is my patient and I should be the one looking after her.'

Abigail took her brother's arm and looked up at him with affection.

'I am sorry, my dear brother, but it simply is not possible for me to think of Eliza as my doctor when I know we are going to be true friends, first and foremost.'

'I am glad to hear it,' he said, patting her hand. 'You see, Dr. Hawksmith, your very presence may be the best medicine Abigail could wish for. And I confess to finding my own spirits lifted by your being here. Can I persuade you to dine with us this evening?'

Eliza felt an unfamiliar quickening of her pulse, a rare flutter of excitement. For an instant, she considered accepting the invitation but shook her head.

'Regrettably I cannot,' she said. 'I have my Whitechapel clinic. This is one of our busier evenings.'

'Another time perhaps?' He cocked his head slightly.

Eliza smiled.

'Another time,' she agreed.

That night Eliza's sleep was troubled by dreams. She dreamed she was at a fabulous ball wearing a gown of the finest cream silk. All around her, love-struck couples swirled and turned to the urgent tempo of a tarantella. Suddenly a man of proud bearing and noble features took her in his arms and spun her onto the dance floor. They danced and danced and danced, her own feet a blur in silver slippers, the music growing faster and louder. Soon the other dancers had melted into a chaos of whirling colors, and Eliza was overwhelmed with dizziness. Her partner held her tight, pulling her body firmly against his. He pressed his cheek against hers, then leaned forward to nuzzle into her neck. Still they danced. Eliza felt his hot breath on her skin, and then his wet tongue sliding across her throat. She struggled to pull away from him. When she succeeded in gaining a small space between them, the sight which met her eyes drew from her a terrified scream. Her dancing partner still retained his strong, lithe body, but his head had been replaced by that of a wolf. Its foul breath forced its way into Eliza's nostrils, and bitter saliva drooled from its mouth into her own as she screamed.

4

In the weeks that followed Eliza came to enjoy her visits to the Astredge household more and more. In Abigail's company she felt more relaxed than anywhere else, and she had even admitted to herself that her affection for Simon was deepening. It quickly became obvious to her that he too had a high regard for her. As was her habit, she fought against such a connection, afraid of the heartache it could bring. But, on occasions, there were moments when she allowed her emotions to overwhelm caution. She longed to be loved. To allow herself to love another. Years could pass where she would put such ideas into some locked place in her heart where they would not trouble her. Then someone would step into her life who held the key, and the yearning of years was set free. She wanted to give in to her desire for Simon. A desire she had not felt in such strength since she was a teenager—since Gideon. Now here was a good man, a kind man, well thought of by those who knew him, a loving brother with a gentle heart. A man Eliza could lose herself to in an instant if she allowed herself.

By the first week in September, Eliza spent more time at number 4 York Terrace than she did at the Fitzroy. She often stayed to dine with Abigail and Simon, no longer the doctor but a dear friend. She was on the point of leaving her office to make her way to the house for just such a visit when shouts from the street caught her ear. She looked from the window and saw a newspaper boy doing brisk trade on the pavement below. He continued to yell out the news as he handed over papers and pocketed coins.

'Latest News! Read it 'ere! The Ripper strikes again. Another woman cut to pieces!'

Eliza closed her eyes, her fingers tightening around the curtain. Another murder. The third, apparently, in the unstoppable killings of the man they had nicknamed Jack the Ripper. Eliza could not face the thought of reading the hideous details, though she knew she would have to. She knew there would be gruesome descriptions of the exact and awful way the poor woman had been slain. She knew also, with a dreadful certainty, that the victim would be another of the girls who visited her clinic. Was it coincidence? Could it be? How long could she go on convincing herself that these poor women were randomly selected, thrown into the murderer's path by chance, nothing more? How many more would die before she allowed herself to think the unthinkable—that they were all connected to her. That their violent deaths had something, somehow, to do with her.

That afternoon Abigail felt strong enough for a short walk. It was a sweet autumn day, warm enough for a light shawl, and the two women made their way through the entrance to the park and along the little path that wound its way through the trees to the ornamental ponds.

'Oh, Eliza, how such a gleaming afternoon lifts the spirits. It is so long since I have taken the air; I have spent too many days shut up in the house. Surely exercise can only improve my health. Will you not prescribe a short walk for me every day? Then I should have to take one, come rain or shine.'

'Light exertion is indeed beneficial to the circulation and to a person's general well-being,' said Eliza, 'but those benefits must be weighed against the risk of fatigue. Your strength is needed to combat the disease that has you in its grip, Abigail. To put yourself in a weakened state would be to undermine your body's ability to win that battle.'

'Oh, pish.' Abigail linked her arm through Eliza's. 'Do not speak to me of disease when the sun is shining and those silly ducks are waddling across the grass, and adorable children are playing among those magnificent trees. I feel my legs could carry me for days without rest. And besides'—she smiled—'I have my very own doctor at my side. What possible harm could befall me?'

'It is good to see you smiling again.' Eliza squeezed her friend's hand. She wanted to enjoy the day, to revel in the peacefulness of the moment, but her mind would not empty itself of thoughts of the murdered women. Terrible thoughts and even more terrible images.

'Oh, do look.' Abigail pointed across the lawn to a gaggle of children clamoring around a cow. The animal stood half asleep, a white-smocked farmer seated on a three-legged stool beside it. He finished milking and stood up. The children arranged themselves into a disorderly queue, ushered by their nursemaids, nannies, and mothers. The cow chewed quietly while the farmer ladled milk into tin cups.

'Let's have some.' Abigail pulled Eliza across the grass. 'Come. Put your fears of fatigue from your mind. A drink of milk is surely just the restorative your patient requires. Do you not think so?'

Abigail took a penny from her purse and handed it to the farmer. He filled another cup and handed it to her. Abigail drank deeply, the frothy milk leaving a delicate line of white above her top lip. She beamed and passed the cup to Eliza. 'It's delicious. You try,' she said.

Eliza put the cup to her mouth and took a sip. Her face contorted and it was all she could do not to start retching. The milk was undrinkably sour, curdled, and ruined.

'Oh, but Abigail. This milk is bad. It has turned sour.'

'What nonsense, Eliza. I have just tasted it.' Abigail snatched back the mug and sniffed at what remained of the milk. She frowned. Her face darkened for a moment in a way Eliza had not seen before. Suddenly she tipped the liquid onto the grass and returned the cup to the farmer. 'I can't think what you mean,' she said. 'It tasted perfectly fine to me. Come along.' She took Eliza's arm once more and marched her away from the cow. 'Let us take a stroll beside the zoo.'

Eliza was at a loss to make sense of what had just taken place. She had seen Abigail drink the milk, but she herself could not take down so much as a sip it was so rancid. Why had Abigail not noticed it? And why had she sought to pretend it was good when it wasn't? It was a small, seemingly insignificant incident but one which bothered Eliza. She found the day had lost its golden glow and was relieved when they completed their circuit of the park and returned to the house.

Two days later, Eliza entered Dr. Gimmel's rooms to find Gresseti already there.

'Ah, my dear Eliza.' Dr. Gimmel sprang to his feet. 'We were on the point of leaving.'

'Oh?'

'I am taking Signor Gresseti to meet a Sir Edmund Weekes. During his stay here, our visitor has developed an interest in circulatory disorders and there is no finer surgeon in the field than Sir Edmund.' He took his hat from the stand and gave her a wave as he disappeared through the door.

'We shall return before afternoon surgery, have no fear,' he called back to her.

Gresseti bowed low before replacing his hat and edging past Eliza. She moved aside, not wishing to have the slightest unnecessary contact with the man. Gresseti paused, clearly aware of her reluctance to be near him.

'I see you are still cross with me, Dr. Hawksmith. I fear I am paying for my outspoken nature. Please, I wished no offense. It is merely my manner, which might seem strange to you. I implore you, do not let a poor beginning spoil our working relationship.'

Eliza feigned brightness. 'Rest assured, Signor, our working relationship remains unaffected.'

'Gresseti? Come along now, we must not keep Sir Edmund waiting.' Dr. Gimmel summoned him from Mr. Thomas's reception room.

Gresseti paused, seemingly about to say something more, then changed his mind and went after the doctor.

Eliza found she had been holding her breath in his presence. She shook her head. What was it about the man that unsettled her so? Was it merely his unfamiliar manner? A thought occurred to her. She opened the door and leaned through.

'Mr. Thomas, has Signor Gresseti signed our register at any time during his visit here?' she asked.

'Why yes, Dr. Hawksmith, I believe he did so on his first morning with us.' Mr. Thomas licked a finger and leafed through the pages of the register on his desk. 'Yes, thought so. Here we are.' He turned the book around and pointed to Gresseti's name written with an elegant flourish.

'Let me have this a moment, would you?' Eliza took the book back into the other room before Mr. Thomas could ask why she wanted it. She shut the door and sat down behind Dr. Gimmel's desk. After a moment's hesitation, and quelling her uneasiness about what she was about to do, Eliza began to search through the drawers. Minutes later she held in her hand the letter of introduction from the Milan Institute. It was written as if by Professor Salvatores and signed by him, but the writing matched that on the register exactly. The letter must have been written by Gresseti himself. His credentials were fake. Eliza was sure of it. Of course, there was a small chance that the professor had asked Gresseti to pen the letter to save himself the trouble, but then surely he would have had his clerk do it. Eliza leaned back in the wide leather chair. She had always harbored suspicions about Gresseti but had quelled them, reasoning his references were impeccable and she had nothing to fear beyond his rudeness. Now, however, things were different. If his letter of introduction was bogus, then they knew nothing about him at all. Who would bother to forge a letter to gain access to the hospital? A rival surgeon? Someone sent to check up on Dr. Gimmel's capabilities? As Eliza's mind teemed with possibilities, she spotted a cane in the umbrella stand. Gresseti's black, silver-topped cane. The sound she had heard in the alley behind her clinic came back to her. The sound made by someone hiding in the shadows. The sound that had spooked her on the night of Martha's murder. Eliza hurried over to the cane and picked it up. It was heavier than she had expected, the wood warm beneath her fingers, the silver top cool. She shook it gently and heard a faint rattle, a minute vibration in her hand. It was hollow. There was definitely something inside. It must, therefore, have a removable lid. She was on the point of lifting it when the door was flung open and Gresseti strode in. When he saw the cane in her hand, he stopped and frowned. He quickly rearranged his features and smiled politely, his eyes remaining unmoved by the gesture.

'Ah, Dr. Hawksmith, I returned for my cane, and here you have already found it. You see how forgetful a man can be when he does not have a wife to train him?' He reached out and gently took the cane from Eliza. 'Thank you so much. Until later . . .' He touched his hat and was gone.

Eliza stood where she was for some time, her heart thumping loudly.

That night Eliza worked late at the hospital. There were only so many hours in the day, and her increasingly lengthy visits to Abigail were causing paperwork to mount on her desk and patients to have passed from her care to that of other doctors. By the time she stepped off the omnibus and made her way down Whitechapel High Street, the day was old and a choking fog had descended. The gas lamps on the broader streets gave at least small pools of light, but the back alleys and side streets were thick with gray air and gathering darkness. Because of the lateness of the hour, the usual muddle of people had dwindled. The weather kept all indoors who did not need to be outside.

Eliza pulled her shawl tighter around her shoulders and quickened her step. Droplets of fog gathered and fell from the brim of her bonnet. As she hurried down Marchmont Street, she became aware of footsteps behind her quickening to match her own. She turned the corner around the draper's shop, closed and shuttered, its friendly proprietor having called an end to the day's business hours before. As she turned, she glanced backward and was convinced she saw a figure moving swiftly, close to the wall, his step purposeful. Eliza licked foggy moisture from her lips into her dry mouth. It took all her will to resist the urge to run. She searched for signs of other people, anyone, but the cobbles were deserted. The fog thickened, a bitter concoction of dirty water, dampened smoke, and the sour smells of the street. The distance left to her lodgings was but a few minutes walk, but it was as though the ground stretched away beneath her feet. Her pursuer was closer now. She dared not look back. She hurled herself around a corner and walked straight into the solid chest of a burly drunk.

'Oi! Why don't you watch where you're going?' His words were slurred.

'I'm sorry. Please, let me pass.' Eliza tried to step round the man, but he grabbed hold of her, his grimy hands closing around her arms.

'Nah, where's your 'urry, little lady? Seems to me you came running into me arms, so you did.' He pushed his body against hers and began to march her backward until they reached the opposite wall.

'Let me go!' Eliza snatched her arms from him, but he pinned her against the rough stone, his weight easily double her own.

'Now then, how about a little kiss, eh?' He lurched toward her face with his own.

Eliza turned her head and screamed, but he was not so easily deterred. She felt a hand forcing its way down inside the front of her dress. She kicked at his shins, but he was so numbed by ale that he barely flinched.

'Like to play a bit of a rough game, then, do yer? All right, if that's what you want, you little pinchprick!' The man wrenched at her clothing, tearing the bodice of her dress and exposing her corset. He plunged his face into her bosom. Eliza opened her mouth to scream again, but at that moment the man was hauled off her with startling speed. Someone possessed of enormous strength had caught him by the scruff and yanked him backward off his feet, throwing him onto the wet cobbles.

'What the . . . ?' The man scrambled to get up, stunned by the sudden switch in his position from attacker to attacked.

From the fog, a tall figure in top hat and swirling cape emerged. Gresseti. Eliza tugged her clothes over her exposed breasts. The drunk stood up and launched himself at Gresseti, who sidestepped, causing the thug to fall flailing into the gutter once more.

'You bastard!' he shouted as he thrashed about in the debris and filth. 'I'll 'ave yer yet! I'll teach yer to lay 'ands on me!' He was about to get up for a second time, when in one fluid movement, Gresseti removed the top of his cane and drew out a gleaming sword. He brought its point to rest at the man's throat. The drunkard froze.

'I think, Signor,' said Gresseti slowly, 'that you would do better to leave this place while you are still able to do so.'

There was a moment of absolute stillness before the man bolted. Gresseti watched him go. Eliza watched Gresseti. After the smallest of pauses, he sheathed his sword and shut the lid. Silently. The silver top of the cane, which formed the hilt of the weapon, was returned to its home with a twist and made no sound whatsoever. Eliza stepped away from the wall. Gresseti turned to smile at her.

'He has gone. I think he will trouble you no more,' he said.

'You . . . you were following me.' Eliza failed to keep the tremble out of her voice.

Gresseti gave no reply, merely raising his chin a fraction and narrowing his eyes.

'You were following me,' Eliza said again, stronger this time. 'Why? What do you want?'

Gresseti took a pace toward Eliza. She instinctively took one back but found herself against the wall once more.

'Forgive me,' he said, his voice the purr of a tiger, 'but you must know I find you . . . fascinating, Dr. Hawksmith. In the short time I have been in your company, I have developed an affection for you that I can no longer hide.'

Eliza took her courage in both hands.

'Signor'—she spat the word at him—'be under no illusion. That affection is not returned. Indeed, I have no interest in you other than that required of me in my capacity as Dr. Gimmel's assistant. Your attentions are unwelcome.'

'Ah, Bess, once again I have caused offense where none was intended. I implore you . . .'

'*What?*' Eliza's voice rose to a shout. 'What did you call me?'

Gresseti was confused. He shrugged. 'I believe Bess to be an affectionate form of the name Elizabeth, is it not correct? And that is your full name, I know this. I have seen it written on correspondence in Dr. Gimmel's office . . .'

Eliza did not wait to hear more. Pushing past him, she fled into the night, letting the fog swallow her up before Gresseti had the opportunity to utter another word.

5

The following Thursday evening, Eliza dined with Abigail and Simon. She had noticed a distinct decline in her patient's strength in the preceding days. After their meal, the three settled in the drawing room by the fire. Eliza made Abigail comfortable on the sofa and she was soon asleep, her breathing shallow. There was something about her when sleeping that made her look so much more unwell than when she was awake and animated. Eliza stroked her hair for a moment. It was clear to her that they could not put off surgery for much longer. She had to remain optimistic, for all their sakes, but in her heart she feared Abigail was not strong enough to survive such a dangerous and grueling operation.

'Come'—she felt Simon's hand on her arm—'sit with me.' He drew her over to the small sofa on the other side of the fireplace. A vase of peacock feathers stood beside it. Eliza touched the delicate edges, sending a ripple through the iridescent purples and greens.

'So beautiful,' she murmured.

'Some consider them to be unlucky.'

'We don't.'

'We?'

'That is, my . . . family.' She corrected herself, surprised at how close she had come to telling him that most witches had them in their homes.

'You have spoken very little about them.' Simon smoothed the fabric of her skirt over her knee as he spoke. Such casual gestures of intimacy between them had become natural whenever they were unobserved.

'There are none living now,' she said simply.

'Like myself, you too are alone in the world.'

'But you have Abigail.'

He glanced at her, then nodded. Eliza wondered if he had accepted the probability that Abigail was going to die. Did he already consider himself alone? How she longed to hold him and tell him she would always be at his side, that he need not fear loneliness ever again. But she could not. How could she allow him to care for her, knowing as she did that at any time she might have to flee, to run from his life forever without explanation. How could she subject him to that when he had already faced losing everyone he loved?

'Why so sad?' Simon asked, slipping his arm around her shoulders and kissing her cheek.

Eliza closed her eyes and savored the delicious moment of closeness. She must stay strong. She must keep her head. Abigail's recovery depended on it. And so did Simon's future happiness. And she wanted him to be happy, very much. She mustered a smile.

'Not sad, just a little weary.'

'You do too much, my love.'

'There is much to be done. The clinic is busy, as ever, and Dr. Gimmel has come to rely on me more and more.'

'He is very lucky to have you. As are we all.' He took her hand from her lap and pressed it to his lips. Eliza gave a little laugh and stood up suddenly.

'Mr. Astredge, I believe you are taking advantage of me,' she teased.

'Don't go.' He sprang from the sofa.

'Well,' she said, walking briskly over to the card table, 'if you promise to behave yourself I will agree to a short game of canasta. It is about time someone taught you how to play properly.'

'Oh, is it now? We'll see about that!' Simon sat at the table and picked up the cards, attempting to shuffle them deftly. He succeeded only in dropping most of them on the floor. Eliza laughed, watching him scrabble about for the cards and his dignity, and thought she had never loved a man more in her life.

In the morning, Eliza arrived late at the hospital. She undid the ribbon of her bonnet as she hurried past Thomas.

'Good morning, Mr. Thomas. Has Dr. Gimmel arrived yet?'

'He has, Doctor, about half an hour ago. I was just going to fetch some tea. Shall I bring another cup?'

'Thank you, tea would be most welcome.'

Mr. Thomas disappeared into the small kitchen behind his office. As he did so, Gresseti stepped into the room from the hallway.

'Dr. Hawksmith, good morning to you. I am happy to find you looking in such good health after your alarming encounter with the drunkard.' He showed no signs of awkwardness, though this was the first time they had met since the incident near her lodgings. It was as if he chose only to remember he had been her rescuer, nothing more.

'I am well, thank you.' Eliza hesitated. She could not go on any longer without confronting him about the letter of introduction. If there was a simple explanation, she wanted to hear it. She had to know the truth about him. Part of her was terrified at the thought of confronting him. Her tactic in the past, where Gideon was concerned, had always been to vanish the moment she was certain of his identity but before he became aware that she knew. This time, however, the matter was more complicated. She could not leave Abigail, not now. And if she was being honest with herself, she knew she did not want to leave Simon.

'Signor Gresseti,' she started, 'I was wondering, how long have you been connected with the Institute in Milan?'

'Many years. Why do you ask?'

They were interrupted by Dr. Gimmel emerging from his office at speed.

'Ah, Eliza, you're here. Thank heavens.'

'Whatever is the matter?'

'I have just heard from Simon Astredge. Abigail has collapsed.'

'What?'

'She is unconscious, and he is unable to rouse her.' Dr. Gimmel strode past. 'We must hurry, Dr. Hawksmith,' he called to her as he went.

Eliza ran after him. Gresseti would have to wait.

At the house, they found Simon pacing the hall waiting for them.

'Thank God you've come.' He grabbed Eliza's hand and pulled her toward the stairs.

'When did it happen?' she asked.

'About an hour ago. Her maid was helping her dress. At first we thought she had fainted, but I cannot wake her. She is in her bed. Come, this way.'

The three hurried up the broad staircase and along the landing. Abigail's room was at the front of the house overlooking the park. Two full-length windows let in soft morning light. Sunshine fell on the brass bed and rosebud linen. Abigail lay propped against feather pillows, her eyes closed but lids fluttering lightly. Her breath was ragged and irregular. Her color was pale, with a blueness around her mouth. Dr. Gimmel reached the bed first. He lifted an eyelid and examined her pupil. Next, he put his stethoscope over her heart and her lungs. Eliza stood on the other side of the bed. She placed her fingers on the pulse in Abigail's neck and measured the irregular beats.

'What is it?' asked Simon. 'What has happened? I know she has been tired of late, but this . . . this is so unexpected. I don't understand.'

Dr. Gimmel and Eliza exchanged worried glances. Dr. Gimmel straightened up and left Abigail's side.

'Your sister's condition, as you can see, has become more serious. I had hoped that medication might arrest the advancement of the disease, but . . .'

At that moment Abigail moaned. She stirred, slowly opening her eyes. 'Eliza? Is that you?'

'I am here, Abigail. Do not be afraid.'

'Oh, how do I come to be back in my bed? Dr. Gimmel? I have put everyone to so much trouble.' She struggled to sit up.

'Lie still, my dear.' Dr. Gimmel smiled at her. 'You must conserve your strength. Bed rest for you. Not the slightest exertion, do you hear? Mr. Astredge, I will send a nurse from the Fitzroy. Your sister must not be allowed to get up and must not be overtired by company, is that clear?'

'Perfectly.'

'Dr. Hawksmith will be in attendance, of course. We will increase your medication, but it is rest that is required, first and foremost, at this point.' He beckoned to Simon and walked with him to the corner of the room. Eliza took Abigail's hand and squeezed it. Despite their low voices, she could clearly hear the conversation between the two men.

'What is to be done?' Simon asked.

The look on his face tore at Eliza's heart.

Dr. Gimmel put a comforting hand on his shoulder.

'I fear we cannot put off surgery much longer,' he said.

'But she is so weak.'

'Indeed, but there remain no further avenues for us to explore. We will let her rest and assess her strength in a day or two. Let us hope this episode will pass so that she might regain sufficient vitality to face the procedure.'

Eliza felt Abigail tighten her hold on her hand.

'I am dying, am I not, Eliza? Please, tell me the truth.'

Her loose hair flowed out against the pillow like seaweed pulled by a gentle tide. Her skin had an alarming tautness to it, and her eyes appeared to sit deeper in their sockets. Eliza felt rage at the unjust nature of disease. She stood looking down at her dear friend, as helplessly as she had stood next to her brother. And her father. And her sister. How could she do nothing when it lay within her power to save her?

She sat on the edge of the bed and forced herself to speak brightly.

'Abigail, you are my patient, and I am not about to let you die, do you hear me?'

Abigail smiled. 'Do you forbid it, Doctor?'

'I forbid it absolutely.'

'Then, of course, I must not. To allow oneself to pass away under such diligent care would be the height of bad manners, do you not agree?'

'I do. Now, you must rest. I will visit the apothecary at the hospital and then return later today. I will send you a nurse.'

'A gentle one, please.'

'A fierce one,' Eliza told her, 'to keep you in your bed, Miss Astredge.' She stood up, tucking the sheets around the girl. 'Sleep. That is my instruction.'

'Very well, Doctor.' Abigail closed her eyes, already beginning to drift. 'I will be a good patient and do as I am bid.'

That night, Eliza headed back to her lodgings with a heavy heart. She had concocted a potion for Abigail that would give her strength and had been pleased to see her a little brighter by teatime, but there was no escaping the fact that surgery would be calamitous for her in her current state. The fog had barely lifted in the day and now thickened again as dusk fell. The market was being cleared away, and Eliza picked her way through discarded rotten vegetables and litter. The music from the organ grinder drifted through the gloom strangely distorted and muffled by the weather. The lamp lighter was just descending his ladder from the lamp outside Mrs. Garvey's house when Eliza felt her stomach turn over. She stopped, straining to listen more carefully. At first she thought her troubled mind was playing a trick on her, but the more she listened, the more horribly real the sound that reached her ears became. The tune flowing through the congested air was unmistakable. Eliza dashed toward its source, bumping heedlessly into other people, ignoring their shouts. She reached the organ grinder at the precise moment the melody came to an end.

'Who asked you for that tune?' she demanded.

'What?' The bearded man's eyes widened in his whiskery face at the urgency of her request.

'You were playing "Greensleeves." Who paid you for that melody? Where is the man who requested it?' She looked about her at the anonymous shapes looming in and out of the fog.

'"Greensleeves" you say?' The organ grinder shook his head. 'I haven't got that one. Could play you a nice waltz if you like.'

'But I heard it. I heard "Greensleeves,"' Eliza insisted.

'Not from me you didn't, love.' He shrugged and began to turn the handle again. The jarring notes of a military march began to assault Eliza's ears. 'Here you go, something to stir the blood and chase away this damp ol' weather, eh?'

Eliza stared at him, shaking her head. She backed away, all the time searching, searching, searching the fathomless faces about her. At last her nerve failed her, and she ran to the door, slamming it shut behind her. Ignoring Mrs. Garvey's inquiries as to her well-being, she tore upstairs and threw herself on the bed, her hands over her ears, her legs curled up, wondering if the nightmare would ever end.

6

Eliza sat at her desk in Dr. Gimmel's room, poring over reports of the Whitechapel murders. The details made gruesome reading. The killer had not been content with merely ending the lives of his wretched victims but had also horribly mutilated them. Martha had dozens of slashes and stab wounds. Mary Ann Nicholls had been partially disemboweled. Poor Annie Chapman had had her head almost cut from her body. Certainly these killings had been the work of an evil and deranged mind, yet there was skill here too. These were not the wild slicings of a frenzied knife but incisions made with deliberate precision. Care, almost. Eliza thought of Gresseti's sword. Certainly such a weapon could have caused some of the broader wounds, but it would not have allowed for the careful removal of specific organs. An instrument far more exact would be required. As would a fair knowledge of anatomy. There had already been theories put forward that the Ripper might be a butcher. Or a surgeon. In Eliza's mind there was no doubt that the man responsible for these terrible crimes must be someone with medical skills and training. The thought made her feel sick. What would drive a person to use knowledge acquired to heal for the purpose of such barbarity and cruelty? What evil mind could conceive of such cold-blooded and brutal treatment of defenseless women?

Eliza knew of just such a mind. Of just such a person. A man who would stop at nothing to achieve his goal. To claim her. Not simply to kill her; he was not interested in revenge. He wanted her to be his. He wanted her soul. Could it be that Gresseti was Gideon? Could it be that these women were dying as a result of his persecution of her? If she stayed, how many more women would be slain? But if she left, who would save Abigail? Eliza let the newspaper fall onto her desk and rubbed her temples. She had to find a way of getting rid of Gresseti, but who would help her? Dr. Gimmel still believed him to have been recommended by Professor Salvatores. Perhaps if she could show his credentials to be false, he would be sent away. She took a sheet of writing paper from the drawer and picked up a pen. She dipped it into the inkwell. She would write to the institute herself, asking them to confirm some detail about Gresseti. As soon as she received a reply showing that they did not know the man, she would alert Dr. Gimmel. It could be that her deep-seated fear and wariness of strangers had warped her judgment. Gresseti might not be Gideon. But even if he were not, she did not trust him. The sooner he was sent away, the better. If the killings stopped, she would have her answer. As long as he remained unaware of how close she was to exposing his lack of bone fides, she felt reasonably sure he would not confront her.

She began to write, fighting off a feeling of panic that Gresseti himself might appear at any moment and discover what she was doing. She chided herself for not having thought of contacting the institute sooner. Her pen scratched its way across the vellum. Abruptly, she stopped. She stared at the words she had just written. For formality's sake she had written his name in full—Signor Damon Gresseti. She snatched up another sheet of paper and wrote the letters of his first and second name in a rough circle, leaving out his title. Her mind raced as she rearranged the letters, crossing them off one by one until she had used them all up to form a different name. A perfect anagram. Precisely the sort of game he would delight in playing. She dropped her pen as if it had burned her fingers and gasped at the words she had formed on the page: Gideon Masters.

Eliza arrived at number 4 York Terrace less than half an hour after her discovery. She was certain now that Gresseti was indeed Gideon and that he had been responsible for the Whitechapel murders. She was tortured with guilt and despair at the thought that the killings had been somehow her own fault. If she had not been living in Whitechapel, if she had not set up her clinic there, Gresseti . . . Gideon, would never have known the place. And Martha, Mary Ann, and Annie would still be alive. By the time she reached Abigail's bedroom, Eliza was beyond concealing her distress. Simon rose from his seat at the bedside, alarmed at Eliza's distraught appearance.

'My dearest Eliza, whatever can have happened? Come, sit by the fire. Tell me what has brought you to this state.' He took her hands and led her to the small sofa on the far side of the room.

'I must tend to Abigail,' Eliza protested.

'My sister is sleeping happily. She will wait a little longer. It is you who needs care at this moment.' He took her bonnet from her head and tenderly stroked her cheek. 'Won't you tell me what is wrong?'

Eliza closed her eyes against the tears that were threatening to spill from them. Tears! The first in so many years. The first since she had stood with her mother in the Batchcombe jail. She had promised her then there would be no more. But now, with Simon so supportive, so attentive, so willing to take on her troubles, now she felt more vulnerable than she had all the long decades that she had dwelled alone.

'I cannot tell you,' she said. 'I wish with all my heart I could, but . . .' She shook her head.

'Is there anything I can do to help?'

'There is nothing.'

'Even so, you might find that sharing your worries with another, that is, with me, well, there is some solace to be had. I would not see you alone in your suffering. I have allowed myself to believe we are friends. Close friends. Friends who should be able to confide in each other. To offer support.'

'All I can tell you is that there is someone I fear. Someone who is not what he claims to be. And I believe him capable of terrible things.'

'Who?'

Eliza shook her head.

'Dearest, you must tell me. I cannot bear to think of you afraid. How can I protect you if I do not know from which direction the danger comes?'

Eliza took a breath. 'Promise me you will not act rashly if I give you his identity. He must not know I have discovered the deception. Do you give your word you will not confront him?'

'Very well, reluctantly, yes. You have my word.'

'It is Signor Gresseti.'

Simon's face darkened. A small muscle at the corner of his left eye began to twitch.

'The Italian at the Fitzroy? But Dr. Gimmel speaks so highly of the man. Are you certain?'

'Yes. Beyond any doubt. The man is an impostor, and he is dangerous. Do not ask me to explain further, I beg of you.'

'Have you voiced your fears to Dr. Gimmel?'

'I cannot, before I obtain proof. I have written to the Institute in Milan. I am awaiting their reply. In the meantime . . .' She trailed off, her voice faltering.

Simon let go her hands and stood up.

'In the meantime you must come to stay here with us. No, I will hear no objections. What manner of friend would I be to allow you to traverse London alone daily while you fear this man? Whatever he has done, whatever his intentions, he will not assail you here. I am sure of it.'

'But my clinic . . .'

'Can do without you for a short while until this creature is exposed and sent packing. As soon as you have the proof you require and have alerted Dr. Gimmel, I myself will take great delight in booting the villain all the way back to the Mediterranean if necessary.' He held up a hand, 'Say nothing further, Eliza. I will not be moved on this matter. I will send a carriage to your lodgings this day to collect what belongings you require.'

Eliza felt such relief at the idea of living under Simon's protection that for a second time she thought she might weep. She met Simon's determined gaze.

'Very well,' she said quietly, 'I will accept your kind offer. Only send your carriage late this evening. I must open the doors of the clinic once more so that I can inform my patients I will be away for a few days. It would not be fair to simply disappear.'

'But you will come? The minute the clinic is closed?'

'I will.' She stood up and stepped into his open arms, resting her head against his chest as his gentle hands smoothed the back of her gown. 'I will.'

It had been Eliza's intention to go straight home after seeing Simon, but she realized there were medicines she required from the apothecary. If the clinic was to be closed for a short time, she would need to ensure that her patients had their medicaments in sufficient quantities to last until her return. She browsed the shelves of the pharmacopoeia, selecting bottles and jars until her bag was almost too full to shut properly. While she was helping herself to a bundle of bandages and dressings, Roland appeared behind her.

'Dr. Hawksmith, what a surprise to find you here.' His grin was pleasant enough, but Eliza caught the chiding note in his voice.

'Roland. I am aware I have not been spending as much time with my patients here at the Fitzroy as I should of late. I have had duties elsewhere.'

'So I understand.' He let the subject drop and passed her a packet of lint. 'Supplies for your clinic? It must be a fearful place to work at the moment. I understand some of the victims were among your patients.'

It was a measure of the widespread horror at the Ripper's actions that Roland did not have to mention whose victims he meant. The murders were the talk of London. Of the world, indeed.

'Yes.' Eliza clipped her bag shut. 'Two of them were, certainly. I am not sure about the third.'

'The third? Then, you have not heard?'

'Heard what?'

'There have been more killings.'

'More?'

'Why yes, last night.' Seeing how shocked she was, Roland sought to explain himself. 'I am sorry, Dr. Hawksmith, I assumed you knew. It was in the papers this morning. Two women this time. Yes, two in one night. Both dreadfully cut up . . . the most awful business.' Roland was left talking to an empty space as Eliza snatched up her bag and ran from the room.

The journey home gave her time to form a plan, so that when she arrived back at Hebden Street Eliza knew exactly what she was going to do. Gideon had to be stopped. And she had to stop him. There was no time to wait for letters from Milan. No time for half measures. She would confront him herself. She would do whatever was necessary to rid the world of this evil being. No more women would die because of him. Because of her. No more.

The clinic was not busy. The fog had been replaced by steady rain. The bad weather and the fear that washed the streets along with it kept all indoors who did not have a need to be abroad. Even those women whose livelihoods depended upon their tramping the alleyways and side roads had largely decided the risk was too great. The girls all knew one another. Some had lost close friends. The nature of the killings was well known and the horror too terrifying to face. Eliza waited until only one patient remained in the small room. A painfully young girl with a heartbreaking cough. Eliza touched her sleeve as she was about to go.

'Wait,' she said, 'just a moment.'

The girl regarded her with shadowy eyes.

'Connie, isn't it?'

'Yes, Doctor.' The girl's voice was hoarse.

'I have a favor to ask of you. I know it may seem strange, but, well, I hope you will simply accept that I have my reasons for asking. Will you help me?'

'Yeah, course I will. Don't see as I can do much, but you just tell me what you want, Doctor.'

'Look,' Eliza said, 'look at this.' She took from the corner table a pretty green dress of fine cotton with lace at the collar and cuffs. 'It is your size, I think. The color would suit you. Will you swap your clothes for this dress?'

'What, these old scraps? What use are they to you?'

'Never mind that. Just say you will.'

Connie reached out and touched the fresh fabric, her face brightening as her fingers glided over the embroidered detail at the waist.

'Go on then,' she said. 'Beats me why you want to, but, yeah, I'll do it.'

'One more thing.' Eliza pulled the dress away from the girl. 'You must go straight home tonight. Do you understand? No working. Straight home. Promise?'

'All right.' Connie shrugged and nodded. 'I promise.'

Within the hour, wearing Connie's shabby but gaudy clothes, with her hair piled up beneath a flowery hat, Eliza was strolling the darkest streets of Whitechapel, the rain quickly seeping through her shawl. She walked slowly, waiting, listening, knowing he would find her. She did not have to wait long.

As she turned into a narrow cul de sac, she could plainly hear footsteps behind her. She passed a cat crouched low at the sight of her. It wailed as the man following her drew nearer. Eliza reached the dead end and turned, keeping her head bowed, her face hidden in the darkness beneath the brim of her hat. A tall figure came to stand only a few paces in front of her. The rain was warm but incessant, puddling the streets. It provided an unnerving, relentless sound, the hissing of a hundred angry snakes. In the distance hoofbeats could be heard as a hansom cab hurried over the cobbles. Somewhere piano music and drunken singing drifted on the night air. With her head lowered, Eliza could see only her pursuer's feet, his highly polished shoes, the fine cloth of his trousers, the hem of his silk-lined cape. And his black cane, its silver top reflected in a puddle by the dull light of a nearby gaslamp.

Gresseti's voice was unmistakable.

'Good evening to you, Signorina. Have you time to spare to entertain a gentleman this night?'

Eliza closed her eyes. The moment had come. It seemed fitting that she should at last choose to confront Gideon on this night. Walpurgisnacht. Samhain. Halloween. During the hours of darkness on the eve of All Saints' Day, restless spirits walked the earth. The underworld was touchable; a door opened and its inhabitants were drawn back into the tangible world. This was the perfect moment to connect with those who would help her. Her sisters in witchcraft. Now she would unleash her own long-buried power. She turned to a place in her mind she had not allowed herself to visit for centuries. A place of hidden strength. A place of wonder. A place of magic. Long-forgotten words began to form in her mouth, filling it up, pressing against her teeth, eager to be spoken aloud. She summoned the strength that she knew dwelled within her, though it had lain dormant for so many years. Behind her closed lids, rainbows of color played out a chaotic display. In her ears, she felt the breath of a thousand voices whispering, urging her on, echoing her own silent incantations. Power surged up through her body, a tide of will, a ferocious heat, a glorious, electrifying, seething energy. As she felt her body transformed, Eliza slowly opened her eyes and lifted her face. A face that had about it now the evanescence of magic.

Gresetti gasped as he recognized Eliza, his mouth opening in wonder at the radiance of her expression. Then he smiled, a long, thin slither of a smile that wound its way around his face like a snake coiling back, ready to strike.

'Why, Bess,' he said, 'look at you. I always said one day you would be magnificent.'

As he spoke his features began to blur. As Eliza watched the man who had been Gresseti twisted and pulsated, melting into the half-light and the rain before reforming into a solid being. Now Gideon stood before her. He was dressed in the same somber black clothes and hat she remembered. His face was still as strong and seductively handsome as ever. The smile he wore was dangerously warm. His body was broad shouldered but lithe and youthful. She could smell desire on him as he took a step toward her.

'I have waited so very long to stand face to face with you once again, Bess. I saw the brilliance shining out of you all those years ago, when you were not much more than a child. You were a Bel fire waiting to be ignited. I was merely the spark that grew to the flame inside you. The flame that fuels your power now. Your power and your desire. You feel it still, don't you, Bess? You cannot lie to me. I know your heart. You liked me well enough once, do you remember? Do you remember how your body burned with desire for me, night after night, hmmm? I told you then our time would come. And now it has. I know how you want me. We were always meant to be together, you and I.'

'Yes.' Eliza kept her voice level. 'The time has come. The time to put an end to all this. An end to the hunting. An end to the fear. An end to the killing.' She lifted her arms, stretching them out and up in supplication, drawing down the force of those she had called upon for help. Those she had summoned. 'Time to put an end to you, Gideon!' As she uttered his name, she brought her arms down to point at him with a whip crack of lightning. As Gideon reeled backward, she screamed the words of the spell, words she had memorized and practiced a thousand times in preparation for this very instant. The instant when she would conquer Gideon or die attempting to do so. One way or the other, her soul would be free of him at last.

Gideon hit the ground with bone-breaking force, but still he sprang up in a second. He seemed to grow before Eliza's eyes until he loomed above her, his own dark power emanating from him in sulfurous waves. He began to spin with such velocity that Eliza found herself being drawn into the whirlpool of his pulsating blackness. She screamed, annunciating the final words of the spell with her last breath before giddiness began to claim her senses.

Suddenly there was silence. Eliza found herself thrown onto the wet ground. She lay gasping for breath, fighting to rid her lungs of the toxic fumes that had filled them. She cast about her wildly, but she was alone. Completely alone. There was nothing to be seen of Gideon. Dumbfounded, she clambered to her feet and felt her way unsteadily along the street, leaning heavily on the stone wall of the buildings on one side, not trusting her legs to support her unaided. She listened for a telltale sound. She craned her neck, peering into the gloom in all directions. She sniffed the air. Nothing. No trace of him remained. Had the spell worked? Could it be true that she was really rid of the evil creature, free of him once and for all time? She had never imagined it would be so simple, that he would not fight against her, countering each blow she inflicted with a greater one of his own. She searched on, but he was nowhere. He had vanished. Had she succeeded in obliterating him, or was he merely hiding? She stayed in the alley, watching and waiting, wanting proof. But she could find none. Only time would tell if she was truly free of him or if he was simply biding his time. Pulling her sodden hat from her head and wiping her sweat-damp brow with the back of her hand, Eliza staggered in the direction of her lodgings to await Simon's carriage.

7

Eliza spent the days directly following her encounter with Gideon in a state of bewilderment. Part of her was still alert to the possibility of his reappearance, still waiting for him to play his final hand. She could not believe she had conquered him with such ease, and she was afraid to let down her guard, aware that he might be marshaling his resources for a surprise attack. Aside from this persistent fear, however, it was a time of wonder. Having utilized and unleashed the full force of her power as a witch, Eliza now walked on a different plane from the one she had inhabited previously. Her senses had become heightened to an extraordinary degree. Smells, sounds, sights, and tastes assaulted her every moment. She found herself unable to stand near a newly lit fire, for the fumes from the coal turned her stomach. She could detect the aroma of baking in the kitchen even while she was upstairs in Abigail's sickroom. She could clearly discern the words of whispered conversations in the street outside the drawing room window. From the bottom of the stairwell, she watched a spider on the ceiling at the top of the house spinning its web while she listened to the *click-clicking* of its legs as it worked. Cook's best soup was intolerably salty. The sweetness of an apple became an incomparable delight. Added to all this, Eliza was more aware of her body than ever she had been. She might be a witch, completely and undeniably now, but she was still first and foremost a woman. It was as if her desire had been trodden down along with her craft all those long, dry years, and now she was alight with it. Simon's presence became exquisite torture. Close proximity caused her breath to quicken, and the touch of his hand made her shiver with pleasure. She dared not let him kiss her for fear of utterly losing control. Her altered state did not go unnoticed. Abigail had recovered her strength a little and was sitting up in bed while Eliza read to her.

'Eliza, my dear, please slow down.'

'I'm sorry?'

'You read at so swift a pace I cannot take in what is happening.' Abigail laughed softly. 'Surely *Dr. Jekyll* was never meant to be understood at such a gallop.'

'Oh, I did not realize . . .' She closed the book and let it rest on her lap. 'How are you feeling? You look very much stronger.'

'Indeed, I am. I should be ready for you and Dr. Gimmel to do your best with me any day now.' She shifted her position against the pillows. 'Would you be so good as to pass me my shawl? Yes, that blue one, thank you.'

Eliza draped the soft woolen stole around Abigail's shoulders and tried to focus on the idea of performing surgery on her friend. She was right; they would operate very soon. Eliza still felt such a procedure might well prove fatal, but she was determined not to transmit her fears to Abigail, who was clearly trying so very hard to be brave. The door opened and Simon came in carrying a vase of flowers so vast he could barely be seen.

'For you both, ladies, to bring a little cheer to the room.'

'Oh, Simon.' Abigail clapped her hands. 'They are delightful.'

'And so many of them,' said Eliza. 'Did you buy up the entire flower stall?'

'I believe I left the odd buttonhole in case someone had need of one. Now, how about over here on this table? Abigail, can you see them from there?'

'I should imagine I could see them from the top of Primrose Hill. You spoil me, brother.'

He came over to the bed and took her hand.

'And why not? I am so happy to see you regain your health. Why there is even color in those cheeks, I fancy.'

'If there is, it is rouge,' Abigail told him. 'Now, why don't the two of you escape this jail and take a turn around the inner circle? I have a park-full of flowers to look at in here. No reason for everyone to sit about watching me. I promise not to do anything that requires either medical attention or brotherly fussing before you return.'

'If you're sure?' Simon made a poor show of reluctance, his eyes on Eliza as he spoke.

Eliza knew she looked radiant. He had already commented upon it several times in the last few days. She knew also that he was aware of her desire for him. She had done her best to hide it, but it was an impossible task.

'Oh, I don't have a suitable hat for walking out,' she said, feebly searching for an excuse not to go. She was torn between wanting to be with him and being afraid of the strength of her feelings in her changed state. She needed more time to become accustomed to herself this way. 'I left mine at my lodgings.'

'Pish,' said Abigail, 'as if I haven't a hat to lend you. Go into my dressing room and choose one and hurry up. The sun does not stay out long in November; you must make the most of it.'

Eliza did as she was told. Abigail's dressing room was through an adjoining door. Trunks and wardrobes of dresses and crinolines and nightclothes and cloaks and capes and shawls lined the walls. There was a shelf filled entirely with hatboxes. Eliza lifted lids here and there until she found two possible hats. She took them to the dressing table by the window to try them on. The first was much too fussy, with a net veil that made her feel so silly she giggled at her reflection. She took it off and put it on the dressing table. She was about to try the next one when she noticed a pretty silver box. It was smaller than a hatbox but the wrong shape for a jewelery box. There was a swirling pattern of dog roses tooled onto it, with green and pink enamel highlighting the leaves and buds. Eliza could not resist picking it up. She held it in the light the better to study the lovely decoration and beautiful craftsmanship. There was a slender key in the lock. She turned it and the lid sprang open. Inside, a tiny figure in an emerald dress twirled on a stage of glass as the music box began to play. Eliza found herself unable to move. She wanted to throw the box across the room and run from the house, but her hands felt stuck fast to the silver. The dancer twirled, a sly grin on her pinched face. Eliza wanted to scream, to cry out, to hurl the offending object through the window, but she sat as if mesmerized by the movement and the melody as the unforgettable notes of "Greensleeves" played on and on.

The next morning Eliza left the house early and was at the hospital before even Mr. Thomas was at his desk. She sat in Dr. Gimmel's room staring blankly out the window. After finding the music box, she was certain of nothing. Everything she thought she was sure of seemed now to be built upon shifting sands. Eliza closed her eyes and tried to calm her whirling mind. Today, she was to operate on Abigail. Nothing must distract her.

The door opened and Dr. Gimmel strode in, newspaper in hand.

'Have you heard?' he asked, jabbing at the paper with an angry finger, 'Have you read the reports? Another murder. Another brutal slaying of a defenseless woman. In her own room, if you please.'

'Another?' Eliza stood up shakily. 'Not the Ripper. That cannot be right.'

'See for yourself.' He thrust the paper under her nose. 'Only a few steps from your own home, Eliza. I tell you that place is a pit of horrors. Why you insist on living there . . .'

Eliza was not listening anymore. Her eyes were fixed on the name of the victim. Mary Jane Kelly. The vision she had experienced weeks ago of the girl's body cut open and reduced to a gory mess had been horribly accurate. She scanned the article, taking in the details, searching for some sign, some assurance that this was not the work of the same man. How could it be? She looked for the hour the body was discovered. It was later than her encounter with Gresseti, though as yet the police did not know exactly when the woman had died. Had he survived and fled to kill again? No, surely there was not time. How would he have found his way to where Mary Jane lived? Or had she been wrong? Could it be that he, Gideon, had had nothing to do with the murders? Nothing made sense. She could not believe that the killings were not in some way connected to herself. The victims had almost all been her patients. And she had been convinced for weeks that someone was following her and hiding in the shadows. And then Gresseti had followed her while she was dressed in Connie's clothes. And the organ grinder had played "Greensleeves." It had to be Gresseti. And Gresseti had revealed himself to be Gideon. But questions remained, questions that would have to wait. Dr. Gimmel finally succeeded in breaking into her thoughts.

'Dr. Hawksmith! Come, we are needed in theater,' he said.

In the operating theater, Nurse Morrison was already busy preparing the table. Fresh sawdust had been placed in the blood tray and carbolic had been liberally sprayed throughout the room. Instinctively, Eliza checked the tiers of seating. All were empty. As she put on her theater apron, she found her hands were trembling. She shook her head, frustrated by the ease with which she was distracted and unsettled. This was no time for nerves. She must remain entirely focused on Abigail. Still her head buzzed and the blood seemed hot in her veins. She occupied herself with inspecting the instruments, trying to turn away from the voices in her mind that were urging her on to use witchcraft. Now, more than ever, she needed to be Dr. Elizabeth Hawksmith, assistant to the revered Phileas Gimmel, dedicated physician and skilled surgeon. Abigail's life depended on it.

'Ah, here we are.' Dr. Gimmel greeted his patient as she was wheeled into the room. 'My dear Miss Astredge, I am delighted to see you looking stronger.' He took her hand and patted it gently. Simon came to stand behind her.

'How could I fail to thrive under Eliza's care?' she asked, smiling at her friend.

'Quite so, quite so.' Dr. Gimmel took Simon's arm. 'Now, Mr. Astredge, if you would take a seat over here, close enough to your dear sister to give her the invaluable strength of your support, not so close as to impede our work. Fear not, she is in the very best of hands.'

'Of that, I am certain,' said Simon, his gaze fixed on Eliza. She felt herself blushing and turned to Abigail.

'How are you this morning?' she asked.

'I am well and happy to be here. Soon you will have done your wonderful work, and I will be free of this wretched disease.'

Dr. Gimmel began to help her out of her chair. 'We are still awaiting the arrival of Roland,' he said. 'Is he late or are we all, in our eagerness, a little early?'

He asked the question of no one in particular, but it was Simon who took out his pocket watch.

'It is four minutes before ten o'clock, Doctor,' he said, and returned the watch to his waistcoat.

'Ah, there we have it. No doubt he will be here directly.'

A stab of fear traveled the length of Eliza's spine. She could not think what had caused it. Though she knew herself to be far from calm, the suddenness and force of the feeling took her by surprise.

At that very moment, Roland entered the room, breathless from running.

'Forgive me,' he said, 'I was detained with a patient, and . . .'

'No matter.' Dr. Gimmel held up a hand. 'This is not the place for excuses. You are here now, Roland, that is all that need concern us for the present.'

Abigail was assisted onto the table and made ready. Eliza touched her brow and spoke softly.

'Sleep now. That is all that is required of you.'

Roland stepped forward and administered the chloroform. Within seconds, Abigail's eyes had shut and she lay motionless, except for her shallow, rhythmic breathing.

Eliza selected a scalpel from the tray and made a broad incision. The nurse swabbed blood from the wound so that Eliza could better manipulate the retractors to gain access to the abdominal cavity.

'Good, good,' said Dr. Gimmel. 'Proceed precisely as you are, Dr. Hawksmith. Gently but firmly, gently but firmly. Excellent.'

Eliza worked steadily, taking the greatest care, but all the time she was acutely aware that such a procedure could be lengthy and she must move forward with some urgency. Abigail was not strong. The longer she remained anaesthetized, the more blood she lost, the more her body was forced to endure, the less likely she was to survive the operation. She was unable to shake off the sense of foreboding and danger that had gripped her moments before. What had caused it? She tried to recall what Dr. Gimmel had been talking about. He had been asking for Roland, she remembered that, but Roland was the most harmless creature she knew. There had been an issue about the time—was it early or late? Simon had consulted his watch.

'Have a care, Dr. Hawksmith!' Dr. Gimmel's voice was uncharacteristically harsh.

Eliza saw that she had allowed blood to flow back into the wound, obscuring her vision. At that moment, it was all she could do to hold the instruments, her hands had begun to tremble so much. The watch. Simon's watch! That was what had alarmed her so. When he had closed it, there was a very definite double click. The exact same noise she had heard in the shadows outside her clinic. Simon? But how could that be?

'What is it?' Dr. Gimmel moved closer to her, peering into the cavity. 'Eliza, is something amiss?'

Eliza shook her head, as much to rid it of the terrible thoughts as to reassure Dr. Gimmel.

'No, nothing. Just . . . pausing. Here, the liver is exposed now,' she told him, leaning back a little so that he might observe her progress. And so that she might search her mind for answers. She raised her eyes to look at Simon, unable to help herself, hoping to see in that good, open face some proof that he was the man she loved and was incapable of such terrible deeds. He was watching her and smiled at her, his most loving, most endearing smile. In a heartbeat, Eliza knew where she had felt the warmth of that smile before. An idea came to her. Simon Astredge. No middle name. Just Simon Astredge. She fought to rearrange the letters in her mind, praying she was wrong but pressing on with awful certainty.

G-I-D, *where is the* E? *and the final* S? *Yes, they are all there. I can see it now. Oh no. No! How can I have been so blind?*

Panic made blood pound against Eliza's eardrums, but there was no escape, nowhere to hide from the truth of it. Simon Astredge was an anagram of Gideon Masters.

Both of them! Gresseti and Simon. Both of them.

She knew Simon was watching her. Had he seen how disturbed she was? Could he possibly know that she had discovered his true identity? The more she thought about it the clearer it all became. Gresseti was a ploy, a distraction. Gideon would have known that Eliza would dislike the man. By creating a figure for her to loathe and eventually fear, he had propelled her into Simon's arms. How could she resist his warm affection when she was so frightened of Gresseti? And, of course, she would be less suspicious of Simon while her concerns were all about the rootless Italian. But what of Abigail? She could not be his sister. Gideon's powers as a warlock and as a mesmerist meant he could certainly have convinced her of it. Where had he found her? Some poor, unsuspecting woman who had stepped into his path at precisely the right moment for him and the wrong moment for her. Abigail clearly had no recollection of any other life. Who knew what heartbreak her disappearance must have caused. Had she family still searching for her? And she was most definitely ill, that was beyond doubt. Even now Eliza could see the diseased condition of her liver. It was a wonder Abigail had survived as long as she had. Eliza bit her lip, willing herself to act as a doctor now, to put Simon from her mind. To put Gideon from her mind.

'What can you tell me?' Dr. Gimmel was still at her elbow, readjusting his spectacles on his nose. 'What can you see, Dr. Hawksmith?'

'The news is not good, I fear.' Eliza spoke more loudly than she had intended because she was so determined not to betray traces of the fear and confusion she felt. Her peripheral vision allowed her a glimpse of Simon shifting in his seat, leaning forward. As he did so, his watch fell from his pocket and swung on its fob chain, backward and forward, backward and forward. Eliza bent lower over her patient. 'There is no tumor. Nothing that can be extracted. There is advanced cirrhosis of the liver. Over eighty percent of the organ is affected to a debilitating level.'

'Ah,' Dr. Gimmel sounded crushed. 'Then there is nothing to be done,' he said, stepping back a little.

It was more than Eliza could bear. She had believed she had defeated Gideon by confronting Gresseti, but Mary Kelly still died. She had thought that in Simon she had at last found love, but all she had found was her nemesis. Nausea threatened to undo her as she recalled how she had let him kiss her and touch her, and how close she had come to surrendering herself to him completely. How much she had wanted to. And now she was to lose Abigail. Poor hapless Abigail who had unwittingly played such a vital part in Gideon's complicated charade. It seemed so unjust. So unfair. As if she had been sacrificed for Gideon's purposes.

'Dr. Hawksmith'—Roland leaned closer to her—'the patient has been anaesthetized for some time. Are you ready to complete the procedure?'

'Yes, yes.' Dr. Gimmel answered for her. 'There is little point in subjecting Miss Astredge to further drains on her already weak resources. Additional anaesthesia will not be required.'

No. I will not let her die. Not like Margaret. I can save her, and I will, whatever the consequences.

Without responding to Roland or acknowledging Dr. Gimmel's remark, Eliza gently pushed both her hands through the incision and laid them on Abigail's liver. She looked down, not daring to risk closing her eyes, not wanting to meet Simon's increasingly probing gaze. She began to mutter the incantations under her breath. Dr. Gimmel fidgeted but said nothing, plainly expecting her to begin suturing the wound. Roland watched her, waiting for further instructions. Nurse Morrison held the tray of instruments out for her selection. Eliza ignored them. A thin wind began to whine around the operating theater. It gathered force until it moaned about the legs of those present, an eerie, chill breeze that wove its way between the figures but brought with it no new air. It was as if the molecules of the space itself were being agitated and rearranged. The nurse looked about anxiously and instinctively moved farther up the bed to stand closer to Roland. Dr. Gimmel began to exclaim and entreat Eliza to complete her task quickly. Simon stood up.

Now Eliza raised her head and looked at him levelly. She could feel the substance of Abigail's internal organ altering beneath her hands. The scarred and pitted tissues were being renewed. Healed. She stared at Simon, daring him to challenge her now, knowing that she would not stop until she was sure of Abigail's recovery. By using her magic openly in his presence, she was laying herself open to him. So be it. She would not let another innocent person die while it was in her gift to save them. Slowly, with neither anger nor any apparent violence, Simon raised his left hand. When it drew level with Dr. Gimmel's eyeline, he snapped his fingers. The doctor fell backward with a cry, landing awkwardly in the first row of seats, clutching at his eyes.

'Dr. Gimmel!' Nurse Morrison quickly placed the instruments on the table and ran to him. When she put her hands over his, she screamed, staggering away from him, staring incredulously at the smoldering burns on her palms. Simon flicked his fingers a second time, and the nurse fell to the ground as if struck. She lay motionless at Eliza's feet, one of her burned hands coming to rest in the mess of sawdust and blood in the box beneath the table.

Eliza did not move. She shouted, 'Run, Roland. For pity's sake, run from this place!'

Roland opened his mouth to protest but was too slow. With a flick of his wrist, Simon caused the tray of surgical instruments to rise up and hover above the bed. The steel blades of the scalpels glinted for a second before three of them lifted from the tray, then sliced through the air with supernatural speed. The first pierced Roland's hand as he flung his arms in front of him in a futile gesture of defense. The second slashed his throat open, and the third embedded itself in his heart as he fell soundlessly to the ground.

Simon turned back to Eliza. He smiled again, the gentle expression a mad contrast to his evil intentions.

'My dear Bess, does it disturb you to see your beloved Simon behaving in this way? Forgive me.' He bowed low, swinging his arm in an elaborate gesture. When he straightened up, it was not Simon who stood before Eliza but Gideon. 'There, is that better? Finally we are come to this point. No more games, Bess. No more running. Just you and I face to face.'

'Stay back,' said Eliza, using every scrap of courage she had to stop herself from fleeing. 'Abigail has done nothing wrong. I will heal her. I will not let you stop me.'

'Oh, please, do not trouble yourself on Abigail's behalf. She is much healthier than you might suppose.'

Eliza looked at Abigail, willing her not to slip away. Her own heart was in danger of stopping when she saw Abigail looking straight back at her. Her eyes were wide open, and she was watching the procedure with an expression of mild curiosity, nothing more.

Eliza gasped. 'Abigail! But you . . .'

Simon interrupted, 'Are a witch, just as you are, Bess.'

'What? No! I don't understand.'

Abigail smiled sweetly. 'Eliza, my dear, do not be cross with me. We can be such friends.'

Eliza shook her head and tried to wrench her hands from inside Abigail's body, but they were stuck fast. Abigail began to laugh, a harsh, discordant noise. Her body shook with it, but still Eliza's hands were trapped.

Simon began to pace casually around the theater.

'Bess, Bess, Bess. What are we to do with you? You surely did not think I would spend centuries waiting for you entirely on my own, did you? Go on, admit it, you are the tiniest bit jealous, are you not?' He laughed, then went on, 'Don't be, my love. There have been many Abigails over the years. Diverting companions, nothing more. Though this one, I'll admit, has impressed me with her fine performance as my ailing sister. Congratulations, my dear.' He nodded politely at Abigail, who blew him a kiss in return.

Eliza wanted to scream but knew if she gave way to hysteria she would be lost. Without her hands free, she could not use her magic effectively against Gideon. Behind her, Dr. Gimmel moaned and stirred on the floor. Eliza prayed silently for him to keep quiet and stay down. It was only chance that Gideon had not already killed him, and she was powerless to protect him.

'You will never claim me, Gideon,' she said.

'So stubborn. So defiant. Why do you continue to struggle against your destiny, hmm? You know we were meant to be together, you and I. Think of it. You have tasted the glory of the power of magic in these last few days. You know what life could be, if only you willed it so. Together, you and I would be unstoppable. Unassailable. We would be magnificent.'

He began to walk around the table toward her. Eliza knew she had to act or she would be lost. But she could not fight him handicapped as she was. If she was not to submit, there was only one option left to her. She twisted round so that she could see Dr. Gimmel more clearly. He was drifting in and out of consciousness. She made herself speak.

'Forgive me, Doctor,' she said.

Then, quicker than the eye could record, she vanished.

Gideon roared.

'Bess! Bess! No!' His thunderous voice shook the room as he spun about, searching for any sign of her.

High up near the ceiling, a butterfly flitted silently toward the narrow open window at the top of the auditorium. It paused on the threshold for a moment, its silver spotted wings flashing in a slender sunbeam, and then it continued through the opening and was gone.

Letter from
Mrs. Constance Gimmel to
Professor Salvatores

My dear Professor,

Thank you so much for your kind letter. It is a comfort to me to know Phileas is not forgotten among his friends and colleagues. I know that when I communicate your good wishes, they will mean a great deal to him. His condition remains unchanged. Indeed, it has not altered in any significant way since the day he was found so terribly afflicted. I thank God that he was spared at all, given the sad fate of both Nurse Morrison and the junior doctor in attendance. Though of course I find his suffering hard to witness, I am ever hopeful of improvement. The nightmares that had been waking him with exhausting frequency do appear to have abated, which is a mercy. His blindness he bears with fortitude, though I know he grieves for his sight and all the things he can no longer do.

He talks often of the Fitzroy, naturally, but never of the events of that terrible day. No trace of Mr. Astredge, his sister, or Dr. Hawksmith has ever been found, and the police can give no satisfactory explanation as to what happened. Poor Phileas is unable to do so. Indeed, I doubt he knows himself. I certainly do not see the purpose in pressing him on details. There is nothing to be done, and he finds it so hard to talk of the things that occurred. I know he misses Dr. Hawksmith, and it is regrettable that she cannot be located. I fear the mystery will never be solved, and I must devote my energies to caring for my husband rather than chasing will-o'-the-wisp notions and theories.

Please remember me to Louisa.

> *Your good friend,*
> *Constance Gimmel*

LITHA

By the time I had finished the story of Eliza, Tegan was properly attentive and bright-eyed. I could see that the tale had once again ignited in her a great curiosity and interest in the idea of magic.

'So she escaped again?' she asked.

'She did. Just. But she was forced to leave Dr. Gimmel with neither farewell nor explanation.'

'And the others? The nurse and Roland, they died?'

'Yes. There was nothing anyone could do for them.'

Tegan got out of her chair and began to roam the room, her mind ablaze.

'Imagine,' she said, 'imagine being able to do magic like that. To heal people. To shapeshift.' She paused and looked at me. 'To kill people. It's powerful stuff. Seriously dangerous stuff.'

'It can be, in the wrong hands.'

'Well, that Gideon sounds like a complete nightmare. But why should Eliza have to run away from him all the time? Why did she have to hide? Surely she could have defeated him if she'd been ready, set a trap or something?'

'Remember, Gideon had been her tutor. He instructed her in the craft. He knew every possible trick or trap. He would have known almost before she did what Eliza was planning. That was why often the only course open to her was sudden disappearance, before he had a chance to stop her.' I paused to watch her and to give her mind a chance to settle. She continued to question me for some time, until at last I held up my hand and silenced her. 'I have a question for you now, Tegan,' I said.

'Yeah?'

'Are you ready, are you truly ready to become my pupil and learn the craft? Are you ready to devote time and thought and focus to the quest for magic? Are you ready to make sacrifices, to work hard, to be attentive and studious and serious-minded? Are you ready to protect the knowledge you gain, to observe the ways of the hedge witch, to use what you learn only for good? Are you, Tegan?'

She stopped pacing and came to stand before me. I stood up. She met my eye unwaveringly and for once did not fidget or gabble or jump like a grasshopper from one thought to the next. She took a slow breath.

'Yes, I am ready,' she said. 'I am.'

'Then welcome, Tegan,' I said, and held out my arms to her.

She beamed a smile of radiant happiness and flung herself at me. As I held her, I wondered how long it had been since her own mother had embraced her.

JULY 12—NEW MOON

It is hard to believe so many months have passed since my last entry. What a summer it has been! I cannot remember a period in my life when I felt so at peace and yet so productive. Tegan has taken to her studies with great enthusiasm, as I think I always knew she would. She devours knowledge the way a starving woman would devour a feast. She has a quick mind and is fearless. Once or twice, I have had to upbraid her for her lack of patience, but then, since this is my own failing too, I am not in a position to be harsh. Her romance continues, but I have not yet been introduced to her lover. It could be that she has taken to heart what I told her about priority and that she does not want the distraction of her man being involved in what we are about here. Or it may be that she has not told him and does not know how to explain. Either way, I am content to have her undivided attention while she is with me. The time she spends elsewhere is not my concern.

I decided the moment had come to formally initiate Tegan into the craft. I felt the act of dedicating herself to the wiccan way, and the solemnity of the ritual, would help her to take her studies seriously, and to feel that she truly belongs. Although often conducted under a new moon, instead I chose the mead moon of a few weeks ago. This is traditionally seen as a time of metamorphosis, so what better occasion for Tegan's moment of change, of transformation from girl to young hedge witch?

We waited until the night had wrapped itself around the landscape and then made our way up to the stone circle in the copse. I had lent Tegan one of my robes, a beautiful garment of heavy silk given me by the members of a coven in Mumbai over a century ago. The sight of her in it quite made me catch my breath.

'Do I look okay?' she asked.

'You look wonderful.'

A light blush colored her cheeks. I sensed her nervousness and took her hand.

'Come,' I said, and led her through the garden and into the copse.

During the preceding weeks, Tegan, on my instruction, had been gathering items for her charm bag—a seashell from Batchcombe beach, a feather from a young kingfisher, the shell of a wren's egg, and an empty butterfly cocoon. She had wrapped them in moss, tied them with some strands of her own hair, and put them in the small velvet bag she had chosen for the purpose. When we reached the circle, I bade her place the charms on the flat stone to the east. I lit a candle, which was to burn down completely before the bag was moved. After the ceremony, her charms would become the first part of her own protective wiccan tools.

Tegan began to pace around the circle, chanting, invoking the spirits of the elements, lighting candles at the four compass points. Her voice was uncharacteristically hesitant.

'*The witch, the magic, the fire, are one. The witch, the magic, the earth, are one. The witch, the magic, the air, are one. The witch, the magic, the water, are one.*'

I drew her into the center of the circle and banged my staff firmly into the dry ground three times and cried, 'The circle is sealed!' I raised my arms. We both turned our faces to a night sky of dazzling clarity and stillness. 'O Goddess!' I called. 'A seeker stands before you. She wishes to join us, to become one with the craft. She is of strong will, clear mind, and open heart. Her soul is free of evil, and she wishes to use the craft only for the good of others. I ask you to hear her. Heal her. Transform her.' I returned my gaze to Tegan and we joined hands. 'Recite with me the Rede of the Wicca, child. Speak from your heart. Consider the words as you utter them, and be sure you mean every one.'

And so we spoke together:

'*Bide the Wiccan Law you must, in perfect love and perfect trust.*
Live and let live; fairly take and fairly give.

Soft of eye and light of touch, speak little and listen much.
Deosil go by the waxing moon. . . .'

I watched as the power and wisdom of the words lit up Tegan's face, and her grip on my hands became strengthened. When we had finished, I asked her, 'What is the witches' creed?'

She answered clearly, her voice emboldened, 'To know, to dare, to will, to be silent.'

'Will you abide by these laws?'

'I will.'

'And will you promise to honor the Goddess, to respect the way of the wiccan, to use the craft only for good, spurning all thoughts of gain or self-aggrandisement?'

'I will.'

I passed her a new candle of pale purple and lit it for her. She held it aloft.

'Now?' she asked.

I nodded.

She took a deep breath and raised her voice to the heavens. 'I call thee down, dear Goddess! Enter my body. Commune with my soul. Be with me as I take this sacred step into your arms and into the sisterhood of the craft.'

There was utter silence. Not a leaf moved. Nothing in the woods stirred, neither flora nor fauna. It was as if every single thing held its breath and waited. The flame of the candle Tegan held aloft began to dance and flicker, though there was not the slightest whisper of wind. It grew brighter, bluer, pulsating. It climbed higher, its phosphorescent radiance casting an ethereal glow that filled our circle. By its light I could see the joy and wonder in Tegan's face. She must have been awed, but she did not falter. Her hold on the candle remained steady. Suddenly, the moment was over, the flame returned to normal, the sounds of the woodlands resumed once more.

I smiled at Tegan and she beamed back at me.

'Is it done?' she asked.

'It is.' I took the candle from her and placed it in the center of the circle. 'Follow me,' I told her.

She stepped carefully over the stones and allowed herself to be led over to the stream and the small consecrated pool.

'Look,' I said. 'Look and see your reflection and know that you are looking at a fine young witch.'

She leaned forward, excitement winning over nervousness, and gazed into the watery mirror. 'Oh!' she gasped. 'I look the same . . . but different somehow.'

I laughed lightly. 'What had you expected?'

'I don't know. Something. Nothing, perhaps. It is so strange. It's just my reflection. There's nothing scary or weird, but . . . I am changed. There is something.' She turned to me. 'I feel it,' she said, joyful tears brimming in her eyes. She sprang to me, wrapping her arms tightly about me, hugging me close. 'Thank you!' she whispered into my hair. 'Thank you!'

JULY 24 — DARK OF THE MOON

I am finding it increasingly hard to keep my irritation in check. Tegan's continued tardiness and lack of commitment to the course upon which we were set is making me seriously question her suitability for the craft.

AUGUST 19 — WANING MOON

I see now that I have, rather stupidly, underestimated the seriousness of Tegan's relationship with her mysterious boyfriend. At first, she would arrive late for one of our sessions, breathless and apologetic. Then she began to miss meetings altogether. Now I feel she cannot be relied upon to keep our appointments, and when she does deign to attend, she is distracted.

AUGUST 25 — DARK OF THE MOON

Things cannot continue as they are. I have attempted to raise the matter of unreliability with Tegan, but somehow the conversation always turns to her boyfriend and she becomes defensive. I see that if I press her, I may lose her completely. I will have to bide my time and hope that the initial flame of passion subsides soon, and sufficiently for her to be able to take a more long-term view of how she invests her time and energy.

SEPTEMBER 2—MOON IN LIBRA

A surprise this morning, and not a pleasant one. I was busy in the vegetable garden taking down bean sticks when I heard the front gate squeak. Footsteps padded up the path, two pairs of young, restless feet. Tegan appeared around the side of the house pink with pleasure and pride, her hand clutching that of a tall, fair young man.

'Elizabeth, this is Ian,' she told me, gazing up at him.

He is older than I had expected, not a teenager at all. In his mid-twenties at least, I think. Not a boy but a man. Surely unsuitably mature for Tegan. His sandy hair and pale blue eyes are undeniably appealing. He has a pleasing face and is soft-spoken. In short, there is nothing about his appearance to object to or which could give obvious cause for alarm. But Tegan knows practically nothing about him. He is not, as I had imagined, part of a family recently moved into the area. He is a loner, living in a narrow boat on the canal, and he has a motorbike. He performs for donations for a living, so he has no place of work. No friends. No past, it seems. I admit he appears open and polite and is charmingly attentive toward Tegan, but why is he bothering with her at all? She is a child. I am aware some girls her age are worldly and womanly, but Tegan is not. She is utterly in his thrall already, to the point where I could barely hold a proper conversation with her. She rabbited on about Ian's gypsy lifestyle and how brilliantly he plays the guitar and how cool his houseboat is. While she spoke, I watched him. He smiled down at her, seemingly enjoying her girlish twitterings.

'Elizabeth?'

Tegan broke into my thoughts, and I realized I had been staring. I pulled myself together and offered to make tea. I was relieved when they declined, saying that they had planned a trip to Pasbury on Ian's motorbike. I waved them off, feigning cheerfulness, but I was concerned for Tegan—she is so very young—what does she know of the ways of men?

SEPTEMBER 8—MOON IN THIRD QUARTER

Tegan has missed two of our sessions. This morning I made myself take a walk along the canal. I was certain I would find Tegan with Ian on his houseboat, and I was no longer content to let him interfere with her instruction. Perhaps the sight of me would remind her of her commitment. I carried my staff and asked the sun god for protection before setting out. It was nearly eleven by the time I found Ian's mooring. The boat itself looked unremarkable and quiet. The motorbike was chained to the aft deck. I approached slowly and was greatly startled when the door opened and Ian stepped out.

'Elizabeth,' he said, his voice honeyed. 'Great to see you. Hop aboard. I've got the kettle on.'

'I felt the need for a walk,' I said. 'Is Tegan here with you?'

'Yeah, she's still in bed.' He watched my reaction, letting the information settle before continuing. 'Great girl, isn't she?' He smiled.

I wanted to seize the moment, to say something to him about there being other important demands on Tegan's time besides him. If he truly cared about her, it might be possible for me to persuade him to allow her more time to pursue her interests. I opened my mouth to speak but was silenced by a noise from inside the boat. Tegan emerged, hair tousled, half dressed, obviously having just got out of bed. Here she was, fresh from the warmth of his arms, a girl enraptured by her first love. She would not be ready to hear a word said against her romance; would not want it in any way diminished. I felt defeated before I had begun.

'Shouldn't you be at school?' I asked.

Her face darkened. 'Are you checking up on me? Is that why you've come? To tell me I should be at school? Didn't bother you if I skipped the odd day to dig your garden or make things for your stall, did it?' Her jaw had already set defiantly. I knew she might still be sulking about my inhospitable response to meeting Ian.

'I was concerned about you, that is all. Does your mother know where you are?'

Tegan laughed. 'Like she cares!'

I could see that by coming to the houseboat I had crossed a line. It had been her choice to keep me apart from her boyfriend, so that we were separate pieces of her life. True, she had introduced us. Not to have done so would have been odd after a while. But I could see, standing there on the towpath, looking at the confusion and distress on Tegan's face, that she had never intended for the two of us to spend time together. She did not want these important and challenging aspects of her life merging. I saw that today but too late. I had trespassed where I was not wanted, and however reasonable my motive, Tegan was furious with me.

'Look, it's none of your business what I do, okay? You are not my mother. You're not my anything, in fact, so keep your weird witchy nose out!' She slammed back inside the boat.

Ian was still smiling. He gave a shrug.

'Looks like she'd rather be with me,' he said.

He turned as if to follow her. I could not bear the thought of Tegan alone with such a creature.

'Wait!' I called out. He paused and looked at me, eyebrows raised in question. I licked my dry lips and raised my staff. 'If you harm that girl, you will have me to answer to.'

'Harm her?' Ian looked genuinely puzzled. 'I'm nuts about her. Why would I harm her?'

In truth, I do not know what made me say such a thing. Even to me, it sounded odd, uncalled for.

There was a moment of complete stillness. Under his gaze, my breath caught in my throat.

A pair of ducks landed noisily behind the boat, breaking the moment. I saw them course through the water in a splash of feathers and quacking. When I looked back, Ian was shutting the door of the cabin behind him.

SEPTEMBER 12—FULL MOON

I have done my best to be sensible about my reactions to Ian. He has given me no cause to doubt his feelings toward Tegan, and yet I still have my misgivings. Could it be that all these years of being persecuted, of looking over my shoulder, of running from the terror of my past, have left me unable to see danger rationally? Have I lost my intuition as a witch that should allow me to detect danger, to be warned, without muddling the signals? Am I no longer able to meet a solitary stranger without instantly feeling suspicious and threatened? I fear I have already handled the situation badly. Tegan has not visited me, and I cannot visit the boat again. I must talk to her. If only she would return to her course of instruction, return to me, I could keep closer watch over her. This evening I will write a note and post it through the door of her house. I only hope she is not too entranced by her lover to listen to me.

SEPTEMBER 14—LUNAR ECLIPSE

My hand shakes as I write this, but write I must. On my way to deliver the letter to Tegan, I called in at the village shop only to find her standing at the post office counter. She was withdrawing money from her savings account.

'Hello, Tegan,' I said, as casually as I could. She gave only a nod in reply. 'On your own today?'

'Ian's performing, if you must know. Went on his bike into Pasbury this morning.' She folded notes into her purse.

'Well, it's been ages since you've been to the cottage. Why don't you come back with me? Have a cup of tea? I've baked some raisin bread.'

'Look, I don't want to be rude, Elizabeth, but I'm busy, okay?' She started to push past me. I stepped in front of her.

'Tegan, please listen to me. Ian . . .'

'For God's sake, I don't want to hear it! Why can't you just be happy for me? What's wrong with you? Are you jealous or what?'

'It's not that . . .' I was stopped mid-sentence by the sound of Tegan's mobile phone ringing. In those few seconds, my world collapsed. I felt time rushing through my head, century upon century, my sanity sucked into the vortex. I watched Tegan fish the phone from her bag, smiling. I saw her lips move, knew she was saying something, but I could discern no words. All I could hear was the tune ringing out of the mobile phone. A tune I knew. A tune I feared. It was the tune of "Greensleeves."

I fled. In fact, I do not remember getting from the shop to my kitchen. No! It could not be him! Not now, not here, not so terrifyingly close to Tegan. And to me. It may be that Ian has a dark secret, that he is not the good and gentle person Tegan believes him to be. But surely that does not mean he has to be . . . Even now, I cannot bring myself to write the thought down, fully formed. I must not give way to panic. But no, I cannot deny the evidence of my senses. I find myself unable to order my thoughts. My first impulse was to pack and leave. I still had an opportunity to evade him if I left before he knew I had discovered he was near. It would be a simple matter to gather the few belongings I care about and disappear. After all, I have done it many, many times before. And yet, I am surprised to find I cannot run. Even though I am certain Gideon has sent me a signal of his proximity. Even though I must surely face the fact that he is close by, watching me, and now using Tegan to reach me. How long has he been so close? And what would be the consequences of my flight? Leaving Matravers would mean leaving Tegan. And if I were to succeed in slipping away and thwart Gideon again, how would he react? And whom might he vent his fury and frustration upon? No, I cannot leave. The time has come to face him. I will not run anymore.

SEPTEMBER 30—NEW MOON

I have not seen Tegan since the night of the lunar eclipse. I am, of course, concerned, though I do not believe she is in any real danger as long as I remain. I encountered her mother in the village shop this morning. It seems all is well. She has met Ian and declares him a well-mannered young man. If she knew only half the truth, what would it do to her, I wonder. It seems to me all she wants is to convince herself that Tegan does not need anything from her. It suits her that the girl is so taken up with her new man; it assuages her guilt at having so little of herself to give. It is hardly surprising that Tegan has thrown herself at the first man who has shown an interest, given the lack of care she receives at home.

I have arrived at the conclusion that there is only one way I can both face Gideon and protect Tegan. I must take her further into my confidence. I must entrust her with the ultimate truth about myself. Only then can I teach her how to protect herself, should the need arise. It had been my intention only to instruct her in the ways of a hedge witch, to give her the skills of a healer. But now, now that I sense Gideon's heavy presence, I must go further. She must learn the craft proper. For only the dark arts are strong enough to be of use against such a foe. Somehow, I must make her understand. She needs to believe that I am Eliza. That I am Bess. And the only thing that will convince her of any of this is magic. Long ago, when I clung to the shadows all those dark and lonely years, I shunned my own powers. I truly thought that to use them was wrong. Of course, I also knew that to do so would be to reveal my whereabouts to Gideon.

Magic travels. He would have been able to detect my craft from hundreds of miles away, perhaps thousands. And as for every practicing witch, access to the forces of magic opens a two-way portal. While I am connecting with the sisterhood of witches, with the strength of the underworld, with the power of magic through all time, those same entities are connecting with me. At that time, I am empowered, but I am also vulnerable. I chose to spurn that power in part because of this. My main reason, however, the thing that had me turn away from what I might have been, was my own guilt.

I still believe I was responsible for my mother's death. She could have saved herself, but to do so would have been to offer me up as a sacrifice to those who wanted retribution. She eschewed her own power so that I might survive. How could I then allow myself the glory of that magic? And it is truly glorious. I have shown Tegan only a glimpse of that wonder by relating Eliza's transformation from earthbound immortal to fully functioning witch. Heightened senses and sexual awakening are but a part of what a truly powerful witch will experience. And I know myself to be of the first order. Gideon saw to that. What pact he made with the devil I hope never to find out, but in me he saw all his dreams of the perfect mate made flesh. Why else would he have pursued me so relentlessly all this time? Gideon had prowled this earth for centuries before he happened upon my family. In me, he saw the potential for what he had yearned for. An equal. He took that raw material and he schooled me and guided me until I was ready. Then he asked for his master's blessing and for my transformation. On the night in Batchcombe jail, when I pronounced the words he had taught me, the transmutation was complete. His equal, did I say? Well, now we shall see.

OCTOBER 2—WAXING MOON

It has taken me all my scant reserves of patience to wait until this day to seek out Tegan. I believe my forbearance will pay dividends. I forced myself to allow time for Tegan's temper to cool. I dropped a letter through her door yesterday asking her to come and see me so that I might apologize for meddling or for presuming to tell her how to live her life. I assured her that I wish only to put things right between us. I promised not to raise the subject of Ian or poke my nose in any of her business. I would never again push my help or advice upon her unless she asked for it. For friendship's sake, I urged her to come. I have brewed some fresh ginger beer, and we could sit in the garden and drink it, which would give her the chance to see how many of the plants she helped me with are now flourishing.

Of course, I recognized that such a letter might not be sufficiently persuasive to bring the child to me. It is vital that she come. To this end I took it upon myself to dress the letter with a spell. A gentle one, designed only to lure and to coax, not to force or frighten. Tegan will be unaware of it, but she will find herself keeping our rendezvous without resistance.

OCTOBER 5—SECOND QUARTER

What a night of wonders! Tegan arrived at my cottage a little after eight o'clock. It was an unseasonably warm evening, the mildness of the waning day still lingering in the sheltered garden. Late-flowering jasmine filled the quiet air with its heady scent. Tegan was a little wary at first and gave the impression she could not stay long. I bid her join me at the table beneath the apple tree, where I had already set out a jug of ginger beer and almond biscuits.

'Yum, this is really good,' she said after downing half a glass. She wiped her mouth with the back of her hand, for a moment seeming worryingly young and childlike. We sat and talked about the garden, remembering what she had planted and how hard she had worked, particularly on the herb beds. She began to relax, but we were talking about everything and nothing. I had promised not to raise the subject of Ian, and I feared talk of my own history might cause her to bolt again. But time was running out. I had to do something.

'Another glass?' I asked.

'Yeah, go on then.' She held out her tumbler.

I moved as if to pick up the heavy glass jug but then stopped. I sat back in my chair, focusing on the ginger beer. Slowly the pitcher began to move. At first it merely shook a little, causing the drink to slosh about inside it. It was a small movement but enough to attract Tegan's attention. She watched openmouthed as the jug rose silently into the air, tipped at

precisely the required angle, and poured the beer into her waiting beaker.
Job done, it settled back on the table. Tegan remained transfixed, arm still
outstretched, staring at the glass in her hand. She glanced at the jug, then
back at her glass, then looked at me.

'Tell me you saw what just happened!'

I nodded.

Her eyes widened further. 'It was you!' she said. 'You did that!'

I nodded again.

Tegan took a swig of the drink before setting it back on the table. 'Oh
my God! Do more,' she said. 'Do something else. Go on.'

I focused on the drink in her glass now. It began to bubble vigorously.
Tegan shifted back a little on her chair. In seconds the cloudy beer had
been transformed to a frothy blue liquid that boiled and bubbled until
foam spilled out over the top of the glass and began to cover the table.

Tegan screamed in amazement.

'Look at that! That's brilliant. Can you show me how to do it? Will
you?' She stood up, dipping her finger into the bubbles that were now
running down the sides of the table. I clapped my hands and the blue
liquid vanished. Not a bubble remained. The drink had returned to ordinary ginger beer. Tegan picked up the glass a little nervously, sniffing the
contents. I stood up and met her gaze, my expression serious.

'Stay with me through this night, Tegan, and I will show you wonders
you have only ever dreamed of. If you decide to come with me and to
witness these things, you must do so with an open mind, a kind heart,
and a steadfast soul. What is more you must tell no one of the things you
see. Do you agree?'

'Yes! Yes,' Tegan replied, her face betraying something of her own
nervousness.

I smiled, wanting her to relax. I walked around the table until I stood
in front of her. I reached out and touched her hair. 'Oh, look,' I said,
'there is somebody who would like to accompany you on this journey.'
From behind her left ear, I produced a whiskery white mouse. Tegan
gasped as she took him in her palm.

'Oh, look at him! He's gorgeous.' She grinned at me, relaxed again
now.

We went into the little copse behind the house and gathered wood.
Soon we had a lively fire burning in the fire pit. I patted the fallen tree

trunk beside it. Tegan came to sit next to me, eager now, not stopping to think too deeply about what was happening, simply letting it happen. The white mouse sat on her lap, washing its face with licked paws.

'Listen,' I said. 'What can you hear?'

She turned her head this way and that. 'Well, the logs crackling in the fire. An airplane somewhere. A wood pigeon, is it?'

'Good. What else? Listen deeper.'

She frowned, head cocked, listening beyond those first available sounds. When she spoke, it was in a whisper. 'I . . . I can hear breathing, really fast.' She looked down at her lap. 'It's this mouse. I can hear him breathing!'

'What else?'

'Rustling. There is something over there in those nettles.'

'Call to it,' I told her.

'How?'

'Just call.'

'Come on,' she called softly. 'Come out. It's okay.'

The rustling stopped for a second, then the nettles parted and a hedgehog trundled out. He poked his snout into the air and made his way toward us, taking a circuitous route around the fire. He halted at Tegan's feet, snuffling at her toes, which peeped out of her sandals. Tegan laughed.

'Hey! That tickles.'

I took a piece of almond biscuit from my pocket and handed it to the hungry hog. He chomped it down and then hurried off in search of a juicy slug or two. I touched Tegan's arm.

'Look behind you.'

She turned slowly and came face to face with a fine dog fox. He flicked his tale, clearly provoked by the proximity of the mouse.

'Now then, Monsieur Reynard, behave yourself,' I told him.

He whimpered and lay down, rolling over playfully to expose his tummy. Tegan leaned down and scratched his rusty fur.

'Wow! You are fabulous. Look at you.'

The fox tolerated her attentions for a few more moments before leaping back onto his feet. He shook his fur into place and loped off into the night.

By now, dusk was beginning to deepen, and soon darkness descended properly. Tegan's face glowed, partly from the reflected light of the flames but mostly from wonder.

'Listen again,' I said. 'Be very still, close your eyes, and let the sounds come to you.'

She did as she was told. The mouse started, sensing something unusual in the air. It darted up Tegan's school shirt and dived into her pocket. Tegan waited with admirable patience. At last she took a quick in-breath, her whole body tensing.

'What is it?' she whispered. 'What is that noise? It sounds almost like . . . like voices.'

I smiled. I had not been sure that she would be able to hear them. I had always believed she had a sensitivity that would help her connect, but you can never be certain until the moment comes whether or not a person is as open and accepting as you wish them to be.

'They are indeed voices,' I said, 'many, many voices. Not everyone can hear them. You are fortunate, Tegan. They trust you. Now, open your eyes.'

I noticed her hesitate but only for an instant. When she did lift her lids, the sight that greeted her made her hands fly to her mouth to stifle a cry. It was undeniably a wondrous sight. In front of us, stepping lightly past the fire and coming to stand in a fidgeting group before us, was a gathering of at least one hundred fairies. The tiny beings were arrayed in a spectrum of the most brilliant colors, their lacy wings fluttering lightly against the heat of the fire. They were all much of a size, no larger than blackbirds, their dainty feet clad in exquisitely tailored shoes. They jostled for position, all eager for a better view of the new human who had come into their midst. One, a little bolder than the others perhaps, flew up and alighted on Tegan's knee. With infinite care, Tegan held out her hand and the fairy hopped onto her upturned palm. Tegan lifted the weightless creature up until it was level with her own face. The two peered at each other, equally enthralled and amazed by what they saw. The fairy tripped along Tegan's arm until she came to her ear, reaching out to touch the silver dragon that dangled against Tegan's neck. Tegan quickly undid the earring and offered it to the fairy, who clapped her hands excitedly before accepting the gift and flying down to show it to her friends. The group was so delighted they started to dance. While we watched, filigree wings flittered and blurred as the fairies danced and danced and danced around the fire. For nearly an hour, with moonbeams as their spotlights and the glow from the fire flashing off their iridescent clothes, they kept us both enchanted and beguiled. Then, as if on some secret signal, they gathered on the fallen trunk, waved good-bye, and disappeared into the woods. Tegan stared in the direction they had gone for many minutes after the last of them had melted into the shadows between the trees. Finally, she turned back to me.

'Magic,' she said somberly. 'It really is magic. And you really are a witch, aren't you?'

I could see the thought processes she was working through in her bewildered mind.

'I am,' I said, 'but there is one final thing I must share with you. I know you will not be truly convinced without it, for you must believe, surely, that all witches can fly?'

She sprang to her feet. 'Don't tell me you are going to fly!'

'No, not me,' I took her hand, '*We*.'

Before she had time to react, I threw my head back, waved my arm, and we were airborne. Tegan screamed with a mixture of terror and delight as we shot up into the night sky. Once we had reached a safe height, I paused. 'Just hold onto my hand,' I told her. 'Spread out your arms, that's right. Now, come with me.'

It had been a very long time since I had flown. I had forgotten the pure joy it engenders. My heart sang with the freedom, the lightness, the grace of gliding through the air, swooping low over treetops, twirling and diving and rising again. I heard Tegan laughing, unable to contain her glee. We passed over the sleeping village and across the rolling fields. A family of bats came to investigate, joining us for a moment or two. An owl screeched in alarm in an oak tree far below. On we went, cutting through the night sky, tumbling and turning, then climbing and soaring as free and as glorious as hawks. Soon we had reached the coast. I pulled Tegan out over the dark water and pointed down to the smooth ocean. Dolphins surfaced. I swooped low so that we might race alongside them, the sea spray refreshing our faces. At last we turned back, and I set us down in the copse beside the fire. Tegan lay on the ground, panting from exhilaration and wonder. Slowly she grew quieter and sat up.

'How?' she asked. 'How can it work? How does any of it work? I mean.'
I looked at her levelly.

'You have listened to my story. You know how I came to be what I am.'

For a moment she struggled to assimilate the information I had just
given her. I could see that her instinctive reaction was to reject such an
idea as nonsense, impossible, fantasy. But then, after what she had just
seen, just experienced . . . She knew now that there were things far beyond what she had hitherto accepted as possible in this world.

'You are Bess, aren't you? And Eliza?'

'And many more.'

She shook her head slowly, not denying the truth, for she could see it
for what it was, but as if to help the thoughts settle in her spinning head.

'Tegan, do you trust me?'

She nodded.

'There are things you need to understand. Things . . . about myself.
And about others who are connected to me. There is danger, Tegan.
Danger which you cannot see but which is nonetheless real.'

'Why would I be in danger? I have you to protect me,' she said.

I felt tears, the first for such a very, very long time, sting my eyes. Oh,
how I wanted to keep this girl safe! It was because of me that she was now
in peril. I could not fail her. I had to make her understand the power of
the force we were to face. The evil. If she were to stand any chance of
survival, I had to take her further into my world.

'You have come to realize that I am not what you first thought. That
outward appearances can be deceptive. There are others who present
themselves as one thing and yet are another. One other, in particular.'

'Ian? You mean Ian?'

I nodded.

'But I love him. *He* loves *me.*'

'Just as Eliza, as I, once believed Simon loved me.'

'You're saying Ian is *Gideon*?' She shook her head vigorously now. 'No!
No, I don't want to hear this.'

'You must.'

'I won't!'

'Tegan!' I knelt beside her and held her shoulders tight. 'I know how
much this hurts you.'

'You don't, you can't.'

'I do! I know what it is to love and to lose. But you must accept what is true; you must listen to me.'

She began to cry.

'Please,' I said softly, pulling her close. 'Listen.' I threw another log on the fire and poked it into life. 'Listen and I will tell you one last tale.'

Passchendaele, Flanders, 1917

I

I stepped off the train at Saint Justine, twelve kilometers south west of Passchendaele, onto what was in fact nothing more than a halt. In peacetime, few feet would have paced its platforms awaiting its infrequent and half-empty trains. Now, even in the hours of the night when most people would choose sleep if it were offered them, it was a scene of constant movement, a place of urgency and purpose. As returning troops and non-combatants disembarked, the wounded were lumbered onto the train, many on stretchers, others on crutches, all battle-weary and setting their sights firmly in the direction of home. Along with the small group of surgeons and nurses, I picked my way through the giddying mêlée, out of the station and down the main street. Saint Justine was a village, nothing more, and an unremarkable one at that. Had it not been for its situation on the railway line or its perilous proximity to the Front, I would most likely never have seen or heard of the place. Instead, it is forever etched into my brain: a name to jolt me from the present, a place ineffably coupled with pain and loss. The words themselves are sweet-sounding and cause the mouth to smile when they are spoken—*Saint Justine, Saint Justine*. But I have never in my life known a place more bowed down under the weight of human suffering and heartbreak. The main street, such as it was, offered a few empty shops, a café, a bakery devoid of warmth or smells, a church with its stained-glass windows boarded up, a deserted school, and a handful of nondescript homes. The dwellings petered out as the road crested a small hill, on the other side of which the temporary hospital had been erected. Or, more correctly, Number 13 Casualty Clearing Station (CCS), Saint Justine. Number 13 seemed appropriate enough. The whole consisted of a hamlet of tents, marquees, and wooden huts. Under the summer moon the canvas gleamed dully, bone-white and inappropriately bright. If one could have shut out the noise of marching feet, of barked orders, of moaning from hastily moved stretchers, and of the distant booming of the heavy artillery, it was just possible to imagine one had stumbled upon a large, hearty agricultural show on the eve of its opening. But it was impossible to block out those sounds. I hear them still, on wakeful nights.

I located the entrance to the reception marquee and, along with a glum-looking young girl from the First Aid Nursing Yeomanry called Kitty, presented myself for duty to the first nurse I encountered: a broad-shouldered girl whose red hair frizzed out at the front of her white head-dress.

'Ah, fresh faces. Splendid! Hope you got some sleep on the crossing; you won't do much of that here. Follow me, I'll take you to Sister's office,' she said, never once pausing in her brisk and somewhat unladylike stride. 'Name's Arabella Gough-Strappington, but for pity's sake call me Strap; war could be over by the time you've got that mouthful out.'

We threaded our way through the ceaseless current of doctors, nurses, orderlies, stretcher-bearers, and walking wounded. Strap covered the ground surprisingly swiftly for one so solid, her nurse's uniform billowing like a wind-filled spinnaker. Kitty and I followed on with hurried steps.

'Don't be put off by our Dear Leader,' Strap said over her shoulder. 'Her bark is worse than her bite. As long as you don't get bitten.' She laughed at her own joke, shoulders shaking as her loud guffaws drowned out the gunfire from the Front.

She led us to the smaller tent that housed Sister Radcliffe's office. Sister Radcliffe, who eschewed her more formal title of Commandant, was a formidable creature. She exuded efficiency and good sense from her very pores and had about her the air of one who was accustomed to unquestioning obedience. We stood in front of her as she sat behind her desk. Despite Strap's introductions, she did not hurry to complete the notes she was writing. At last she put down her pen and looked up at us over metal-rimmed glasses. She gave a sigh, as if already disappointed by the caliber of her new recruits. She consulted her register.

'Assistant Nurse Watkins . . .'

'Yes, Sister. Kitty Watkins.' The girl could not have been more than twenty-five years old, but her expression was one of weary middle age.

'With the FANY since 1916,' Sister read. 'Slow to answer the call, were you not?' She looked up at Kitty with genuine bewilderment.

'Yes, Sister. That is to say, no, Sister,' Kitty quickly became flustered under such scrutiny, her cockney twang growing more noticeable. 'I was needed at 'ome. Me mum was poorly, y'see. And me baby brother, well, he's only twelve. . . .'

'And is your mother recovered now?'

'No, Sister. She died, ma'am.'

For a moment Sister Radcliffe said nothing and I wondered if she was about to make a comment on the ineffectual nature of Kitty's nursing skills. Instead, she said simply, 'I am sorry to hear that. Kindly do not address me as 'Ma'am.' You will be stationed in the Evacuation Tent.' She turned her attention to me. 'And you are . . . ?'

'Nurse Elise Hawksmith, Sister.'

'A professional nurse, I see.' She took off her glasses and looked me full in the face, daring me to drop my gaze. 'And which do you consider to be your particular skills, Nurse?'

'I have been assisting in the surgical ward and in theater at Saint Thomas's hospital in Manchester for over two years now. I do enjoy the work very much, Sister. But of course I shall be happy to do whatever is asked of me.'

'Indeed.' She replaced her glasses, made two swift marks in the register, and then put it away. 'Let's start you off in the resuscitation tent. See how "happy" you are there, shall we? Nurse Strappington, show them to their quarters.'

Morning came quickly. Kitty and I found the refectory and queued up for breakfast. We were given weak tea and gray porridge. I looked for Strap, but there was no sign of her. I wondered how long her shift could be. She had been working when we arrived and must surely be in need of food and rest by now. Looking around at the taut, pale faces near me, I could see grim determination written over sad resignation. Kitty saw it too and was looking glummer than ever. I finished my food, gave Kitty a few words of encouragement, and made my way to the resuscitation tent. It did not take me many minutes inside it to understand that Sister Radcliffe had sought to test me. The pre-op and operating tents would offer action, treatment, and hope. The ward tent allowed those still too weak to travel to heal a little before their journey or to receive further treatment. The evacuation tent prepared patients for the longed-for trip home or return to the front. The resuscitation tent was a limbo. A purgatory.

Here it was that men too weak to withstand surgery, however much they needed it, must cling to life and wait for an improvement in their conditions that frequently did not come. Here those horribly burned and too frail to withstand the bustle of the ward tent would writhe behind screens and undergo all manner of painful and often ineffectual treatments. Here those half-dead from languishing in the muddy stretches of No Man's Land for fear-filled days, suffering their wounds alone and unaided, would be placed in heated beds in a desperate attempt to bring warmth back to their failing hearts and rotting flesh. I soon learned that more men died here than in any other part of the CCS. And they died here slowly and in pain.

'Nurse Hawksmith!' Sister Radcliffe's voice jolted me from my daze, 'I am not familiar with the way the wards are run at Saint Thomas's, but here there is no time to stand idle.'

'I'm sorry, Sister.'

'Corporal Davies needs his dressings changed.' She indicated the bed nearest me with a curt nod before stepping past me. 'When you have finished there, you will see to Private Spencer and Corporal Baines. There is a list of daily dressings and treatments pinned up at the nurses' station by the entrance to the tent. Kindly read it the minute you start your shift. I do not expect to have to remind you of your duties again.'

'Yes, Sister.' I fetched fresh dressings from the cupboard in the center of the room and hurried to do as I had been instructed.

Corporal Davies was a short, ruddy-faced young man with a shock of black hair and twinkling blue eyes dulled by pain and fatigue.

'Don't let Sister put the wind up you, Nurse,' he said in a soft Welsh lilt. 'She's our secret weapon, see? When they've run out of men at the Front, we're going to send her over the top. Those Germans won't stand a chance.' He tried to laugh, but this caused him to cough horribly, his whole body going into painful spasms. The effort of it left him further weakened and quiet. I glanced at his notes. He had been felled by shrapnel during a bombardment while out on nighttime operations. Unable to move, he had lain in a water-filled shell hole for three days and nights before stretcher-bearers had been able to reach him. While most of his wounds were not serious in themselves, the sheer number of them was incredible. His face had mostly escaped harm, and his tin hat had no doubt saved his life, but his chest and abdomen were riddled with cuts and holes, many still containing sharp pieces of metal, since he was too weak to face surgery. Most of his ribs had been broken in the blast, and a larger piece of shell casing had smashed his left knee joint and tibia and fibula. His right foot had been almost severed at the ankle. He claimed it was the coldness of the muddy water that had saved him from going mad with the pain, and the angle at which his right leg had been stuck up that had stopped him from bleeding to death. Indeed, he had even managed to cake the wound in his ankle with mud to staunch the flow. But that same slime and cold that had kept him alive were now responsible for what would, without hope or doubt, kill him. The filth of the mud had worked together with the hot metal in his wounds to render them septic, turning the flesh around each painful tear and cut purple and swollen. The only thing that might now stop the poison in his blood from killing him was the pneumonia his watery mantrap had given him. The two deadly conditions were engaged in a macabre race to claim the poor man's life. I began the slow task of redressing his wounds. Despite the agony he must have been experiencing, he did not offer one word of complaint or even moan as I peeled lint from his wet and festering skin. Not for the first time I marveled at the human capacity for bravery; at the strength of spirit some possess. And at the ability of man to inflict such merciless suffering on his brothers.

I worked my way through the list of patients who needed dressings changed. Each soldier seemed to present a more ghastly set of injuries than the last; some sightless and terrified, some burned beyond recognition, others limbless and helpless. And each bore his suffering with a calm fortitude that humbled me. At first, I wondered if they were so quiet because they were too weak to complain or because they had simply given up the struggle and were waiting to die. But I quickly came to see this was not the case, at least not for most of them. Each man was locked in his own personal torment, and the heavens only knew what terrors they relived in the darkest moments of the night, but still they were able to find the strength to fight on. Was that what it meant to be a true soldier, I wondered. Not only to be able to fight on the battlefield, but to be able to conquer one's own personal demons, again and again, over and over, in any way that was asked of them? There were very few in the resuscitation tent who wished to die, and those who did could hardly be blamed for it.

At the end of my first shift, some twelve hours after I had unraveled the first bandage, pausing only for a half-hour lunch of watery soup, I returned once again to Corporal Davies. He was sleeping fitfully, his breathing shallow and ragged. All at once, a fierce bout of coughing woke him. He struggled to raise himself and I hurried to help him. He leaned forward, hawking up blood, fighting to drag air back into his failing lungs. When at last he slumped backward onto his pillow, a hideous gurgling noise accompanied each feeble breath. He gazed up at me, his eyes full of panic, and clutched at my hand.

'Don't . . . !' he spluttered.

'Shh, no need to try and talk.'

'Don't . . .' He tried again, each word wrenched from his body with Herculean effort. *'Don't leave me to drown!'*

I let him cling to me and forced myself to hold his gaze. He knew what lay ahead. Hours, perhaps days, of battling for every breath, of choking and retching and suffocating and ultimately drowning on his own blood. I slowly placed his hand on his chest and drew the covers tight around him. I searched for some words of comfort, of hope, of reassurance that I might offer him, but none came. For there was no hope. And he and I both knew it.

I left his bedside and flung myself through the door of the tent. It was already dark outside and the air felt blissfully clean and cool. I walked, head down, not knowing where I was going, wanting only to put some distance between myself and the suffering in the resuscitation tent. I rounded a corner and walked straight into Strap.

'I say!' She caught me as I reeled sideways. 'Steady on, old girl. Can't have you joining the casualties now, can we?' She examined me more closely. 'You look all in. Come along, time for a sit down and a couple of gaspers.' She steered me behind the nurses' hut and onto the step of the seldom-used back door. We sat down, not caring that the wet wood and mud would soil our uniforms, not caring about anything except the need to stop. She pulled a packet of cigarettes from her pocket and offered me one. Seeing me hesitate, she said, 'You might as well. It's the one thing we can all do out here.' She struck a match and I leaned forward. We sat and smoked in silence for a while. I rubbed my temples, wondering how she managed to stay so cheerful in the face of what challenges she must rise to day after day. My weariness had not gone unnoticed.

'No need to ask what you thought of resuss,' she said. 'Miserable post. Was in there myself for a couple of months. Blessed relief to be given pre-op, don't mind telling you.'

'Some of them are so very young.'

'Babes. Mere babes.'

'And we can do so little.'

'Better at blowing people to pieces than sticking them back together, that's the sad truth of it, I'm afraid.' She leaned back against the door-frame. ''Twas ever thus, I suppose.'

'At least in pre-op they have a chance,' I said, feeling slightly sick after my third lungful of cigarette smoke. 'In resuss, well, most of them won't even make it to the operating theater. Some of them would be better off . . .'

'Don't say it!' Strap was suddenly furious. 'Say anything else you must, but never, ever, *ever* say what you were about to say. We are here to heal, to help these men recover.'

'And you really believe that's best for all of them? That we patch them up and send them home no matter what state they're in, no matter how terrible their . . . existences would be?'

'Of course I do. I have to. Otherwise, what's the point?' Her voice dropped again. 'What the bloody hell's the point?'

I looked at her strong, open features and wondered at her clarity of thought. At her sense of purpose. At her resolution. I thought of the burned shadow of the boy in the corner bed, and of the pointless suffering of Corporal Davies, and I couldn't agree with her. Life at any cost? I wished I shared her passion, but I did not. Was it because I considered some suffering to be intolerable, or was it because I had, at times, come to see life as a curse? I, who had shuffled about on this planet for centuries observing the ceaseless fighting and battling and struggling that people endured. Could death be such a terrible thing? Were there not times when it was the right thing? Or did I wonder that because it had been denied me? I could not be certain.

Strap stood up, grinding out her cigarette stub with her heel.

'Come on,' she said brightly. 'Better get some supper down our necks. Brace yourself—the horrors of resuss are as nothing when compared to what's served up as stew around here.'

As we entered the refectory, the smell of the food hit us. It was so vile

I wondered how anyone could sit in the room, let alone actually eat the glu-
tinous mess of rancid meat and salty gravy that slopped about in our bowls.

'I'd like to tell you one gets used to it,' Strap said, pushing up her
sleeves, 'but it would be cruel to give you false hope. Just pray for a speedy
delivery of parcels from home and for pity's sake write to anyone you've
ever met who might be talked into sending us Bovril and biscuits.'

An hour later, my stomach struggling to hold onto the revolting supper I had inflicted upon it, I washed quickly in cold water, took off my
uniform, and crawled into bed in my underwear. I hadn't the energy to
dig out my pajamas and had no wish to waste what precious time for sleep
there might be. This proved to be a wise decision. My eyes could not
have been shut for more than an hour when I was roughly shaken awake
by Kitty.

'Wake up, Elise! Sister says everyone's to be on duty in five minutes.
Get a move on, do!'

'What's happening?' I asked blearily. Strap finished lacing her boots
and stood up.

'Failed attack. There's a convoy of ambulances heading our way. It's all
hands on deck, I'm afraid.'

I flung on my uniform and raced after her. Sister Radcliffe was outside
the nurses' hut issuing orders.

'Nurse Strappington, Nurse Hawksmith, reception marquee. Quickly
please.'

Strap glanced at me. 'Oh Lord,' she muttered, 'you really are getting
thrown in at the deep end, aren't you, old girl? Never mind. Hold your
nerve and don't expect to work miracles. You'll need these.' She shoved
a packet of cigarettes into my hand.

'Surely there won't be time to take a break . . . ?'

'They're not for you, you goose, they're for the men. Half the time it's
all they want. Most of the time it's all you can do for them anyway.'

I was about to follow her when I sensed I was being watched. Of
course I have spent my life glancing over my shoulder, listening for unfamiliar footsteps, and generally staying alert to the possibility that I have
been found. It is no more than any other creature that has become prey
would do. But by the time I found myself in Flanders, it had been many
years since I had felt his presence. Gideon's presence. I had put this down

largely to the fact that I had taken to moving even more frequently. And to my not having used my magic. Whatever the reasons, I believed I had not come close to being in his company for decades. And even now, at the moment when I halted in my stride because of the overwhelming feeling of someone's eyes being focused on me, I was certain that still this was not him. This spirit was powerful but utterly benign. I moved my head minutely and scanned the bustle of people pressing about me. I soon found him. He was a tall, broad-shouldered young soldier. An officer, his uniform suggested. He wore his mustache fuller than most, and his eyes were gentle. He leaned on a stick but looked otherwise fit and strong. He stood quite still, looking directly at me. In the midst of all that chaos and fear, he was a small point of calm. Of peace. I stared at him and experienced an unexpected and confusing longing for my childhood home in Wessex. Puzzled, I continued to watch him, that is, to watch myself being watched by him. In the darkness and at a distance of twenty yards or so it was hard to see his face clearly. Indeed, I did not feel that I *saw* him at all, rather that I connected with him. We both stood motionless, locked in this strange meeting, until I heard Sister shout my name and was galvanized into movement. I stumbled through the crowd of scurrying orderlies and nurses toward reception. When I looked back, the soldier was gone.

2

I slept so badly that by five o'clock the next morning I had given up trying. I slipped out of the dormitory and exited the clearing station, heading away from the sound of the artillery. The darkness was just lifting into its pre-dawn pallor so that I was able to find my way quite well. I was very soon clear of the village and picked my way through fallow fields as yet undisturbed by war, except for their state of neglect. It was bliss to be free of the madness of the tents and their tragic occupants. Here I could convince myself normal life, whatever that was, continued. And would continue, beyond the chaos that raged only a few miles away. I found a moss-covered gate and sat on it to watch the sun rise. The light began to alter, lending an amber tinge to the flat landscape that stretched out before me. The first birds of the day started to sing out. There were larks, rooks, and finches. In the grass, poppies and marigold vied for attention, so clean and bright and unashamedly pretty. How I needed to remind my weary heart that life would go on. That there were still good things to be discovered, even in this fearsome place. I found myself weeping. For the men whose eyes had been permanently closed and would never witness such loveliness again. For the mothers back home who had lost their boys and would never see joy in anything again. For the pointlessness of it all. For my own uselessness. At last I could ignore that small voice in my head no longer. The ancient voice, the voice that I had silenced and refused to listen to after what had happened at the Fitzroy. I had promised myself I would turn my back on my magic. I would never again draw Gideon to me by using it or subject other innocent people to his evil power. And so I had lived a half-life, a lie—a tense, benumbed existence, denying what I truly was. I knew, as I sat there on that gate surrounded by beauty and goodness, I knew that I could pretend no longer. The bravery of the wounded men humbled me. What sort of coward would I be to put my own safety above theirs? What sort of woman would I be not to give help and care where it was so sorely needed? What sort of witch would I be not to use everything in my gift to heal? I stopped crying and lifted my face to the sun. I let its warm rays bathe my features. I took in its energy. I breathed in the sweet country air.

'So be it,' I said aloud. 'So be it.'

By the time I arrived back at the CCS, it was too late for breakfast, so I went directly to the resuscitation tent. As I approached, strange sounds reached my ears: strangled, unearthly cries that made my skin crawl. Corporal Davies was locked in a nightmare of delirium.

I glanced around the ward. None of the other patients would meet my eye. All were clearly greatly affected by their comrade's suffering. In the bed behind me, another soldier hissed between clenched teeth. 'Shut him up, Nurse,' he begged. 'For Christ's sake, shut him up!'

I passed my shift in a blur of confusion and anxiety. I knew what I had to do, but I was aware of the risks and of what the consequences might be if I was found out. I bided my time. At six o'clock that evening the doctor finished his rounds, and I watched Sister Radcliffe head across the campus to her office. I was left with one other nurse, a nervous young girl from the Home Counties.

'You go and get some supper,' I told her. 'I can finish off here.'

'Are you sure?'

'It's very quiet tonight. I can manage. Go on. If you're quick, you might even get some fresh bread with your meal.'

She needed no further persuading and disappeared with something approaching a spring in her step. I checked that the patients were comfortable and settled and then quietly positioned screens around the bed of Corporal Davies. I picked up his notes and read his first name. Danny. Not Daniel but Danny. To somebody he was a son, a husband, a father, perhaps. Danny Davies from a far, far away place with mountains and viridian grass and speeding clouds in the sky. I looked at the wheezing, trembling figure on the bed and thought how cruel it was that he must suffer so very much and so very far from home. I moved to kneel beside him. I reached out and took his hand in mine. He stirred and looked at me. He had not been asleep, merely closing his eyes against the ghastliness of his painful waking world.

I met his gaze and leaned closer. 'I cannot heal you, Danny. I am sorry, but I do not have it in my power to undo what has been done to your poor body. I cannot return you to the fine young man you once were, at least, not here. But I can help you; I can put an end to your suffering. Danny, I can send you to a wonderful place, a place free of pain, a place of happiness and love, a place where you can be whole again. Do you understand?'

He peered at me through flickering lids. For a moment he made no response, then, almost imperceptibly but quite distinctly, he nodded.

'Is that truly what you want, Danny? Tell me. I must know that this is what you wish.'

His breathing grew quicker. His mouth moved painfully. At last, in a rasp of exhaled air, seemingly from his very heart came a single, vehement word.

'*Yessss!*'

I nodded and straightened up. I closed my eyes but kept my hand softly on his the whole time. Slowly I focused my mind; I directed my soul. I looked inward, deep into my own essence, searching, searching. Searching for the long-buried treasure. Gradually it began to stir. Haltingly at first, and then with increasing strength and speed, I felt the magic within me welling up, filling my being once more. It coursed through my veins; it charged through my nervous system; it pumped through my heart. It engulfed me. I could feel myself glowing with the power and the wonder of it. It felt so good to be complete again, after such a long time asleep and alone. I opened my eyes. Danny was watching me closely, but I saw no fear in his expression. I let my head fall back and began to whisper a chant. Softly at first, then as loud as I dared without disturbing the sleeping men on the other side of the screen. Over and over I repeated the incantation, putting all the longing of those dry, barren years into each word. In no time at all my calls were answered. They had joined us. The swirling green mist grew thicker and brighter, so that very soon I could make out the faces and shifting shapes of many of my sisters within it. Danny moved his head, trying to follow the whirling progress of the beautiful figures as they danced around and above him. I squeezed his hand, confident that he would feel no pain. The air was filled with an almost overpowering scent of roses. He looked at me again now, wonder in his eyes.

'Do not be afraid, Danny. The Summerlands is a glorious place. Go now. Be free. Be strong and happy again.'

My sisters spun about him faster and faster until in one pulsating maelstrom they moved upward. There, in the midst of them, I saw Danny's spirit rise up too. This was not the wretched, ruined, husk of a man like the one who lay in front of me. This was Danny whole and vibrant and youthful once more. He looked down at me and smiled, a smile of such joy it moved me to tears. I knew in that instant I had done the right thing. Whatever was to come, whatever the consequences, this was what I had to do. There was no other path to be taken. Suddenly, in a heartbeat, they were gone. The small space was still and silent once more. Danny's body was empty. I let go his lifeless hand and hurried out of the tent.

In the nurses' quarters I found everyone else asleep. I sat on my bed, my heart still pounding, my mind fizzing, and my body tingling. For the first time in a very long while, I felt properly alive. I sat for almost an hour, unable to proceed with the mundane business of undressing and getting into bed. Knowing, in any event, that I would not be able to sleep. I was lost in rekindled memories, in rediscovered bonds and friendships, in the bliss of magic filling my being once more. I was so distracted I did not notice Sister Radcliffe enter the hut until she was standing in front of me. Startled, I sprang to my feet, convinced my altered state could not go unnoticed. She regarded me severely for a moment, her mouth set and tense.

'Nurse Hawksmith,' she said, her voice even more stern that usual, 'my office, if you please. This instant.'

3

It would not be an exaggeration to say Sister marched me to her office. I braced myself for what was to come. I presumed that by now Corporal Davies' death had been discovered. I could only imagine someone must have said something about my sitting with him shortly after the end of my shift. Had the other patients heard the strange sounds coming from behind the screens? Could they have seen the apparitions or heard my incantations? I had administered no drugs. There could surely be no evidence to suggest I had had anything to do with his death. However, even in his extremely fragile state, Danny had not been expected to die so quickly. Sister Radcliffe sat down behind her desk and, to my surprise, bade me take a seat myself.

'I have been watching you closely since your arrival, Nurse,' she said. 'I admit I find some of your methodology, shall we say, unorthodox. Nevertheless, you have proved yourself to be hard working, diligent, competent, and, possibly most important of all, able to keep your head.'

I was taken aback. The last thing I had been expecting from Sister was praise of any sort.

'Thank you, Sister,' I said.

'In peacetime these would have been qualities I would have expected from my nurses without exception. However, this is not peacetime. These are extraordinary circumstances, and many of the girls here would never have thought to unravel a bandage had it not been for the war. Suffice it to say most of them are not natural nurses. In truth, there are few here I consider worthy of the name. But we must make the best of what we have. To this end, my job is to see to it that the most expert care is given to those who require it, and this often means my best nurses find themselves overstretched and under considerable pressure.'

She paused and I wondered if she was waiting for me to say something. I still had no idea where this speech was leading, so I sat still and remained silent.

'The upshot is,' Sister continued, 'I face a dilemma. Should I, at all costs, keep the most able of my staff here at the CCS, where I know their talents will be well used? Or should I, as I have been asked to do, relinquish a valuable pair of trained hands to lend support to a woefully undermanned field hospital?'

'A field hospital? You mean, at the front?'

'Precisely.' She pulled a letter from the neat pile of papers on her desk and studied it. 'The request has come from the commanding officer himself. He does not ask lightly.'

'Is it customary? To send nurses, female nurses, so close to the battlefront?'

'It is not. However, there is soon to be a major offensive. I give away no secrets in talking about this, as you will have heard the Allied bombardment of the past few days. It precedes the order to attack. It is believed this may be the final push. Such is the nature of our sustained artillery fire that it is considered the risk to our own men will have been minimized. Heavy casualties are not anticipated. However, the number of soldiers involved is great, and it is felt that the medical officers need more support. All the CCSs have been asked to send someone.' She looked up from the letter. 'Well, Nurse Hawksmith, do you consider yourself equal to the task?'

'Why yes, Sister. I am willing to do whatever is needed. I am flattered to be asked.'

'Don't be. I would have sent Nurse Strappington, but we simply can't spare her. You are the next best choice. Have your things packed for the morning. You will be taken in one of the ambulances along with the requested medical supplies. Now, go and get some sleep.'

I stood up, 'Thank you, Sister,' I said. 'I won't let you down.' I had almost reached the exit when she spoke again.

'One thing more, Nurse. Corporal Davies passed away this evening.'

I was glad I had my back to her. I composed my features into as blank an expression as I could muster and turned around. 'I'm sorry to hear that, Sister,' I said.

'Are you? Are you really, Nurse? I wonder.' She looked at me through narrowed eyes and then returned to her paperwork. 'Hurry along now,' she said.

The next day I said brief farewells to Kitty and Strap and climbed into the front seat of an ambulance. The bonnet of the vehicle bore a deep gash. The driver told me with grim relish it was a shrapnel scar from a perilously close encounter with a German shell. I wedged my bag beneath my feet and clung onto the doorless frame of the open-fronted van as it rattled its way out of Saint Justine and toward the Front. Soon we had left the roads and joined the rough track that served as conduit between the railway station and the front line. This was the main route for all supplies, as well as being the most direct path for transporting the wounded to the hospital, and for troops going to join battalions in the trenches. As the ambulance drew closer to the location of the Allied artillery, the sound of the guns became utterly terrifying. And the farther we drove from the village, the more sinister the landscape was. Gone were the fescued fields and bird-filled hedgerows. Gone, indeed, were all signs of normal farming activity. A relentless combination of wagons, bombs, booted feet, and unseasonal rain had rendered the low-lying fields a muddy wasteland. All that could be seen was a gray-brown wetness pocked with waterlogged shell holes. The mud was riven with zigzagging trenches and entrances to subterranean dugouts. At random points, stretches of wire remained, all that was left of an earlier measure of the army's advance: a previous line drawn on a map somewhere that translated to a wound on the skin of the landscape, jagged and barbed and filled with the blood of young men. The rain that had been falling steadily for many days showed no signs of stopping. Even so, it could not hope to wash away the stains such slaughter had left upon the gentle countryside. Nor could it cleanse the ground of the all-pervading stink of death. The smell was overwhelming. I pressed a hand to my mouth, amazed at how none of the passing soldiers seemed to notice the intolerable odor that filled my nostrils and threatened to make me retch. I was forced to the conclusion that they no longer detected it, so accustomed were they to the stench. It was the smell of stagnant water and rotting vegetation, of cordite and smoke, and above everything, the smell of decomposing flesh. I had encountered it so many times before, and in so many ways. The dead sheep behind the hedge. The plague corpse left too long in a house. The unmissed vagrant disintegrating in an alley. The hospital morgue on a warm day. There was no mistaking it.

At last the ambulance stopped.

'This is as far as I go,' said the driver. 'I'm unloading the medical supplies here, and they'll be carried up the line to the field hospital. If you hang on a mo' you can follow on.'

I climbed out of the van, moving awkwardly with my gas mask strapped over my heavy greatcoat, and did my best to keep out of the way as men were mustered to transport the crates and stretchers. The driver made no attempt to conceal his eagerness to leave, and the moment the last item was handed over he revved up the coughing vehicle and was gone.

'Stay close,' a sergeant addressed me as he passed. 'Watch your step now, Nurse. Don't want to lose you, do we? Right you are, lads. Let's get this lot to the medical officer, quick as you can now.'

We were still some distance behind the foremost trenches, but there was no road. Instead, we stepped onto a complex network of duckboards. The wooden slats were coated in a layer of slippery mud and tipped in places at unhelpful angles. Some of the tracks sank and wobbled as we made our halting progress, so I was amazed to see teams of horses and mules using these makeshift paths as they pulled supply wagons and even gun carriages. The animals plodded stoically on. Constant exposure must have inured them to the cacophony and flashing lights ahead of them. That or extreme fatigue. We stood aside to let one team pass. The lead horses' mouths were foaming, and their brown flanks were sleek with sweat from the effort of their work. Their hooves slithered on the treacherous surface, but still they leaned into their collars, urged on gently by the driver atop the biggest of the four. Two gunners rode the hind pair of the outfit. Behind the carriage walked an officer. His gait was confident and brisk, but there was an unevenness to it. As he drew level with me, I recognized him as the soldier I had seen outside the reception marquee. He saw me and stopped. Surprised, he smiled, and I found myself smiling back. After a moment we became aware we were being observed.

'Forgive me, Nurse,' he said. 'Manners fare badly out here in the salient.' There was a laugh at the edge of his voice, and the faintest trace of Caledonian origins. 'Lieutenant Carmichael, Ninth Battalion, Royal Scots Regiment, surprised but delighted to meet you.' He offered me his hand and I took it.

'Nurse Hawksmith. I've been sent out from the CCS at Saint Justine to assist at the field hospital.'

'Ah, is that what they're calling it?'

'I'm sorry?'

'It's not much of a hospital. More an advanced first-aid post, really. But you are absolutely what they need, I'm sure of it. I'll take you there myself. You'll like the MO. Looks like a light breeze would blow him over, but the man's a trouper. Couldn't wish for better.'

I fell into step beside him, though I had to slow my pace to do so.

'Surely you should be recuperating, Lieutenant. Your leg . . .'

'Is perfectly fine, thank you so much for your concern. I may never be a sprinter, but I could still tramp the heather from dawn till dusk. Seems a good enough test of a man's fitness to me.' He broke off abruptly, raising his eyes to the sky. He seemed to hear something I did not. In a second he had hurled me to the ground and flung himself upon me. Only as I landed on the boards did I hear the approaching shell. The random bombardment was swift and merciless. I pressed my eyes shut and threw my hands over my head in an ineffectual reflex as the deadly metal ripped through the air and exploded only yards from where we cowered. The noise of the shell was replaced by the screaming of the horses. We scrambled to our feet. Three soldiers lay dead, having taken the main force of the blast. It was their misfortune that killed them and our good luck that decreed we should live, nothing more. The terrified horses had bolted and charged from the duckboards, dragging their weighty cargo into the mud. One had taken a piece of shrapnel to the chest and lay lifeless on its side, while the other three thrashed and screamed in the silt-filled water that was already up to their bellies. The two gunners clambered onto the howitzer. The driver clung to his horse's back, frantically trying to calm the panic-stricken animal. His words were lost in the noise and chaos as the horses plunged and roared in desperate attempts to escape the sucking mud into which they had run.

'Get out!' Lieutenant Carmichael shouted at the men. 'Climb back along the gun!'

'Got to untie the horses, sir!' the driver replied, reaching down to grope for the chains and straps, which were already submerged.

'There is no time.' The lieutenant organized other soldiers to form a human chain to reach the gunners, who were now kneeling on the end of the gun carriage, only the barrel of the weapon visible above the liquid mud that was dragging it down. 'Leave the horses, driver, that's an order! Now, man, while there's still a chance we can reach you!'

The young soldier shook his head.

'No, sir! I can't leave them, sir!'

The weight of the sunken gun speeded the descent of the doomed horses into the mud. Their struggles were futile. Within moments only their heads—eyes rolling, nostrils pink and distended—remained above the soupy waterline.

Lieutenant Carmichael grabbed a nearby ladder. 'Corporal, hold the end of this,' he said, flinging the ladder ahead of him onto the mud. He lay on top of it, spreading his weight, and crawled toward the petrified driver. He reached him just as the lead horse was finally swallowed by the mire. Its last, exhausted groan was replaced by a heartbreaking silence, disturbed only by the ever-present booming of the guns. The officer grabbed the young soldier's arm and dragged him onto the ladder. Too shocked to protest, the driver lay beside him, shaking, as the gunners and two more soldiers struggled to drag the ladder back to safety. The lieutenant sat on the boards and held the sobbing lad in his arms, the two of them coated in a layer of filth, the young soldier's tears washing clear trails down his grime-covered face.

Quietly, people returned to their duties. The dead soldiers were near enough to be recovered and were taken away for burial. There were, miraculously, no further casualties. Lieutenant Carmichael instructed the gunners to take their driver back to their unit in the reserves. He stood in front of me and took hold of my hands.

'Are you all right?' he asked.

'I am unhurt. I dropped my bag,' I began to look around. He spotted it and picked it up. Taking my arm, he directed me along a short stretch of boards that led to one of the trenches.

'Come along,' he said, 'the MO can wait a little longer. I have some brandy in my dugout.'

We picked our way down a flight of uneven and slippery steps into the trench. I was surprised at how deep and how narrow it was. How could men spend hour upon hour, day upon day, often night after night in such inhospitable, wet, stinking places? Although the trench was hundreds of yards long, it was zigzagged, the better to protect its inhabitants from blasts, so that I could only see a short distance ahead. The effect was claustrophobic, while at the same time offering scant protection. Indeed, if a trench was to take a direct hit from a shell such as the one I had just encountered, there would surely be no hope of survival for anyone in it. One young soldier sat on his haunches over a tiny stove, entirely focused on stirring stew in an improvised tin pot. Another leaned against the sandbags and played a harmonica softly. A movement caught my eye on the floor. A rat, bigger than any I had ever seen, scuttled among the debris. It was fat and sleek and clearly thriving. I thought it strange, at first, knowing how scarce rations were at the Front and how jealously supplies were guarded. Then the awful truth came to me. There was no shortage of food for these creatures. Indeed there was a limitless supply of meat, freshly slaughtered by sniper or barrage or machine gun, readily available in the wastes of No Man's Land. Now I saw that the narrow passage was alive with rodents, many spiky with mud, others caked in gore. I fought the desire to vomit and followed the lieutenant down another short flight of steps. The dugout was surprisingly dry inside, with boards on the floor, four bunk beds, a locker, and a table and chairs in the center of the space. Little light penetrated from the outside, so two Tilley lamps dangled, rasping from nails in the beams, swinging with each shudder of the assaulted earth above. As my eyes adjusted to the gloom, I could make out two figures, one standing beside the table, the other reclining on one of the lower bunks.

'Please, take a seat.' Lieutenant Carmichael pulled out a chair for me, taking off his cap to dust it. 'Oh, this is Lieutenant Maidstone, and that lazy creature over there is Captain Tremain. This is Nurse Hawksmith. Break out the RAD, Maidstone.'

'This is more like it,' said the mustachioed officer, 'company and cocktails. Why, I could imagine myself back in Berkshire.'

The captain stirred himself and rose slowly from his bunk. He was tall and lean but moved stiffly, as if life in the trenches had rusted his very joints.

'Here we go,' said Maidstone. 'RAD, or Rarely Arrives at Destination, as we call it. Glasses, please.'

The three of us held out tin mugs while he tipped brandy into them. We did, indeed, for all the world resemble a little gathering enjoying pre-dinner drinks. If only one could block out the distant rumble of the artillery. If only one could stop the stink of rotting flesh from creeping up one's nostrils. We drank in silence. Lieutenant Carmichael smiled at me. Lieutenant Maidstone openly stared, making me wonder how long it was since he had seen a woman. Captain Tremain was standing a little too close to me for my comfort. Then, to my astonishment, he leaned closer still, closed his eyes and breathed in deeply. He was actually smelling me! This bizarre action had not gone unnoticed. Maidstone let out a rattle of loud laughter.

'I say, Tremain, you're aiming to get your face slapped!' he said.

'Hmmm,' he murmured, opening his eyes slowly, 'it would be worth it.'

Maidstone laughed some more. I stole a glance at Lieutenant Carmichael and was reassured to see he did not think the incident in the least bit amusing. Nor did I. More than that, I was unsettled. A coldness settled about my shoulders, provoking an involuntary shiver. The ridiculousness of this struck me. After all I had experienced on the duckboards, after all the horrors I had dealt with at the CCS, why was I now so disturbed by one man's harmless impertinence? As if I needed an answer to my question, from the trench outside the dugout came the whining strains of the young soldier's harmonica, distorted by the mud wall and the distance but unmistakably the one tune guaranteed to strike fear into my heart.

4

The rain worsened. It was not cold, and there was no wind to speak of, it simply fell relentlessly and pitilessly upon the sodden ground and upon the battle-weary soldiers whose world had been reduced to a few miles of bleeding earth. Lieutenant Carmichael escorted me farther along the meandering boards to my new post. He explained that I was to wait there for the MO and that he himself would call back that night to make sure I was well provided for. There was no compulsion on him to appoint himself my protector, but I did not protest. In truth, I was pleased that I would be seeing him again. Already I found I was altered in his presence; affected in a way I had almost forgotten existed.

The field hospital was, in fact, nothing more than an abandoned German pillbox. I could not believe that this cramped, dark, single room was to be all we would have. It was certainly a solid structure and, from the look of it, had already withstood many blasts, but it was so small. I was still staring wordlessly about when the medical officer in charge arrived, blocking out the precious light allowed in through the doorway. He was, as the lieutenant had told me, a slender reed of a man, with wayward wisps of gray hair and a sparse mustache. His gaunt features and generally cadaverous appearance did nothing to inspire confidence that he would be able to look after himself, much less anyone else. However, there was indeed a steely core to the man.

'Ah, reinforcements!' he declared on seeing me, grabbing my hand to shake it with surprising vigor. 'Captain Young, exceptionally pleased to see you.'

'Nurse Hawksmith,' I said. 'Hardly the cavalry, I'm afraid, but . . .'

'. . . infinitely more welcome, and no doubt more useful,' he assured me. He let go of my hand to stride about the interior of the concrete box. 'We were lucky to get this,' he said. 'Last advanced aid post I set up was in a dugout. All very well being tucked in among the trenches, but we had the devil's own job getting stretchers in and out. And a few sandbags and a bit of wood won't keep the shells off a person.' He patted the rough walls with pride. 'This will do very well. They can throw the worst they have at us, to no avail. Ironic, really, that we should benefit from the enemy's engineering skills.'

'Isn't it a little on the small side?' I asked.

'Compared to what? No, no, don't you worry about that; space can be a mixed blessing. The more room you have, the more stretchers you can take, the more casualties pile up around you. This way we have to send them on quick sharp. No dithering. You don't dither, do you, Nurse? No,' he answered his own question, 'I can see that you don't. There will be no time for it. We are here to clear airways and staunch the flow of blood sufficiently to enable the wounded to survive the trip to the CCS. That's the long and the short of it. No time for frills and furbelows. Forget cleaning wounds. Bind 'em up and send 'em out.'

'But surely,' I protested, 'the risk of sepsis . . .'

'. . . is considerably lower than the risk of a bomb falling on a casualty's head if we have to start lining them up outside. And don't go dishing out morphine like sweeties, whatever you do. Save it for the ones who can't do without.'

I wondered how I was to decide such a thing and imagined myself refusing pain relief to an agonized soldier. I closed my eyes briefly. There were things I could do. There were other remedies at my disposal. And I knew that I would use them to ease suffering. Just as I had used them for Corporal Davies.

'Are you quite well, Nurse?' Captain Young asked. 'You're not given to fainting? Not squeamish, I hope?'

'I am perfectly well, Doctor.'

'Last thing we need is women swooning all over the place . . .'

It was my turn to interrupt. 'I assure you I have no intention of swooning. Even if I had, I doubt there would be room for it.'

He looked at me in amazement, failing entirely to see the joke of the comment, rather applauding my logic.

'Quite so, Nurse, quite so. No fainting then. Excellent, excellent. Now, if you will assist me, we must organize our supplies. Everything must be to hand, d'you see? Organization is the key.'

My dugout was situated only a few yards from the pillbox and still bore evidence of the German soldiers who had fled from it when the Allies had gained a few yards of ground and extended the salient farther into Flanders. There was a biscuit tin of German manufacture, the smiling child depicted on the front shown enjoying one of the long-gone *brötchen*. Beneath the lower bunk was a torn photograph of a young woman. In the stillness of the dugout, in an unaccustomed moment of idleness, my mind coasting, I became aware of a stirring of my sixth sense; a restlessness in the part of me that intuits rather than thinks. I should not have been surprised. I was in a situation, a time, a location so steeped in the blood of sacrifice, so echoing with the cries of the wounded and dying, so imbued with suffering that it was to be expected that the power of evil would be ever-present too. There is a dark energy that surrounds the battlefield, that feeds off the violence and cruelty of war. It is a frightening force. A potent one. And one in which those who practice the dark arts thrive. I shuddered, attempting to shake off the notion of Gideon being drawn to such a place. At that moment I sorely missed the company of my fellow nurses back at the CCS. Hearing light footsteps on the wooden stairs behind me, I turned to find a tiny woman, her overlong greatcoat trailing in the mud, her nurse's headdress threatening to slip down over her eyes.

'Oh, hello, dear,' she said. 'They told me there was already a nurse down here. I'm Annie Higgins.' She held out a dainty hand.

'Elise Hawksmith. Have you been sent up from a CCS somewhere?'

'That's right, dear, down at Beaumonde.' She unbuttoned her coat and looked for somewhere to put it. 'My word, this is a bit of a gloomy place, isn't it? Never mind. I don't suppose we shall be here long.' She sat on the lower bunk and looked about her. She had an aura of motherliness and warmth. She was considerably older than any of the nurses I had encountered at the Front so far, and I wondered about her reasons for being there.

'I'm glad you've come,' I said, sitting down beside her. 'I have a feeling we are going to be impossibly swamped.'

'Well, we shall do our very best. You can't do more than that. That's what my Bert always says.'

'Is Bert your husband?'

'That's right, dear. Married twenty-five years last month. Or would have been, had God seen fit to spare him.' She glanced up at me and then down at her lap. 'Lost him at the Somme. Still can't get used to talking about him in the past. Still feels as if he's with me, if you know what I mean.'

I nodded. 'Is that why you're here? Because of him?'

'He did his bit. Seems only fair I should do mine. Mind you, I wouldn't have come when our boy Billie was still out here. He had to have someone back home to write to, didn't he? But now he's gone too.' She fell silent.

'I'm so very sorry,' I said. 'To lose both your husband and your son . . .'

'I'm not the first, and I dare say I shan't be the last. No use me sitting at home feeling sorry for myself.' She summoned a brave little smile. 'Better to keep busy. See if I can help out.'

She looked at me now, and in her gentle face and delicate features I saw the sorrow she had endured, the sorrow and the unbearable loss. I knew that she would indeed be a comfort to the young wounded soldiers. I knew also that they would in some way be a solace to her in her grief. I put my hand on hers.

'We will do our very best, then, you and I,' I said. 'Our very best.'

It was nearly midnight by the time we had been given our rations and made our bunks tolerable. Annie had clambered into the bottom bed and fallen immediately into a sound sleep. I was about to retire when I heard a now-familiar voice calling my name, and Lieutenant Carmichael stood in the entrance to the dugout.

'I hope I am not disturbing you. I wanted to make certain that you have everything you need,' he said, swiping his cap from his head as he stepped into the damp little room.

'It was good of you to trouble yourself, Lieutenant,' I told him, 'but we have been well looked after. Nurse Higgins is already asleep.' I indicated the slumbering form beneath the gray blanket.

'Ah, good,' he said more quietly. 'That's very good, then.'

Seeing him hesitate, I stepped aside. 'Won't you stay for a few moments?' I asked him. 'I'm sure I shall never sleep anyway with the guns so close.'

He allowed himself the slightest of smiles and joined me on the low bench.

'I'm not sure I should be able to sleep without them,' he said. 'I've grown accustomed to the noise.'

'It is a curious lullaby.'

'Isn't it?'

I noticed he had succeeded in brushing some of the mud from his uniform, and some must have been washed off in the rain. It was still hard to get from my mind the image of him with the sobbing young gunner in his arms.

'That was very brave, what you did when the horses bolted,' I told him. 'I'm certain that poor soldier would never have left them if you hadn't been there.'

'The shell holes are death traps. I've seen men lost in them in moments. Tanks even. Swallowed up. It's no way to die.'

'Is there a good way?'

'I suppose I have to think so. Otherwise, how could I, in all conscience, order my men over the top tomorrow? Most of them won't survive the attack, you know.'

'But the bombardment . . . surely the enemy's defenses must have been weakened?'

'They might. Then again, they can retreat and wait for it to stop. They may lose a few positions but nothing of importance. We don't even know if the wire is still there. If it is, we'll be trapped. And we have lost all possible element of surprise. Even if we advance under a creeping barrage, they will know that as soon as the heavy guns fall silent we are preparing to attack.' His knuckles blanched as his grip on his army cap tightened. For a moment, neither of us spoke. 'Do you know,' he said at last, 'I truly believe that out here more soldiers die of drowning than anything else? Imagine that, so far from the sea. Oh, I know it's different in the clearing stations, and back home some suffer terrible wounds from which they never recover. But you don't see what happens out there, in the salient, with nothing but bog and stinking water. It's the accoutrements as much as anything. The packs are so heavy, and the guns, and the gas masks, and God knows what else they won't go a step without. If they are hit, bullet or shrapnel, it doesn't matter; unless they are blown off their feet, they nearly always fall flat. Onto their faces or backs, doesn't make much difference, they start to sink the moment they hit the ground. Some pass out. Others simply can't move. So they drown. Just like that. In a few rotten inches of water. It takes days for the stretcher-bearers to gather everyone in after a push. Some are never recovered. They just sink. And every time we gain a bit of this hellish territory, we walk over them. We've been doing it for weeks now. If one steps on a firm piece of ground, chances are it's an Allied casualty beneath one's foot. Sickening thought. Sickening.'

I felt deeply sorry for him, and I badly wanted to take his hand, to hold him, to tell him everything would be all right. But I could not. For one thing, it would have been a lie. He was in as much danger as any of his men, possibly more. There was no guarantee we would ever see each other again. I could not bring myself to patronize him with empty words of encouragement and optimism. But there was something else that made me hold back. I realized that, had he been any other soldier sitting next to me sharing his fears of the coming battle, I would not have hesitated to take his hand in mine. Had I not spent my life trusting in the healing power of touch? But with this soldier, there was more to be considered. There were my burgeoning feelings for him. The way the sound of his voice had made me catch my breath. The way my body stirred beneath his gaze. The way I had already spent so many hours thinking of him, imagining him, wanting to be near him. And there was the way the closeness of him made me feel that I had come home. I remembered how I had thought of my family cottage at Batchcombe when I had first seen him. In his company, I had the sense of being where I belonged. A sensation that was so strong and so unfamiliar to me that I was afraid of it.

'Don't let's talk of war,' I said. 'Tell me about your home. Tell me about your life before all this madness. You spoke of tramping the heather.'

'Do you remember my saying that? How strange. In the middle of bedlam you remember heather.'

'Tell me. Please.'

I could see the tension ebbing from his body as he began to describe his home in the Scottish highlands. The taut muscles around his mouth relaxed, and his handsome face lost its haunted look.

'Our family home is called Glencarrick. It is a truly remarkable place. The house is stone and ridiculously large but quite magical. It was built in the fourteenth century, and I don't suppose it's any warmer to live in now than it was then, but I adore the place. From the turrets on the west wing, you can see for thirty miles in any direction. If you look south, you can see the village of Glencarrick Ross, all of which used to belong to the estate originally. To the north and east are hills and open moorland, the most beautiful landscape you would wish for. And if you turn your face west, I swear you can taste the salt from the sea that lies over the blue horizon. In the summer, when the heather is at its best, the air is filled with the song of skylarks and curlews, and bees from our hives make splendid honey from visiting the blossoms. There are red deer, of course, and otters on the river nearby, and the swiftest mountain hare of anywhere in the world. I used to go shooting; everyone did. I doubt I shall ever pick up a gun again after this.' He closed his eyes and leaned back against the gritty wall of the dugout. 'When things get really very bad here, whenever I fear I might not be able to do what is asked of me, I shut my eyes and travel back to Glencarrick. If I listen very carefully, I can hear the mewing buzzards and the whirring larks. I can smell the wet autumn bracken or taste the damsons from the trees that grow wild behind the house.'

He sat still as stone, his breath held. I watched him, and I shared his longing to be in such a place. Suddenly his eyes sprang open and he looked directly at me.

'I wish I could take you there,' he said. 'One day.'

'Perhaps you will. One day.'

'You know, I'd like it very much if you would call me Archie. Would that be all right, d'you think?'

'I think that would be perfectly all right,' I said, 'and you can call me Elise.'

'Elise?' He seemed surprised. 'Strange. I would never have guessed that was your name.'

'No? What name would you have given me?'

He thought about it for a several seconds then said, 'Bess. A good Scottish name. Yes, definitely Bess. Why, whatever is it? What's wrong? If I've upset you, please forgive me . . .'

'No.' I struggled to regain my composure, knowing that my face must show my surprise, my shock at his choice. I should have been afraid, perhaps, and yet, hearing my name, my true name, in Archie's gentle voice . . . I was not alarmed. Far from it. I knew at once I wanted to hear him say it again, and again. 'You haven't upset me,' I assured him. 'On the contrary.' I smiled at him now, the most heartfelt smile I had bestowed upon anyone in a very long time. 'Bess will do very well,' I said. 'Very well indeed.'

5

While it was still dark, Annie and I got up and went to the field hospital to take up our positions. Dr. Young was already there, pacing about the small space in an agitated fashion. Suddenly, just before dawn, the guns stopped. The silence that replaced their rumble was even more terrifying than the guns themselves. There was such an intensity to it, such a sense of anticipation and of dread. Annie gave my hand a squeeze.

'Good luck, dear,' she said.

Dr. Young was dismissive. 'I shouldn't put your hopes in luck, Nurse. Lack of the stuff is what has brought us all here in the first place. Trust in your own abilities, that's my advice.'

His last words were all but drowned out by the sound of shrill whistles and urgent shouts. The order to go over the top had been given. I remember experiencing something close to a thrill as the voices of our soldiers were raised in their battle cry and immediately feeling disgusted at such a response. For a few seconds, there was only the sound of those determined shouts and their own rifle fire. Then the machine guns started. I saw Dr. Young's face darken.

'They were supposed to have been taken out.' He voiced what we were all thinking. 'The machine guns were supposed to have been obliterated by the bombardment. There shouldn't be any left.'

But there were. Soon the air rattled to the continuous sound of the deadly weapons as they cut down the advancing troops in their hundreds. We barely had time to register what the full impact of this would be when the first casualties began to arrive at the entrance to the pillbox.

'Nurse Higgins!' Dr. Young barked orders as he worked. 'You are not dressing that soldier for parade. Get that wretched bandage in place and move on to the next one. We have no time for pretty finishes. Stretcher-bearers! This one's ready to go, and that one. Take them down the line and come back. There will be plenty more,' he said, his left hand struggling to stop a fountain of arterial blood that threatened to end the life of the pitifully youthful corporal in front of him. Within minutes, the pillbox was full and casualties were being left outside. I stepped out to treat one with a leg injury and another who had taken a bullet to the shoulder. I heard Dr. Young shouting my name.

'Nurse Hawksmith, if you please!'

I hurried back in.

'Stay inside, Nurse.'

'I was just trying to . . .'

'Well, don't. You're no good to anyone if a shell falls on your head. See to it that the casualties in here are dealt with swiftly, and then there will be room for more. You are not to attend to patients outside these walls. Either of you. Is that clear?'

We assured him it was. Even so, I found it hard to focus on my work knowing that there were dangerously wounded men lying helpless in the mud only a few feet away. A rifleman clutched at my arm as I stooped to bind his head wound.

'The wire!' he gasped, his eyes wide. 'Dear God, the wire.'

'Shhh, lie still. We'll soon have you away from here.'

'They're caught on it. Like rabbits in snares. The more they struggle, the more it cuts. They're easy targets. Tommy Barret lost his arms. I saw them shot right off. What chance did he have, stuck in that wire? What chance?'

'Dr. Young, could I have some morphine for this soldier? He has a head wound and needs to keep still, but he's so agitated . . .'

'If I had any left, I'd give it to you, Nurse.'

'It's all gone?'

'Half an hour ago. There's a drop of brandy, but go steady with it.'

There were moments when it was almost a blessing not to have time to talk to the casualties, for what words could I offer them? I set my jaw and followed Dr. Young's example. For hour after hour, we applied rudimentary dressings, splints, and bandages. We gave water and brandy. On and on the nightmare went. More and more soldiers were left outside the pillbox.

'Why don't they stop it?' Annie asked me. 'Why do they keep sending them up when it's so hopeless?'

Dr. Young turned on her. 'Be quiet, won't you! If these lads see fit not to question their orders, then it is of no concern to you. There is a gunner over there likely to lose his arm if you fail to help him. Nurse Hawksmith, assist me here please.'

He positioned himself at our makeshift operating table. On it lay a soldier of indeterminable rank or age, so covered in mud was he. He did not shout or make any complaint, but his breathing was shallow and rapid and his body rigid with pain. I saw that he had sustained a shrapnel wound to the stomach.

'Now then.' Dr. Young put his own face close to that of his patient. 'You've a nasty bit of metal in you. It needs to come out. I can do it here or you can wait until you get to the CCS. Thing is, by the time you get there, you could be in trouble. I have to tell you we've no morphine left. Well, what's it to be?'

With great effort, the soldier summoned his voice. 'Best get it out, sir. If you wouldn't mind.'

'Good man. You there,' he called to two stretcher-bearers, 'hold him for me, will you?'

Fear flashed across the soldier's face as the men approached.

'That won't be necessary,' I said.

Dr. Young shot me a look.

'He must stay still, Nurse.'

'He will. Just give me a moment.' I took the young man's hand in mine. 'Look at me,' I told him. 'All you have to do is look at me.' I made myself shut out everything but his face. I met his unsteady gaze and held it. I pressed his hand to my heart. 'See how slowly it beats? Your heart can do the same. Let go. Think no thoughts. Hear no sound but my voice. Feel nothing but the pulse of life beneath your hand. I will keep you safe.' As I spoke, I swayed minutely from side to side, never blinking, never letting his eyes stray from my own. Very soon, his breathing became slower, his own heartbeat more regular. His eyes lost their focus but did not close. His body relaxed. I turned to Dr. Young.

'He is ready now,' I said.

The bearers waited for instructions. Dr. Young hesitated for only seconds before shooing them away. He snatched up a scalpel and began to incise flesh around the point of entry. The soldier did not flinch but lay quiet. Dr. Young glanced at him, then proceeded. Within minutes he had dug deep enough to expose the piece of shrapnel. He lifted it out with a pair of surgical tweezers and quickly sutured the wound. I gently let go of the soldier's hand and stroked his cheek. He blinked a few times and then smiled at me.

'Right,' said Dr. Young, 'let's get you off to the CCS. Well done, Nurse.' He turned to me. 'I have heard of mesmerism, of course, but I have never seen it used. I confess up until now I would have described myself as a skeptic. Up until now.'

'I am only glad I could help.'

'Stay close. I may have need of your talents again before the day is done.'

The battle seemed interminable. However hard we tried to keep up with the stream of casualties, we were inundated. Dr. Young became increasingly ruthless about who was allowed to stay and indeed who was to be admitted at all. He screamed at one corporal who assisted a limping and profusely bleeding man through the entrance.

'Stretcher cases only!'

'He was one, sir, only a shell tipped him off and killed the bearers,' the soldier explained. Dr. Young tutted loudly but saw to the corporal himself. Of growing concern was the nearness of the bombs. One landed so close it shook the walls, and for a moment I feared the roof would collapse on top of the patients. It held, but only just, and the explosions did seem to be getting worryingly near.

'Surely we are behind the battle line,' I whispered to the doctor. 'Why would the enemy waste their weapons?'

'Naturally they know the positions of all of what were once their own bunkers,' he told me, 'and naturally they know we would put them to good use.'

'You mean they are deliberately targeting us?'

The ground shuddered again in answer to my question.

I hardly had time to think of anything other than the task at hand, but even so images of Archie repeatedly formed in my mind's eye. I tried to hold him there, as if that would keep him from harm. Every time an officer was brought in, I held my breath. Toward the end of that terrible day I did see a face I recognized. It was Captain Tremain, whom I had met in Archie's dugout and who had so unnerved me. He had a gunshot wound above the left knee, and his hands were deeply lacerated—I supposed by the barbed wire—but he was not in danger. I dressed his wounds and dared to ask him about Archie.

'Haven't seen him since we went over,' he said. 'We were positioned some distance apart.' He watched my face the whole time I worked, and I felt the familiar prickling at the back of my neck. Even now, he had the audacity to stare, to lech. I had to force myself to finish his dressings. I stood up.

'Try not to move,' I told him. 'We'll send you down the line with the next available stretcher-bearers.'

I turned my attention to a soldier in the corner of the room who was coughing badly. I saw he had taken a bullet to the abdomen at an upward angle, and it was likely that his lungs were being filled with blood. I knelt beside him and took his hand. He spluttered and choked, fighting for breath, every spasm inflicting further pain upon his ruined body. His distress was heartbreaking to witness. I knew that he was drowning, and there was nothing to be done to save him. I put my lips close to his ear and whispered to him.

'Shh, do not be afraid. Listen to me. You will feel no pain. No pain. Sleep now, a deep, refreshing sleep. Sleep. Sleep.'

As I spoke, he stopped his paroxysms of coughing and his eyelids fluttered and closed. His breathing became shallow. I heard a gurgling sound from deep within his chest, but he no longer fought or suffered. He merely slept, as he would continue to do until his body failed him and his soul was finally set free. I stood up and turned to find that Captain Tremain had been watching me. I made a move to pass him. He grabbed my wrist.

'That's some strong medicine you have there, Nurse,' he said levelly. 'Strong indeed.'

I snatched my arm from his grasp. I was about to respond to his comment when I noticed Annie slipping outside. Like me, she was troubled by the wounded left unattended and in need of nursing. I glanced at Dr. Young, but he had not noticed her go. I looked back at Captain Tremain.

'I would be grateful . . .' I began, but the expression on his face made me pause. I was aware of shells falling close by, and to me the whistle of this particular one was no different from the others. To Captain Tremain's more experienced ear, it was very different. He grabbed me again and wrenched me down onto the floor beside him just as the mortar exploded at the very entrance to the pillbox. The thunder of the blast was followed instantly by a storm cloud of concrete dust. Everyone in the pillbox began to cough. As the air started to clear, I heard Dr. Young shouting. 'Nurse Hawksmith? Are you unharmed?'

I clambered to my feet, righting Captain Tremain as I did so, his wounded leg causing him great pain and making it hard for him to move unaided.

'I am all right, Doctor,' I called back.

'The walls have held, and the roof, thank God. Where is Nurse Higgins?'

Now I remembered seeing Annie leave the safety of the hospital. I ran outside. There were mangled bodies and groaning casualties everywhere. Annie lay next to a young rifleman. I sank to the ground beside her.

'Annie? Annie?'

She stirred slowly, opening her eyes. 'I know Dr. Young told us to stay inside,' she said, 'but these poor boys . . .' She smiled. 'So like my Billie. They just needed a bit of care. A mother's touch, you know?'

I nodded.

Her eyes narrowed and a frown creased her brow. 'We did our very best, didn't we?' she asked.

'Oh, yes, Annie. Our very best,' I said, and watched the light of life go out behind those kind eyes.

Three exhausting hours later, the attack was at an end. The machine guns fell silent. As the last stretcher was carried out of the pillbox, Dr. Young spoke to me.

'Go with them, Nurse. There is nothing more to be done here.' Seeing my face, correctly reading the despair growing there, he squeezed my arm. 'There is nothing more to be done. You have saved many lives here today. There are some you can help'—he swallowed hard, his voice breaking—'and there are others . . .' He shook his head and left the sentence unfinished.

I accompanied the wounded back along the duckboards to the waiting ambulances. I have heard of people being numbed by shock, by terrible experiences. How I wished for such a release from the ache in my heart. I tried to tell myself I had done all I could, and for once at least I knew this to be true. I had used my skills as a nurse, I had used all my fortitude as a woman, and I had used my magic in the way a witch should—to ease suffering and to heal. As weary soldiers trudged past me, I searched their faces but did not find Archie. Was he alive? I wondered. I somehow believed he was, even though I knew the odds to be heavily stacked against such a supposition. So many had died. He would have been leading his men into those terrible guns, onto that merciless wire. And yet, something inside me knew him to be alive. It was as if I were aware of his life force, connected to it in some way, and it still burned bright.

I climbed aboard the last ambulance. The driver revved the engine and began to move off. Then, above the noise of the rickety vehicle, I heard my name being called. My real name.

'Bess! Bess!' Archie appeared at the side of the ambulance. The driver reluctantly slapped his foot onto the break.

'Quick as you like, sir,' he said to Archie. 'These lads don't need to hang about here any longer than they have to.' He jerked his head at the casualties in the back.

'A moment, Corporal. One short moment.' He grabbed my hands, 'Bess, thank God you're safe.'

'Archie! I knew you were alive. I just knew.'

'I'll drag you over those heathered hills yet, you wait and see if I don't.' He grinned.

The ambulance began to move forward. Archie limped alongside it, my hands slipping from his. 'I'll come to you at the CCS,' he called after me, 'as soon as I can!'

I leaned out of the side of the van and waved at him until lines of troops obscured my view and he was lost in a muddle of khaki. I sat back in my seat and wondered at the capacity the human heart possesses for experiencing both despair and joy at one and the same moment.

6

In the nurses' quarters at the CCS there was great excitement at the delivery of some post. Three days after my experiences at the field hospital, I had yet to recover my sense of reality, of normality, and was finding it difficult to join in the glee the others were enjoying at the arrival of supplies of Bovril and biscuits and cakes from home. Strap stood in front of the stove warming her ample backside and chomping on a gingernut. Kitty sat on her bed reading and re-reading a letter from her younger brother. I sat on my own bunk, caught somewhere between relief at being away from the front line and restlessness born of a longing to see Archie. I had tried to concentrate on my work, but everything seemed to send my thoughts back to him. A particularly strong reminder lay in the ward tent in the shape of Captain Tremain. His wound was healing fast but not quickly enough for me. I found it difficult to be in the man's presence, though I could not fully understand why. Although he made me uneasy, I was certain he was not a real threat. I sensed nothing of Gideon about him, and yet there was something unsettling. I kept revisiting the time in the dugout with Archie and Tremain and Lieutenant Maidstone. I had experienced such a strong sense of danger, but why? Tremain himself continued to make unwelcome and inappropriate remarks, and I was well aware that he had witnessed some of my unorthodox healing methods in the field hospital. I did my best to avoid him and hoped he would soon be sent home on leave to fully recover from his injury. At least I could cling to the hope that I would soon see Archie again. I had received a note from him, and we planned to spend our two days of leave together that coming Saturday. The thought of it made me feel like a giddy teenager. Such moments of wistful joy were not without their price; I was beset by guilt immediately. How could I be contemplating fun, laughter, love even, when so many had died or were suffering? Could it be right? Strap caught sight of my expression in an unguarded moment.

'Good Lord, Elise, you look positively dyspeptic. Here, have one of these. No better pick-me-up to be had in these parts,' she said, proffering her precious biscuits.

I took one without enthusiasm. 'Thank you.'

'So, any word from your soldier yet?'

I had already told her Archie's name and of our encounter at the Front. It was against my natural inclination to share such information with any-body, but I had been missing him so badly, and talking about him was a way to bring him close, if only for a few moments. I glanced over my shoulder to check that we could not be overheard.

'He sent a note.'

'A note, you say? Well, there's a thing.'

'He has forty-eight hours' leave, starting on Saturday.'

'Which would be of no interest to you, naturally, being fully aware as you are of the rules forbidding nurses from stepping out with officers.'

'Naturally.'

'And knowing that if our Dear Leader were to get one whiff of any sort of *liaison* between one of her staff members and a man in uniform, the consequences would be most unpleasant.'

'Extremely unpleasant, I should imagine.'

She left the stove and sat down beside me.

'So, where are you meeting him?' She grinned.

'I'm to take the train to Gironde, three stops southwest from here. I'm supposed to wait for him on the platform and he'll find me.'

'Ah, a clandestine rendezvous! How ridiculously romantic.'

My own smile faded. 'Or perhaps just ridiculous.'

'Why so?'

'Oh, I don't know, it doesn't feel right. Going off to enjoy myself, sneaking around, forgetting why we're here in the first place.' I ran a hand through my hair and let my shoulders sag. Strap was having none of it.

'Now you listen to me, Nurse Work-Till-I-Drop Hawksmith,' she said. 'If anyone around here deserves a few hours off, it is you. I absolutely insist you do jolly well enjoy yourself and completely forget why we are here. That's the whole ruddy point! Good grief, girl, you don't know when you're well off. Last time I did any sneaking about, it was breaking back in to the dormitory at school. Make the most of it, I say. And come back and tell us loveless creatures all about it. Or tell *me* at any rate. Quite see you might not want to broadcast your peccadilloes . . .'

'Peccadilloes!' I laughed, 'Strap, you're a tonic. If we could only bottle whatever it is that keeps you so relentlessly cheerful, we'd empty the wards.'

'Gingernuts,' she declared, biting into another one. 'Legions could march on 'em, I swear.'

We giggled together, and I realized how long it had been since I'd heard the sound of my own laughter.

The days crawled by until finally Saturday evening arrived. I had no clothes but my uniform and for the first time felt the lack of something pretty to put on. I washed my hair, rinsing it in a little of my precious rose oil, and borrowed a lipstick from Kitty. Although I played down the occasion as much as I could, the others must have sensed my excitement and teased me pitilessly until I managed to slip away. I had packed a few overnight items in a small bag lent me by Strap, not wanting to draw attention to the fact that I was planning to be away two days. And nights. The seven o'clock train for Gironde was packed with off-duty soldiers and noncombatant volunteers, all intent on a short time away from the grimness of the war. Some were headed for the coast and a boat home. Others were, like me, settling for a few snatched hours as far from Saint Justine as their passes would allow them to go.

I found a window seat and gazed out at the deserted landscape as the locomotive huffed and puffed away from the front. With every passing mile, the countryside looked more normal, more peaceful. Under the setting sun, crops grew, livestock grazed, and rooks circled stately trees in preparation for their nighttime roost. I began to feel excitement stirring within me. Not only at the thought of seeing Archie again but also at the realization that there was hope, that all would one day be well again.

By the time we reached Gironde, it was properly dark. I made my way along the platform, away from the stream of people heading for the exit. I secreted myself in the shadows and waited. I felt a tightening in my stomach as the stream dried to a trickle and the last of the passengers alighted. Still there was no sign of Archie. Would he come after all? Had I been deluding myself about the sincerity of his feelings for me? Then, suddenly, I saw him. He stepped from the train carefully, his damaged leg forcing him to lean heavily to one side. He stood alone on the platform. I emerged from the dark corner where I had been waiting. He saw me and smiled at once, hurrying to me. For a moment, we stood facing each other wordlessly. At length, Archie began to laugh and offered me his arm.

'Well, Nurse Hawksmith,' he said, 'I diagnose nervous excitement and prescribe two large glasses of the best local wine we can find. What do you say?'

'The perfect remedy.' I took his arm and let him steer me toward the town.

'And,' he went on, 'I further prescribe some of Madame Henri's excellent *cassoulet*, followed by a cup or two of the finest coffee outside Paris. How do you think we feeble patients will fare on that?'

'I think the prognosis is good, and the treatment should be repeated at frequent intervals.'

Café Henri was located down a side street off the small square that constituted the center of the little town. We slipped beneath the awning and pushed open the door onto a scene of welcoming warmth, light, and gaiety. It was clear Archie had been here before, for Monsieur Henri greeted him like a favorite son and showed us to a cozy corner table. The café was already close to full, and we had to squeeze our way past the other drinkers and diners. Monsieur Henri pulled out my chair for me and handed us our menus with a flourish.

'What's good tonight, Albert?' Archie asked.

Monsieur whipped out his notepad and licked his pencil. When he spoke, his accent growled and he swallowed his words, 'Ah, Lieutenant Carmichael, *ce soir* I can highly recommend the cassoulet. Madame Henri prepared it by herself and it is'—he gave an expression of ecstasy— '*magnifique!*'

'Cassoulet it is, then.'

Monsieur Henri snatched the menus from us and was gone, shouting urgent instructions to the elderly waiter to bring us wine *tout de suite*.

Archie leaned forward. 'I hope you don't mind my choosing for you,' he said, lowering his voice. 'Fact is, everything else on the menu has been "off" since the war began. It's cassoulet or nothing, I'm afraid. But you won't be disappointed. It's always excellent.'

'*Magnifique*, even.'

'Precisely.'

The waiter brought glasses and a bottle of wine, which he opened with some effort and then placed next to Archie.

'How ever did you find this place?' I asked.

'A fellow officer brought me here, first week I came out. If I have to be away from home, there is nowhere else I'd rather be. Do you like it?'

I took in my surroundings. The walls were painted deep red but were almost entirely obscured by a Victorian hang of paintings, mostly oils.

Some were landscapes of the area; others appeared to be portraits of regulars, with a particularly grand one of Monsieur and Madame Henri above the door to the kitchen. The bar was polished and worn by a thousand sleeves as their wearers clamored for wine or absinthe or coffee. From the high ceiling, three impressive chandeliers of black glass were suspended over the center of the room, with matching wall lights illuminating the corners. To the left of the bar was a small piano. The window had two tables in it, which were occupied by a party of inebriated soldiers. I judged from their uniforms and accents that they were Australian. Most of the diners were soldiers, in fact, apart from an elderly couple in the far corner and a small group of fresh-faced young French girls sitting in the center of the room pretending not to notice the blatant admiring gazes of the men. The entire space was filled with the buzz of people enjoying themselves; with the excitement of flirtation; with the smell of coffee and wine and cologne; and with a determined sense of *joie de vivre*. This was France as it always had been, as it would always be. This was a million miles from the brutality that was taking place only a short train ride away. I understood then what Strap had meant: it would be sinful not to enjoy oneself in such a place. The opportunity to revel in normal, friendly human interaction should indeed be celebrated and savored to the very last drop.

'I like it very much,' I told Archie as he handed me my wine. I looked at him as I raised the glass to my lips. 'I can't imagine anywhere I would rather be.'

'Nor I.'

'Not even Glencarrick?'

'At this moment, no. This moment is already perfect. Let's drink to it. Let's hold it in our memories forever, how ever long that might be.'

We drank our toast, our eyes lost in each other's gaze. I felt that Archie had the ability to look at me and to know me, to see deep into my being. There was something wonderfully comforting in that realization. It was as if all the loneliness of the slow years I had lived was lifted from me as long as his eyes fell upon me in that way. As if he had read my thoughts, his expression became more serious. He put down his glass.

'I think I should explain something,' he said. 'I was an only child and very close to my father, but it is my mother I most resemble. My father is gone now, sadly. I miss him dreadfully, as does my mother. She will never leave Glencarrick. I suppose it is part of the reason the place means so much to us both—it is where he was. Where he is. Anyway, my mother is a very singular person. She was brought up in Edinburgh but moved out to the highlands, where she was introduced to my father. They loved each other from the moment they met.' He paused and smiled at me, then continued. 'I think my father knew at once that there was something different about her. He didn't care. He accepted her absolutely as she was. Though there were some in the family who thought her a little . . . odd. But she soon settled into Glencarrick, and the local people adored her. They were more accepting of her . . . unusual talents.' He took another swig of his wine. 'Fact is, my mother is a medium. She makes no secret of it, gives no excuses or explanations. She simply has an ability to communicate with spirits who have passed over into the otherworld, as she calls it. I was never frightened by it, not even as a child. I grew up with séances and with strangers appearing at the door asking for my mother's help in contacting their lost loved ones. She never turns anyone away. When I was still quite small, about eight or nine I suppose, my mother spotted something in me too. I had the gift. She noticed it first when I spoke of the little boy who visited me each night. My father passed it off as dreams or an imaginary friend. I don't think he was keen to admit that he had another "odd" member of the family, not at first. But my mother knew straightaway that my visitor was a spirit. A ghost, if you like. He was the first of many. After that, I regularly met up with all sorts of people in the hours of darkness. Most of them had lived at Glencarrick at one time or another. Sometimes I would help my mother contact people's relatives and friends. As I say, it never frightened me. It was just how we were.'

He stopped talking as Monsieur Henri arrived with steaming platefuls of cassoulet.

'Madame, here you are. I hope that you will enjoy your meal.'

'It smells delicious,' I said.

'Lieutenant Carmichael, *bon appétit*.'

'Thank you, Albert.'

As he left the table, we both stared at our food in wonder. After weeks of rations and the ghastly fare we had been surviving on, the meal in front of us was indeed magnificent. I could detect marjoram and rosemary and garlic and sweet onions amidst the tomatoes and beans and chunky pieces of rabbit and sausage. Never had I anticipated a plateful of food with such relish. But I dearly wanted Archie to continue. I didn't want the moment of confidence to be lost.

'Go on,' I said, 'you were telling me about your mother. About you. Please don't stop.'

'Do you know I've never told anybody else out here about this? None of the men. Nobody. But I wanted to tell you. I want you to understand. I want you to see that I'—he hesitated—'that I understand *you*.'

At that moment it was as if the rest of the room ceased to exist. I was no longer aware of anything except the very special man who sat in front of me. And of the true meaning of what he was saying. He knew me. He knew what I was! I did not have to hide or pretend. I did not have to try to explain or excuse. His ability to see what others could not, to connect with the otherworldly, meant that I was laid bare before him. I was not Nurse Elise or even Bess. Well, I *was* them but not only them. I was everything I had ever been. Elizabeth Anne Hawksmith. Born when the world was so much younger. Changed from simple healer to immortal. Once and for always, for good or bad, a witch. My heart began to sing with the joy of it. Before I could stop them, tears dripped from my chin. Tears of pure happiness.

'Careful now.' Archie handed me his handkerchief. 'Albert will be offended if you add more salt to his already perfect cassoulet.'

'You don't . . . despise me?'

'*Despise* you!' He shook his head and reached across the table to take my hand. 'My love, my dear sweet Bess. I adore you. You have my heart completely and utterly. For all time.'

I let him squeeze my hand. He smiled at me.

'Come on,' he said, 'let's eat.'

We had just begun to tuck in to our heavenly food when I saw Archie's attention taken by someone entering the café. His face darkened a little, and I turned to see Lieutenant Maidstone stepping into the room, accompanied by two other officers. He saw us and approached our table smiling.

'Carmichael, you are a dark horse.' He slapped Archie on the back and beamed at me. 'Well, well, Nurse Hawksmith, I recall. How delightful to see you again.'

'Lieutenant Maidstone, I hope you are keeping well.'

'Tip-top, my dear. Tip-top. I say, that looks good. I'd heard about this place, but this is the first time I've been here. Think I might get a bowlful of that for myself.'

'Reg, old man!' A shout came from one of his companions now standing at the bar. 'Don't be shy with that money of yours, come and pay for the drinks.'

Lieutenant Maidstone smiled and gave a little bow. 'Enjoy yourselves, children,' he said to us, before turning and threading his way between the tables to the bar. Archie seemed strangely bothered by his friend's appearance.

'How far does a person have to go to find some privacy in this wretched war?' he wondered aloud.

'He's very jolly,' I said. 'I suppose you make good friends, thrown together in those dugouts.' I scooped up a forkful of beans.

'Lieutenant Maidstone is no friend of mine,' he said quietly.

I was surprised. I glanced over my shoulder. The lieutenant was engaged in animated conversation with Monsieur Henri, who seemed happy enough to talk to him. There was something overbearing about him, it was true. And I recalled the way he and Captain Tremain had both stared at me in the dugout. I remembered how unnerved I had felt. I had assumed it was the captain who had made me uneasy, but clearly Archie saw something in Lieutenant Maidstone. I stopped eating and started to focus on him, to tune in my witch's intuition, but Archie drew my attention back to him.

'I don't want to hurry you,' he said, his mood distinctly altered, 'but can we eat up and go from this place now? I have found us somewhere where we can be together. Just the two of us.'

'Yes, of course,' I said. 'I would like that. I really would.'

We finished our supper in a silence filled with a curious tension not altogether born of the anticipation of the night ahead.

7

Archie summoned Monsieur Henri, and after much conspiratorial whispering we were led out via the kitchens and through a back door. In the small yard at the rear of the café, the portly restaurateur tugged back a canvas sheet to reveal a gleaming motorcycle. He handed the keys to Archie and took pleasure in explaining the bike's finer points to him. Archie strapped my bag onto the back and helped me climb aboard the pillion seat. With three determined kicks, the vehicle roared to life. I clung to Archie, snuggling up to his strong, warm back. As we left Gironde and took the country road south, I could not have felt happier. I had no idea where we were going or how long our journey would take. I trusted Archie completely. We were together, we were away from the war, we had precious time ahead of us, and for now we could be utterly selfish. Nothing else mattered. We traveled along increasingly narrow roads through shadowy countryside. It must have been half an hour later that Archie turned the motorbike down a bumpy farm track. We passed the farmhouse itself, rattling across the cobbled yard. An arthritic dog raised the alarm, but the front door remained closed. We negotiated the ruts and potholes of the increasingly uneven path until we came to a tiny cottage sitting among a small group of silver birch trees. It was a single-story stone dwelling with a steeply sloping roof and a stout chimney out of which ghostly smoke drifted up through the still night air. Archie stopped the motorbike and switched off the engine. The quiet of the place was glorious and punctuated by nothing more than a hooting owl here and a barking fox there. Archie took my bag and led the way to the low wooden door, which was not locked. I stepped across the threshold and breathed in woodsmoke and cut flowers. Archie lifted an oil lamp from the mantelpiece and put a match to the wick. The room flickered into focus. A fire had been lit some hours ago and burned bright and hot in the large hearth. A scrubbed-pine table in the middle of the little room boasted a bowl of roses and a box of groceries. There were two wooden chairs by the table, as well as a rocking chair and a faded leather armchair by the fire. In the far corner was a washstand with pitcher and bowl. A mirror hung on the wall. Beside these stood an iron bedstead with a deep feather mattress and a patchwork quilt.

'It's not the Ritz, I'm afraid,' said Archie, lighting a candle in a brass holder and placing it on the table, 'but it's ours for the remainder of the weekend. No one will disturb us. The farmer is a cousin of Albert's.'

'It's wonderful,' I said, 'quite wonderful.' A thought occurred to me and I was unable to stop myself asking him. 'Have you . . . have you been here before? With anyone?'

'Not with anyone.' He shook his head and then stepped close to me and took both my hands in his. 'I promise you, I'm not given to whisking beautiful young nurses off to remote cottages in the dead of night. I have been here only once before, on my own. I badly needed a little time away from the front, but I had only a few days leave. I wanted somewhere quiet. Somewhere I could let my mind rest, if just for a short time. I mentioned my wish to Albert. He is a good man. He offered me this place. When I said I wanted to visit the cottage again, this time with a friend, well, he saw to everything for me. It is heartening, isn't it, to find such small acts of kindness in the midst of all this misery?'

I smiled at him, nodding. 'I can't believe it's for us.' I circled the room, touching the rough lintel above the fireplace, pausing to sniff the showy roses, wrapping myself in the warmth and tranquillity of the place. 'Just us.'

'Just us. Now.' He rubbed his hands together and peered into the box of provisions. 'Let's see what treats Monsieur Henri has found for us.'

The box yielded fresh bread, a truckle of hard cheese, some waxy tomatoes, brown eggs, apples, a pot of honey, and even a few precious grains of coffee. Besides these wondrous delights were a corkscrew and two bottles of red wine. Archie beamed, holding one up to the light.

'I'll find glasses,' he said, and proceeded to dig about in the one and only cupboard in the room.

I unbuttoned my coat, slipped it from my shoulders, and draped it over one of the kitchen chairs. I knew exactly where I wanted to sit, but something made me hesitate. I approached the rocking chair slowly, as if it might spring into movement without warning. I became aware of Archie watching me. He must have thought my behavior strange. To him, it was just a chair. To me, it was such a powerful reminder of my mother that here, in this cottage which was so very like my childhood home, long-stifled emotions threatened to overwhelm me. Tentatively, I touched the smooth wood. The rockers shifted and creaked minutely; the faintest tilt, the lightest whisper of a sound. I sat down and leaned against the rounded wooden bars of the backrest. Slowly I let the chair move. It gathered momentum smoothly. The light from the flames beside me blurred slightly as I rocked forward and back, forward and back. I looked across at Archie, who stood, glasses in hand, waiting for my reaction.

He knows, I thought, *he knows so much about me.*

I smiled again, aware that I had not done so with such frequency or with such genuine happiness for a very, very long time. Instantly, I felt guilty for enjoying myself when so many were suffering only a few empty miles away. I could only guess at what conflicting emotions Archie must have been struggling with.

'It's difficult, isn't it,' I said, 'to forget the others? To put all the ghastliness of the war out of one's mind and just . . . be here.'

He nodded, contemplating the inky wine in his glass and lowering himself heavily into the old leather chair. 'I was fortunate,' he said, 'during my first weeks out here I had a terrific CO. Brunswick, his name was. He noticed I wasn't taking my leave and spoke to me. "Get away from here every chance you have," he told me. "Get away and don't give the place another thought. It's the only way to remain sane." He was right. Dead now, of course, but that doesn't make him any less right. I've learned to do what he said.'

'I think it's an excellent plan. No more war until we leave. Agreed?'

'No more war. I'll drink to that.'

That evening we sipped our wine and talked long into the night. We talked of our childhoods and our lives before ever we had heard of Passchendaele. I longed to hear more of his family, of his origins, of him. What he had said in the café came back to me and I wanted, *needed,* to know more.

'You say you used to help your mother, assist her in her work as a medium. That you had the gift. Do you have it still?'

Archie allowed a rueful smile to alter his features. 'I think now it would be not so much a gift as a curse. Out here, in this Bedlam, what tortured souls would come to me if I were able to see them, I wonder. What would they say to me?' He shook his head. 'I am very sure I could not stand it.' He paused to pour more wine into my glass and to refill his own. When he continued, his voice was hoarse with emotion. 'I was fifteen when my communications with spirits who have passed over ceased. Just like that. It was as if a light inside me had been snuffed out. I felt bereft, as though I had lost my family. Can you understand that?'

'I can, yes. To lose that connection . . . how could you not feel a tremendous loneliness? But why? Why did things change? And why then, do you know?'

He shook his head. 'My mother told me it had something to do with my transition into manhood, that's the only way she could explain it.'

'I have heard that children are more naturally susceptible. More sensitive to vibrations on planes other than those in our own, normal, waking world. By becoming an adult, you stepped beyond their reach. And yet your mother . . .'

'My mother is an exceptional woman. Clearly, I am a lesser being. My connection was tenuous. My gift only viable when it was enhanced by my being a child. It could not withstand the brutal business of my becoming a man.'

'But you still retain a sensitivity. You must. How else would you know . . . know about me?'

'A person would have to be blind not to see that you are someone truly extraordinary, Bess. The light shines out of you. A powerful energy.'

'It is powerful, certainly. Though that power is not always a force I am thankful for.' I turned and studied the low-burning fire. The heat had eaten through a lump of hazel to expose an old copper nail, so that tongues of green danced among the orange flames. 'There are times when I feel cursed. When I allow myself to let what-might-have-beens twist and turn in my gut. What if I had been able to save my mother somehow? What might have happened had I been strong enough to resist Gideon? Could I have led a simple life, with husband, family, a home to stay in and love in and feel safe in?' I closed my eyes briefly, shutting out the familiar pain. When I opened them again, I saw how strongly my words had affected Archie. 'I'm sorry,' I said. 'I should not be gloomy. Not here. Not now. I suppose I'm letting myself think of these things because of you. Because, somehow, I know you will understand. Understand something of what it is like to be . . .'

'Different?'

'Yes, but not just that. More than that. To be connected to something else, something wonderful, and yet not quite to belong there either. As if we are suspended between two worlds.'

Archie nodded. 'I know, my love,' he said softly. 'I know. But it's not all bad, is it?' He leaned forward, eyes bright with curiosity and awe. 'I mean, what I had, what I could do, it was special, yes, but it was insignificant compared to what *you* can do, to what you are. I understand what you say about being lonely, truly I do. And it breaks my heart to think of you, all those years, with no one by your side, no one to trust, to share your gifts and your life with. That's hard, Bess. But, well, the magic!'

I smiled, his boyish enthusiasm lifting my mood. 'Yes,' I agreed. 'The magic is splendid. To feel it coursing through your veins, to feel it inhabit you so utterly, mind, body, and soul, well, there is nothing I can compare it with. It is as if you are connected to an energy so infinite and so ancient . . . I am a conduit for that power, nothing more. But in that moment I am blessed, I know it. And yes, when I experience that wonder, and when I see the good it can do, and I know that I am a part of that goodness, then I am no longer alone. For the briefest of moments, no longer lonely. It would be impossible to experience separateness at that time.'

'It sounds like bliss.'

'It is. It is. And yet . . .'

'You pay a high price for it.'

A stillness settled between us, and we were silent for a while. There was no need for further words. It was the first time since my dear mother had died that I believed myself to be completely accepted, for all that I was, by another human being.

We talked on and listened to each other until the last of the logs had burned down to a scarlet glow, and then Archie took my empty glass from me and pulled me to him. We stood in front of the dwindling fire holding each other as if nothing could ever part us. He lifted a hand to my brow and touched the white swath of hair. Self-consciously, I pulled away a little, but he shook his head and let his fingers trace the line to the pins that secured it at the back. Gently he pulled my hair free of its restraints and watched it fall about my shoulders. He leaned forward and lightly kissed that snowy trail, that gleaming streak that he knew stood for the streak of magic within me. He slipped one hand beneath my hair at the nape of my neck, whilst with the other he held me firm about my waist. He lowered his lips to mine, and we shared the sweetest kiss of my whole long life. There in the warmth of the embers, we undressed each other, slowly and with infinite care. The shadows from the lamp and the shortened candle filled the dips and hollows of our bodies, and the irregular pools of light lent a sheen to the curve of a shoulder or the angle of a hip. Archie picked me up and carried me to the bed. The coldness of the linen made me gasp, but I was not aware of it for long. Archie proved to be the most imaginative and exciting of lovers. In him, I found that ideal balance of tenderness and aggression that results in exquisitely intense and satisfying sex. We fell asleep with limbs entwined, hearts locked together, enveloped in the gentle harmony of the ancient cottage and our own deep love.

The next morning when I awoke in our warm bed, Archie was gone.

A jolt of fear lurched through me before my ears became attuned to the sound of axe splitting firewood outside the cottage. I climbed out of bed, wrapping myself in the pretty quilt. I opened the door to cheerful sunlight and a morning sky painted baby blue. The air was autumn fresh and revived my sleepy brain. Archie stood with his back to me near the log pile, hefting the axe methodically as he chopped blocks of oak and ash for the fire. I was about to call out to him but stopped. Instead I sent my thoughts to him silently.

I'm going to brew some coffee, would you like some?

He stopped splitting the wood and turned to smile at me. He put down the axe and walked toward me. Had he heard me? Had my voice sounded the words inside his head, or was it merely coincidence that he chose that moment to cease his work and come to me? He stood close and gently pushed my hair back from my face.

'Not before I have taken you back to bed and made love to you again,' he said, in answer to my question. This was beyond any expectation I might have had regarding our ability to connect with each other. Oh, the joy of it! I leaped into his arms, the silky quilt slipping from my shoulders as I did so. Archie laughed as he carried me into the house.

It was not until some time later, when we sat in front of the newly stoked fire, sipping the bitter coffee, that a tremendous and fantastic idea came to me. An idea so enormous in its significance, so potentially life altering for both of us, that it took my breath away. For a moment I did not know how to give voice to such a thought. There sat Archie in the shabby leather chair, mellow from our lovemaking, refreshed by a cold-water wash and the strong coffee, with no notion of what I was about to suggest. Or had he? How much, how often, how successfully could he enter my mind and discern my thoughts if I did not will him to do so? I finished my coffee and went to kneel at his feet, taking his hands in mine. He looked down at my glowing face.

'Well?' he asked, waiting for whatever it was that had clearly so inspired me. If he already knew, he did not say but let me find the words myself.

'Join me,' I whispered, then again, stronger this time. 'Join me! Be as I am. Take the step that I took all those centuries ago and become immortal. Stay with me through all time. I can do this for you, for us. I know I have the power if I choose to use it. I'm certain I can do it. Think of it, my love. No more partings, no more death. The two of us sharing our lives, never having to be alone again.' I stood up, dropping his hands, too excited to remain still. 'Imagine what it would mean, what we could do. And we would always have your wonderful home to live in, away from the rest of the world. No one would bother us there: you've said yourself how the local people love your family. They would not question our longevity. They would not fear it, not as others might. Don't you see? It could be the answer.' I was alive with the possibility of it now, transformed by the thought of sharing this love forever, and of never having to be alone and frightened again. Archie got up and wrapped his arms about me. 'I will show you such wonders,' I told him. 'I will teach you everything I know. You are attuned, you have the spark of magic, the sensitivity to the otherworld, already within you. You cannot imagine the bliss of filling your being with the power of magic, with the gift of healing and of eternal life. Together, we will be happy. We will be safe.' I closed my eyes and rested my head against his chest, his steady heart beating lightly against my eardrum. 'Let me do this for you. For both of us,' I said.

He kissed my head and let his lips rest against my hair. When at last he spoke, his voice was faint and hoarse with emotion. 'Oh my Bess, my lovely, lovely Bess,' he murmured, holding me tighter still, 'I am so sorry, but I cannot do as you ask. I cannot.'

I refused to believe what I was hearing. I stayed pressed against him, willing him to say the words that would change my existence beyond measure.

'But . . . Archie, think how it might be. How wonderful. How magical. The two of us . . .'

'I know, I know, but still I cannot, Bess.'

I pulled away now. My hope and joy was quickly replaced by hurt and anger.

'You mean you can, but you won't,' I said. 'Why not? I thought, I believed, that you loved me. That you wanted nothing more than to be with me.'

'I do, truly I do.'

'Then what is to stop us? What reason can you have for not wanting us to be together?'

'I do want us to be together, my love. And so we shall. But I am not what you are. I can never be. No amount of teaching or spell casting can change that. Yes, I have a gift myself, an ability to reach through the veil that separates this world and the next. I am thankful for that gift. I cherish it. But it is not magic, Bess. I am an ordinary man with an extraordinary gift. I am not a witch. I cannot change myself beyond recognition to be what you want me to be. I am as I am. You are as you are. And I love you for it.'

'But it is within your reach, Archie, I know it is. You have sufficient sensitivity, sufficient connection with the otherworld—your mother, your own ability to hear my thoughts. All else that is required is my use of the craft and your willingness. Together, we can make this happen.'

'My love, I do not doubt for one second the marvelous strength of your magic. I know what you are suggesting is possible. No, please, try to understand. I love you for who and what you are. I accept the gulf that lies between us. I know you love me. But me, Bess. Lowly, mortal me. And that is how I want you to love me. As I am. Not as a . . . creation of yours. Not altered so that even I might not recognize myself. If I have learned nothing else in this wretched, filthy war, it is that we must be true to ourselves. Our raw, basic, imperfect selves. I cannot follow you into the craft, Bess. I wish us to share our lives as we are now. I am prepared to embrace the consequences. I will give myself to you completely for whatever time we might have. And however long or short that might be, I will be content because I will have been allowed to love you.'

'How can you talk of love and yet know that it will end in death?' I let my anger out now, unable to weather the storm of my emotions. 'Will you be happy, then, to grow old while I remain young? To wither and die while I look on, unable to help you, unable to save you? Would you condemn me to the gnawing loneliness with which I have been forced to live all my adult life when there is another way?'

'There is not, Bess, not for me.'

'Then it is not love you feel for me at all! It cannot be!'

I ran from the cottage and did not stop until I came to an ash tree at the far side of the paddock. There I crumpled on the ground and allowed myself to weep. It seemed just when I believed I had found the solution to the solitary torture, the loveless drifting that was my life, my hopes had been dashed. I was too distressed to see clearly the sense of Archie's thinking and the wisdom of what he was saying. Only later would I come to accept that he was right.

I heard soft footsteps behind me. Archie stood close but did not try to touch me.

'Bess.'

I stayed where I was. Slowly he knelt down beside me.

'Bess,' he said again, with such tenderness, such longing in his voice, that I could stay angry no longer. I turned and burrowed into his warm embrace.

'For whatever time we might have, then,' I whispered.

'Yes, my love, for whatever time.'

8

Back at the CCS I found myself able to work with more enthusiasm, with more energy than ever before. I had, reluctantly, accepted Archie's terms for our relationship, for our future. I knew, of course, that he was right; we are what we are. In a less emotional moment I recognized that I loved him as he was, and I would not want to change him, to alter him in such a significant way. We would survive the war, we would go to Glencarrick, and we would have a future together; that was what mattered. In the meantime, there was work to be done. I was relieved to find on my return that Captain Tremain had been discharged and sent home. Archie had listened to all that I had told him about Gideon and warned me that he sensed a presence among his men. Someone different. Someone dark. I had assured him that I was forever on my guard. And yet, suspicious as I was of Tremain, I did not believe him to be Gideon. Perhaps he was, after all, simply a man whose manner I found offensive, nothing more. Even so, it was hard to dismiss the fact that "Greensleeves" was being played the first time I met him.

On Tuesday morning, Strap, Kitty, and I were detailed to see to the beds in the ward tent. Many of the casualties had gone home, so that there were fewer than ten patients for us to tend, and Sister Radcliffe saw this as an opportunity to turn mattresses and scrub lockers and generally see to chores that in busier times might have been neglected.

'Here, this should cheer you up,' Strap said in a stage whisper, holding out a folded piece of paper. 'One of the ambulance drivers gave it me. Asked me to see it got to you.'

I took the note and unfolded it, my heart speeding up at the thought of Archie. Strap tactfully stepped away as I read the short message.

Bess, my love, meet me at the old schoolhouse tonight.
Six o'clock. Yours always, AC.

I was surprised. It was not like Archie to arrange something with such short notice. He was only too keenly aware of how difficult it was for me to steal a few moments or hours away from the CCS and to meet him without our being found out. But then, he was sometimes granted leave at the last moment. I glanced at my watch. It was already past five. I tucked the note into my pocket and glanced at Strap.

'Strikes me,' she said, shaking a cigarette out of its packet, 'that a person who has been working so hard deserves a bit of time off.' She lay back on her bed, boots on, gasper between her teeth, and closed her eyes. 'Strikes me that's only right and proper,' she said.

The old schoolhouse presented a gloomy aspect in the drizzle that spat at its gray walls. The gate to the schoolyard was unlocked. I pushed it open and walked across the empty space, abandoned so long that no hop-scotch chalk or even paint marks remained, only the ghostly echoes of children's voices. When I reached the main door of the building, I hesitated. It would surely be locked. I glanced behind me, but no one was abroad. The depressing weather and spate of air raids had put people off leaving their homes unless they were compelled to do so. I tried the large brass handle and jumped a little when the door latch clicked open easily. I pushed the door and stepped inside. The vestibule was drafty and lit only by the gray light falling through the door behind me. I continued on to the first interior door, which stood ajar. It creaked loudly as I opened it farther. I found myself standing in what must have been the main school-room. It was large enough to accommodate several dozen children and was filled with dusty light filtering through high windows. There was a dais at one end in front of an impressive blackboard. All the desks and chairs had been removed, no doubt commandeered for war purposes or burned for firewood by desperate villagers. In the far corner of the room stood an upright piano, and to the right of that a large chest of drawers, its doors swung open to reveal empty shelves. The heels of my boots sounded rudely loud against the polished wooden floor. I walked slowly to the blackboard and ran my fingers over the gritty surface. What had happened to all those children? I wondered. Where were they now?

My thoughts were brought to an abrupt halt by music coming from the piano. I swung round. The instrument was at such an angle that I could see only the back of it, and the player was entirely obscured. The music was nothing I recognized, merely notes, scales, and arpeggios. I opened my mouth to call to Archie, but something made me pause. I could not recall him ever mentioning he played the piano. Whilst there was no reason why he should not be able to do so, it somehow didn't fit. I found myself walking toward the music, not wanting to speak and yet not prepared to flee. Then, when I was but a few strides from the wooden back of the upright, I began to discern a tune among the random notes. A tune I knew well. Very well. It was "Greensleeves." My feet refused to move. Adrenaline charged my blood, sending shocks to my fingertips and making my heart bang beneath my ribs. It was then that I began to smell the sour, sulfurous odor I had first encountered in Batchcombe woods so many lifetimes ago. My first clear thought was to berate myself for being so gullible. Had I learned so little from my years of evading my pursuer? Had my instinct as a witch been so strained by the grief and suffering of the war that I had been unable to detect him in my presence? It seemed so. For here I stood, not more than a few yards from the one who wanted at the very least my destruction and more probably my soul. There was nowhere to run. There was nothing left to do but to face him. I forced myself to walk forward, to step around the piano. As the loathsome melody continued, I gained sight of the player, his head down, bent in rapt concentration over the keys. He straightened up unhurriedly as I approached and turned to smile. It was the same affable smile with which he had greeted me that first time we had met in the dugout.

'My dear, I was beginning to think you might not come,' said Lieutenant Maidstone as he continued to play, 'but then I should have had more faith in the strength of true love.' He made the word *love* sound ridiculous, piteous, despicable. At last, the tune came to an end and he swiveled round on the piano stool to face me. He narrowed his eyes. 'You are grown pale and thin, Bess. This war does not suit you, I think. For myself, I find the energy here . . . invigorating.' He stood up, stretching, his arms wide, embracing the dark power that is always to be found where there is violence.

At that moment I experienced a painful longing for Archie, for his comfort, for his love.

Oh, Archie. Archie. Archie.

I lifted my chin, determined not to let my fear show.

'Will you never tire of hounding me, Gideon?' I asked. 'Can you never find it within yourself to let me go, to set me free of your obsession?'

'Oh, *obsession*, is it? Is that how you see it? Perhaps you are right. I have no intention of giving up what is rightfully mine. What I am owed. What you promised me.'

'I made no promise.'

'You knew the terms of our bargain, Bess; do not pretend otherwise. I offered you the power of the craft and you took it. That was your decision, remember?'

'And it is a decision I have been paying for ever since. There is not a day goes by that I do not try to make amends, to use my gifts for the good of others. To heal. To end suffering.'

'Oh, please, Bess, credit me with a little more sense, a little more insight into your character. You may try to convince yourself that you are different from me, that you are a saintly servant of the oppressed and the needy. I've heard that speech before. I didn't believe it then, and I don't believe it now. The truth is you and I are the same.'

'No.'

'Yes, exactly the same. We are not flimsy white witches bothering ourselves with herbs and potions. We are immortal sorcerers, Bess; we have transcended death by use of the dark arts. The same power that keeps me alive sustains you also.'

'No!'

'Yes! You know it. You feel it. And what is more, my dear, tortured little Bess, *you desire it.* Just as you once desired me.'

'It's not true!' I turned to run, but the lieutenant conjured a whirlwind to spin me, again and again, so that I was unable to move forward. When at last the vortex released me, I slumped to the floor. I looked up to see the figure of Maidstone beginning to dissolve. His features seemed to first distort and then melt until the being before me was no longer recognizable as human. It was a pulsating, swirling mass of light and energy. The colors of the miasma burned orange and smoky red. Then I caught glimpses of flesh, of blood, of bone, until a new being stood before me, fully formed and as solid and real as any man. Gideon. Unchanged since our time together when I was just a girl. Gideon. Possessed of the same malignant force, the same fascinating aura, the same powerful physique that had at one time both repulsed and enthralled me. I clambered to my feet.

'I do not want you!' I cried. 'I never wanted you!'

'Now you know that is a lie. Or perhaps you have forgotten. Don't you remember, Bess? Don't you remember how your body ached for me? How you longed for me to come to you at night? How you lay sleepless in that bed, yearning for my touch? Don't you remember?'

'You had bewitched me. I was not myself.'

'Oh, on the contrary, you were more yourself than you have ever been, before or since. Why must you fight against your true nature? Against your destiny? You know, in that poor perplexed heart of yours, you know we are meant for each other.'

'I will never be yours. Never!' I summoned all my strength and threw up my arms, mustering my magic, calling on my sisters to help me, focusing my energy into one piercing beam of light. I flung the bolt of power at Gideon. The unexpected swiftness and ferocity of the blow caught him off guard and he staggered backward, an arm thrown across his face. For a second I thought he might fall, but he soon regained his balance. He lowered his arm and frowned at me.

'Upon my word, Bess, you have not been idle since our last encounter. The power of your magic is growing. Do you deny how wonderful it feels when your whole being is possessed of that power? Is it not glorious? Is it not divine, the pure strength of that sorcery?'

'There is nothing pure about it.'

'You are alive with it. If you could see now how it transforms you. Imagine how we could be together, my love. Just imagine.'

'I would rather die than exist with you.'

'Sadly, that choice is not yours to make, now, is it? Or at least, you could achieve some sort of corporeal death, but then I would be waiting to claim your soul. Such a waste, I would far rather have you by my side, living, breathing, feeling.' He started to float upward, his feet lifting effortlessly off the ground. He drifted forward so that he loomed above me, his black clothes and dark features forming a deadly cloud that threatened to envelop me completely. I wanted to run, but the unaccustomed use of my magic had left me drained. Slowly he lowered himself, taking me in his arms, his face close to mine, his lips curled back to reveal unnaturally sharp teeth. His breath was hot against my cheek. I felt his tongue slide around the outline of my lips, testing and tasting. I tried to pull away, but my limbs had become enfeebled.

'Let me go,' I whispered, my whole being enervated. 'Please, let me go.'

'Hush, Bess,' he said, pulling me closer, lifting me to him so that we hovered together, suspended in an evanescent cloud of his dark magic. 'Do not be afraid. I have waited so long for this moment. We both have. The time is right, Bess. Here, amidst all the madness these foolish mortals have created. Drink in the energy their futile thrashing releases. Feed upon it, as I do. Join me in eternal bliss.'

I felt my will weakening. Despite my horror at being so close to him, despite the revulsion I felt at his touch, I was aware also of a stirring of desire. It was as if his hold over me was so strong, so far in excess of anything I myself could understand, that I had no chance against it. I was certain I was moments away from being lost forever, from being made his for all time, when a voice, clear and strong, cut through my stupefied consciousness.

'Let her go!' Archie's words were full of barely controlled anger. 'I said, let her go!'

Gideon altered his grip on me to glare down at Archie, who stood in the open doorway. Gideon growled as he saw the gun in Archie's hand. The unearthly rumble echoed through his chest and shuddered through my own body.

'How dare you!' he hissed at Archie. 'How dare you try to come between us. She is mine.' He grabbed me by the scruff of the neck and held me aloft, 'Mine! To do with as I please.' He shook me like a cloth doll.

Archie shouted at him to stop, pointing the Webley revolver squarely at his head.

'Let her go or I'll shoot.'

Gideon let out a roar and with his free hand summoned a ball of sulfurous fire, which he flung toward the door. Archie leaped to his left, but the flames caught his shoulder. He rolled on the ground to extinguish the fire but could not put it out before it had burned right through the serge of his uniform tunic. I could smell the smoldering fibers. Gideon raised his hand to fling a second charge.

'No!' I screamed, at last managing to reclaim my wits. I countered his spell with one of my own, spoiling his aim, so that the fireball fell harmlessly to the floor. Enraged, he hurled me to the ground. I felt a rib crack as I connected with the wooden floor.

'Bess!' Archie scrambled to his feet.

'Archie, look out!' I could see Gideon spinning, gathering strength, preparing to strike again.

Archie raised his gun and fired, but Gideon vanished into nothing, reappearing in the far corner of the room. Archie shot at him once again, but before the bullet could reach him he became as insubstantial as a cloud, letting the charge pass harmlessly through him before rematerializing. I pulled myself painfully to a sitting position, raising my arms, summoning desperate force. I sent a silent message to Archie, not knowing if he would pick it up but certain that working together was our only hope.

Wait. Wait while I hold him.

Archie threw me a glance before diving behind the piano to avoid a further fiery blow. He looked at me steadily and nodded. I turned my attention back to Gideon, thanking our luck and his arrogance that he had not noticed what had passed between Archie and myself. Let him believe he is indestructible, I thought; his pride will be his downfall. I took a deep breath, deeper than a pearl diver, sucking in the air around me until my lungs burned. In my mind, I called my sister witches, imploring them to aid me, to protect me, to assist me in ridding the world of such a rancid soul. I felt my body infused with the power of the ancients, the strength of the craft, the dangerous force of the supernatural. I gathered every atom of that power and hurled it at Gideon. He hurtled backward, slamming against the wall of the schoolroom. He let out a roar of rage, but he was unable to move from the spot.

'Now, Archie! Now!' I screamed.

Archie sprang out from his cover and took aim. Gideon saw at once that he could not evade the bullets that were about to be fired at him. He was trapped. I fancied, in that fleeting instant, I saw real fear flash across his face. It was quickly replaced by fury.

'What?' he bellowed. 'You dare to face me with your puny weapons and your repulsive affection for each other!' His features distorted, dissolving into a monstrous visage of scale and horns with blood-red eyes and snakes coiling from his nostrils. His body doubled in size, the clothes falling from it in shreds, until a tailed beast with cloven hooves and the chest and arms of a giant loomed above us. Archie was frozen by the apparition.

'Shoot, Archie! Shoot him!'

Still, he was unable to move. The hideous creature that was Gideon's spirit-made-flesh drooled as it grinned.

'So brave, your little soldier, is he not?' He laughed. 'See how he trembles. See how his hand shakes now that he knows who it is he dares to face. Thought you would do anything for your lovely Bess, didn't you, hmmm? And yet now you lack even the courage to use that silly weapon. Now you see what it is that confronts you, all your fine words come to nothing. Disappointing, isn't it, Bess? To see such weakness in someone you had thought to honor with your attentions.'

Gideon was straining against the magical ties that bound him, and I knew my strength would soon give out.

'Archie! Archie, please . . .'

'Save your breath, Bess. I must say I expected better of you. Do you really prefer him to me? Can you truly want to spend your life with . . . *that?*'

My vision began to blur and my limbs to ache. The effort of the spell was draining the last scrap of energy from me.

'You know, Bess,' Gideon sneered at me, 'I grow tired of this. Tired of these games. Tired of your pious resistance. Tired even, I have to admit it, of you.' He exhaled a great, malodorous sigh. 'Perhaps it is time, after all, to finish what was begun.'

I frowned at him, uncertain of his intentions. I struggled to hold him and to focus my thoughts.

'Finish?'

'Yes, why not. After all, there are other women, other witches. All this unrequited desire, it's beginning to feel . . . undignified.'

'You mean . . . you mean you will let me go?' My voice was little more than a whisper.

Gideon set his jaw and spoke through gritted yellow fangs.

'Let you go. *Let you go!* Hah! I will be humiliated no longer by a foolish woman. You are not worthy of me! But you will pay for your stubbornness, for your stupid refusal to accept your true destiny. You will pay for it with your life!'

So saying, he bounded forward, breaking free of his bonds as if they had never been. In two bestial strides, he was almost upon me. I flung my arms over my head in what I knew would be a futile act of self-defense. I waited for the fatal blow. It did not come. Gideon hesitated. I still do not know what made him pause. Could it be that there was, in that devilish creature, still some vestige of a human soul, some spark of love that stayed his hand? Whatever it was, it allowed the fraction of a moment in which Archie chose to act. Seeing what was about to happen, he made a swift and crucial calculation. Gideon was about to use the full might of his magic to kill me, that was plain to see. No man-made bullet could have stopped him. And there was no time for Archie to pull me from danger. He did the only thing that was left for him to do. The only thing that a man who loves beyond reason, beyond life, would do for his beloved. Archie flung himself in front of me at the precise moment that Gideon struck. The demonic energy that hit him was meant for me. It was conjured with sufficient force to extinguish the life of a sorceress, a witch, a possessor of the craft. Archie had no hope of withstanding it. Even so, as he threw himself in the path of Gideon's wrath, he held his nerve and pulled the trigger. The shot struck home a heartbeat before the sledgehammer of magic collided with his mortal body, snapping his spine and ending his short life before I could even cry out his name. Gideon let out a roar as blood spurted from his shoulder. The unexpected pain of the injury sent him spinning and squealing; the room filled with the unearthly sounds so that I was forced to cover my ears with my hands. The last sight I had of him was as his grotesque form shifted shape again and again before re-forming as a raven and flying from the room.

Gasping for breath, I crawled to Archie. His face looked so gentle. So peaceful. I stroked his pale cheek as my own tears fell unchecked onto him.

'Oh, Archie! Archie, my love. I am so sorry. Forgive me.' I wept. Then, with startling clarity, I heard his voice in my head.

For whatever time we might have, my love. For whatever time we might have.

POST OFFICE TELEGRAMS

Office of Origin: Edinburgh.
OHMS Received here at: 10:30 A.M., 24/9/17

To: Lady Lydia Carmichael.

REGRET 1ST/LT A.T.W. CARMICHAEL 9TH BATTALION ROYAL SCOTS REGI-
MENT WOUNDED 23/9/17 STOP TAKEN TO CCS SAINT JUSTINE STOP DIED
OF WOUNDS SAME DAY STOP LETTER TO FOLLOW STOP

SAMHAIN

Tegan listened to my story in silence. When I had finished, she turned away from me. We had sat beside the dying light of the fire all the long night, and now a reluctant dawn began to further dim the glow of the fading embers. I added more logs and dusted moss from my hands. I felt a great deal of pity for Tegan. She had so much to contend with. To come to terms with. And time was not on our side.

'Tegan,' I said, gently but with a firmness to my voice I knew she could not miss, 'you must see him now, see him for what he really is.'

'No.' She shook her head. 'I don't want to. I can't. I let him touch me, you know? We . . .'

'I know. I know. But you must see him now. Come.'

I took her hand and led her along the path that followed the stream up a few yards to the pool. I drew her close to the water's edge and pointed at its dark surface.

'Look in the pool and say his name so that you may know precisely what it is that we are confronting.'

Reluctantly, Tegan edged forward. She knelt down and leaned toward the water. The mouse, her constant companion now, who had been slumbering in her pocket, ventured out to sit upon her shoulder. Tegan sniffed loudly, wiping her nose on her sleeve. After a deep breath, she said in a trembling voice, 'Ian. Show me Ian.'

For a moment nothing happened; then the water began to turn as in a whirlpool. Round and round it went until the surface shimmered and pulsated. Then, atop the vortex, a face could be discerned. Ian's appealing features swam into view. Just as they had formed, they began to change. First, they darkened, became more angular, still handsome but most definitely altered. I recognized the face at once as that of Gideon. Then the face distorted, changing again. Tegan began to cry loudly. While we watched, the features melted into the water and then re-formed into a hideous, terrifying visage. It was a face from a nightmare. A demon. A monster.

Tegan got up, staggering backward, her hands over her eyes. I went after her and caught her up in my arms.

'Shhh, there now,' I said. 'It's all right. It's gone. It's gone.'

'*It* has,' she sobbed, pointing a shaking finger toward the reflection in the pool, 'but *he* hasn't.' She looked at me directly now, her expression desperate. 'He hasn't, has he? He is still here.'

She sees plainly now what I have known in my heart all along. What the pool has shown us is the true nature of the man Tegan had fallen in love with. He may give the outward appearance of a gentle young drifter, but there is something very rotten hiding behind those pretty eyes. And that thing will do Tegan great harm if I do not stop it.

I nodded at Tegan, slowly. 'Yes,' I said, 'he is still there. And you and I are going to do something about that, aren't we? Together.'

OCTOBER 14—DARK OF THE MOON.

We have talked at some length of what must be done. I recognized that Tegan needed a little time to digest the events of the other night. I told her to stay at home, claim a cold or some such to avoid having to see Gideon, to give her time to accept there is no such person as Ian, and to simply allow herself a brief moment of adjustment. It is not every day one's entire system of beliefs and understanding of the way the world works is turned on its head. She is young and often impulsive, but she has a good soul and a kind heart. She knows, deep down, what is right and what is wrong. She knows also that Gideon will have to be dealt with, once and for all time. She was appalled at the thought of spending time in his company and unsure if she could feign affection and normality in his presence. I told her she must. To arouse his suspicions now, before we are ready, would be highly dangerous. She can avoid him only so far. Beyond that, she must stall him. My hope is that we are able to maintain the pretense until the All Hallow Eve. There is much to do and I must prepare. The auspicious date I am sure will be of great help. It is a day when departed spirits are near at hand, and I will have need of them. Although All Hallows is a night for remembering and communing with the dead, it is not, contrary to popular myth, a time for darkness or fear of death. I must also find a way to bring about the confrontation on blessed ground. I am under no illusions—Gideon's power far exceeds my own. I must use everything at my disposal if I am to defeat him. There is a place near here that will serve our purposes well. It is fitting that we should return to it, Gideon and I, at last. I know I have been putting off revisiting the spot where it all began, where I, Elizabeth Hawksmith, witch, began my long, singular journey. No doubt the area will have undergone changes, but the woodland itself is protected and still stands, albeit smaller. There is a timelessness in the trees.

We have been much occupied with readying ourselves for the battle ahead. I have had to move Tegan's instruction forward at an unseemly pace, but necessity dictates speed. To begin, we followed a week of rituals, each bound to the traits and strength of the given day. We made particular effort with our incantations and spell casting on the Tuesday, this being the day for addressing the resisting of negative spells. It is hard enough for Tegan to have broken the thrall of love; I must do my utmost to free her from Gideon's darker hold. At the week's end, I consecrated two charms—a silver pentagon for myself, to aid my own magic, and an amethyst for Tegan. This stone is linked with the Sabbat of Samhain, and will help protect her.

Yesterday I asked Tegan to stay for the night so that we could perform rituals and prayers to weaken Gideon. She was keen to take part, but I sensed a nervousness as we walked toward the copse. It was a coal-black night, and she carried her candle low so that I could not read the expression on her face. The querulous note in her voice, however, gave her away.

'Will he be able to hear us?' she asked.

'Hear us?'

'When we're chanting. I don't mean hear our voices, but, well, you know, pick up what we are saying somehow. What we are doing.'

We had reached the center of the copse, and she set down the bundle of things I had given her to carry.

'All magic sends out signals,' I told her. 'So yes, he will be aware of our . . . activity.'

'But will he know it's aimed at him? At weakening him?'

I could see she sought reassurance, but honesty was imperative if I was to maintain her trust.

'Yes,' I said. 'He will very quickly see precisely what we are about.'

'Isn't that going to be dangerous? Won't he try to stop us?'

'Knowing Gideon as I do, I suspect he will merely be amused.'

'What? He'll laugh at us?'

'At our attempts to in some way threaten him, yes.'

Tegan gave a derisory snort. 'Bloody marvelous! That *creature* has got me terrified half out of my mind, and he thinks that's funny.' She was cross now, and I was pleased to see it. She stomped about, lighting the fire, muttering insults.

'Let him laugh,' I said. 'Better he does not consider us a real danger. That way we can continue to summon all the help we might find without him stopping us. Here, add these bay leaves to the fire. Then come over to the stone altar. It should be you who writes his name on the parchment.'

'Why me? You're the one he's been stalking for centuries, not me.'

'There is strength in unity, Tegan. The greater part you take in these proceedings, the better we work together, the more effective we will be.'

She stooped over the low stone and scratched the word *Gideon* onto the rough creamy surface of the parchment.

'Good. Now roll it up and come and stand beside me close to the fire. First, I will say a prayer to speak to the departed, to aid those who might linger between worlds. If I help them to find their true home, they may help us when our moment comes. After that, we will consign your writing to the flames.'

I closed my eyes and focused on the stirring magic within me. The late autumn air was chill but calm. An owl screeched encouragement from the oak tree behind me. Tiny voices whispered from myriad unseen beings. I held my arms open to the fire and began to chant,

> *O flame that burns glory bright*
> *Be a beacon on this quiet night*
> *Light the path for all the Dead*
> *That they may see the way ahead*
> *Lead them to the Summerland*
> *And shine till Pan comes to take their hands*
> *And with Your light, bring them peace*
> *That they may rest and sleep with ease.*

I moved my hands and blue flames joined the scarlet and the orange, then yellow and green too. Tegan gasped.

'Step closer,' I told her. I raised my voice again,

Cleansing inferno, take this name upon this advent of Samhain.
Feed on the strength it bears, claim it for your own. Take from our
foe and give to us you power.

I indicated to Tegan that the moment had come. She raised the parchment, holding it high for a moment before throwing it onto the fire. For a few seconds, nothing happened. Then, with alarming ferocity, the flames leaped skyward, the blaze so intense it lit up the heavens and forced us both to stagger backward.

'Hold fast!' I grabbed Tegan's arm. 'We must stand our ground.'

She cried out, turning her face away from the source of the heat, shielding her eyes with her arm. 'We'll be burned!'

'No! We must not retreat!' Even as I spoke, I could smell singeing hair. The whole night had been illuminated by the fire so that the brightness as much as the temperature became painful. Tegan let out a scream of terror. I took my athame from my belt and held it aloft. 'We will prevail!' I shouted into the maelstrom.

At once, everything was silent. The blaze vanished, leaving only smoldering embers. Soothing darkness returned. The moment passed.

Tegan dared to look around her once more. When she met my gaze, I saw a mixture of awe and fear. I knew what she was thinking. If this was a tiny fraction of Gideon's rage and power, what chance would we have when we finally faced him?

OCTOBER 18—THIRD QUARTER

I have been pleasantly surprised by Tegan's resilience. She herself admits to being a little uncomfortable at how easily she is able to lie when she needs to. I tell her it is for a righteous cause. She has been inventive and resourceful in finding ways to avoid any more contact with Ian than she can stand. I noticed yesterday that she has made the transition from fear to anger. This is a crucial step, which has lent her great strength, every bit of which she will need in the coming days.

OCTOBER 26—GIBBOUS MOON

Our preparations are nearing an end. I kept vigil at my shrine two nights ago, making small offerings and praying to anyone who might listen. I asked the Goddess for her help. I am going to need it. I am fearful for Tegan. I must not fail her. Whatever happens, I will not allow her to become another of Gideon's victims in his pursuit of me. There has been enough dying. Enough heartbreak. Enough killing. It ends now.

NOVEMBER I

It feels weird, writing in someone else's diary, but I think it is what Elizabeth wanted me to do. Someone has got to write down what happened, and nobody else is going to do it, are they? I still can't believe that what went down last night *really* happened. Every minute of it is sharp in my head, but it's too mad. It's too much to take in.

I persuaded Gideon to take me to the woods like Elizabeth told me. I can't think of him as Ian anymore. I'd hate myself if I did. So, we went on his bike, took a rucksack with some food and a few beers. I told him I'd heard it was a really spooky place, great for Halloween. We could camp there all night. And Gideon was cool with the idea. Did he suspect? Did he know it was a trap? Maybe it was what he wanted. Beats me. Point was, he agreed to go and didn't ask too many awkward questions. We must have got there about eight. The woods were much bigger than I'd expected. I thought, oh my God, how am I supposed to take him to the right spot? But it was like he knew where to go. Took us straight to it.

We got the bike in quite a long way, then walked a bit. It was seriously spooky. Really, really still. Silent. We had a torch and a paraffin lamp from the boat. We got to this sort of clearing. About the size of a football field. Lots of brambles and nettles but no trees. Just a few stumps. It was weird, all these tall trees around, oaks and beech—Elizabeth taught me which was which. There was this seriously uncool vibe. I tried to keep it light, opened a couple of bottles and sat down with the food, but I could tell he was really affected by the place. Elizabeth said he would be. She said he knew it from long, long ago. I think, now that I've seen it, I know what she was talking about. There was no house, but there could have been once. And the clearing and the stumps? It looked a lot like I had imagined when she told me about Bess. In the woods. With Gideon.

'Do you want a beer?' I asked him. The way he was pacing about was just making me even more nervous.

For a moment, he didn't seem to hear me, then he turned and smiled.

'Sure, why not?' he said, as he sat down beside me.

I handed him a bottle and he held his hand over mine as he took it. I had to make myself let him, when all I really wanted to do was pull away.

'Lovely Tegan,' he said. 'So young. So sweet.'

'This is a great place. All this fresh air is giving me an appetite.' I withdrew my hand so that I could dig in the rucksack for food. 'I'm going to have a sandwich, d'you want one?'

'Maybe later.' He gently took the bag from me and set it down. He held my hand, stroking my palm with his thumb. With his other hand, he brushed my hair from my face. He seemed to be searching my expression, studying me. I felt his fingers stroke my cheek and then travel down my throat. He leaned forward and kissed me, soft and slow. I shuddered—I couldn't help myself. If he noticed, he didn't show it. He let his hand wander down and started undoing the zip on my jacket. 'It's been a while,' he whispered, never for a second taking his eyes off my face, watching my reaction.

Oh God, I thought, *I can't! I just can't.*

'I've been busy,' I said lamely.

'But now we're here. Just the two of us. In this lovely place.' He kissed me again, harder this time.

'Wait,' I said, wriggling away.

'Wait?'

'I mean, it's early. Let's have a drink. Help us relax a bit.'

'Aren't you relaxed with me, Tegan? What's making you so nervous?'

I couldn't think of anything to say. It was as if he was looking right into me, reading everything I was thinking. As if he was just playing with me now, enjoying my suffering.

Then, suddenly, Elizabeth was there. Standing behind him. I never heard her come, never noticed the slightest movement, but there she was. She looked amazing. I had never seen her looking like that. Never seen anyone looking like that. She was wearing this green dress, long, with a raggedy hem with gold braid, and the same sort of thing going on with the sleeves. Her hair was loose—I never knew it was that long. It sort of blew about like there was a wind, but there wasn't. It was completely still. Not a leaf moved. She glowed. All of her just glowed. Like she was lit up from inside. She was like a goddess of the woods. She had her staff with her. And a knife in her belt, the black-handled one.

Gideon knew she was behind him. His expression changed. He didn't look round, but he knew all right. He stood up really slowly. Then he smiled and blew me a kiss. Bastard! Like he was reminding me what we'd done. What I'd let him do. Then he began to change. Made my skin crawl to watch, but I couldn't look away. Soon he was the Gideon I had seen in the pool, all dark hair and seductive eyes. Nothing left of my Ian. Gone. Completely gone. He turned his back on me. Elizabeth didn't flinch when she saw his face—she must have been expecting it.

'Bess,' he said, making the end of her name sound like a hissing snake, 'or would you prefer Eliza? Elise? Elizabeth?' There was that dangerous smile again.

Elizabeth seemed taller than usual. Now I could see that her feet didn't touch the ground. She was levitating, just about a foot or so, but it made her well taller than him. When she spoke, her voice was different. Sort of louder but not harsh. Like a giant bell that's been rung and the sound still hangs in the air.

'It matters not what you choose to call me, Gideon. I am your nemesis.' There was a calmness about her. A strength I hadn't seen before.

'My dear, you do like to try to provoke me, don't you? All these years I have done my utmost to help you realize you are my true bride, and all you can do is think of my destruction.'

'You will be destroyed, Gideon. Too many people have been harmed because of you. I won't allow it to continue, not in my name.' She glanced over at me. Gideon noticed.

'How it must have tortured you to know that I had seduced your new little friend,' he said. 'Were you jealous, Bess? Did you envy her or me? I wonder.'

'Leave the girl alone. You have caused her more than enough pain already.'

'She was'—he started to wave a hand in my direction—'a pleasant diversion, though a little ingénue for my taste. What did you think I would do with her? Besides the obvious, I mean. Which, I have to say, she enjoyed very much.' As he spoke, I could feel this terrible cold cover me, like I was under an avalanche. I started to shiver. My teeth began to rattle in my head. I could tell by the look on Elizabeth's face that something bad was going down. I looked at my hands and screamed. They were all wrinkled and shriveled, like an old crone. I pulled up my sleeve; my arms were the same. I felt my face. It was all sagged with deep wrinkles all over it. I was so close to panicking. Then Elizabeth raised her staff. She banged it on the ground and pointed it at me. And it stopped. Whatever Gideon was doing to me, it stopped. Just like that. My skin went back to normal. The coldness went. As if it had never happened. I so wanted to run. But somehow I stayed.

'Why, Bess, I am impressed. You must have been practicing. And here I was thinking you had shunned your magic. Could it be that you have at last given up trying to pretend you are not a witch, eh?'

'It was not being a witch I rejected. It was being empowered by you. A witch born of a warlock's magic is cursed, you know that.'

'I so dislike the name *warlock*.'

'It is what you are. No good witch, female or male, would do what you do. Your power should be a force for good, or have you forgotten that?'

'Should, shouldn't . . . how can one apply rules to such a thing as magic, Bess?' He began to drift upward, then lay down in midair, as if he was on a sofa, resting on one elbow. 'You know it still isn't too late—you could join me. You know how powerful we would be together. You have tasted a little of that power, and I think you rather like it, don't you? Of course, you are not going to admit it.' He sighed. 'There is a prim streak in you, Bess, that is really most unappealing.'

'You are wrong, Gideon, it is too late. Much too late.'

Behind Elizabeth, the woods began to move, to heave and twist, as if all the trees were coming alive, as if they were pulling at their roots, try-ing to get free. A thin, cold wind started whistling through the branches. It seemed to come from nowhere, but of course it didn't. It was Elizabeth who summoned it up. Now the trees started swaying and lurching all in unison, as if they were dancing. It was the most incredible sight, the whole forest alive and moving because Elizabeth willed it. I found myself standing completely still, as if I had sprouted roots while the trees had abandoned theirs. I wondered, for a second, if Elizabeth had bewitched me too. Had she cast some sort of protection around me, maybe? It was odd, but I didn't feel like running away anymore. I was where I was meant to be.

The ground started to tremble, then shake. Dry leaves flew up in a whirlwind of rustling, bronze and gold glinting under the supernatural moonlight. At last the trees broke free! One or two at first, and then more and more. Huge oaks and ash trees and all types, their trunks sucking in and out as if they were breathing, their great branches reaching forward as they marched toward Gideon. Elizabeth held her ground as they advanced, letting them stomp past her, closer and closer. Gideon didn't move. He didn't so much as register surprise. He waited. Waited until the trees were so very close, almost close enough to reach out and smash him with their enormous limbs. Almost but not quite. He put his hands on his hips, threw his head back, chest puffed out, and drew in a deep breath. One of the biggest oaks was level with him now, and for a moment I thought Gideon had mistimed things badly and that he was about to be hammered into the ground, but I should have known better. Should have known *him* better. He exhaled, sending his foul-smelling breath forward with an ear-shattering roar. It wasn't human, that breath, and it wasn't just air, either. It was yellow and sulfurous and rancid, and it came out with a force you could never imagine. A force that blew all those trees, all those mighty oaks, hundreds of years old and weighing God knows how much—it blew them all back into the forest as if they were straws. And it blew Elizabeth with them. She was knocked backward, flung through the air, and landed awkwardly against some of the fallen trees. At the exact same moment, I felt myself freed. Freed and exposed, as if whatever protection Elizabeth had constructed around me had been broken. I turned to run to her, to help her, but suddenly the sky went black, as if the bright moon had been blotted out by something. I looked up and wished I hadn't when I saw what was gathering above me. Bats, thousands of them. And not just harmless little pipistrelles. These things were huge, bigger than crows, and they shrieked as they began to swoop down. I barely had time to cry out before they were on me. They knocked me down and clutched at me with their unnaturally sharp claws. I tried to beat them off, but there were too many. One bit my hand, its fangs cutting straight through the skin and deep into the flesh. I wanted to scream, but they were after my face, my eyes, everywhere. And through it all, I could hear Gideon laughing. Laughing! One tried to latch onto my throat with its hideous vampire fangs. I thought it was going to get me. I couldn't see a way out, but then there came another sound. More shrieking. No, *screeching*. Owls! They came from nowhere, hundreds of them, glowing white with their own light, scything through the swarm of bats, snatching them from the sky. More and more came. The bats were terrified and tried to get away, but the owls were too many and too quick. Now I could see Elizabeth standing again, her staff raised, commanding the owls.

At last the sky cleared again, and the moonlight returned. I wiped blood from my cheek and grabbed a length of ivy, wrapping it tightly around my hand to stop the flow from the painful bat bites.

'Why are you wasting your energies, Bess?' Gideon shook his head, like he was telling off a naughty child. 'You must know I would never have equipped you with sufficient power to prove a real threat. I have far more of an instinct for self-preservation than you credit me with. Do you really think I would have created a witch with the ability to kill me?'

Elizabeth didn't answer. I could see her lips moving, really fast, but I couldn't hear what she was saying. There were weird sounds now. Like voices. Or singing. No, not singing, chanting. And all through it, that bastard kept on smiling his sickly smile.

Her words were drowned out by the howling wind and by the chanting. Then I noticed these shapes among the trees. People. No, women. No, witches. Four, five, six, seven . . . a dozen of them, I think. It was hard to count, they slipped out from behind the trees and began whirling about in the clearing. Gideon frowned. He didn't look frightened, more pissed off.

'Welcome, my sisters!' Elizabeth greeted the other witches as they flew about. Gideon stood scowling at her as these fabulous creatures darted about the place. These weren't old hags, not witches out of fairy tales. They were beautiful, all dressed in shimmering colors, their hair streaming, all with the same fantastic glow radiating from them, like the brightest fireworks. They were glorious. Elizabeth was really pleased, really touched that they had come to help her; you could see it on her face. I've never seen her look so happy.

'You foolish creature,' Gideon was yelling at her now. 'You think I can't deal with a few dried up harridans?' He sent one of them sprawling and knocked another against a tree. 'Did you really think this sorry mother coven of yours could kill me?' he screamed.

He was so powerful and so mad by now that I was really scared. He was hurling those lovely witches about as if they were dolls. Smashing them, breaking them, as if they were nothing. No matter how fast they moved or how much they used their magic, he was too strong for them. And still they whirled about him, dancing, flying, chanting. I couldn't understand it. It was almost as if they knew they stood no chance, and yet they kept on and on, making him madder and madder. Then Elizabeth rushed at him. Straight at him! She got so close—too close. Gideon grabbed her and held her up, choking her.

'I had not imagined you would be so foolish, Bess,' he spat at her. 'So foolish as to truly believe you could overpower me, you and your feeble crones.'

I ran at him. I couldn't help myself. He was squeezing the life out of her. I had no idea what I was going to do, I just knew I couldn't stand there and watch him throttle her. I snatched up a rock as I went and swung it at his head. He had been so focused on poor Elizabeth I actually caught him with his guard down, and the stone hit him hard, right on the back of his skull. He staggered, just for a fleeting second, and loosened his grip. Elizabeth seized her moment and got away. Then he turned on me. I was lying practically at his feet. That was the moment I thought I was going to die. He was steaming with rage, roaring at me, cursing and spitting, his eyes flaming. Before I had time to wonder what he would do next, I felt a searing pain in my shoulder, as if a fireball had exploded against me. I screamed—I know I must have, it hurt so much—but I don't remember hearing the sound. Just this terrible sizzling noise as the magic fire burned into my flesh. Elizabeth rushed to my side. She placed her hand on my shoulder, and the burning stopped. It still hurt and I could smell the revolting stink of burning flesh. My burning flesh. Elizabeth sprang up, high into the air, and circled around Gideon with dizzying speed.

All the witches formed a circle around me, protecting me. Looking up, I could see Gideon and Elizabeth flying, hurtling around the enclosure, exchanging phosphorous blasts and spears of flame. One of the other witches, a girl not much older than me, touched my wound. At last the pain stopped completely, but I could feel raised lumps and knew the scar was mine to keep. The witches started to move away from me, to go to Elizabeth's aid, but she shouted at them to stay with me and protect me.

It didn't take long for Gideon to bring her down. She crashed onto the smoldering woodland floor and lay there, totally still. Everything went quiet, deathly quiet. No wind, no howling or crashing or screaming or wailing anymore. Just this awful lifeless hush. Had he killed her? Was that it? Could that really be the end? Nobody moved—none of the witches, not even Gideon, who was now standing a few yards away from where she lay.

'Elizabeth?' I called, my own voice hoarse and breaking. 'Elizabeth!'

Then there was this tiny movement. Not Elizabeth but the ground beside her. It seemed to stir. Then, silently, slowly, a shape rose up from the leaves and plants. It twirled and spun about, growing, still noiselessly, gently shifting and pulsating until it formed into a woman. Another witch. This one was tall and slender and looked a little older than some of the others. She wore flowing, soft robes the color of the darkened woodlands, all smudges and bruises. She leaned over Elizabeth and touched her tenderly.

'Bess,' she said, her voice like a crystal wind-chime moving in the breeze. 'Bess, my child, wake up.'

Elizabeth stirred. She moaned and opened her eyes. She struggled to focus for a little while, and then she saw who it was that had called her name.

'Mother!' Her voice was weak, but there was no mistaking the joy in it. Her mother had come to her. After so many, many years.

Elizabeth tried to get up. 'There, Bess, there,' her mother said, brushing her daughter's hair from her face, gazing at her with such love, such pride.

'Mother, I am sorry.' She shook her head. 'I was never as strong as you were. Never as good.'

'Hush. You have nothing to be sorry for, Bess. It is I who should beg your forgiveness, for ever placing you in the hands of such a monster.'

'You were trying to save me, that is all.'

'And instead, look what you have endured. What you have suffered for so very long. On your own.'

'No, Mother. I knew you were always there beside me.' Elizabeth stood up now, and the two women embraced. And as they did so, the light went back into her—you could see it. You could see the strength and the magic pouring from the older woman into her daughter, filling her up, making her whole and healed again.

Gideon was clearly fuming that she had found someone capable of helping her.

'I lose patience with this mother-daughter reunion,' he said. 'You, Anne Hawksmith, you would have us all believe you did what you did from the very best of motives. Out of love as a mother for her child, nothing more. Well, I saw how you took to the magic I showed you, Witch, do not forget that. I saw how you lapped it up, how you reveled in it, just as your sorceress of a daughter does. As she always has. This false piety sickens me. The two of you were born for magic, for celebrating the dark arts. In your souls you both know it.'

Anne and Elizabeth faced each other. They held hands and they exchanged smiles of pure bliss. And Elizabeth, when she stepped away and turned to Gideon, was incredible. If she had looked fabulous before, it was nothing compared to how she shone now, how she fizzed and pulsed with the light of magic, *good* magic inside her. Her mother dropped back a little into the moon shadows. Elizabeth glided forward on silent feet until she stood only inches from Gideon. Then she did the weirdest thing. The weirdest and the bravest. We had talked about it before. We had spent hours planning, going over and over what would happen, but I still can't get my head around it. I still wish there had been some other way. She offered him her hand. She smiled and she held out her hand to him. He was stunned. Lost for words. At last—something he hadn't been expecting!

'Well, Gideon,' she said softly, 'I am offering you my hand. Will you take it? Do you truly wish to be with me?'

He smiled a really cheesy I've-won sort of smile. 'Yes,' he said. 'Yes, my love. It gladdens my heart to see that you have, finally, come to your senses. That you know yourself. That you see that we were always destined to share our journey through time. Imagine how we will be together, imagine what we can accomplish!' He seemed to grow, to pulsate with energy. At last he had what he wanted, what he believed was his right. 'And so yes, as it was written, and as you were created witch in my name, most certainly, I do wish to be with you.'

'Then you shall,' she said. A heartbeat later, the other witches transformed themselves into fire, their whirling circle becoming a ring of flame around Elizabeth and Gideon in the center, who were now a good ten feet off the ground. White spheres of phosphorous swirled through the air. Sparks and burning leaves and pieces of wood were falling onto the forest floor. All about the clearing things started to catch fire. Anne floated upward, blending into the ring of flame and light. In the middle of it all, Gideon and Elizabeth remained calm and focused only on each other. Hand in hand, they began to rise up and up.

'You are right.' Elizabeth's voice was clear even above the racket of everything else. 'We could not kill you, Gideon. That was never really an option. But we can take you.'

The tiniest flash of fear showed in his face.

'We can invite you to join us,' she went on, tightening her grip on his hand, 'and if you come willingly, if you agree, as you just have, then you can be our guest in the Summerlands.'

'No!' he roared, but it made no difference. He struggled to free his hand, but nothing he could do would make Elizabeth let him go. Not now.

'You will cause no harm there, Gideon. Who knows, perhaps among us you may even learn a little humility.'

He was screaming now, his face changing all the time. He transformed wildly, madly, red eyes, fangs, tusks, horns. He bellowed and writhed and thrashed about, but she held him fast.

She turned her head slowly and looked down at me. I knew she was saying good-bye. I wanted to be brave for her, to show her I understood and that it was all right. To thank her for all she had done for me. But my heart was breaking. I couldn't bear the thought of her leaving me.

'Elizabeth!' I called out to her, tears streaming down my face. 'Elizabeth!'

She shook her head and smiled, and though I couldn't hear her, I saw her mouth the words *Be strong!*

And then, in the blink of an eye, they were gone. There was nothing. Just me and the woodland. I couldn't move. I felt stunned. Only when I realized that the forest was on fire properly now, was I able to make myself think about getting to safety. I was about to run when I noticed something, a small movement on the ground. My white mouse! I went to scoop him up, but the little rat ran off.

'Hey! This is not the time to play around.' I went after him. He hopped onto a stick. It was Elizabeth's staff. I picked it up. The mouse jumped into my pocket. I looked around, checking, just once more, but I was alone. I ran. I knew I couldn't manage the bike, so I kept going on foot. I stopped when I got to the road and used my mobile to call the fire brigade. I threw the phone in the ditch after that, glad to be rid of the last thing he had given me. Then, keeping to the shadows, I walked home.

Well, I say home. Funny, that's how I think of this house now. It is mine, after all. Elizabeth showed me her will. Imagine, a whole house. Mine.

I don't know what Mum is going to make of that. But I'll deal with her. She'll be so pleased to have a rent-free place to live I don't think she'll ask difficult questions for too long. The main one being, where is Elizabeth? Tough one to answer that. I mean, I know where she said she was going, but I don't really get it. And no one else will, that's for sure. The Summerlands, that's what she said. Like a heaven for witches; only it's not forever. They come back. When the time is right, they come back. And she will too. One day. She promised me. Meanwhile, here I am, in her cottage, with all this stuff to find out about, all these books. Her *Grimoire* full of spells and recipes. And this, of course, her *Book of Shadows*. Well, I'll be ready. When she does come back, she's going to be seriously impressed with me. I'll finish this now. It's not really the end of Bess's story, or Eliza's, or Elise's, or Elizabeth's. But she'll want to start a new journal when she returns. And who knows, one of these days I just might write my own *Book of Shadows*.

BATCHCOMBE WOODS ABLAZE

Three fire tenders and nineteen firemen battled with a blaze at Batchcombe woods at around midnight last night. The fire, which spread as far as Batchcombe Hall to the west and the A324 to the east, was believed to have been started by campers. The remains of a burnt-out motorbike were found at the site. There were no witnesses, and the fire was reported anonymously. Batchcombe Hall was never under direct threat, thanks to the firebreak which lies behind the house. However, many acres of ancient oaks and beech trees were destroyed in the blaze. Police say they are investigating the fire, although they consider it to be carelessness rather than arson. A spokesman for the fire service admitted they were so far baffled as to what had actually started the blaze. They were unable to find evidence of a recent campfire. There is a theory that fireworks may have been set off in the woods, as remnants of phosphorous-like substances have been taken from the scene.

So Ends *The Book of Shadows*